"More of the absolutely up-to-date news from Tula Springs, Louisiana, the venue of Wilcox's comic jewels. . . . Not even John Updike is writing this well about American social reality and absurdity—and as the gags rise and then fade into something more melancholy, Wilcox again persuades that he's a master."

—*Kirkus Reviews*

"Each time out, Wilcox gets better—subtler, more complex, closer to the fusion of pathos and joy that makes for the highest comedy."

—Walter Kendrick, *Village Voice*

"Displayed in a series of inane small-town connections, Wilcox's characters are entertaining bundles of quirks and contradictions. . . . A virtual parade of risible personalities."

—*London Review of Books*

"Wilcox has amazing assurance and a nearly perfect ear. . . . One of the most promising fiction writers on the national scene."

—Peter Heinegg, *Los Angeles Times*

Miss Undine's Living Room

Miss Undine's Living Room

JAMES WILCOX

LOUISIANA STATE UNIVERSITY PRESS
BATON ROUGE

10 09 08 07 06 05 04 03 02 01
5 4 3 2 1

Library of Congress Cataloging-in-Publication Data

Wilcox, James.
    Miss Undine's living room / James Wilcox.
      p. cm.— (Voices of the South)
    ISBN 0-8071-2699-3 (pbk. : alk. paper)
     1. Tula Springs (La.: Imaginary place)—Fiction. 2. City and town life—
Fiction. 3. Louisiana—Fiction. I. Title. II. Series.

    PS3573.I396 M5 2001
    813'.54—dc21

                         00-067283

The paper in this book meets the guidelines for permanence and durability of
the Committee on Production Guidelines for Book Longevity of the Council
on Library Resources. ∞

FOR
TOM CARNEY AND MAUREEN LAMBRAY

• ACKNOWLEDGMENTS •

The author would like to express his special gratitude to the Guggenheim Foundation for its support while this book was being written. And he would also like to thank his editor, Richard P. Kot, for his most helpful and intelligent guidance.

"Our Sun is not motionless in space; in fact it has two proper motions. One is a seemingly straight-line motion in the direction of the constellation Hercules at the rate of about 12 miles per second. But since the Sun is a part of the Milky Way system and since the whole system rotates slowly around its own center, the Sun also moves at the rate of 175 miles per second as part of the rotating Milky Way system."

Information Please Almanac, Atlas & Yearbook
34th Edition

". . . and where thou lodgest, I will lodge . . ."
Ruth 1:16

PART ONE

Chapter One

"MRS. UNDINE COMES FREE FOR SHUT-INS," Olive was saying to the old man as she pressed a strip of electric tape to his plump, womanish loins. The sturdy tape, she hoped, would help secure the disposable diaper, which was far too small for him. They were out of the adult pads, though, down at the drugstore, and she had to make do with something. "Don't you dare give her any money, hear?"

Encased in a shiny waistcoat that seemed to choke all four of the antique humors into his massive square head, the old man shifted his weight to make it as difficult as possible for Olive to finish putting on the Pamper. With her own hard-earned money she had bought the jumbo box of diapers, lugging it up the stairs in this heat along with a variety pack of Weight Watchers Quiescently Frozen Confection, something she thought he might like as a change from his regular diet of bananas and Vienna sausages. But was there the slightest grunt of appreciation from the old bulldozer? Try as she might to focus on his good qualities, after five minutes in his cramped, stuffy apartment she could not help thinking of him as a bulldozer, always getting his way, bossing everyone around, flattening any attempt at normal conversation with his two-ton lectures on the Peace of Ghent and the goddam YWCA. When he shifted again, she gave him a poke in the ribs to let him know she meant business. "I haven't time for any of your games, Uncle L.D. Now turn so I can yank it under."

"Why must you use my good electric tape?" he demanded, his eyes squeezed shut with outraged modesty. Sometimes he would open them a little to make sure Olive had kept hers shut, too, which explained why she squinted during this, the most difficult part of his toilet.

"You're too fat, that's why. You tell Mrs. Undine to work on that pot of yours. Maybe then I could get you dressed without killing myself." Mrs. Undine came every Wednesday to give the old man an exercise class, and Olive was anxious to have him presentable before she arrived. It was quite a chore and seemed to be getting more difficult week by week.

After his wife had passed away, Uncle L.D. had fended for himself in an efficiency apartment over the Sonny Boy Bargain Store. Then one day on the way back from staring out the window he had stumbled over a toaster oven and broken his hip. Bedridden ever since, he had been cared for by a series of home attendants. The latest, a certain Mr. Versey, did not appear to be overexerting himself. Olive usually stopped by on Mr. Versey's day off and tried to make what improvements she could, picking up the blackened banana peels, washing the dishes Mr. Versey had left in the sink, and spraying some of the old man's Right Guard over the pile of laundry Mr. Versey should have done weeks ago. She was planning to come here one day with Duane, her husband, to give the place a good once-over. How satisfying it would feel to scour the grease off the linoleum, paint the smudged khaki walls a cheery yellow, and maybe hang those Van Goghs that were cluttering up her garage. Trouble was, Duane was always able to come up with some excuse why he couldn't lend a hand. Either he was too tired or too busy, the story of his life.

"In my own dull, retarded way may I suggest that I might be able to make up my own mind about paying Mrs. Undine?" the old man said after she had tugged the Hart Schaffner & Marx trousers up over his scrawny legs. In contrast to his barrel of a torso the frailty of his smooth, boyish limbs always gave her a pang.

Olive trudged over to the only window in the one-room

apartment, an oversized window that would have provided plenty of light if only he didn't insist on the shade being drawn. "Mrs. Undine is a volunteer," she reminded him. Her knees bent, she vainly attempted to raise the sash. The effort left her dizzy, her heart pounding violently. And to think, not that many years ago—at least it didn't seem that many years ago—she used to tear up and down the basketball court, all-parish guard at Tula Springs High, without feeling the least bit winded. "The Ladies' Aid Society isn't supposed"—she took a few deep breaths—"isn't supposed to get any money from you. And besides, it upsets Mr. Versey. How do you think it makes him feel when he sees you doling out five bucks to her for doing nothing?"

"Mr. Versey is well provided for," he said with a significant wink, as if the home attendant's salary were coming straight out of his own pocket, not the government's. "Now, if you'd be so kind, my coat, sir."

At the beginning of the summer she had brought him a bundle of short-sleeve Lacostes that Duane was tired of, but not once had she seen him wear anything but the yellowed white shirts that Mr. Versey refused to iron. It made her swelter just to see him in one. And yet for Mrs. Undine's visits even this get-up was not sufficient: He must wear his vest and the hundred-per cent silk coat from Marshall Field's in Chicago, which was where he was from, or someplace near there. He always liked to make a big deal out of the fact that he had never set eyes on a Louisiana highway until he was fifty-five years old, the same as the speed limit—and then you were supposed to laugh or act impressed or something.

Holding up the double-breasted coat, she said, "Here, let's go."

"Not so high."

With a set look on her face she lowered the sleeve opening to accommodate his bad arm and never changed her expression as a series of vague, urgent orders—"Watch it! Left, left!"—mixed with the grunts and sharp moans that always accompanied this procedure. Not so long ago Olive would have winced in sympathy, but by now the novelty of his distress had worn off, and in this heat it was all she could do to keep from giving him a good belt in the kisser. After all, he did like to exaggerate. The pain couldn't be that bad.

"O.K., now," she said once the coat was on and she had adjusted his pocket handkerchief so that three starched points peeked out the way he liked, "this water's getting tired of waiting around for you."

"Later—I'll drink it when you go."

"Uh-huh, tell me another one, Mother Goose." She picked the wineglass up off the tv tray and held it to his lips. The doctor had told her that unless he drank seven glasses of water a day, the old man was in danger of dehydrating. Yet all he ever wanted was that sickly sweet port that made her gag. Of course, it would have helped if she had some ice to put in the water, but Mr. Versey hadn't defrosted the mini-refrigerator. It was impossible to get the tray out. "Come on, down the hatch."

His lips white, resisting the glass pressed against them, he made low, growling sounds while Olive studied herself in the mirror above the bed. Her girl friend Carol had talked her into cutting her hair stylishly short for the summer, a big mistake since now her firm jaw seemed more prominent than ever, downright manly. She thought she might as well join the Marines.

"Fine, have it your way," she said, taking the still-full glass back to the sink. While she was there she removed the rubber gloves she always wore in his apartment, not so much to protect herself from all the germs as to avoid bringing them home to her boy. He had an extremely delicate digestive tract.

As someone clomped noisily down the stairs from the floor above the old man cleared his throat. A speech was on its way. "Shall we pass the calumet, Olive?" The red had left his face now, and it looked as sleek and placid as a warden's. "May I say you're a remarkable woman? From now on I'm going to make it a point to listen and learn from you, as I hope, in my own dull, retarded way, that you will perhaps learn just a little from me. I will consider myself a student of yours and you a student of—"

"Oh, hush," she said wearily, retrieving her purse from a handsome rocker with a slightly damaged seat. Like the other basically good, solid pieces of furniture in the apartment, the rocker seemed to be in storage, waiting for the real owner to take it away. "I'm sorry, man, I got to run."

Consulting the gold pocket watch that dangled from a bedpost, he announced, "Seven minutes. A record, I believe. Fastest Social Call of the Decade was achieved by Mrs. Olive Mackie of Tula Springs, Louisiana, on September—"

"Look, I've been here longer than any dang seven minutes. Been more like a half hour." She leaned over and pecked him on the forehead. Despite the fact that he rarely bathed, he had a pleasant smell, something like a baby's. "By the way," she added, smoothing a wisp of his fine, reddish hair, "you don't happen to have a few bucks you could shoot this way?"

In order to economize, Olive had been driving forty-five miles to Ozone, twice a week, for appointments at a dental college that Mrs. Undine had recommended to her. Mrs. Undine's ex-son-in-law was a student there, and she had promised Olive he would take good care of her for half the cost of a regular dentist. Olive's husband, though, claimed that the gas she ate up driving there and back wiped out any savings on her teeth. This was why she sometimes felt it necessary to cheat a little by borrowing a few unreported bucks every now and then from the old man. Actually it wasn't cheating when you considered that she was forced to take the Cadillac to Ozone. If she were driving a sensible compact, like she wanted, Duane wouldn't have a leg to stand on.

"My fine feathered friend," he said, clasping her hand in both of his, "I wasn't going to mention it, but didn't I lend you twenty last week? Not that twenty dollars means anything at all to me. I mean, the fact that Mr. Versey didn't have enough for groceries this week, don't let that trouble you. After all, not by bread alone."

"Don't you dare talk to me about food." Wrenching her hand free from the grip that was surprisingly powerful for a ninety-one-year-old's, she looked straight into his dim, clouded eyes. For some reason or other one of them couldn't move. He had told her why once, but the explanation was so long and complicated that she had purposefully forgotten it so as not to clutter up her brain. "Who was it trudged up here twice with Food Stamp applications? Who was it tore them both up right in front of my eyes? And furthermore, I don't think it was a twenty. Remember, I asked for change for a twenty, but I only took ten, you know."

The bedsprings creaked as he tried to raise himself against the carved headboard. "Forgive me, but may I remind you that you're talking to a mnemonician. It has always been my job to be accurate. You'll observe that in the past . . ." The more he droned on about his reputation as a memory expert, the more certain Olive became that he had only given her a ten, or maybe it was five. In any case, nothing had been said about a loan. She had accepted the money in the spirit of a gift. After all, she never expected him to repay her for all the Pampers and treats she bought. That would be tacky.

"Why do you think I possess such a king-size noggin?" the old man concluded—as he had concluded the same lecture about a million times before. Olive was scribbling a note for Mr. Versey about the laundry and the defrosting. "It's because it's chock-full of facts. Ask me the population of any town over five thousand in Illinois, ask me who was the mayor of Kankakee in 1929, how many votes he won by. I'm trained to retain."

"In my own dull, retarded way, Uncle L.D., may I ask what happened to that brand new can of Comet I gave you last week?" She stuck the note to the mini-refrigerator with a magnetic letter *B*, which didn't stand for anything as far as she knew. "God, this place is like a black hole. I know there was another box of those adult wee-wee pads, and now they've disappeared too. I may as well take all my money and throw it right out the window. Which reminds me, when are you going to get that landlady of yours to fix that thing? I don't know how you can stand it in here with the window shut and—"

"Knock, knock," came a timid voice from the door Olive had left ajar to help ventilate the place. Glancing over her shoulder, she saw the tall, shapeless figure of Mrs. Undine poised uncertainly at the threshold. Her neck was thrust out slightly, as if to sniff the air before proceeding any farther. "It's just I," she said, venturing into the apartment.

"May I say, Mrs. Undine, that I think you're remarkable," the old man fairly shouted from the bed on the far side of the room. In a more normal tone of voice he added, "Where's your manners, Olive? Offer the young lady a glass of port. And while you're at it you might bring me a smidgen. And don't forget the cube."

The young lady, who was well into her sixties, ignored the old man's greeting as she settled her overstuffed handbag on the rocking chair next to the window. "I couldn't find a parking place," she said in a hushed voice, as if they were in a library, "and then . . . How are you, Olive? You look a little pale. Heavens," she added, rooting about in her bag, "I can't see a thing. I wish he'd let me raise that shade."

"The green bothers him," Olive said. One of the N's from the neon Sonny Boy sign cut across the panes and gave the apartment a greenish tinge if the shade wasn't down. The shade, though, did not affect the nervous hum of the neon; even with the window shut it popped like bacon on a hot skillet.

"May I say, Mrs. Undine, that I think you're remarkable," the old man shouted again, his voice strained and anxious.

"Yes, yes, I'm coming," she muttered as she made an entry in an official-looking black book. Olive was reminded of the conduct book Mrs. Undine used to keep on her desk when she taught civics. Long ago, though, she had retired. "Now, have I got everything? The keys—did I leave them in the car? Oh, goodness." Unzipping a compartment in the bag, she pulled out a large key chain that said I ♡ NY, took a good look at it, then stuffed it back inside.

"The port, Olive, what about the port!" the old man demanded as Olive crossed to the door. She would have to hurry if she was going to make it to the dentist on time.

"You know what the doctor says about alcohol. It dehydrates you." She glanced at her watch. "Give him a Weight Watchers, Mrs. Undine. I'm sorry, I got to run."

"Yes, dear, we don't want to keep Dr. Bates waiting."

" 'Bye, y'all. You be good, Uncle L,D. I'll see you next week."

She was halfway down the stairs before it struck her: How did Mrs. Undine know she had an appointment in Ozone? Had she mentioned it to her? No, she was sure she hadn't. Lord, what a busybody, Olive thought as she opened the downstairs door, which led, not to the street but into the Sonny Boy Bargain Store. With her sharp eye for bargains Olive was usually distracted from whatever might be bothering her the minute she set foot inside the dimly lit store. Today was no exception, and Mrs. Undine was soon forgotten as Olive made a beeline for a stack of slightly damaged stoneware.

"She's not really a blood relation," the old man explained as Mrs. Undine handed him a glass of watered-down port sans the requisite ice cube. He hoped she understood how little time he had to work with Olive. It seemed like only five or ten minutes a week. Given an hour or two, he was sure he could have made some headway, knocked off some of those rough edges that caused him such embarrassment in front of company. Imagine, just breezing out of the apartment like that. "I let her call me Uncle L.D. All her folks are the same, calling everyone Uncle This, Aunt That. You'd think they just came off the farm. You see, my late wife, Artis, she was Olive's great-aunt. No blood at all between us. Say, it looks as if you've forgotten my cube again." He managed a jovial chuckle. "And Mrs. Undine, did I catch you trying to put water in my port again? Ha! Shall we try once more?"

"Perhaps we don't need our port today," Mrs. Undine said, setting the glass aside. But she was wrong. Leaning across the bed, he hoisted it from the tv tray and drained the glass in two or three gulps.

Although Mrs. Undine was very strict about allotting only twenty minutes to a client per week, the old man always tried to induce her to stay a bit longer. Not that he really thought that much of Mrs. Undine herself. A plain, somewhat dowdy widow, she was not exactly the most alluring female he had ever encountered. But after nearly an entire year of Mr. Versey anyone, even a Mrs. Undine, began to look good to him. At least she spoke without solecisms. To someone as finely tuned as Uncle L.D. there was nothing more painful than to hear *hopefully* misused.

"Manners were never the girl's forte," he resumed.

Mrs. Undine appeared to consider this a moment before observing in a bland, even tone, "I suppose Olive will always be Olive." A fly that had been perusing the frizzed bangs of her mousy hair whisked off suddenly of its own accord. "All right, Mr. Loraine, enough chitchat. Let's place our two hands in front of us. Now we're going to loosen up those wrist joints. Down, up, one, two—"

"You used to 'teach' her, didn't you?" The old man flexed his wrists in time to the beat. "Of course, I put 'teach' in quotation marks. Seems like the minute Olive landed on this great emerald orb, she made up her mind right then and there that she wasn't going to be improved. Why, when I was her age, I was improving myself every chance I got. The day began at four-thirty A.M. for me. Four-thirty A.M. I was on my way, servicing all the vending machines from Evanston to Waukegan. Had to keep an exact account in my head of each and every Ace comb I put in, all the Wildroot hair tonic, the Old Spice, those Trim toenail clippers, and the whole time I was driving, madam, you wouldn't catch me wasting a second: I had a book propped up on the dash, a textbook on memory. Of course, in those days there weren't as many cars coming at you. But still, the way young folks today who have every opportunity, the government begging them to stay in school, why it makes my blood boil. I could take out a gun and . . . Now, I've offered Olive the chance to come learn from me, gratis, three times a week, an opportunity I would have given my right arm for when I was her age. I promised to teach her how to remember any fact she wanted. People with facts in their heads can double, triple their salaries. That's been proved, scientifically proved by all the top experts. Someday I'll show you how—"

"Quiet!"

Startled, the old man looked up and saw that Mrs. Undine had drifted to the window. He hadn't noticed earlier since he found it easier to pretend she was someone agreeable by not looking at her when he talked.

"Do please hush down there," she said after having raised the shade and striven vainly against the sash. A persistent whining and yapping now settled down into a methodical bark.

"Use the sink, Mrs. Undine. Give a good shout into that air duct by the sink, that's where all the racket comes from. It's that blasted store downstairs."

The neon *N* tinted the exercise instructor's hair a sickly green as she stood before the window in an awkward pose. It seemed as if she was about to turn away, and yet she remained where she was. "I don't believe they'd let a dog in the store, would they?"

"Young lady, anyone with two cents in his paw is welcome there. Now, would you mind pulling down that shade?"

"It's so dark in here. I really think you'd be happier . . ." The look aimed at her from across the room cut her short. "In any case, something should be done about that window. I think it's painted shut. Oh, well, it's stopped," she added, referring to the barking. "I don't know how you stand it. That dog sounded as if it were right here in the room with us."

"Dogs I can take. It's when they start talking about their nails and their hair, that's when I'd like to take a gun and . . . You have no idea how many hours those salesgirls down there waste when they could be learning something. I sent Mr. Versey downstairs a couple times, told him to invite them up here for their coffee break. Give me fifteen minutes a day with those girls, that's all I would need. And it wouldn't cost them a cent. I tried calling down a few times, through that air duct there, but I guess it's a one-way connection.

"Now, this dentist business," the old man went on when Mrs. Undine had rejoined him by the bed, the shade down. "A tragic mistake. How many times have I told Olive, if you're going to have your spleen taken out, would you go to a student surgeon, someone who was just learning how to remove spleens? If you want to learn about memory, would you go to a student of memory? No, sir, you would want the best, a top expert in the field, just as I did when I was her age. I went straight to the top, the man who taught Dale Carnegie himself how to retain. I was only a kid then, no hope of going to college, had to support my mother, my siblings, after my father lost everything in a land deal that— "

"Neck rotation. And one and two and round we go and three and four and by the way, Mr. Loraine, I do believe Olive is being sensible about the dental college. For one thing, the students are thoroughly supervised by a staff consisting of the finest practitioners in southeast Louisiana. Furthermore, the students themselves are of the highest caliber, with only a few exceptions. Now, please, dear, try to rotate. It won't do you a bit of good to sit there admiring your walls."

"Well, some people might be content with Cutty Sark," the old man expounded, making the recommended figure eight with a neck that seemed far too frail for the extra-large head. "Me, give me Chivas or nothing at all."

"I hope you still aren't blaming Mr. Versey for that."

The old man suspected his home attendant of having taken a bottle of his best Scotch, even though Mr. Versey claimed that his doctor didn't allow him to drink. It was just like Mrs. Undine to bring up something disagreeable, he mused. The world was filled with so many remarkable people who had accomplished so many remarkable things, and yet she must bring up this pitiful specimen.

"If you keep on annoying Mr. Versey," she went on after putting a few X's in her exercise chart, "you just might find yourself without a friend to help you out."

He winced. How could anyone be so dull, so retarded as to believe that Mr. Versey did anything but drive him nuts. "Yes, that's Olive for you," he said, veering sharply away from this subject, which would only result in words being exchanged, "penny wise, pound foolish. You mark my words, that dental school is going to cost her in the long run. Reminds me of the Thanksgiving she came over. Artis had just about everything imaginable you could want—turkey and homemade stuffing, T-bones for anyone who didn't like turkey, string beans, potato puffs, and her special gravy— you haven't lived until you've tasted my wife's gravy. Olive was just a little runt then, eleven or twelve, but already she had a scowl a mile wide. Just between you and me a lot of folks used to mistake her for a boy, the way she used those fists. Seems like everyone in the family was afraid of her, too much to cope with, so they let her have her way. And what's the first thing out of her mouth the minute we all sit down to eat: I'm not hungry. Here it is Thanksgiving, and she's not hungry. I'd have liked to give her a good belt. But her mother says, that's fine, dear, you run along. So off she goes, and I'm so mad I don't taste a thing. Finally I can't stand it any longer, I'm boiling. So I excuse myself and go out in the back yard, where we used to have a little cement frog pond. Artis had a soft spot for frogs, used to go out and feed them around sunset. Anyway, it was just as I thought. Olive was out there by the frog pond, and you'll never guess what I saw. There she was lying on her belly and—"

"And eating Cheez Whiz and crackers. Yes, terrible, Mr. Loraine. You could have shot her, right? Now let's reach up with our hands and try to touch the ceiling."

Mrs. Undine's thin arms, prickled by unsightly patches of heat rash, swayed over her head while mild complaints wafted from the air duct. Someone in the store was wondering where she had put her tweezers. Someone else noticed a run in her stockings. "Up, up, reach for the . . . Now what?"

He had managed to twist himself around in bed so that one hand could get a grip on the wheelchair. "I'm going to fix you a nice cool glass of port, Mrs. Undine." A decent drink would help him decide whether he was hungry or not. He thought he was, but he couldn't be sure. So often he was confounded by the signals from his body. Flashes of pain would assault him from an uninjured calf or toe, or a violent craving would issue from a spot an inch or so in the air above his stomach, as if he had suffered an amputation of that organ and was remembering hunger. The port with one cube always seemed to block the false signals. Without the cube it didn't do the slightest good.

"I don't care for any port." She shoved the wheelchair out of reach. "And you know I'm not strong enough to help you into that chair. You let Mr. Versey do that."

With a conspiratorial wink he leaned toward her and whispered, "I can make it worth your while. Just one glass."

"If you're thirsty, Mr. Loraine, I'll be happy to get you a nice glass of water. I shouldn't have let you talk me into that first glass of port. I think I've been too lax."

The old man kicked out viciously with his right foot, hoping to crack her a good one on the shin—at least that was his intention. The leg stirred feebly, unnoticed by Mrs. Undine, who had risen and was tying a pale scarf about her head.

"It's only eleven-forty-three." He jabbed a thick finger at the watch dangling from the bedpost. "You came at eleven-thirty."

"I'm surprised at you, sir. Being a mnemonician, you certainly must recall that I arrived at eleven-twenty-five." She dabbed at her nose with a threadbare embroidered handkerchief; a repressed sneeze made her eyes bulge.

"I suppose you don't have time to fix me a grilled cheese? I haven't eaten all day, and Mr. Versey has been under the weather lately. He may not be able to make it in tomorrow, and I won't see Olive for another week. But I'll understand if you must go, of course. What's food, after all? Not by bread alone."

"Honestly, Mr. Loraine, do you have to wait until the very last minute to ask me? You know I have other clients who depend upon me. Do you think it's fair that I should sacrifice their peace of mind just so one man can have his way? I'm afraid that ethically it doesn't hold water." She was standing in the doorway, neither in nor out. Then, just as it seemed she was making an exit, she turned and added, "And besides, I fixed you a grilled cheese last time and you barely touched it. And you got all that nice Vienna sausage right by your bed in that nice Tupperware. And what's that I see, five, six bananas? You can't fool me, sir. I know you're not really hungry."

She was right, of course, for after she finally left—there was one more false exit, when she returned to look for her good pen, which was behind her ear—he forgot all about food as he waited, with clenched teeth, for the voices from the sink.

Chapter Two

WHEN SHE RETURNED TO HER DESK and found Dr. Bates writing in her appointment book, Louise, the receptionist for Group 3W at the Gregg College of Dentistry, wondered aloud if she was going to make it through the day without coming apart at the seams. Didn't he realize that no one was authorized to write in that book except her? she demanded in front of an audience of three patients waiting in turquoise molded chairs. Hugging herself against an onslaught of fierce air conditioning, Olive shook her head slowly as Dr. Bates attempted to justify his action. *He shouldn't have to explain anything to that hussy,* she thought sadly. *A fine man like him, so bright and sensitive. . . .*

"I didn't know how long you'd be gone, Louise." Dr. Bates's voice was hushed, almost reverent.

"What? That don't make no difference." Louise put her head phones on and told her three-year-old boy, who was leashed to the leg of her desk, to stop using up all the Scotch tape. The man who ran the play school was sick today, Olive had heard the receptionist say to various friends on the phone. Might be gallstones.

"The rules say it's only me supposed to write," Louise muttered while Dr. Bates smiled meekly down at her son's golden head.

The first time Olive had set eyes on her dentist—this was about three months ago, shortly after she had affixed her signature to a legal document stating that she would not sue the college for anything that might occur during, or as a result of, her treatment—she thought he had the kindest face she had ever seen—for a man, that is. He would have made a good preacher, except for the fact, as she found out later, during a root canal, that he was Jewish and didn't believe in God. Bates didn't sound very Jewish to her, but she didn't bring this up until two or three sessions later, when he told her it was his mother who was Jewish. His father was English, actually born in England, but now lived in Netcong, New Jersey, which was where Dr. Bates had grown up. Although she did not consider herself the prying type, Dr. Bates's extreme reserve often made Olive feel a little pushy. She was careful not to ask him too many direct questions about himself. Instead, she gave him the chance to volunteer information by reminiscing from time to time about her own high school days and casually dropping the name Kay Undine. Kay was his ex-wife, and Olive was just dying to know what had gone wrong with the marriage. Was Kay still as snobby as she used to be in high school, looking down her long nose at Olive? In any case, Olive hoped it was Dr. Bates who had dropped Kay, and not the other way around. But Dr. Bates was very closemouthed on the subject. And as for Mrs. Undine, it was impossible to get anything out of her about her daughter other than the most superficial pleasantries.

"Oh, uh, Mrs. Mackie," Dr. Bates said, redirecting the kind smile from the receptionist's boy to her. Yes, that was why he would have made a good preacher: He had the same gentle manner with everyone, and it was beginning to bother Olive. Why should she and someone like that ignorant Louise, who wore plastic sandals, be given the same kind of treatment?

"I'm sorry I'm late," she said, following him past a row of cubicles from which feet and heads protruded as in restroom stalls. "My uncle, though, just wouldn't shut up. I had to stop in and see him today."

With a vague "How nice" he ushered her into the last cubicle on the window side of the room. During the course of her treatment Olive had been casually observing the comings and goings at the local Midas muffler shop across the street. Much to her annoyance several of the employees there were now appearing in her dreams. She knew she should be dreaming about people who were important to her, untangling troubling interpersonal relationships with her subconscious and not, Lord knows, wasting time on a bunch of muffler specialists. Dr. Bates picked up her chart while she tried to close the dimity curtains before settling into the leatherette chair. She discovered that they were only "show" curtains, though, without enough material to actually close.

"This inlay that came out, Mrs. Mackie, you're sure it was the one I put in?" Being rather short, Dr. Bates would adjust Olive's head so that it was slightly below the level of her feet. One day, after nearly blacking out when she tried to stand up, she had suggested, in as polite and unpushy a manner as possible, that he might want to use a stool in the future. He was now perched upon a stool, but he didn't look comfortable. She wondered if it was possible to indicate to him that he really didn't *have* to use the stool. It had only been a suggestion.

"Well, I suppose it could be a, uh . . ." With a loud hum the contour chair was raised and then tilted back to the old prestool angle. Of course, the inlay was indeed the one he had put in yesterday, the one he had gotten his first A on. She just hated having to tell him it had fallen out. Never before had anyone worked on her teeth so conscientiously. Redoing each filling several times before he was satisfied, he would then polish and buff it to perfection, his hands trembling with eagerness. And yet he was always ending up with B−'s and C's. Olive had found herself actually rooting for him. When he didn't get the grade she thought he deserved, she would sometimes have a word in private with his supervisor, trying to get him a higher mark.

"Maybe you better check the chart to see for sure. And Dr. Bates, I wonder if you would mind raising my head just a tee-tiny."

After he had drilled and picked at the bits of inlay remaining in her number five, he asked to be excused for a moment.

Olive had an idea what he was up to and laid a restraining hand upon his arm. With a rubber dam in her mouth it was impossible to talk. But since the dam was slightly askew and hurt like the devil, she didn't feel too guilty about yanking it loose. "You're not going to get Dr. Schexsnyder, are you?"

With a frown he took the bloody dam from her and rinsed it off. "I have to show him."

"Why? So he can give you an F? Now, look, Dr. Bates, I know you worked hard on this inlay. Just fix it up for me, and no one has to be any the wiser." She gave him a wink, and he blushed. She blushed back, afraid he might have gotten the wrong idea.

"It won't work." His voice sounded solemn, almost profound. "I'll have to get the gold from Louise, and she'll have to charge you. If it's my mistake, the school pays for it, see? Which reminds me, Mrs. Mackie, I've been getting some flak from Louise about your bill."

"I've been meaning to tell you—if you don't mind my being personal, Dr. Bates—well, it's really disgraceful the way you let that girl push you around. With those kind of people you really have to put your foot down. They don't understand anything else." Olive folded one thick ankle over the other. They were her worst feature, and she tried to make them as inconspicuous as possible, especially around Dr. Bates. For some reason, his gaze often wandered to them, or at least in their general direction.

"Mm, well, Louise is not really the issue here. You see, I don't get any credit for the work I've done until you've paid up. Collecting the money is part of the assignment. Now, I know a lot of this has been my fault, like I haven't mentioned your bill after every session and all. Quite frankly . . ." Pressing a silver explorer to his nose, he stared into space. "Quite frankly," he resumed just as Olive started to say something about Louise.

"Go ahead," she said.

"Quite frankly, I . . ."

"Money," she prompted, "you were talking about money."

"Yes, uh, quite frankly, I find this the hardest part of my

job. Money is something I'd rather not think about. I've never been good at . . ."

Her neck corded as she tried to raise her head, which seemed to weigh a ton. "Seems to me you're evading the issue. Let's face it, Dr. Bates, like I said before, you're a horribly attractive individual. And what happens to horribly attractive individuals? Nine times out of ten, people try to take advantage of them, am I right?" Actually Olive had never found her dentist to be so horribly attractive. Good-looking, yes; cute, indeed. But for her horribly attractive meant someone like Clint Eastwood, and this boy was about as far from Dirty Harry as you could get. Nevertheless, she could not help noticing how virtually every female in this joint eyed him—Louise included. All he had to do was give the signal, and they would throw themselves at his feet.

"Well, I don't . . ." He was blushing like a schoolgirl. "I'm not actually . . . just ordinary. Anyway, let's see if we can get this dam back in. Maybe I better give you a little more Novocain."

" ' . . . Someone left the cake out in the rain—' Dr. Bates, front desk . . ." Olive narrowed her eyes as Louise's voice pierced the Muzak in a flurry of static. " ' . . . take it 'cause it took so long to bake it . . .' "

"I'll be right back," he said, putting down the needle.

She gave him a significant look, which said, Be firm. After he had left, she glanced anxiously at the watch that she could wear, if necessary, two hundred feet underwater. Nine after one. If she got out by two and drove seventy, seventy-five miles an hour and didn't get held up at that train crossing, she might be able to make it back to Tula Springs for the Zoning Board meeting. Vondra, her boss, would have a conniption fit if she missed it.

"Well, I hope you . . ." Olive said when he returned. "What's wrong?"

"She's not going to give us any gold until you do something about your account."

"You got to be kidding. Listen, I mailed something in last week, I forget how much. But I know I sent a check. And anyway . . ." She swung her legs over the edge of the chair and sat up. "Anyway, this is just a replacement. You owe me this."

Clutching the chair arm while the spots faded before her eyes, she announced her intention of having a good talk with Louise. Dr. Bates, though, requested that she stay where she was and let him handle Louise. "Just give me something now, anything, as a sign of good will. You got twenty, fifteen, anything?"

"All right, all right." She dug in her purse for her checkbook. So what if she didn't have enough money this month for her son's tuition? So what if her pool cleaner was threatening to take her to small claims court? Louise must have her pound of flesh. She wrote out a check for fifteen dollars and handed it to Dr. Bates. "I'd like a receipt, please."

Every day, usually at three on the dot, they took their coffee break in Dead Records, a musty room on the third floor of Tula Springs' hundred-and-fifty-year-old City Hall. Crammed with Army surplus file cabinets, all stuffed to the gills with useless information that should have been thrown out years ago, the L-shaped room could have provided desperately needed office space. No one, however, was courageous enough to sign a written order, fearful that some memo or edict from a past administration might turn out to be important after all. Mrs. Sanchez, the mayor's appointment secretary, had domesticated a corner of the bleak room with a fringed tablecloth that covered a pair of waist-high files. There the drip coffeepot and china cups were set beside a vase of dried asters. Although she and Olive had known each other for the nearly fifteen years Olive had worked as secretary to various Superintendents of Streets, Parks, and Garbage, it was one of those friendships that existed solely within the confines of the office. If Olive happened to see Mrs. Sanchez browsing through patterns in the Vogue Shoppe or testing perfume at the Rexall counter, she would make a guilty detour around this older, somewhat heavy-set colleague. On the few occasions when they couldn't avoid saying hello in public, Mrs. Sanchez tended to gush in nervous, confused detail, as if Olive were a store detective.

Today Olive was late for the coffee break, not getting back from the dentist until after four. After apologizing to Mrs. Sanchez she settled into a large, misshapen wing chair and began to complain about her husband. He had come home the other day with yet another video game. "I said to Duane, enough, that's it. Here we can barely afford to pay the light bill and you got to get yourself another toy. If you want to play, I said, why don't you go play like you're mowing the lawn."

"Mm . . . Try this." Mrs. Sanchez handed Olive a Danish butter cookie from the flowery tin beside her beeper. The mayor made his secretary carry an electronic pager with her at all times, a device that caused her much misery. Every time it sounded, she would visibly start and then, clutching her ample bosom, commiserate with her poor heart before dutifully obeying the summons. As a witness to these tortures, Olive had once taken it upon herself to ask the mayor to give his secretary a beeper with a less piercing beep. But Mrs. Sanchez, when ordered into his office, denied that it was as bad as Olive said. Since then Olive had thought twice about doing Mrs. Sanchez any favors.

"Twenty-nine ninety-five for Donkey Kong."

"Mm, terrible," Mrs. Sanchez murmured as she gazed out the dormer window with her blue, not very Spanish-looking eyes. Olive knew she was married to a man who had something to do with the Bay of Pigs invasion, but whether she herself was Latin was another question, one that Olive was too tactful to pose. Brushing some crumbs from her generous lap, Mrs. Sanchez let out one of her elaborate, rococo sighs. "Listen, pumpkin, I thought you ought to know. Vondra came by my desk right after that Zoning Board meeting you missed today. She seemed pretty steamed, said she wanted to know just where the—where you were."

The current Superintendent of Streets, Parks, and Garbage, Vondra had had the gall to name a fountain after her nephew, a lieutenant or something who shuffled papers at the Pentagon. Olive had wanted to name it after her high-school basketball coach, whose house had burned down the year before, uninsured.

"She knows darn well I was at the dentist. I told her myself."

"Right, but she's beginning to wonder." Mrs. Sanchez pressed a bare, pudgy arm against the cool metal of one of the filing cabinets that hemmed in the cozy nook the women had made for themselves. "She said she never knew anyone who went to the dentist as much you and still had any teeth left to talk through, or something like that, I forget."

"What's that supposed to mean? Boy, she has some nerve. It's her fault I got to tramp all the way over to Ozone. If she paid me a decent salary, I could afford a regular dentist here." The night before, Olive's son, Felix, had criticized the way she sat with her knees so far apart. Remembering this, she brought them together. "You'd think she'd understand I have a kid in private school with a ton of tuition to pay. But no, thanks to Vondra all I can afford is a dentist who lives with his mother-in-law, his *ex*-mother-in-law."

"Hm?" Mrs. Sanchez inquired delicately with a flutter of her lashes.

Olive hadn't really meant to say that. She realized instantly how odd it sounded. But it had been preying on her mind ever since Dr. Bates had informed her, toward the end of her session that day, that he was living on Pine Street in Tula Springs with Mrs. Undine. She had mentioned to him, after he had removed the dam, that Mrs. Undine had known she had an appointment with him. "Isn't that creepy, Dr. Bates," Olive had observed, "the way everyone knows everything about you in a small town? Must make you want to head back up North, I bet."

"Not really, Mrs. Mackie," he had replied in a flat, noncommittal way. "You see, I told Mrs. Undine myself, at breakfast."

"Poor darling," Olive exclaimed. She had assumed, naturally, that one would not be on the best of terms with an ex-mother-in-law, especially if the ex were someone like Mrs. Undine. Olive had gone on to sympathize with Dr. Bates for having to eat breakfast with Old Lady Undies, which was what the students in her civics class used to call her. All sorts of memories sprang up, clear and vivid. There was Old Lady Undies with bubblegum stuck to her behind, Old Lady Undies nearly fainting when Franki Simms pretended to cut off her little finger. Olive was getting the biggest kick out of retailing these stories when she noticed the peculiar expression on Dr. Bates's normally sweet face. That was when he had told her that he happened to share a house with Old Lady Undies and that he found Old Lady Undies to be one of the few bearable aspects of Tula Springs.

"Oh, she *is*," Olive hastened to assure him, "she's real bearable, just one of the nicest people I ever met. All those things I was saying, that was way back, you know. I used to be such a twit, a real jerk. I can hardly stand to think of myself back then. Did you ever take out your high school yearbook and, you know . . . I think Mrs. Undine, the way she goes around cheering up the shut-ins, it's so nice. A shame she had to retire from teaching, but she's still doing good for people, isn't she?"

All the way back to Tula Springs, driving fast as she could, Olive had brooded about these living arrangements. It seemed so sad that someone as cute as Dr. Bates had to be cooped up with an old lady. Surely it would make more sense for him to get a little apartment of his own closer to the dental college. She might even be able to help him fix it up with some of the odds and ends in her garage. There was that Japanese bamboo screen. He might like that even though it had a hole in it. Bachelors weren't that particular, anyway. And there was that maroon chest of drawers that really didn't look right in her guest room. She pictured herself dropping over from time to time to fix him a nourishing meal. Put a little meat on those bones . . .

"Your dentist what?" Mrs. Sanchez asked after spooning Cremora into a second cup of coffee.

"Oh, it's nothing."

"He lives with his ex-mother-in-law?"

A warning went off in Olive's head. She knew it would be best to change the subject. Nothing good could come of such a discussion. "What would you think of a grown man who chose to live with his ex-wife's mother?" she asked, over-riding the warning. "Doesn't that sound strange to you?"

"Not if he likes her."

Olive tried to hide her irritation with a few gulps of tepid coffee. "Mary, we're talking about Mrs. Undine. Even her own daughter couldn't stand living with her. They used to fight all the time."

"Who's Mrs. Undine? Have I met her?"

"She's the reason I've never been to Washington, D.C. Everyone I know has seen the Capitol and the White House and all that, but thanks to Mrs. Undine I don't have the slightest curiosity. You can't believe how boring she made everything seem in civics. And I had her in study hall, too, for four years straight. What are you doing?"

"I'm freshening your cup," Mrs. Sanchez replied as she leaned over with the glass coffeepot that Olive had charged to the tax collector's expense account. Unlike Vondra, he would sign whatever you put in front of him, no questions asked.

"I really shouldn't. I heard it causes cancer of the prostrate or something. . . ."

"One more cup won't do any—oh, my!" Mrs. Sanchez exclaimed with a jerk of her outstretched arm.

"Mary!"

"Oh, I'm sorry." With delicate imprecision Mrs. Sanchez dabbed at the coffee that had spilled onto the papers beside Olive's cup. "I'm really sorry, puss." She took another pink tissue from the packet tucked inside her wide vinyl belt. "I just had a premonition that my beeper was going to go off. It's always when you don't expect it, see. There, it's just fine now. Can't even tell."

Too put out to comment, Olive just sat there gnawing on the inside of her tingling, still half-deadened cheek. The papers that Mrs. Sanchez dabbed at were lists of questions submitted to City Hall by local junior high school students. Three days Olive had spent trying to find out the number of parking meters in town, the name of the first woman ever hanged in Louisiana, whether any fish swam upside down in Lake Pontchartrain—nonsense like that. And now Mrs.

Sanchez insisted on dumping coffee all over the answers Olive had so neatly typed underneath each question.

"There, look," Mrs. Sanchez said, letting the papers flap in front of the portable fan that oscillated fairly between the two ladies. Each got a swish of stale air every five seconds. "Good as new."

Wearily Olive took the papers from her. "I suppose I better get back, Mary. Do you mind washing out my cup for me?"

Later that afternoon Olive was brooding at her desk about certain uncalled-for remarks Vondra had made about the dental college when she was interrupted by a phone call from Mr. Versey. The home attendant wanted to know if it would be all right if he didn't come in and see the old man tomorrow as he was feeling sickly.

"What are you asking me for? That's between you and Uncle L.D.," she said as His Honor, the mayor, walked right by her into Vondra's office without so much as a nod.

"Who's going to feed him?" Mr. Versey said in a weak voice after loudly, vulgarly clearing his throat. A former Grand Exalted Something-or-other of the Ku Klux Klan, Mr. Versey used to work in the post office until he learned that he was allergic to the padding in jiffy bags. He quit and shortly afterwards began a second career at age forty-one as a home attendant. When Uncle L.D. had informed her of the Klan connection, Olive had agreed that Mr. Versey should be replaced by someone a shade more respectable. But after consulting Four Sisters HomeCare, Inc. and hearing about all the red tape involved, Olive had decided to let sleeping dogs lie.

"I was hoping you could maybe drop by his place on your way to work tomorrow, Miss Mackie, and give him an egg. I'm trying to get him interested in eggs this week." His dull, flat voice droned on unsteadily, in and out of focus, as if he were calling long distance from China.

"Good night, Mr. Versey," she finally broke in, "I got Parents' Day tomorrow and Vondra's giving me hell about taking the morning off to see Felix's school. And besides, I was just there today and I want you to know that the smell in that apartment is disgraceful. A whole pile of wet sheets just lying there on the floor—and don't tell me Uncle L.D. doesn't give you money for the laundry."

"Just the day before yesterday I tried, Miss Mackie. But this heat, you know. I was starting down the stairs with a load and I says to myself, I says, 'Ernest, you go one step farther and you're going to drop.' "

"And the grease on the fridge and—"

"Look here, every time I try and clean, Mr. Loraine, he starts hollering at me. He just wants me to sit there and listen to him talk about wars and all, and when I start moving around, he blows his stack, tells me to stay put."

"I told you not to pay any—"

"I hate to interrupt you, Olive," Vondra's voice suddenly broke in on the line, "but I wonder if you might spare a moment of your valuable time and come take a letter."

"Yes, ma'am, if you'll just give me a second, I happen to be . . . Mr. Versey, hello, Mr. Versey, you there? Oh, good, now he's hung up," she muttered as she set the receiver down. Looking under a package of Contempo placemats she had to wrap as a going-away present for the girl down the hall, Olive finally found her dictation pad. It had something sticky on it, which she tried to pick off as she wandered into Vondra's office. Since His Honor was in there, she might as well remind him about that raise he had promised her three months ago. And yes, this might also be a good time to bring up that parking scheme of hers. Diagonal parking in the business district would save a lot of space, despite what Vondra thought. With more parking spaces shoppers might be lured back downtown, away from the mall just across the state line in Mississippi. In fact, Olive was going to suggest that they do away with metered parking altogether. What revenue the city lost would be more than made up for by increased sales-tax income from local businesses. Besides, Vondra was always having personnel problems with the meter maids. They wanted new, more stylish uniforms, a demand Olive could readily sympathize with. She herself had once donned the stiff green meter-maid jumper years ago for a summer job after high school. She would never forget how foolish the uniform made her feel in front of her classmates.

"Olive?"

"Coming, I'm coming."

Chapter Three

DRESSING ON THE MORNING OF PARENTS' DAY, Olive had tried on one outfit after another before hitting upon the right look. This turned out to be an off-white linen jacket with the Cheryl Tiegs navy skirt that she was going to send back to Sears since she had ordered a pale apricot from the catalogue. Halfway through the tour of the school grounds, though, she noticed dark patches on the armpits of the jacket. She thought about taking it off, but then remembered that it was covering the blood stains on her blouse. It had been a big mistake wearing a ninety-one-dollar designer blouse to the dentist the week before. She must have been out of her mind. Certainly Dr. Bates couldn't be blamed for the blood that the dry cleaner couldn't get out. Most people would have thrown the blouse away, she supposed. But Olive wasn't made of money.

As he showed them around the gym Dr. Munrow, the school principal, informed the handful of parents in the Q through Z group that he didn't believe there was any such beast as religion. Perched on a narrow bleacher, her arms folded over the perspiration stains, Olive exchanged a puzzled glance with the parent beside her, a homely man in a too-tight gray business suit and studded boots.

"That's right, you heard me," the principal said, thrusting his meaty hands into his pockets. With his large, comfortably padded body and receding hairline Dr. Munrow did not look like the youngest principal in Louisiana history, which was how he had introduced himself to the parents earlier that morning. What's more, although he was only twenty-five years old, he claimed he had racked up enough experience to fill twenty-five ordinary lifetimes. Olive found all this unsettling. She was not sure she wanted someone *that* experienced in charge of Felix's education.

"You show me that tame furry little animal they let out of its cage every Sunday morning for an hour or two and I'll show you a genuine hybrid jackalope fraud. Here at Robin Downs we don't believe in any kind of religion you can keep locked up ninety-nine point four per cent of the time. No, sir, I say no, sir, Mr. Waters. I say, no way, José, Mrs. Trenie. I say, no, ma'am sirree, Mrs. . . . Mrs. . . ." He squinted toward the back row where Olive was sitting.

"Mackie," Olive supplied, realizing suddenly that she belonged in the I through P group that was being conducted by the life sciences teacher.

"No way, Mrs. Mackie. The Almighty will not be confined to a cage at Robin Downs, no minutes, no hours of the day can keep the Creator of time itself barred from my students. He is sitting there for the full fifty minutes in Miss Johnson's algebra class. He is straining his ears to catch every word Mr. Howard is saying in history about this One Nation Under God. And yes, even here, right where I'm standing"—the principal stamped the floor with a white gum-soled loafer— "on the foul line of this here basketball court, He is here teaching your children the difference between right and wrong. And that difference, folks, is as plain and clear as this great big fat line I'm standing on. Now, if you'll follow me."

After the gymnasium, with its gleaming hardwood floors and whirlpool baths, the actual classrooms at Robin Downs were something of a letdown. Although Dr. Munrow hastened to assure the parents that these were just temporary structures, Olive couldn't help wondering just how temporary something almost twenty years old could be. Connected by covered walkways, the classrooms were a series of prefab geodesic domes that had been hastily erected not long after Tula Springs High was integrated, in the late sixties. Many of the domes, including the domestic science room the Q through Z's were now being ushered into, resembled igloos during a heat wave. Begrimed by close proximity to the highway, they were far from their original gleaming whiteness, and some even sagged in places. "Y'all just pretend we're not here," Dr. Munrow instructed the students as he herded the parents to the back of the class.

"All right, girls, in just a moment you will be divided into three groups," a familiar voice announced. The parents were huddled against a curved wall beneath a sign that advised the happy homemaker to keep a slice of ordinary bread in the cookie jar. Wondering why one was supposed to do this, Olive looked to the front of the room and saw that it was Mrs. Undine behind the lectern. Bridling, as if Mrs. Undine had walked into her living room uninvited, without even bothering to knock, Olive couldn't figure out what business a retired civics teacher had in a home ec classroom. But then Dr. Munrow whispered loudly to the parents that Mrs. Undine was substituting for Mrs. Brown, who was indisposed.

Although this explanation didn't entirely dispel the sense of intrusion, Olive recovered enough to smile pleasantly in her general direction. She was seeing her, or at least trying to see her, in a new light now, as one of the few bearable aspects of Tula Springs. *What could Dr. Bates have meant by that?* Olive asked herself as she scrutinized the woman for some clue. Years had gone by since she had taught Olive civics, and yet Mrs. Undine had hardly changed at all. There was the same stiff smile, the same overbrushed, static-frizzed hair. Even the cameo brooch disarraying the thin material of her dress seemed familiar. Perhaps there were a few extra lines on her face, but these were timid squiggles, about as interesting to Olive as a laundry list. In general, all Olive could come up with was that Mrs. Undine was not quite as unpleasant-looking as she had imagined. The woman, though, seemed to go out of her way to camouflage what could be a normal, somewhat soothing face with her continual, uncalled-for wincing. It reminded Olive of her own mother, a sort of minor prophet who could look at a cup of hot coffee balanced on a knee and know for certain it was fixing to be spilled.

"Before we set the tables in the correct manner"—Mrs. Undine's extended little finger indicated the three card tables ranged beneath a portable blackboard—"I would like to review the history of napkins for you. It's important that we don't take our household objects for granted, that we see everything in its proper historical context." She raised her voice to compete with the shifting gears of a tractor trailer. "First we find napkins being used—"

"Hey."

"Yes, what is it?"

"We was supposed to do julienne today."

Stuck behind a clump of fragrant ladies, Olive shifted for a better view and caught a glimpse of the girl who had interrupted. She was surprisingly lovely, at least in profile.

"The lesson plan from Mrs. Brown indicates that table settings are to be pursued this week," Mrs. Undine replied. She gave a nervous tug to the loose print dress that hung like an irregular on her shapeless frame.

"We never got to julienne last week," another girl whom Olive couldn't see put in and was quickly seconded by a chorus of whines and complaints.

Her face blotched by a patchwork of fear and confusion, Mrs. Undine reached for the Jergens on the desk and gave her hands a good squirt. The girls' unrest worked like caffeine on Olive's hot, weary body, rousing her with the expectation of a scene. In the guise of wondering aloud to a neighboring parent what was going on, Olive made her own contribution to the revolt.

"That's enough, quiet!" a boy's voice called out. "She's already got the tables set up, so let her do what she wants."

"Stuff it, Felix," the lovely instigator said.

Standing on tiptoe, Olive saw with a sinking heart that it was Felix who had spoken up. Why in the world did it have to be *her* son who was the only boy in class? And why hadn't he told her that he was planning to take home ec this year? Olive believed strongly in communication between parent and child, or rather, between friends, because that was what she liked to think of herself as—a friend to her son, not a mother. As a friend, she would have commended Felix for having enough confidence in his masculinity to be in an all-girl class, and then she would have asked him if the wisest way to express this confidence was to take home ec. Felix was always doing things like this that puzzled her. For instance, although he refused to go dove hunting with his father, he spent enough hours at a firing range to win a medal last year at the parish fair. Then, instead of going out for football, he had taken up boxing with an amateur team of middle-aged men who met in the home of a Mormon bishop. Although Felix had managed to find himself a girl friend, a somewhat dour young woman who wore no make-up, she didn't go to Robin Downs. As a result he was excluded from a lot of parties he should have been invited to. It really bothered Olive that someone as good-looking and athletic as her son had not won a thing last year, not Most Likely to Succeed, Most Witty (Olive had won this her senior year in high school), Most Athletic (Olive had won this all four years), or Most Handsome, much less Class Favorite. This year she was determined to see Felix make himself more popular by advising him about the little things that mattered to girls his age.

"No one asked you to talk, Felix."

"All right, girls, quiet. Leave Felix alone." Mrs. Undine adjusted a drooping bra strap. "Let's see now," she went on, her eyes darting anxiously from her notes to Dr. Munrow's benign, impassive face in back. "Before we perform our table settings, let's spend a moment reviewing the role of napkins through the ages. First we find napkins being used to wrap money up in, something that I'm sure many of the boys here in school might still do—right, Felix?"

"Right, Felix?" came a dim echo from somewhere in the class.

"Luke Nineteen, Verse Twenty," Mrs. Undine enunciated, " 'Then another came, saying, "Lord, behold, here is thy pound, which I have kept laid up in a *napkin*: For I have feared thee, because thou art an austere man." ' Miss Barnes, please put that away; you'll be eating soon enough. Next we see napkins being used to get rid of illness in Acts Nineteen. Finally Saint John, Chapter Twenty: 'Then cometh

Simon Peter following him, and went into the sepulchre, and seeth the linen clothes lie, And the napkin, that was about his head . . . ' Back then napkins were used to cover the heads of corpses. Any questions? Now I believe we're ready to fold. Felix, would you help me pass out the napkins?"

Since Olive had promised Vondra to get back to the office by twelve-thirty, she wasn't able to eat with the Q through Z's in the lunchroom after the domestic science class. "I'm disappointed in you, Felix," she said, pausing in the walkway on her way to the parking lot. "You made me feel very small."

"Huh?"

"I thought we had no secrets."

"Look, Ol, I just didn't want to get into a squawk session with you. It's no big deal these days, you know. Lots of guys take it."

"I noticed."

"Not here. I mean at the decent schools."

Being an only child, Felix was used to getting his way, except in this one regard. She insisted that he get the best education that he possibly could, which meant Robin Downs. Of course, Olive found it rather silly, all the emphasis placed on religion here, but it was a small price to pay when you considered the alternative. At the public school half the sophomores were said to be virtual illiterates, and the senior class was full of twenty-year-olds. It was no wonder Mrs. Undine had retired early. Who could expect anyone to teach in a public school these days?

"Felix, I have nothing against boys taking home ec." She reached for his rough hand, which became elusive. It was always easier for her to be cross with him in the abstract. Once he was near, all her principles melted under a steady beam of pleasure that made her feel talkative. "In fact, I think it's sort of brave. But don't you think . . . Oh, hello," she added as Mrs. Undine emerged from the dome. Blinking in the harsh noon glare, she raised a hand to ward off a sidelong gust, gritty and smelling of exhaust fumes.

"Yes, fine." Mrs. Undine nodded abstractly, with a fixed smile, as if Olive were a stranger. Olive wondered if she should say something to her about her last trip to the dentist so that Mrs. Undine would know that she had learned about her living arrangements. But then again, what did it matter? They so rarely saw each other these days. In any case, the question became academic as Mrs. Undine, with a fretful word or two about the weather, wandered off toward the lunchroom.

"You know, I never could stand her. She's such a priss."

"Who?" her son said. "Her? She's not so bad."

"She's a very hostile person. Watch out for her, boy. She seems so nice and sweet on the outside, but underneath . . . In high school she was always putting me down. It took me a while to figure it out, but she was."

Felix shifted his books from one arm to the other. "High school?"

"She taught civics, and I had her in study hall. If I'd listened to her, I never would have gone on to college. Can you imagine, she advised me to enroll in some dumb secretary school or something. She actually refused to write a recommendation for me, too. I needed one once for a summer job."

"You want to go eat?"

"No, hon, I'm late." Kay had gotten that job as a lifeguard at the city pool, Olive remembered now. And Olive could swim rings around the girl, everyone knew that. "By the way, you got a few bucks you can swing this way? I forgot to ask Duane. . . ."

Felix dug into his pocket. "How much you want?" Olive was dismayed by her son's job, bagging groceries at the A&P. But no amount of pleading could make him quit. She did wish he had more of a nose for what was and was not done. The idea of anyone from Robin Downs working at such a job was simply ludicrous.

"Will ten do?"

"Fine." She counted out the dirty bills he handed her. "I'll pay you back, of course. And my darling, please don't wear those pants to school anymore." She glanced at his baggy imitation seersuckers. "Let me buy you a nice pair of Calvin

Kleins, the stone-washed kind. Let's apply the ten bucks to that, what do you say? Listen, I just got to run. 'Bye, hon.''

As she headed for the parking lot Olive congratulated herself for not bringing up the tattoo that Felix had gotten on his upper arm the week before, some sort of tiny snake that was, thank goodness, hidden by his sleeve. Oh, it had nearly killed her when she first noticed it. But she wasn't going to be like her own mother, who had nearly ruined Olive's adolescence with all her restrictions about make-up and dresses. No, Olive had not gone into a swivet when she had walked into the bathroom and asked Felix, who was taking a shower, what he would like for supper. Instead, she had simply informed him that the snake was the tackiest thing she had ever seen and that now he was sure never to find a decent girl from Robin Downs to go out with. Then she had told him, after he explained that it was no big deal, that everyone was getting one, that she never wanted to discuss this subject with him again. The milk had been spilt, and that was that.

The front seat of the Cadillac was so hot that Olive had to stand outside a few moments while she ran the air-conditioner. Duane, not trusting the car dealers in town, was trying to sell the Brougham himself. It seemed so crude, the sign he had painted on the back window giving everyone their telephone number. If he had used a stencil, it wouldn't have been so bad. But no, Duane was too worn out to go look for one. Testing the seat with her hand, Olive figured she had better drive home first and change her jacket before going to the office. Of course, this meant that she wouldn't have time to drop by Uncle L.D.'s, but she simply couldn't let everyone at City Hall see those perspiration stains. She would give him a call instead.

Although she had to admit they could no longer afford the car, Olive was doing everything she could to convince her husband that they didn't also have to give up their house. They had bought it only three years ago, when Duane was making money hand over fist at a real estate agency. He had been one of the top salespersons, always getting his name in the paper, when, for some reason having to do with licensing and a state legislator who was declared insane, the agency had gone bankrupt. Until Duane could find something better, he was working for a friend of Olive's who owned a cheese shop in the mall. His salary barely covered the mortgage payments, but Olive was determined to work herself to the bone to keep the house. For her it had been a case of love at first sight. Situated in the middle of Tula Springs' most exclusive development, Cherylview Estates, the three-and-a-half bedroom Tudor combined rustic charm with the most modern conveniences, including an intercom system that let Olive summon Felix for breakfast without raising her voice.

"Listen, I've only got a second, I'm supposed to be at work," Olive said into the phone as soon as she had stepped inside the door. The phone was sitting on the méridienne she had bought, along with a kidney-shaped pool, with the money she had inherited from her grandmother, who had won a Publishers Clearing House Sweepstakes just before she passed away. Olive still had seventeen thousand dollars of this inheritance tucked away in various C.D.'s for Felix's college education. "You'll never believe what just happened, Gail," she went on. "I was at Parents' Day and—"

Gail, a friend since kindergarten, asked if they could maybe talk some other time. She was in the middle of discussing a loan with a client at the bank, where she had recently been promoted to vice-president. Olive had her largest C.D. at this bank, even though they didn't give any bonuses like the electric blanket she had got at the Ozone bank.

"Hang on, girl. This'll only take a sec. So like I was saying, I was at Robin Downs and—"

"Olive, are you sure this can't wait?"

"Remember Mrs. Undine? She's come out of retirement, and guess who she's teaching now? Felix! Gail, I swear, I nearly died. There I was in the middle of a home ec—I mean where does she get off teaching home ec?—and then I hear—"

"I got to go. I'll call you tonight, I promise."

"Oh. Well, I may not be in. Anyway . . . Yeah, 'bye."

Olive found the blouse she was looking for in the kitchen, where she had left it to drip-dry over a wandering Jew that was turning yellow. A note on the refrigerator reminded her to pick up dental floss at Sonny Boy so she could hem Duane's jeans. Dental floss held so much better than regular thread, her friend Carol had informed her.

On the way to City Hall Olive pulled into a Taco Bell and ordered a number 3 burrito with fries. She had no particular fondness for Mexican food, but this was the only drive-in in town that let you order and pick up without getting out of the car. One of the new banks had this system, too, and what with this heat, Olive considered whether it might not be worth her while to pull their joint account out of Gail's bank and open up one where she could stay in an air-conditioned car. In order to save time, Olive ate hurriedly while driving to City Hall. This didn't turn out to have been such a good idea, for when she got to her desk and checked her make-up, she noticed that there was a little gap between her two front teeth. One of Dr. Bates's fillings had come out on the side of an upper front tooth.

"It's not his fault. I probably just wasn't careful enough when I was eating," Olive explained to Harry Leroy, whom she had called after explaining to Vondra why she was late. Harry Leroy was the friend who owned the cheese shop in the mall, as well as five Quik Stop franchises and a condominium in Panama City, Florida, and he had the most darling wife, Desirée, who was a state trooper. For months now Harry had been advising her to dump Dr. Bates and get herself a real dentist, while Olive had defended her choice by reminding him of such old-fashioned virtues as loyalty, trust, and thrift.

"What are you telling me, Olive? You telling me you can't eat a burrito without having to be careful? What sort of dentist is that?"

"I know, but . . ." She gazed at her teeth in the compact mirror and winced. She would have to remember not to smile today in the office.

While Harry lectured her about Dr. Bates, Olive glanced

over her shoulder and saw that Vondra had opened the door to her office just enough to spy on her. In her late fifties, Vondra Hewes was a handsome woman with a neat mound of platinum blond hair and nicotine-stained fingers that trembled slightly whenever she talked. Olive often had trouble understanding her boss because she ran her words together, talking like people who couldn't work a clutch drove: in rapid, uneven spurts.

"Hold on a sec," Olive said, covering the mouthpiece with her hand. "Yes, ma'am?" she called out to Vondra.

"Huh?"

"You want me?"

"Huh?"

"You're looking at me like you want something."

"I'm not looking at you."

Swiveling her chair back around, Olive said to Harry Leroy in a low voice, "Careful what you say. She might be listening in. Anyway, I was at Parents' Day."

"Oh, right. You were saying something about Felix."

"He's taking home ec, Harry. I like to die when I saw him sitting there in a class full of girls. What do you think he means by that? Is he trying to kill me? I mean, first it's boxing with some goddam bishop, then it's a tattoo, and now home ec. I'm so afraid he might get warped, but I don't want to alienate him."

"It's hard to imagine someone boxing in a miter."

"Oh, it's just a Mormon bishop, some guy who owns a catfish farm out on the Old Jeff Davis Highway. That's where I drop him off every Wednesday after school. I mean, the bishop looks nice and all, clean-cut, but he must be fifty years old. I don't think teenagers should have fifty-year-old friends, do you?" Her tongue probed the gap between her teeth. "God, I just remembered. Duane and I are supposed to go to Carol and Emile's tonight for dinner. I can't go with this hole a mile wide. . . . Look, I better hang up. Let's have lunch soon, O.K.?"

After typing up a memo on the disputed water meter readings for August, Olive felt she had better check on Uncle L.D. She dialed, and while the phone rang she wondered if what she had heard recently about Harry Leroy was true. Missy McBaine, a sorority sister from St. Jude State College, claimed that Harry had give his nephew a Halston bathrobe that he had shoplifted from Penney's at the mall. If that was true, Olive wasn't sure she should be asking Harry for advice about Felix. There was no telling what he might say.

"Come on," Olive muttered into the phone as it continued to ring. "Pick up, man. I haven't got all day."

"Olive, would you come in here a minute?" Vondra called out.

Hanging up, Olive wandered into the office, where Vondra, whose entire body seemed to hum, occasionally to shudder, with enormous reserves of repressed energy, told her to bring the second draft of some letter or other to the city attorney. Then she was supposed to wait for something or other, Olive wasn't sure what, since she was worrying about whether Uncle L.D. was all right. The old man sometimes didn't answer his phone just to give her a scare. At the same time she was also worrying about how she would break it to Vondra that she absolutely had to go to the dentist that afternoon to get the gap repaired.

An hour or so later, while she was headed south to Ozone with the air-conditioner going full blast, Olive's vivid daydream of impeachment proceedings against Vondra was interrupted by a stray thought. As she ran her tongue over the gap Dr. Bates was going to fill, it occurred to her how sad it must be to be Jewish. How could anyone in his right mind go through life thinking he was going to die and that was that? Why, it would just kill her if she thought that one day Felix was going to turn to dust and not rise up again—not just in a spiritual way, but with his whole entire body, every last finger and toe. If the Good Lord had just died on the cross like the Jews thought, then what the hell was the point? Why bring children into such a world? Of course now, as far as Uncle L.D. was concerned, she could feel a little more Jewish about him. After all, he was so old and mixed up, it would be sort of cruel to resurrect him—unless he could be resurrected as he was when he was twenty or so. For a moment Olive tried to imagine a twenty-year-old Uncle L.D., but failing to do so, her mind reverted to more important matters, such as what she was going to give Felix to eat tonight. Maybe she would let him take his Harley-Davidson to the BurgerMat. That would be a nice treat for him since she usually didn't allow him to go there on a school night. And it would give her time to do something with her hair before the dinner party.

Chapter Four

"Leave it," Uncle L.D. snapped at Mr. Versey, who was worried that it might be someone important on the phone. "Let it ring."

"Could be Miz Sill," Mr. Versey muttered as he stirred uneasily upon the tv tray that reinforced the rocker's broken wicker seat. Mrs. Sills—with an *s* that Mr. Versey was too lazy to pronounce—was the home attendant supervisor at Four Sisters HomeCare, Inc. From the way the phone was ringing, though, with that unmistakable impertinence, the old man knew exactly who it was. And he had no intention of giving that someone the satisfaction of finding out that he was O.K. For all she knew, he could be lying on the floor, groaning for just a drop of water. Yet did she bother to take thirty seconds to drop by on her way to City Hall? Because of the girl's complete and utter selfishness Uncle L.D. had been forced to bribe Mr. Versey, who had the flu, to come in today. Twenty dollars he was paying him, over and above what Mr. Versey was getting from Medicaid, to sit there in that rocker and soak up all his port. (Mr. Versey indulged for medicinal purposes only, of course, since his doctor didn't allow him to drink.)

The main problem with Mr. Versey was not his basic lack of anything even remotely resembling intelligence, ambition, or personality. Long ago Uncle L.D. had learned how to sidestep this deficiency in the lower orders he had encountered at various diners, filling stations, and such like—and had managed nonetheless to carry on reasonably entertaining conversations. What prevented Uncle L.D. from getting anywhere at all with Mr. Versey, though, was the absence of any trace of plain and simple curiosity. Though he prided himself on bringing out the best in everyone, no matter his race, creed, or color, Uncle L.D. could not spark even a glimmer of interest in this man's dim, watery eyes. Hundreds of topics had been brought up over the past year, everything ranging from Polonius to canvasbacks, and yet not once had Mr. Versey shown the slightest inclination to broaden his horizons with a sensible question or two, aside from the time they had gotten into a discussion about religion. Religion just happened to be the one thing Uncle L.D. did not know or care a thing about. Mr. Versey had informed him that Christianity was nothing but a Jewish plot to ruin the world. After all, the Jews had started it, and Mr. Versey believed they were still secretly behind it, financing the Vatican.

"Well, I hope you're satisfied," Mr. Versey said when the phone stopped ringing. "Might of been someone trying to tell you you won a million dollars. Now you'll never know."

Bleary-eyed, Uncle L.D. looked over at the rocker, where Mr. Versey seemed to waver insubstantially like a sunken wreck. At forty-three Mr. Versey was young enough to be Uncle L.D.'s grandson, yet his litany of complaints about various aches and pains made him sound more like a grandmother. With more things wrong with him than even he, a memory expert, could keep in mind, Uncle L.D. nevertheless held firm that a gentleman did not discuss such matters. Consequently whenever Mr. Versey launched into a disquisition on his kidneys or described the funny feeling he had in his neck at night, like there was a mouse loose inside him, Uncle L.D. would block out what he was hearing by humming snatches of Berlioz. Or he would attempt to elevate the tone of the conversation, as he did now, when, without any preamble, Mr. Versey began to deliver a white paper on the state of his clogged nostrils.

"Yes, yes, very unfortunate, Mr. Versey, sorry to hear.

Now you remember, of course, the date of the Peace of Ghent."

"You run a rubber tube up far's it can go in one nostril, then get you some lukewarm salt water and—"

"The date, Mr. Versey."

During the Depression Uncle L.D. had enjoyed a modest success lecturing at various YWCA's in East Chicago, Gary and Hammond, Indiana. His most popular talk had been called "Pointless Battles" and took as its primary example the Battle of New Orleans, which had occurred between two countries that were officially at peace. The Peace of Ghent was signed on December 24, 1814, but because the news could not travel fast enough, a battle took place on January 8. The girls were properly astonished and having managed to open up their minds, he would then go on to explain the pointless battles they fought in their own lives due to delayed communications. Afterwards he offered to enroll them in his memory course at a special introductory rate. A defective memory was, of course, the prime reason for delayed communications.

"I'm asking you the date, Mr. Versey. What's the key word?"

"Shoes," Mr. Versey muttered, a finger on his pulse.

"No! High heels!" With a groan Uncle L.D. turned his weary head and spat on the floor. The springs creaked as he tried to find a more comfortable position on the plastic sheet. "It's so simple, sir. Eighteen fourteen is what? Dumpy yellow gals. Twenty-four? Look repellent. December is twelve, the twelfth month, and twelve is what? High heels. High heels look repellent on dumpy yellow gals: the Peace of Ghent, December twenty— Now what? What are you doing?"

Clad in a dun shawl that Mrs. Undine had unintentionally left behind some months earlier, Mr. Versey had risen from the tray and was shuffling toward the breakfront where the port was stored.

"I told you that was it," Uncle L.D. said crossly. "There's no more."

Mr. Versey looked anyway, pawing through shelves of books, cups, lone socks, bananas, screws, underwear, and greeting cards. "Well, since I'm up," he said, abandoning the search, "you may as well go now."

"But it's not time yet," the old man protested, dreading the ordeal of being wrenched onto the portable potty beside the bed. "I'm not ready."

"Now, look," Mr. Versey said, advancing on Uncle L.D., whose body had become rigid enough for a magician to stretch between two chairs, "I don't want to get back in that rocker and have you tell me then you got to go. Come on."

As he took hold of the old man's arm Uncle L.D. winced. The pain was always so much worse than he remembered, as if his arms, his legs, had withered to a jellied mass of nerves. "Let's get them hamhocks over here," Mr. Versey said, tugging at the frail legs with what seemed like red-hot pincers. "Half-dead, can hardly breathe . . ." Mr. Versey muttered through clenched teeth. "Come all the way over here when I should be in my own bed. . . ." He yanked the blanket, which was tangled in the old man's wing-tip shoes, the ones that had the sides cut with a razor to help get them off and on. "You trying to kill me, that it? You want to kill me, Mr. Loraine?"

"Tomorrow, I'll go tomorrow," the old man pleaded.

Mr. Versey thrust his face so close, Uncle L.D. could feel every syllable on his cheek: "You think I'm coming in tomorrow to wipe up after you, you got another thing coming. Now, I'm going to count three. One, two, up we go!"

Despite his desire to take it like a man, Uncle L.D. let out a sharp cry as he was half dragged, half lifted onto the plastic commode. For a moment, dangling between the bed and the white seat, he was certain Mr. Versey was going to lose his grip and deposit him on the flowered linoleum, as he had done twice before. But somehow he landed safely, if a little askew, with one leg mashed against the armrest.

"Help, God help me," Mr. Versey moaned, letting the shawl drop from his round shoulders. "This is it, I'm a goner." Wheezing in shallow gasps, he sank onto the foot of the bed, smushing a box of Cap'n Crunch.

It was customary for Mr. Versey to go downstairs to the lunch counter at Sonny Boy's for a cup of coffee while Uncle L.D. tried to make something happen. But it looked now as if he was not going to leave. This was, of course, intolerable.

"Go," the old man ordered. "What are you waiting for? Get going."

Mr. Versey just sat there, tugging the lank, greasy strands of hair that ribbed his sallow pate. "You go ahead, pull down them trousers. I ain't looking."

The old man gripped the plastic armrests, as if rage alone would give him the strength to rise, but he succeeded merely in making his arms tremble. There was only one other person who could affect him this way—his late wife and former YWCA pupil, Artis. Even dead, she was able to work him up into a frenzy as he nursed with mnemonic accuracy a string of indignities suffered at her hands. It was her pettiness that had nearly finished him off, her complete inability to appreciate anything that was truly marvelous or awe-inspiring, such as the night he had relinquished nearly a half century of purity for her. Yes, he had been a forty-seven-year-old virgin. And what had she said afterwards? Was she at all grateful for the gift he had bestowed upon her? No, it was the sheets she was thinking of. He was barely through when she was hustling him out of bed so she could change the precious sheets her mother had given her, Irish percale that she claimed you couldn't buy anywhere for love nor money. A month afterwards, during which time he had steered clear of her, she had shown up in class and passed him a note informing him that she was expecting. Being a man of honor, Uncle L.D. had done his duty.

"Don't you touch those sheets," he said in an oddly constricted voice, interrupting one of Mr. Versey's better groans.

"What? I can sit here much as I like. This here's a free country." A faint, Camille-like cough escaped his lips. "No way I'll make it down them stairs. You go ahead and do your business, pops. I ain't got all day."

Groping about for something loose, something heavy, which he could use to strike Mr. Versey, Uncle L.D. nearly toppled from his seat. After some effort he righted himself and then managed to pry free an umbrella that was wedged behind the headboard. By this time, though, Mr. Versey was no longer within reach to take the beating he so richly deserved. He had migrated, with tiny, complaining steps, to the window, where he was straining against the sash with all his might.

"Lord, I can't breathe. I need me some air."

"Get out!" Uncle L.D. commanded, brandishing the umbrella.

"It won't budge. Come on, you son of a bitch"—he groaned with the effort—"open the goddam hell up!"

"How sweet, your initials," Olive said as she examined the monogrammed copper dish that Carol had used to make the shrimp mold. Carol, though, looked askance at her friend, as if the comment had been sarcastic. Ever since eighth grade, when she had conceived an intense admiration for Carol's quiet, contained beauty, which had not faded with age, at least not as much as Olive thought it should have, Olive had always felt Carol held the upper hand in their relationship. Somehow this seemed wrong since Olive was obviously smarter and had all the leadership qualities her friend, who was just a housewife, lacked. Yet whenever Olive tried to assert herself, Carol would invariably take offense, and it would always be Olive who, later, was forced to back down and apologize. Deep down, Olive knew the real reason for this state of affairs: In her own dull, retarded way Carol could easily go through life without giving Olive a second thought, while Olive, for some reason she couldn't quite figure out, really needed Carol as a friend. Consequently whenever they were together, Olive remained vaguely puzzled and deferential, anxious not to provoke her friend into acting too polite, which was how Carol expressed her anger.

"No, I mean it," Olive said, having caught a glimpse of the look directed at her. She leaned closer to better appreciate the monogram in the mold itself. "It's so distinctive."

"Olive, that's not our initials. It's Emile's mother's, the

stupidest thing I've ever seen. I got to use it every now and then, O.K., because, like, Emile's feelings get hurt if I don't."

Emile Deshotel, Carol's husband, was a radiologist who was an authority on stamps and General Custer, two subjects Olive had begged her own husband not to bring up this evening. Although Duane rarely had a thing to say around his own house besides "Where's my socks?" or "Where's the cumin?" (he enjoyed cooking), the minute he was out in public, he had an opinion about everything. It was so embarrassing to hear him spouting off about Geronimo while Emile sat there with a pained expression on his face, too polite to contradict him. This was what had happened the last time the four of them had had dinner. Carol had evaded Olive for a full three weeks afterwards, even though they lived only four houses apart in Cherylview.

"How's everything, boys?" Olive said, peering into the living area after having put the shrimp mold out on the Lucite dining table.

"Is it time?" Emile asked with a dim smile. Looking like a normal-sized man when he stood next to his petite wife—a little on the soft side, perhaps, with his pear-shaped torso and round, balding head—Emile was reduced to childish proportions on the futon next to Duane, who had a habit of crowding both men and women when he talked, squeezing their arms, patting and poking for emphasis. Olive signaled with a jerk of her head, hoping her husband would get the message and move over, give poor Emile some air. But Duane went right on talking, as if she weren't there.

"Just a few minutes, Emile."

Back in the kitchen Olive very politely turned down a sample of Carol's pickled cauliflower, murmuring something about calories. She was afraid to eat anything hard so soon after having the gap refilled in her front tooth. Of course, she would rather not tell Carol this, since then she would have to admit that she had been to Ozone that afternoon. Not that it really mattered so much that Carol knew. But if Carol knew, ten to one Duane would find out before the evening was over, and Olive was not that anxious to explain to him how it wasn't Dr. Bates's fault that the filling had come out. It was Louise the receptionist's fault. Louise, God bless her, had supplied him with the expired composite they had bought cut rate, inferior stuff most dentists didn't use anymore. Actually Olive was quite pleased with the results of the trip. Although Dr. Bates had given no real clue why he lived with Mrs. Undine, Olive had had a chance to tell him in detail how much good she thought Mrs. Undine was doing for Uncle L.D. They had also chatted a little about boys taking home ec, which Dr. Bates seemed in favor of, although it was hard to tell since he had a good word for everyone and everything. In any case, he had called her Olive, not Mrs. Mackie, and had walked with her all the way to the stairs. And yes, they had both laughed when they discovered they were the exact same height. O.K., so maybe she shouldn't have kissed him. But it had been an impulsive, friendly kiss, like two girl friends do sometimes. He hadn't seemed to mind so much, though he had blushed. . . .

"You're so queer, Olive," Carol said a few minutes later, when they were all seated. Because Carol didn't believe in eating anything substantial after six in the evening, daylight flooding through the French windows gave a make-believe atmosphere to the candlelight supper, as if it were a children's sitting. "You know you like my cauliflower. At least, that's what you've always said. And then, O.K., you won't even take one little bite."

Olive smiled appeasingly in her direction while Duane, a former tackle for St. Jude (she had heard him mention this to poor Emile at least three times this evening), went on about the dish he had brought over to the Deshotels'. Emile's face was a polite blank as Duane explained how he had mixed a twelve-ounce can of diced Dole pineapples into a bowl of mashed potatoes, adding by feel a cup or so of sugar and cinnamon, and then let the whole thing set in the freezer. (He had had to make this last week since he was so busy this week.) Just before coming over he had popped it into the microwave for twelve minutes. "Then I got some miniature marshmallows and browned them on top. Course you know, Carol, I don't mean to sound critical or anything, but this isn't supposed to be a dessert. It's a vegetable. My mamma always serves it with her glazed ham."

"Honey, Carol already has plenty of veggies," Olive said with a smile in Emile's direction. How nice it would be, she was thinking, if she could transfer Emile's polite, considerate brain into Duane's nice firm body. A latent Frankenstein, Olive often fantasized about rearranging friends and loved ones into more desirable composites. Carol, for instance, could use some of Mrs. Sanchez's *embonpoint*. It would loosen the girl up, make her a little less conceited, while a slimmer Mrs. Sanchez would have more self-confidence. She wouldn't let the mayor push her around so.

"Darling?" Emile inquired as Carol stood up. He was looking a little peaked this evening, Olive noticed. And he barely touched the delicious shrimp mold and flower-cut zucchini.

"If Duane says we should have it now . . ." Carol said with an ominous sweet smile. "I'll just take these things away. I mean, according to Olive my cauliflower, O.K., it's too fattening, and so we'll just have Duane's casserole now instead."

Everyone, including Olive, made appropriate demurring noises about the proposed substitution while Carol stood there, the mellow daylight haloing her simply coiffed hair, her lovely gray eyes wide, as if she didn't quite understand. When she finally sat down, she sighed and put her head to one side, as if accepting defeat.

"Y'all will never guess who they got teaching at Robin Downs now," Olive put in quickly, before Duane had a chance to start dominating the conversation again. "Old Lady Undies. Remember how she used to erase the blackboard so slow and . . ." A twinge of disloyalty made Olive pause. But then she remembered that she had no reason to be loyal to that woman and continued with a silly story that no one listened to except Emile, who hadn't even gone to Tula Springs High. He had gone to Benjamin Franklin in New Orleans.

"Well, anyway," she concluded, avoiding Emile's puzzled gaze. Hobbled by guilt, Olive's story had limped about in a long and pointless semicircle while Duane and Carol talked to each other. Olive had started to say funny, nasty things about Mrs. Undine but had pulled her punches, leaving Emile hanging. "Anyway, even with her there, I still wouldn't have it any other way. Felix doesn't really like Robin Downs very much—Duane, Carol wants the salt; pass Carol the salt—but I'm determined that he get himself a decent education, I don't care what it costs. You know what Harry Leroy told me the other day. He's got his son in Tula Springs High now. Anyway, he said"—she reached across her husband's plate and passed the salt to Carol—"he said that there was a little black boy in the ninth grade that didn't know the parts of his body. That's what we're dealing with, Emile."

"Olive, you're such a racist," Carol said, still looking at Duane, who was telling her his views on the Canadian Football League. "Emile and I are planning to send Cindy to the public school next year, you know." Cindy was the Deshotels' only child, an eighth-grader who studied classical guitar.

"It's not a question of color," Olive tried to be heard over her husband's voice. "Carol, listen, I work side by side with blacks every day and I love them dearly, I mean it. It's just that I don't think it's fair that Felix should be penalized and held back because of . . . You realize what the average SAT score is of people from TSH? Duane, please, Carol and I are trying to . . ." He finally stopped talking and poured himself another glass of Emile's 1979 Tokay. That was his fourth, and he and Emile had been drinking margaritas before dinner. "Quite frankly, I don't think it's fair to Cindy. She's such a talented child. I'd think twice, Carol, before, you know. . . ."

"Would you like some more shrimp?" Carol said, passing the quivering mold to Olive. "I got them fresh this morning."

A dismal pall settled over Olive. She realized she had overstepped her bounds again, that Carol, who was smiling so hard at her, would probably not speak to her for at least another month. She must do what she could to repair the damage. "Of course, y'all know Harry, the stories he tells. I mean, he's always exaggerating. There's this black boy Felix knows, he's from the public school, and I swear he sounds like he went to Harvard or something."

"That the nigger you won't allow in the house?" Duane inquired.

Emile and Carol looked at their plates while Olive, with a fluttery, unnatural laugh, told her husband that he had an awful sense of humor. "I'm always begging him not to tell jokes when we go out," she said, rapping him lightly on the knuckles with her knife. "By the way, did y'all know that Harry Leroy stole a bathrobe from Penney's and gave it to his nephew as a birthday present? And his wife, Desirée, she gave Gail a ticket the other day. Gail went through two stop lights in a row, and Desirée was so embarrassed because she knows Gail, but I think it's wonderful how that didn't matter, her knowing her, I mean . . . she did her job. Not many people these days do their duty like that and . . ."

Duane had started talking to Carol again, and Emile, angel that he was, helped pull Olive out of her nose dive by pointing out the finer points of the wine she was gulping. Presently the dinner was humming along smoothly enough, Olive chiding Emile about the food left on his plate, Duane absorbed with Carol. But then suddenly, for no apparent reason, Emile stood up, his round face grim and quite pale. With a muttered apology he hurried away from the table.

Somewhat shaken, Olive asked in a small voice, "What's wrong?" She wondered if it might have been something she had said. "Is he all right?"

Carol smiled graciously at her guests. "Please forgive us. I'm afraid Emile has a touch of the flu, some sort of stomach virus. It's nothing, really. He gets it all the time."

"Oh, but why didn't you tell us?" Olive asked, genuinely upset that they had imposed on the Deshotels like this. "I wouldn't have dreamed of coming over. Really, Carol, I insist that you tell me these things beforehand. We're too good friends to be coy with each other."

"I did try, like maybe two or three hundred times today. But every time I called, O.K., you weren't in the office."

"Oh, there was Parents' Day this morning."

"I tried all afternoon, too."

Vondra had long ago given up taking messages for her on Olive's own extension; she just let the phone ring. "This afternoon? Oh, yes, I was at Uncle L.D.'s this afternoon."

"Good Lord, girl," Duane said, fooling with one of the dried flowers in the centerpiece. "You spend more time cleaning that old geezer's place, and your own home is . . . You ought to see, Carol. If any vacuuming ever gets done, it's you know who, Ernest Bombeck here."

"For your information, sir, I *had* to go there today because Mr. Versey was sick, and if I didn't, Uncle L.D. wouldn't have gotten a thing to eat." Which reminded her, the old man never did answer the phone today. She hoped he was all right.

"I better check on Emile," Carol said brightly.

"Duane, I can't believe you said that about me," Olive complained once they had the alcove to themselves. "Using that word."

His features, usually fine and strong, seemed blurred by too much drink. "It's true, isn't it?" he said calmly. The bright, unfocused eyes wandered over her with vague curiosity, then drifted to the slow-motion wave, an expensive novelty item that decorated the blond Danish-modern highboy.

"It's not because he's black. I'm just trying to encourage Felix to have friends from his own school. You've been very obnoxious tonight."

"Me? I can't go anywhere these days without you blabbing about that Mrs. Undine. When are you going to get off this kick, man? Nobody knows what the hell you're talking about."

"I don't talk about her. This is the first time I—"

"Don't make me laugh. What about—"

"Hush, she's coming back. Do you think we ought to volunteer to help with the dishes? Poor Emile . . ."

Although Uncle L.D. was fully aware they were dreams once he had awakened, while he was having them they seemed more real than anything he experienced during the interminable waking hours. When he wasn't sleeping, his life seemed to go in and out of focus in a dreamlike way, what with the sink filling the room with ghostly, disembodied voices. But in his dreams, if a person was there, he or she was firmly there in three solid dimensions. Often, too, there was a marvelous sense of proportion that he would savor afterwards, as he did now, awakening from a brief nap. In this most recent dream he had been addressing a roomful of young women, explaining the advantages of the 1040 short form. The girls had been asking such intelligent questions, all of which elicited witty responses from him. In fact, several times he was required to pause to let the laughter die down. Next to him was a large American flag, and in the audience not one girl had on slacks or jeans. Their dresses, sensible and neat, were so fresh-smelling that it was almost as if he could still enjoy that springlike scent.

As if? Vaguely alarmed, the old man realized he *was* smelling something delightful. Trying to prop his head up for a better look around, he discovered that there was no mattress beneath him, just air. No, it wasn't that, he figured out after a moment. The fact was, he wasn't lying down at all; he was sitting up, slantwise, on the potty. With his legs so frequently numb, Uncle L.D. often had a devil of a time figuring out which way was down, especially when he was being moved about by Mr. Versey. Then it seemed as if there were three hundred and sixty degrees of down. Which reminded him, where was that man, anyway?

As he reached with trembling hands for his trousers he began to wonder if Mr. Versey had come at all today. Hadn't he phoned to say he had the flu? Getting a hold on the stiff tweed bunched about his feet, he began to haul with both hands like someone weighing anchor. But just as one would expect a boat to drift with the anchor up, the old man had the ghastly feeling as he tugged on the pants that the potty was indeed gliding. Either that, or the room itself had come unmoored. Once again he yearned for the solid world of his recent dream. Everything had seemed so normal and right there, not just the girls but the hall itself, a room of such wonderful proportions, with just enough columned height to make everyone feel a bit grand and exalted.

Before he could become too anxious about the potty, the old man realized that he was not on the potty at all. He was in his wheelchair. But why had he been sitting there with his pants down like that?

"Hey, you here?" he called out gruffly, trying to hide his anxiety. Nothing upset him more than not being able to remember correctly. To test himself, he muttered the dates Louisiana was French when it thought it was Spanish (1801–03), American when it thought it was French (1803), and what he had had for breakfast on the day he reached his majority (two fried eggs, sunny-side up, a blueberry muffin, three and a half cups of coffee). Unfortunately it was the things that had happened to him most recently, which he hadn't yet had a chance to properly digest, that he had the most difficulty remembering. Fragments of recent experiences would bob about like flotsam until he was able to reassemble them into a reasonable approximation of what had occurred. Usually this was accomplished quite effortlessly, at least on the days that Olive and Mrs. Undine showed up. He could rely on them for continuity and, with a minimum of improvisation, get by splendidly. With Mr. Versey, though, it was another story. The man tended to be so vague at times about what he had said and done that Uncle L.D., bereft of a true north, would find himself at sea.

As Uncle L.D. tried to wheel the chair around to face the window he noticed the bruise on his aching wrist. Curious, he paused a moment to examine it and was reminded of Mr. Versey's sour breath. Yes, he had been here a short while ago, and they had been arguing. It was here on the left wrist that Mr. Versey had gripped him so cruelly while yanking down his trousers. But Uncle L.D. had still refused to do anything until he left the room. Then hadn't he swatted Mr. Versey with the umbrella? Yes, and Mr. Versey had jerked him into the wheelchair, as a punishment, and shoved him into this corner. Probably he had dozed off here, exhausted by his rage. But now, remembering, he was determined to have it out with that man once and for all.

Unable to turn the chair around, he inched backwards,

straining with all his might against the wheels, which seemed to only want to go forward, toward the walls. Pausing to catch his breath, he noticed something odd about the laundry piled by the door. What had Mr. Versey done to his sheets? "All right, sir," he said, resuming his agonizing backwards trek, "I know you're here. You answer me now, right this minute."

Another inch or two—never had the apartment seemed so vast—and he caught sight of a pair of drawers hanging from the mini-refrigerator. Why, they were green! In fact, now that he noticed it, everything in the apartment looked slightly discolored, the sheets, his shirts, the dishes. "You goddam son of a bitch, what have you done!"

Having never used such language, not once in his entire ninety-one years, the old man couldn't help feeling somehow sullied. It was as if he had given up something precious for nothing—exactly the way he had felt on his first night with Artis. When he was eighteen, he had taken a solemn vow on his knees with his mother's hand resting lightly upon his head: Never would he drink, never would he use foul, unseemly language. Well, the drinking had gone by the wayside soon after he was married. But the language, that part of the vow had stood firm all these years. And now, because of this loathsome creature, Mr. Versey, this last remnant of honor was stripped from him.

With a moan he gripped the spokes and edged another creak or two backwards until suddenly he felt a breath stir the untrimmed down on the nape of his neck. Unable to move, he sat there a moment, the blood pounding in his ears like waves on a shingle beach. There it was again, that breath, but it couldn't be Mr. Versey's. No, this was as sweet as a young Christian woman's. *Who is it?* he tried to say, but the words would not sound. Delight and terror, one spicing the other to unbearable pungency, had rendered the old man speechless.

Finally, using his last ounce of strength, Uncle L.D. managed to angle the chair around so he could confront his silent visitor. Ha! It *was* Mr. Versey, after all. There he was, leaning out the window, which he had somehow managed to open. His behind, broad as an old lady's, was bulging over the sill in a manner most unbecoming for a gentleman's domicile.

"Get in here, you old fool," Uncle L.D. said, tremendously relieved now that he discovered everything could be explained. The breath was simply the unfamiliar fresh air wafting through the window that had been stuck shut for so long. And the discolored laundry was just the result of the neon *N* glaring in, unhindered by the shade Mr. Versey had raised against the old man's standing orders.

"You got enough air now, I expect." Uncle L.D. wheeled himself closer. "Now, come on. Look, it's dark. Time to go home."

Noticing the umbrella on the floor, Uncle L.D. picked it up and prodded the broad distasteful moon before him. "Come, now. Enough nonsense," he said, his temper rising with his anxiety. Strange a creature as Mr. Versey was, it was still unlike him to spend long periods of time in any posture other than sitting or reclining. "You hear me? Time to pack up, go on home." Dropping the umbrella, Uncle L.D. grabbed onto Mr. Versey's pants and gave him a good shake or two. "Hello, you been drinking my good Scotch, huh? You found my . . . Hello! No, where do you think you're going? Hello, help!"

Uncle L.D. continued to protest as Mr. Versey's broad moon began to set over the sill, dragging the old man up from his chair as he clung desperately to the cloth. "No, Mr. Versey, stop!" he protested, but it was no use. Gravity had Mr. Versey now. Try as he might to hang on, Uncle L.D. was no match for this giant, which not only defenestrated the home attendant but, almost as an afterthought, deposited the old man upon the flowered linoleum.

PART TWO

Chapter Five

Mrs. Undine was contemplating the envelope of her telephone bill when Dr. Bates wandered into the room. Forgetting what he had come there for, he asked her if it was supposed to rain that day.

"Mm?" she said, holding the envelope up to the light. Mrs. Undine was a very thorough woman. She never mailed a bill without wondering if the check inside had been signed. Often, heeding the notice on the back flap, she would reopen envelopes that she had just sealed to make certain that she had indeed put her account number on the check for VISA or Louisiana Power and Light. Rarely did they leave the house together without Mrs. Undine's returning inside for a moment to check that the stove was off. And it was not uncommon for her to pull the car over after leaving a self-service island to make sure she had put the cap back on the gas tank. Whereas Kay had found her mother's behavior irritating beyond endurance, Dr. Bates could regard it with furtive amusement. And as he grew more accustomed to it he hardly noticed it at all.

It was odd, but the moment they had met, Dr. Bates and Mrs. Undine had hit it off. A modest reception had been given after the civil ceremony in Netcong, New Jersey, and there he had found himself enjoying the company of his new mother-in-law. Admittedly he had at first suspected that much of Mrs. Undine's old-fashioned primness was something of a put-on, that she was secretly mocking him and his let-it-all-hang-out friends. But when he realized that she was for real, that she operated without a sense of irony, he was somewhat enchanted. It was almost as if a character from another age were paying a visit, a mid-Victorian gentlewoman in modern dress, or at least a semblance of modern dress. The deference he showed her, pulling out her chair for her, opening doors, little things that Kay forbid him to practice on herself, quickly won over his mother-in-law. Around her he found himself in a world he had always secretly yearned for, where there were things one simply did or did not do—no questions asked. Euphemisms abounded, a welcome relief from the overdose of honesty that liberated friends and colleagues had subjected him to.

Quite soon it became apparent that they both shared a certain feeling: neither he nor Mrs. Undine liked to make waves. As result of this deeply ingrained tendency Dr. Bates's divorce had been so amicable that it had put little or no strain on his relations with Mrs. Undine. She had been told that both parties agreed that the marriage had been a rash attempt to deal in a superficial, cosmetic way with loneliness. Kay, a graduate student at New York University, had met Martin Bates through a personal ad she had placed in *The New York Review of Books*. Three weeks later they were married and looking for an apartment. Kay's was simply not large enough for two, and she refused to live with his father in New Jersey. Finally, after realizing they would not be able to afford even a halfway decent apartment in the city, the newlyweds decided to move to Louisiana. There they planned to save for a house of their own by living with Kay's mother while Kay completed her post-graduate work at L.S.U. and her husband investigated dentistry. It was while living in Tula Springs that Kay and Dr. Bates discovered that they were basically friends, not lovers, a distinction that Mrs. Undine could not quite grasp but nevertheless learned to accept. Kay moved out, first to Baton Rouge, later to New Orleans, where she found a high-powered job that enabled her to buy her ex-husband a five-hundred-and-ten-dollar jacket for his birthday. But neither Dr. Bates nor Mrs. Undine could get used to the hoodlum look of the prebattered leather, and consequently it was only taken out of the closet during Kay's infrequent visits to Tula Springs.

"Yes, Martin, what is it?" Mrs. Undine inquired as she opened the envelope she had just sealed. Dr. Bates was gazing out the bedroom window at nothing in particular. It could have been Netcong out there, except that the houses were a little closer together than at his widowed father's, where he had used to live before Kay put her foot down. She had decided that it was unhealthy for a father and adult son to live together. Turning from the window, he made a vague effort to remember why he had disturbed Mrs. Undine. Something to do with his car, he imagined, though he was not sure what. In any case, since he was here, he might as well prod her again about that job of hers.

"Fern," he began as she dabbed Elmer's glue on the envelope to reseal it. "What about Dr. Munrow? Have you talked to him?"

"How many times must I say it? Yes, I did. He's trying to find someone else. You ought to know it's not easy."

"That's *his* problem."

Mrs. Undine had promised that next week would be her last as a substitute teacher at Robin Downs, a school that Dr. Bates could not approve of. Not only was it racist (Mrs. Undine denied this, claiming blacks were as welcome as anyone else who could afford the tuition), but also it taught some cockamamie theory of creationism. "They might as well teach that the sun revolves around the earth," Dr. Bates had gently lectured her one evening after dinner, and Mrs. Undine had agreed that, yes, this was pernicious. Yet she was still coming up with all sorts of excuses why she really shouldn't quit just yet. They could use the extra money she was bringing home, after all. And was it her fault that Mrs. Brown was still suffering from dizzy spells?

"You made it clear to him that you're leaving after next week?" he asked.

"Hm? Yes, yes, we'll see. Now, where did I put my coupon wallet?" She rubbed the red stripe on her nose and resettled her half glasses. "Is lunch ready?"

"In a minute. By the way, I won't be able to go shopping

with you this afternoon. Louise called. Some sort of emergency."

"Well, for a dentist, you get more em— You haven't seen my yellow coupon wallet, have you? Oh, here it is. It's always running away from me, the naughty."

In the kitchen, while the bratwurst simmered, he brooded about the crack she had made about emergencies. Just what was she trying to say—that he was incompetent? That was a fine thing to think when it was her own daughter who had landed him in this business. Kay had gotten her Ph.D. in psychology by specializing in vocational guidance. It was only after she had put him through an endless battery of computerized tests—he had been part of her dissertation— that she had arrived at the conclusion that he would be happiest as a dentist. This was fine with him. After all, he was interested in helping people in some scientific way that didn't involve physics or astronomy, both of which he had almost flunked in college. But there was one slight drawback to dentistry for him. He greatly feared being the source of any pain or discomfort for a fellow human being. It was this that made him proceed tentatively, admittedly rather slowly. Those insensitive hotshots in the class, the ones who were getting all the A's, didn't give a damn about their patients' feelings. Is that what Mrs. Undine wanted him to be, a butcher like Frank Estee, who had got a 96 on Mrs. Lovell's inlay even though the poor lady was literally in tears the whole time? What a shame they weren't graded for common decency.

"You think it's done?" Mrs. Undine inquired after he had summoned her with a brisk shake of the porcelain milkmaid, a vaguely Germanic figurine of gross good health, concealing a bell beneath her skirt. "You know one must be so careful with sausage."

"It's done. Eat, Fern. Eat."

Thoroughly chewing a small bite, he washed it down with a gulp of the Chivas Regal that had been given to him last month by one of his odder patients. He had tried desperately hard not to accept the gift and failed. "You're not eating."

"I am," she said, spearing a parsnip.

The window shade that she had hung behind the stove to catch the grease made a barely perceptible rustling sound. Both Dr. Bates and Mrs. Undine glanced anxiously at it. Yesterday during supper it had, for no apparent reason at all, automatically rewound itself with a tremendous clatter that had made her shriek and knock over her buttermilk. They had subsequently Scotch-taped the end of the shade to the wall, but Dr. Bates was not sure this would hold.

"Will you remember to get some electric tape?" he asked. "And would you mind returning that drain guard I bought for the back bathroom? It's too small."

Mrs. Undine said something so soft he could not hear.

"What?"

"I said I don't know if I'll have time." Her long face betrayed the deepest doubt and worry, as if he had just asked her to deliver state secrets to the Russians. "I've got a few clients to see, and I don't know if I can fit them in—my exercise clients—if you make me stop by the hardware store as well. You know how slow they are there. Anyway, I had to transfer some of my Wednesday clients to Saturday, that's today."

"Oh, is it?"

"Yes, today's Saturday," she said, missing, as usual, the irony in his voice.

While she pondered her exacting schedule aloud Dr. Bates finished his Scotch, hoping it would dim the dental-school anxieties that made eating such a chore. In an effort to put some weight on his hundred-and-twenty-four-pound frame, Dr. Bates had asked Mrs. Undine if he could experiment in the kitchen on weekends. Her repertoire of bland, cheesy casseroles was just not doing the trick. But then again, this bratwurst he had picked out was not the answer, either. He wished he could find something he really liked.

"I'll be home around four or so," he said, leaving most of the sausage untouched.

"Two hands on the wheel, Martin."

It turned out, though, that he was home earlier than he had expected; the emergency patient had not shown up. When one worked with these types, Dr. Bates reasoned, people who were basically uneducated, forced to seek out bargain rates, this was the price one had to pay. It was amazing how much confusion arose over dates and times, causing poor Louise to be in a permanently bad mood. Of course, he figured he had better get used to it, for his plan was, after graduation, to continue working with the underprivileged, preferably blacks and, if they had any down here, Native Americans. The last thing he wanted to do was hook up with someone like Dr. Schexsnyder, who had already asked Frank Estee to join his clinic in New Orleans next year. No, Dr. Bates was determined to work as close to cost as possible, perhaps at the Parish Health Center in Ozone. At least there he wouldn't have to put himself into hock for the rest of his life for office equipment. It was obscene how much the chairs alone cost, much less the X-ray machines and drills.

"Hi, it's me," he said into the phone, glad to have the house to himself. Mrs. Undine was still out shopping, which meant he could talk freely. "I just can't seem to get it together," he went on after adjusting the cushion behind his head. He was lying on the living room sofa beside a whitish patch of K2r spot-lifter. The night before one of Mrs. Undine's canasta regulars had spilled a dose of liquid Tylenol during a heated tournament, and the stain still hadn't come out. "Like today, my day off supposedly, I drive all the way to Ozone and wait for someone who doesn't even bother to—"

"Sweetie, would you run these off for me—yes, you, Brett. Sorry, Martin, go on." Kay was at her office on the nineteenth floor of a brand-new skyscraper that looked out over the bankrupt World's Fair. She was a consulting psychologist for several management consultant firms in New Orleans.

"I'm still not gaining any weight. In fact, I lost half a pound this week. And I'm still drinking too much coffee. It's the only thing I seem to look forward to, the next cup of coffee."

"Have you been going out?"

"I don't have time." He caught a glimpse of his reflection in the glass covering the framed photograph of the deceased

Mr. Undine, a large, florid-faced man posed beside a dangling bass. It always disconcerted Dr. Bates to see how exceptionally good-looking he himself was, since most of the time he went around feeling like a troll. "Besides, who's there to date? This town is dead."

"Babe, if I were you, I'd be out of there so quick it'd make your head spin. A doll like you, you'd have your choice of any girl you wanted in New York."

"How do you think I ended up here in the first place?"

"What? And don't start giving me all this bull about school. You know you could probably transfer to NYU or something. They have a great dental school. Brett, the invoices, too."

"Well, like I was saying last time, I figure I must be going through some sort of delayed Oedipal thing with my father. Remember how you used to tell me it wasn't natural for me not to resent him, how I liked him too much and all? Well, I think I had some sort of breakthrough the day before yesterday. We were on the phone and he said something that really pissed me off about your mother. I told him *of course* I realized Fern was a mother figure, and then I explained how this is all right as long as she's not a subconscious mother figure. The real danger comes when you project an unconscious mother figure onto wives and friends and all. But if you got an actual motherlike person . . . Anyway, he sounded sort of jealous, and then it started getting weird because it was like *he* was the child and . . . Kay, you there? Kay?"

No response. Then a few seconds later: "Sorry, Martin. I had to show Brett where the key was. By the way, I meant to ask you, do you think I ought to go on that cruise with Mario? I'm so conflicted about him. He's a little like you, you know—not physically, but every now and then he'll say something or do something with his hands that reminds me of you, and I'll say to myself, 'Oh, God, what is going on here?' It's like this nightmare where the same thing keeps happening over and over. I mean, not that you're a nightmare or anything. It's just that I can't afford to make the same mistake again by getting involved with someone. . . .

Even your names are sort of alike. Martin, this is your bill, isn't it? You can't afford . . . The whole point, save up. Let me call you back."

"It's all right."

"No, now, listen."

"Wait, hold on a sec. There's someone at the door."

Getting up off the sofa, Dr. Bates felt his heart thud with dull anxiety. The phone, the doorbell always raised his blood pressure, for he lived in fear of a mad threat, maybe a summons, from a patient who had gone around the bend. And there were plenty who seemed on the verge. He had had no idea how demented most people were until he had started going to dental school. One of his patients, Mr. Washingtons, had shot his favorite hound because of something his wife had done to the greens or his jeans—Dr. Bates wasn't sure which since he only understood about half of what Mr. Washingtons ever said.

"Oh," he murmured, opening the front door and seeing Carol Deshotel standing there. She looked a little tired, anxious.

"Yes, thank you, I'm just fine. And how are you doing, Marty? No, I wouldn't mind coming in out of this heat."

"I'm sorry, yes, come in," he said lamely as he closed the door behind her. "Uh, Fern isn't in right now," he added. Carol's mother, Mrs. Rawlins, was one of Mrs. Undine's canasta regulars. Every now and then Carol would have to drive Mrs. Rawlins over herself when her mother had fortified herself on the golf course with one too many swigs from her flask of Rob Roys. Of course, Mrs. Rawlins, a severe, formidable-looking woman, never showed it, except perhaps by becoming even more severe. While waiting for her mother Carol would sometimes have a cup of coffee with Dr. Bates in the kitchen. He found her, in the main, rather agreeable and attractive, though at times she did exhibit a certain uncalled-for coyness that seemed rather juvenile. Since he would always be thinking he should be studying, these chats were somewhat constrained, and once or twice in jest she had called him a bookworm. Or was it a worrywart? In any case, it was some quaint-sounding word that had made him smile, the way she had said it.

Following her into the kitchen, he said, "I'm on the phone," and then, picking up the extension by the microwave, discovered that Kay had already hung up.

"I just had to talk to somebody," Carol said, yanking out a tray of ice cubes from the freezer. "I'm at the end of my rope, and there's just nobody in the world I can— They're red. The ice cubes are red."

Dr. Bates explained that Mrs. Undine sometimes froze Kool-Aid in the trays. He did not add that he liked to suck on the cubes while studying.

"She's nuts, isn't she?" Carol said, putting the tray back. "Is it possible to get a plain cold glass of water? Oh, Lord, why does everything have to be so complicated?" She collapsed into a vinyl dinette chair while Dr. Bates fetched her a plain cold glass of water. Usually when he saw her, there wasn't a hair out of place, but this afternoon her blouse was wrinkled, and her eyes looked puffy, as if she had just woken up.

"How's your mother?" he ventured.

"Here I am about to go over the edge, O.K., and he asks me how my mother is." She unscrewed the sugar jar and poked a few grains of bloated yellow rice that sat atop the sugar. "Marty, please."

He stood there uncertainly, wondering if perhaps he should apologize. They were nothing but the most casual of acquaintances—for Christ's sake, she couldn't even get his name right (he loathed Marty). Yet here she was behaving as if they had some sort of long, intimate history of shared confidences. Why was it so hard to maintain a simple, shallow relationship? That was all he had ever asked of anyone these days. Perhaps after his final exams he would be ready to be a better friend. But for God's sake, not now.

"I suppose Fern will be home any minute," he said, hoping to forestall the lengthy emotional outburst that her clouded, very comely face forecast.

"Have you ever been in a situation," she asked before he

could finish his sentence, "where it just seemed there was no one you could turn to? This town is so narrow, no one would understand. I know you probably laugh at us, and I don't blame you. Sometimes I think I'd be much better off, O.K., living, like, up North in some big city where everyone's not prying into your life with their big fat noses, you know what I mean?"

He gave a vague nod, trying not to encourage her with too much sympathy but at the same time loath to hurt her feelings by appearing too callous. "More water?"

"Well, to make a long story short," she said, poking a manicured nail into the sugar jar, "Duane and I have just called it quits. It's over, finished, that's it."

He tried to look appropriately surprised or shocked or upset, but having never set eyes on her husband, this was not easy. "What about your little boy?" he asked, knowing this wasn't the most original response imaginable but unable to come up with anything better. "Shouldn't you give some thought to how it might affect him?"

"Cindy?"

"Uh, yes, her."

"What's she got to do with it? Christ Almighty, you think for one second I'd tell her?"

"But I mean, Duane, if he's leaving, won't she notice or something?"

Shoving her chair back to get a better look at him, she said, "Marty, dear child, please try not to be so dense. Duane is, O.K., like this big secret. He's the husband of this girl I went to high school with, and the only one who knows anything about this is you and Mamma, and Mamma always did hate Duane, and I don't want to give her the satisfaction of knowing it's all over." With the suddenness of a child she lost all composure, her lovely face crumpled by gut-wrenching sobs. Rarely had he seen such perfect misery displayed in an adult with no thought of pride or self-consciousness to take the edge off it. For a few moments it seemed she would never recover. But then, with equal suddenness, she was once more sitting erect, one shapely, tanned leg folded neatly over the other. She asked for a sip of Perrier.

"I don't think . . ."

"Club soda?"

"There's some Pepsi."

"Oh, never mind. Well," she added somewhat cryptically, "this is the price you pay for being good. To tell you the truth, I'm a little embarrassed. I mean, I'm normally not like this. But I just thought I'd die today if I didn't . . . I hope you don't mind, Marty."

"Oh, no, really." He shifted positions, leaning awkwardly against a counter. "It's, yeah . . ."

"I don't know, somehow the fact that you're from Connecticut, it made me feel, like, O.K., you'd understand. Connecticut is so sophisticated, I imagine—all those white houses and people going to the theater and all."

"Actually I'm from New Jersey."

Her gray eyes widened slightly. "I thought you said—"

"I went to school in Connecticut, Wesleyan."

"Well, anyway," she said, dipping a moistened fingertip into the sugar, "this is the price you pay. Duane, you know, he was ready to leave her. He wanted us to go to Baton Rouge and start a new life together. The trouble with me is, I'm too softhearted. I just couldn't stand to do that to my girl friend. I don't think you realize what a big sacrifice I made for her—and she probably never will, either. Because, O.K., I really love Duane, I really really do. I've loved him ever since high school, only I didn't know it back then." She sucked the sugar off her index finger. "We used to date a lot, but then I broke up with him, and not long after that he married my friend on the rebound. I'd tell you her name, but I think you might know her through some other connection, and I don't want to betray any confidences, if you know what I mean. Anyway, she's a good kid, I suppose, except I'm not sure she realizes that she really doesn't deserve someone as good as Duane. Lots of girls were after him, and he went and married this . . . She's not really bad-looking, but she's certainly not what you'd expect someone like Duane to pick. I mean, she's not exactly Miss America." Her eyes were filled with a soft, almost motherly amusement. "You know, Marty, it's like we were on a plane, you and me.

Have you ever sat next to a total stranger on a plane and suddenly told him all sorts of things you wouldn't ever tell anyone, not even your best friend?"

"No, I haven't."

"That's how I think of you. Like, here you are now, O.K., and then I'll never have to worry about seeing you again. You'll get off at Kennedy Airport and disappear into the crowd, and that will be that. It's sort of neat, isn't it?"

He pondered this a moment, feeling somehow slighted, yet glad to be off the hook. Perhaps this relationship was in fact as shallow as he had desired it to be. "What makes you think I'm getting off?" he asked, not quite satisfied with this glad feeling.

"Someone like you could never make his home here," she said blithely. "You just don't fit in."

"I'm planning to stay down here once I graduate, you know." He had settled into a dinette chair that was some distance from the table, the chair Mrs. Undine used to reach the high shelves in the cupboards. "Probably in Ozone. I like the lake."

"What lake?"

"Pontchartrain."

"Oh, that thing." She gazed sadly at the avocado plant on the sill. "I can't believe it. Here I am, thirty-seven, and I'm all alone. I swear, I've never felt more alone." She blinked back a tear, which, despite her rather doubtful logic—wasn't she married to a rather nice doctor?—still managed to move him. It was evident she was quite sincere. "I guess this is what growing old is all about. Oh, by the way, you won't breathe a word of what I said to anyone? I mean, you got to swear. My whole life, O.K., it could be ruined, just completely wrecked." She adjusted the girlish barrette that held back her hair. "That's the choice you have here in Tula Springs, being completely ruined or dying of boredom. There's no in between."

"Don't worry, I'll never, I don't know anyone to . . ."

"Oh, and one other thing. His name isn't Duane. I just made that up, you know. His real name is, uh, Bill." He pretended not to notice the violent blush on her delicate cheeks.

"I don't know anyone anyway," he said again, trying to reassure her, but it was almost as if another person were getting up from the table now. Looking as paranoid and resentful as an upstanding citizen shortly after finishing his business with a whore, she went to the sink and rinsed her glass out thoroughly. "I don't know what came over me," he half expected her to say.

"I've got to go."

"Don't worry, Kay, I won't—"

"Carol. Listen, I'm sorry. I shouldn't have just come barging in here like this. My . . . It's been . . . Anyway, I . . ."

"Hey, it's no big deal, really. Uh, you better unlatch that first," he added as she tried to shove open the screen door next to the refrigerator. "Careful, let me help."

"Oh, I see. Thanks, Dr. Bates."

From the living room window he watched her gray Mercedes pull away from the curb.

At supper that evening Mrs. Undine seemed almost cheery, which was very unlike her. Normally they got through meals with her placid observations on the state of the furniture, the look of the houseplants, leaving him plenty of room to wander in his own thoughts. Occasionally she would voice anxieties about the neighbors' children or the speed limit in various sections of town. It was such a relief from the churning, emotional meals he used to engage in with his father. Judaism, Marx, sex, the Third World—everything became a personal issue. But on this particular evening Mrs. Undine seemed to want more from him. "Isn't that funny?" she said after relating an incident that he was only half listening to, something to do with the neighbor's maid. "That's exactly what Moab said, you know, Mrs. Keely's girl." Her face, usually resigned, was eager, and when she laughed, it sounded genuine. Somewhat curious, Dr. Bates inquired if anything had happened that afternoon while she was out.

"As a matter of fact, yes," she told him with a trace of pride. "I ran into Dr. Munrow at Shoe-Town, and it looks as if I won't have to teach home ec any more. Oh, those girls, they were just dreadful."

"Well, it's about time."

"There was just one nice student, a boy, except he made me nervous—I don't know why. Martin, it's cold in the center,"she added, prodding the potato-chip topping of what she called her Chinese casserole. She had taken it from the freezer and heated it for forty-five minutes at three-fifty. "I better put it back in the oven."

"No, come on. I want to eat now."

"But—"

"Fern," he said testily. Carol's visit had left him somewhat moody. All the signs were there; she was definitely on the verge of becoming another friend—and by friend he meant just that. Not lover, for Dr. Bates had a stern puritanical streak that had hardened over the years in response to his father's "liberation," which had occurred in the early seventies and resulted in one messy, self-indulgent affair after another for Cecil, the handsome widower. That was why, over the years, married or otherwise engaged women had honed in on Dr. Bates as a safe bet. Some sixth sense let them know he could be trusted. Even Kay, who was supposed to have broken this pattern, had turned, ultimately, into that dreaded specter, yet another real good friend.

Not that he hadn't derived a good deal of pleasure from these charged relationships. From time to time they would go over the edge with a furtive, guilty coupling that was later denounced, after much discussion, as an aberration. But he was tired, dreadfully tired, of relating to women merely as a friend. What he was looking for now was an unattached, highly intelligent, socially conscious female who was interested in only one thing: sex—wild, romantic sex such as he had eyed on the cover of trashy paperbacks in the A&P. The fact that he was thirty-five and still hadn't discovered such a woman was beginning to weigh on him, although he did give himself some allowance for being in school. After all, most of his energies were taken up with study. There was precious little time to go searching for a mate.

"Is there something wrong with your throat, Fern?" Dr. Bates inquired after they had eaten silently for a few minutes. It was a question he had always wanted to ask, for whenever she swallowed any food, she would first close her eyes and then gulp, as if a horse pill were going down. "Is the passage too narrow, or what?"

She looked quizzically at him over a forkful of Chinese tuna.

"You close your eyes, you know," he persisted. "It looks like it's painful for you to swallow. Is it painful?"

"A lady never looks when she swallows," she replied. "I'm sorry that good breeding disturbs you, Martin, but there's little I can do about that." She tried to spoon more tuna from the casserole onto his plate, but he held up his hand. "You eat like a bird," she commented, redirecting the spoon to her own plate. "You know, dear, I'm beginning to worry about you. You need to start getting out more, having some fun. All work and no play makes Jack . . ."

"Mm."

"Would it have killed you to go to that social on Friday?"

He would as soon have put a bullet in his head as spend an evening with young singles from Frederik Episcopal Church. "Mm."

"I don't think in this day and age a young person should feel so stigmatized by divorce," she went on. "Do you think that maybe you're taking it a little too much to heart? I know when I was your age, I used to let things like that bother me. I don't mean divorce. Of course, in my day divorce was unthinkable. It's just that, well, I don't know if Kay ever told you, but I didn't get married to Mr. Undine until I was thirty. In those days, of course, that meant you were an old maid. I had given up on myself at twenty-eight. . . ."

Only half listening, Dr. Bates perked up when he heard "thirty." Was that possible? Since Kay was thirty-seven, that would make Mrs. Undine at least sixty-eight, maybe even seventy. For some reason, perhaps it was because she didn't have any gray in her hair, he had always thought of her as being in her late fifties. He looked hard at her and saw that, yes, she could be over sixty-five. It was a disconcerting discovery, as if he had just found out that she had always worn a wig.

". . . met Mr. Undine in a sporting goods store," she was saying. "I'm still not sure what I was doing there, because I never used to frequent sporting goods stores. In any case, he was selling someone an Evinrude motor for a boat. I remember the brand to this day. Now you see what I mean? If I had stayed inside my little house all day, I never would have met Mr. Undine. One has to go off the beaten track sometimes, because you won't find Mr. Undine looking at draperies in Penney's or checking out the latest styles at the Vogue."

Any comparison between his situation and Mrs. Undine's seemed to him too ludicrous for words. He was just about to inform her of this when she began to fuss about the chill in the center of the casserole again—and the fact that she had put potato chips on a Chinese casserole. "I can't imagine why I would do such a thing," she mused aloud, but then it occurred to her that this wasn't her Chinese casserole, after all. "Didn't we eat that last week, the one I had in the freezer? Of course, this is my tuna casserole."

"By the way," she said later, as she was clearing the dishes away from the table, "do you think you'll be able to drive me to school next week for a day or two? I want to get the tires rotated on my car and . . ."

Dr. Bates was standing by the screen door sipping coffee. The view of the woods would have been quite pleasing at sunset were it not for the water tower set in the midst of the pine and scrub oak. Painted on the tank was a large faded tomato with a message only half visible from this angle, something about Tula Springs being Friendly. "I thought you just told me you were through. Please don't save that cobbler," he added as she spooned his untouched dessert into a plastic container. "It's already three days old."

"Yes, but you might get hungry later on. And Martin, dear, I said I was through teaching home ec. You see, Dr.

Munrow was finally able to get a little graduate student from St. Jude to come look after the girls."

"Good."

"Now, wait, I'm not through. There's been a terrible tragedy. The brother of one of our teachers, well, Dr. Munrow just told me today at Shoe-Town that he did away with himself. Luckily he's not Catholic, so they'll be able to give him a decent funeral. But you see, Nesta—it was her brother—Nesta won't be able to come teach for a while, and Dr. Munrow asked if—seeing as how I've gotten a feel for the place now—if I could take her place until she recovers."

Dr. Bates set his cup down. "No. You tell him no, you can't."

"See?" she said, holding up the peach cobbler in the container. "I'm putting it here, on the second shelf in the refrigerator. Now, Martin, I know you're not going to be unreasonable about this. I know you don't expect Nesta to teach, feeling the way she does. How would *you* feel if *your* brother had leapt out a window?"

"I'm terribly sorry about that," he said, allowing a moment of sympathy for this Nesta, whom he had never heard of before. "The point is, that is no place for anyone with the slightest sense of decency to be teaching. It's a disgrace, Fern."

Rinsing the plates so thoroughly that they really didn't have to be put in the dishwasher—and yet she did—she said, "It is a disgrace when children aren't given the chance to learn about life sciences."

He was almost out of the kitchen, but hearing this, he paused. "No, you got to be kidding. You were going to teach science?"

"I *am* going to teach science. For your information, Martin, I've already promised Dr. Munrow he could count on me, and I have no intention of going back on my word."

"Now, listen, you know what sort of science they teach there, don't you? Creationism. You're going to be teaching kids that evolution is wrong, that God created man out of dust and a whole pack of fairy tales." He had gone to the sink and turned off the faucet to make sure she was listening. "You're going to send those kids right back to the Dark Ages with that crap. Is that what you want?"

Mrs. Undine dabbed at her eyes with the edge of her apron. It was the first time he had ever seen her cry. As bad as this made him feel, though, he had no intention of backing down. "But can't you see, I won't be . . . Just a couple days. I'm not going into evolution or anything, I'll just . . . Her poor brother, and what will I say to Dr. Munrow? I can't. I don't have any choice."

"You got a choice, Fern." He had never felt so tall before, so strong. Finally he had a chance to make some difference in this world, just as he would later, when he worked with poor Louisiana blacks and Indians in his clinic. So what if everyone he knew, all his former friends, had forgotten the dream of the sixties? There would be one person who wouldn't go to his grave cynical, resigned. "You got a choice: either me or that school. Make up your mind."

"I don't understand," she said, reaching for a napkin and blowing her reddened nose.

"I am not living in the same house with someone who teaches creationism. Period."

"But, Martin"—she blew again, hard—"I'm not sure I even understand what creationism is. I'll only be filling in for a while, a few days at most. I can't just go back on my word. And really, all they're talking about now is cells or something."

"No deal. I want you to get on the phone to Dr. Munrow right this minute."

With a sigh of resignation Mrs. Undine tossed the napkin away in the trash. "Well, dear, if that's the way you feel about it. I put your suitcase in the hall closet, behind that broken fan. And I believe there's still some of your underwear in the dryer. I'll sort it out for you after I do the dishes."

"Now, Fern," he said, not quite believing his ears. Surely she had no idea what she was doing, unless she was bluffing. But Mrs. Undine was not the type of person to bluff. She seemed to be perfectly sincere. Yet hadn't she the slightest notion of how fortunate she was to have an intelligent young man looking after her? How many old ladies wouldn't give their eye teeth for just such an opportunity? "Maybe you need some time to think this over. I know it must be—"

"Oh, yes, I just remembered. Your suit coat, that nice one from Brooks Brothers, it won't be ready from the cleaners until Wednesday, I believe. Where shall I be sending it to, dear?"

Chapter Six

ITCHING TO BREAK OUT HER FALL WARDROBE, Olive was distressed when October turned out to be as stifling as September, with only a few uncertain days, when the brassy sun, muted by a smoglike haze, granted a confusing hour or two of relative chill. Down at City Hall everyone seemed out of sorts whether they chose, like Olive, to look unseasonably comfortable in light summery pastels or, like Mrs. Sanchez, to look seasonably uncomfortable in tweeds and earth tones. On the twenty-ninth of that month, in a special ceremony held in Vondra's office, the mayor presented Olive with a trophy for fifteen years of dedicated service to the city of Tula Springs. Unfortunately Vondra happened to come down with a cold that morning and was unable to attend the 3:25 P.M. ceremony. Flushed with a sense of achievement, Olive allowed herself a day or two of slacking off, coming in late and going home early. She felt she really owed herself this after fifteen years with her nose to the grindstone. But then one afternoon, while she was updating Vondra's Rolodex, it suddenly occurred to her that she had been had: A raise, not a three-ninety-eight trophy from Jaydee Signs, was what she deserved. The mayor, whom she confronted later that day at the shredder in the annex, saw her point and promised to look into it.

"Can you believe I fell for that?" Olive was saying to Mrs. Sanchez during their coffee break in Dead Records shortly after her talk with the mayor. "I mean, remember how I burst into tears when he handed me that two-bit . . . I must be about the dumbest mule alive."

Mrs. Sanchez said something about her not being dumb and then returned to the subject of Olive's low-maintenance hair. "It's fine on someone like you," she remarked, "but I just don't believe it's me, doll." For the past fifteen years Mrs. Sanchez had worn the same high-maintenance hairdo, a helmet of dark ash blond that could stand up to a hurricane. Olive, who had been informed this morning at breakfast that she had a patch of gray on the back of her head, thought it was high time Mrs. Sanchez got with it.

"It would take ten years off you, Mary."

"Well . . . Oh, by the way, I was wondering—now, I want you to be honest with me. If it's any inconvenience, just say no. I hate to ask people for favors, you know, especially—"

"Mary."

Mrs. Sanchez had put down her cup and was probing her face with her middle finger, as if trying to locate a sore spot. Olive wished she would learn to use her index finger more; it would be less disturbing. "I know how it is when people impose," Mrs. Sanchez went on, her baby-fine skin blossoming with white spots that quickly melted into pink again, "but anyway . . ."

"You're not imposing. You never ask me to do anything for you, Mary. I'd be only too glad to help out."

"Oh, cupcake, you're a dream. You don't realize what a favor it is. I've been worrying about it for weeks now. I just can't stand to leave things undone, but I simply haven't had the time to go all the way to Ozone. See, I was wondering if the next time you go to the dentist, I have this picture that needs framing. My niece sent me a snapshot of her parakeet that would look so nice in the guest room, where there's this water stain that's been driving me nuts, see."

"Mary, I wouldn't mind a bit if—"

"Oh, goody. Now, listen, my yard man told me there's a shop that frames things catty-corner to that drive-in daiquiri place they just opened up."

"But I'm through with the dentist. My teeth are all fixed. I'm really sorry, but . . ."

"Oh, gosh, you mean . . . And all this time I've been working up the courage to ask you. Wouldn't you know."

Mrs. Sanchez went on to talk futilely about the type of oak frame she had envisaged for the parakeet while Olive, with a sympathetic nod or a "How nice" in her general direction every now and then, puzzled over an elaborate frame of carved vine leaves that had come to mind. At first she thought it must be the frame to the mirror over Uncle L.D.'s bed. Then it occurred to her where she had seen the vine leaves before: over the mantel of the nonworking fireplace of whitewashed brick in Mrs. Undine's living room. But it was strange that she should remember the leaves now since at the time of her visit, two or three days earlier, she had hardly noticed the frame at all. It was the pastel the leaves framed, of Kay in an orangish-pink prom dress with a Jackie Kennedy hairdo, that had drawn her eye. Nowhere near as attractive as Carol Deshotel, Kay had nevertheless managed to insinuate herself into Tula Springs High's most exclusive circle. For years Olive had revolved around this in-group in a desperate, erratic orbit, sometimes close enough to be smiled upon with favor by a lesser member, but more often feeling the tug at a chill, elliptical distance. The fact that Kay had found a secure place there, in spite of her mother, who was ridiculed by everyone who was anything, had always mystified Olive. What did Kay have that she didn't? Olive was much better coordinated, yet it was Kay who was elected a varsity cheerleader. Neither Olive nor Kay belonged to the country club, yet it was Kay who was invited to all its dances, wearing dresses that were no more expensive than the ones Olive's aunt used to lend her from the dress shop she owned, the Vogue.

"Quite frankly, dear," Mrs. Undine had said once Olive had explained her reason for dropping over, "I agree with you. Perhaps young Felix should not be enrolled in home economics. Unfortunately all this is out of my purlieu now. You see, I've been transferred to life sciences. I was replaced by a girl from St. Jude for a while, but now it seems Mrs. Brown has recovered and is back at the helm, as they say."

"It's not that I'm against men learning how to cook and all that," Olive said, refusing an aged mint from a silver candy dish that Mrs. Undine proffered at arm's length. "As a matter of fact, my husband, Duane, does most of the cooking at home. But I just think Felix could spend his time more wisely in school. Chorus, for instance. I've always felt that music was a good way for boys to round off their education. They go on trips together, don't they? It's a real good way to make friends."

Idly caressing a darning egg, Mrs. Undine said, "Perhaps this is something you should bring up with Dr. Munrow, Olive. As I told you . . ."

"It's just taking Felix a little longer than most boys to get adjusted to, uh . . ." Footsteps in the hall behind her made her heart skip a beat. He was here. She must make a severe effort to appear totally calm, totally normal. After all, she had a perfectly good reason to drop in on Mrs. Undine. She *was* worried about Felix. "I thought putting him in an environment like Robin Downs, you know, with kids from a basically better class of people than you'd normally find . . . I don't know if you're aware of it, but we've had trouble with Felix in the past. He went to the public junior high school, you see, the one out on North Hazel. Well, first he was suspended for three days. He got in a fight with a black student. Then he was almost shipped off to a reformatory because of this same black student. They were friends by then and decided that it would be a good idea to steal some hubcaps."

It was Mrs. Undine's practice to keep the shades drawn in order to protect the carpet and furniture from too much sunlight, a household hint she now encouraged Olive to adopt. Feeling that maybe she hadn't been heard over the loud hum of the wheezing air-conditioner, Olive repeated her story about the hubcaps, all the while keeping her ears pricked for the creak of footsteps. Perhaps he was standing in the hall at this very moment, peering into the stingily lit room. The elephant on the coffee table, the dried flowers in the fireplace, her hostess's pale, anxious face—all seemed as stiff and faded as a tintype gathering dust. Instinctively Olive reached out to turn on the pole lamp beside her chair, but Mrs. Undine, with a vigorous shake of her head, stopped her. "No, dear, we mustn't." She nodded toward the huge, droning air-conditioner that made the window sash vibrate in its none-too-snug frame. "You might blow us up."

"Well, anyway, I—"

Mrs. Undine said something in a low voice that was drowned out by the air-conditioner.

"What? I was saying about Felix, that he—"

"I'm very sorry about Felix," Mrs. Undine said a little louder, in a strained tone of voice, "and I do admit he is something of a concern at school. But really, this is Dr. Munrow's province, I'm afraid. I really have nothing at all to— Please, do be careful with that," she interrupted herself, looking past Olive.

"Oh, I didn't expect to see you here," Olive said casually without bothering to turn her head to see who had walked into the room from the hall. "I just dropped by to see about, I mean, I was on my way past here anyway. It's on the way to the post office, you know, from my house, and I was wanting to talk to Mrs. Undine about my son, and I said to myself, why not just drop by and see if she's home?"

"You know each other?" Mrs. Undine asked, her pale eyebrows, as vague as down, arching slightly.

"Of course, we . . ." Olive began, shifting casually in her chair for a glimpse of Dr. Bates. A tiny, wizened black woman met her gaze with a stony mask of contempt. Without saying a word she let the sponge mop she was carrying fall to the gleaming woodlike floor and retreated into the kitchen.

"I declare," Mrs. Undine commented softly, almost to herself, "nowadays it's like asking the Queen of Sheba for a hand. Can't say anything." Clutching the darning egg, she rose to her feet and went to pick up the mop. "I try to borrow Moab a couple hours every now and then from Mrs. Keely next door. It's impossible for me to do everything around here myself, not with this teaching and my clients. Which reminds me, when you see your uncle, you give him my best, poor man. It must have been such a terrible shock. Imagine, having someone kill himself, right in your own home. People are so ill-mannered nowadays."

Olive was about to say that actually she wasn't that surprised that Uncle L.D. had driven Mr. Versey to suicide. If she had been in Mr. Versey's shoes, she, too, would probably have leapt out the window. But she didn't want to get into a big discussion with Mrs. Undine about him. She had already spent hours talking to the coroner, the sheriff, Mr. Pusey from the Citizens Patrol, and Uncle L.D. himself. Sometimes she thought if she heard Mr. Versey's name mentioned one more time, she would scream. "I'll say hello for you."

"Yes, do," Mrs. Undine said in a faint, distracted voice. "It is a shame Mr. Versey didn't have a little more breeding. I met him once or twice . . ." The voice became lost again in the wheeze of the decrepit air-conditioner which shuddered like the single engine of a Piper Cub. As Olive sat there in the guarded living room she had the feeling of low, tentative flight and wondered what flock of bright flamingos, like in the old Tarzan movies, was on the horizon. That was how the plane would go down: a flash of pink, the engine choked by feathers.

Remembering the vine leaves as she sat in Dead Records, Olive would also remember, incorrectly, that she had been offered tea out of an orangish-pink teacup; the Tarzan movie she had seen with Duane on one of their first dates had been completely forgotten. Reattaching her beeper to the wide patent-leather belt that bit cruelly into her waist, Mrs. Sanchez dispelled the troubling image of the somewhat lurid cup when she said, "Listen, hon, if I were you, I'd take it sort of easy around Vondra for the next few days."

Olive tensed, and her attention, which had been wide, grainy, and diffuse, immediately came to a sharp focus. "You mean . . ."

Mrs. Sanchez nodded. "She was in the office this morning. Her final ultimatum. Either you or her. His Honor said—"

"Oh, her and her ultimatums," Olive said crossly. About six months ago, and then again six months before that, Vondra had threatened to resign unless Olive was fired. The mayor had always managed to calm her down with the promise of an extra assistant, who never materialized, since the only way there would be any help was over Olive's dead body. She'd be damned, Olive had told the mayor, if she was going to let the city throw away one red cent on another secretary for Vondra when they claimed they hadn't the money to give her, Olive, a twenty-dollar raise. Either Tula Springs had the money or it hadn't. There was no two ways about it.

"I think she means it this time," Mrs. Sanchez ventured timidly after Olive, in the middle of a brown study, had suddenly smacked a file cabinet with her fist.

"Good, I hope she does. She's been coddled enough around this joint. Let her go out in the real world and find out what it's like. Any real boss would have had her out on her ear ages ago. Everyone knows darn well who it is does all the work around here. Good night, Vondra doesn't even know how to order a paper clip, much less a sewer pipe. That so-called mayor of yours, Mary, he's nothing but a marshmallow. He's always beating around the bush, trying to make everyone happy. And anyone with an ounce of brains knows that whatever makes half the world happy is going to kill the other half, and there's no getting around it. No, ma'am, there isn't."

Mrs. Sanchez tried to say more on the subject, but Olive got up abruptly and stalked out of the room. What with all she had on her mind the last thing she needed was to be forced to listen to anything concerning Vondra. Had she had the slightest consideration, Mrs. Sanchez would have known better than to try to upset her with this kind of talk. Back at her metal desk on the second floor, Olive corrected a memo concerning the sewer lift station on Coral Street and answered a query from the Cemetery Board about the ruts in the Catholic cemetery, explaining that it was up to the Catholics to fix them. These were her memos; she had composed them on her own without one bit of help from Vondra. As she typed in commas it dawned on her: Why not her? Why couldn't she be Superintendent of Streets, Parks, and Garbage? If Vondra really was so fed up, let her quit. Then His Honor could appoint Olive to take her place for the duration of Vondra's term. And why not? Hadn't she served faithfully for fifteen years? Didn't she know as much as anyone about the way things ran? Plus, it didn't hurt that she knew the whereabouts of a buried body or two, certain financial indiscretions concerning the mayor's beloved Citizens Patrol. Of course, it went without saying that she would never bring this up, not unless His Honor forced her to. To think that she had been begging for peanuts—an extra twenty a week —when a superintendent's full salary was within reach. Imagine what she could do with Vondra's salary! First of all, she would get herself a new Head tennis racket. Then she would hire a maid to come in twice a week, a white maid, of course, because she wouldn't dream of holding a poor black woman down the way people like Mrs. Undine did. Felix could get a few clothes for himself, good designer outfits. Oh, and maybe they could get a new motor for the speedboat that was sitting in the garage. The Evinrude they had now didn't have enough pickup for Duane's two hundred and thirty-two pounds, and so they hardly ever got out to Warsaw Landing to ski.

"Sorry to disturb you, Olive." Vondra loomed over the cluttered desk where Olive had laid her head a moment while she surveyed the vast landscape of possibility that had opened up before her in the last few minutes. "Would you mind stepping into my office? It won't take long."

Embued with an unfamiliar and slightly heady sense of power, Olive got out her dictation pad and, without saying a word, walked briskly into Vondra's office, where she was given two weeks' notice.

The janitor at Robin Downs had told her he was out back, but all she could see was a ragged line of boys in maroon gym clothes trotting along a Cyclone fence. Olive continued walking around a long row of candy and soft-drink machines to see if Dr. Munrow might have gone inside the gym. A week had gone by since Vondra's triumph, during which Olive had lain abed, regrouping her forces. At first it had seemed she would never be able to get up again. The humiliation was too severe. And the injustice—after all she had done for the town . . . The more she had thought about it, though, the angrier she had gotten, until finally she had rallied and marched herself over to City Hall to give the mayor a piece of her mind. She wasn't going down without a fight.

R. Vine Binwanger had admitted that, yes, he had given in to Vondra's demands, but only because he believed in Olive. Election time was coming up this spring, and he wanted to make sure Olive had the time to work up a first-rate campaign for Superintendent. Did that mean he was going to endorse her? she wanted to know. Was the Pope Catholic? But why couldn't he have let Vondra quit and appointed Olive in her place? Because, the mayor explained, Vondra wouldn't have quit without stirring up a ruckus of some sort. She had some pretty influential friends, after all. No, it was best to let her finish her term and then, come spring, die a natural death at the polls.

Olive hesitated at the back door to the gym, not sure if it was a boys' or girls' entrance. The effect of the mayor's pep talk was beginning to wear off. No matter what he had said, she couldn't help feeling that the starch had been knocked out of her. She was a nobody who couldn't even hold a stupid secretary's job. She would end her days a nobody, trying to keep house in a trailer park. Duane would blow up to three hundred pounds, still selling cheese logs. They would have to use Food Stamps. . . .

Straggling behind the others, one of the boys, a wide-hipped fellow in black socks, peeled off from the group as they rounded a goal post, and limped over to the door where Olive was standing. Quickly putting away the tissue she had been dabbing her eyes with, she inquired, without really looking at the hefty lad, if he had perhaps seen Felix. She had decided that she was in no state now to interview Dr. Munrow about the possibility of getting his support for her upcoming campaign; so she pretended to be looking for Felix, who she knew was out riding his motorcycle somewhere or other.

"Oh, Dr. Munrow," she said, flustered, for the hefty lad was he. She hadn't realized this until he muttered something she didn't understand. His hands on his dimpled knees, he was leaning over, trying to catch his breath. Apparently he had been working out with the students.

With a sigh the principal wiped his plump, hairless chest with the maroon T-shirt that had been tucked into his gym shorts. "Might as well be in Calcutta. I don't think I'll ever get used to this heat." He was squatting in the shade of the brick building. With a wave of his hand he invited her to sit on a blue gaspipe that sprouted dials and valves.

"I'm Felix's mother," she said, remaining in the sun. "I just came by to see . . ."

"Fine boy. Wish he'd come out for football this year. We could sure use him." He flicked his shirt at a lizard that had crawled out on one of the dials. "Sit down."

"I'm fine," she said, stepping into the shade. With him squatting there, half-naked, like an overweight, slightly weirdo schoolboy, her courage returned. After they had exchanged a few desultory remarks about Felix and his athletic prowess, she decided that she might as well go ahead with her original plan. "You know, I was thinking," she began in an offhand way, gazing out at the stark, unshaded playground, "seems to me this school could use a few trees or bushes or something."

"Don't stop!" he shouted to the boys, who had clustered around the goal post. Like a magician, he waved the listless stick figures into motion. "That's the least of my worries, Mrs. Mackie—trees. What we need here are proper classrooms. You ask me, it's disgraceful all this money went into a gymnasium at the expense of—"

"I know," Olive said quickly before he got off the track. She didn't want to start discussing the previous principal, who had resigned under a cloud. Dr. Munrow had been imported from somewhere out West—Oregon, was it? or maybe Idaho?—to get the foundering school back on its feet. Given the slightest encouragement, he was apt to run Mr. Eddie, the disgraced principal, into the ground. This bothered Olive, since Mr. Eddie was one of the nicest people she had ever met, personally speaking. She didn't know and didn't want to know anything about his business affairs. All she knew was that whenever they needed dry ice for a party at City Hall, he brought it over himself, free of charge, and often threw in a bottle or two of champagne.

"It is terrible," she went on, "but I can't help thinking, Dr. Munrow, I mean, it seems so bleak the way the highway runs so close to the classrooms and nothing to shade the poor kids when they come out." She leaned against a comfortable-looking valve. "Did you ever think that maybe the town might be able to give you a hand, like a few bushes or something, things left over from the Cemetery Board?"

He squinted up at her. "Correct me if I'm wrong, but isn't this a private school, Mrs. Mackie?" It wasn't so much what he said as the way he said it that gave Olive pause. His accent was so different, so refined-sounding, almost prissy. It made her wonder about his down-home speech to the parents.

"O.K., but a lot of time, what I'm saying, things just go to waste," she ventured tentatively. She had stuck her big toe in and now wasn't sure she wanted to take the plunge. But at the same time she couldn't bear to think of herself as a coward. "Nice shrubs and hedges that we sometimes just have to dump—there's no room for them. And the workmen —Lord, I know for a fact they put in about two hours a day mowing and bill us for eight. Now, listen, your garbage, too. Route B in the Third Ward is only a few blocks away. It doesn't seem like it'd be that much trouble if they swung over here once or twice a week."

"But how—"

"You see," she said, patting him on the shoulder as Duane would have patted him, "all I want is a chance to help you out. I know things are tough for the school right now and . . . If you could just . . ." She faltered. This was the hard part. She tried to think how the mayor would get his case across without appearing too obvious. "This spring we're going to need to put in office someone who cares about our students, O.K., and that's why, I mean, I know lots of people here in Tula Springs look up to you, and I think they'd listen to what you had to say about the crisis we have in education and what— Even though you're new, you still, anyway, what I'd like to count on is your endorsement. See, it's like I'm going to be running for . . . uh, Superintendent of Streets, Parks, and stuff this spring, and I think it would be nice to count on you for . . ."

The look on his smooth, boyish face made her voice trail off. "Mrs. Mackie," he said, digging the heel of his New Balance into the dry earth, "I'm going to pretend I didn't hear a word you said. You read me?"

Olive stiffened. "But I—"

"I'm going to pretend you didn't stand here in front of an ordained minister of God and try to bribe him with bushes and garbage. I think that what just happened was that my ears got to buzzing in this heat and I misheard what this good Christian mother standing in front of me just said. Tell me I misheard, Mrs. Mackie."

"Well, I . . ." Red with shame, Olive actually began to stammer, which made her blush even more. *The nerve of this young twerp to make me feel like I've done something wrong,* she was thinking while she tried to explain to him that he didn't understand what she had meant and at the same time to apologize. Perhaps this was why everything that came out was a little garbled.

"Please, stop while you're ahead, Mrs. Mackie. Enough."

As he stood up, Olive noticed that he shaved under his arms.

She had never seen a man who shaved under his arms before. "Now I think," he said, opening the door to the gym, "a nice cold shower will be just what the doctor ordered."

"Seems like you misunderstood what I was trying to say about—"

"No more, please." He was leaning against the jamb, holding the metal door open with a foot. Behind him echoed the sharp squeak and thud of sneakers on a basketball court. "Oh, by the way, how's that uncle of yours doing?"

"Which uncle?"

"Mr. Loraine—that's his name, isn't it? Must have been a terrible shock to the poor man."

"He's fine, Dr. Munrow," she said coolly. Everybody and his dog had to ask about Uncle L.D., and Olive was getting darn tired of it. As if she didn't have enough troubles of her own: fired from her job, her husband still working in a cheese shop, a Cadillac that no one would buy, mortgage payments, tuition. Yet did anyone put in one word of sympathy for her? No, it was always, How is Mr. Loraine—oh, the poor dear old man. Then they would make her go through the whole song and dance. Yes, she had told Gyrene, the hairdresser at the beauty college she went to, to save money, she had spoken to the coroner right after it had happened, but no, she didn't actually see Mr. Versey's body on the sidewalk. Yes, it was like they said in the paper, a smashed skull. He had jumped out the window and smashed his skull on the concrete sidewalk. Yes, she had said to the produce man at the Winn Dixie, she had spoken to the sheriff and the Citizens Patrol, and they were nice as could be. No, she had said to Gail at the bank, who suddenly had plenty of time to talk, she did not think Paul Lamont, one of the sheriff's deputies, looked that much different from high school. Paul Lamont had questioned her on the night of the suicide. Olive used to turn him down for dates in high school, not because he was that bad-looking but because she suspected him of being queer. In any case, he had been real stiff and pompous when he questioned her: "Now, you say, Mrs. Mackie, that a character-disordered-type person, someone basically unstable to begin with, might have been driven into a deep, psychosislike depression by your great-uncle, who is something of an aggressive, domineering type?" "Yeah, Paul, and besides, it stank in there." Afterward he had shown her pictures of his three children and a poem he had gotten published in the Amtrak magazine.

"I imagine he must be pretty—" the half-naked principal began.

"Listen, if it's all right with you, I'd rather not talk about Uncle L.D. just now. You have no idea what trouble he's caused me. They tell me at the home care agency they don't have anyone to replace Mr. Versey, and I say, that's just great. Now I'm going to have to . . . Anyway, I can't talk about it."

Still holding the door open, Dr. Munrow regarded her with raised eyebrows, a schoolmarmish pose that didn't quite fit with the exposed, large pink nipples she was trying hard not to look at. Olive shifted her weight from one leg to another. After a false start or two she said, "You know I do the work sheets for the maintenance men. It really burns me up the way they goof off. Takes them three days to mow that cemetery, and I know I could get it done in one afternoon by myself with one of those riding lawnmowers. That's why I thought . . . I mean, the corruption there is terrible and . . ."

Like one of the three monkeys, Dr. Munrow clapped his hands over his slightly protuberant ears. "I hear nothing, Mrs. Mackie. Nothing."

Not amused by his antics, Olive tried to explain herself over a sudden stampede of sneakers, which soon exploded into a roar of triumph. "If you'd just listen, I'd—"

"Come in. Let's talk inside. There's something I'd like to discuss with you."

Another roar, this time sharpened by a girlish scream of defeat. Olive's pulse quickened in a confusion of anxiety and old excitement—the memory of her own triumphs on the court. She did not like this man, she realized. There was something funny about him.

The passage behind him was dark as the ones that led, in all those drive-in movies Duane used to enjoy, to the bright arena where gladiators and Christians were greeted with the deafening roar of a handful of extras. "I'm sorry," she said, turning away. "I've got to run."

"It'll only take a minute. It's about Mr. Versey."

"Felix wants me to pick something up for him, and . . ." She was already walking toward the parking lot. "I've got a million things to do."

Chapter Seven

Dr. Bates had discussed his situation several times, long distance, with Kay, and they both agreed that subconsciously Mrs. Undine did not want him to move out. She may have claimed that she would be perfectly happy living alone, that she found him more of a hindrance than a help, and that she still didn't consider it seemly to board an ex-son-in-law, but all this was nothing but a smoke screen. The truth was, Mrs. Undine was crying out for help. She was, whether she realized it or not, a very sick woman, and Dr. Bates was the only person who could help her now. Basically what it boiled down to, Dr. Bates had told Kay, was a severe case of agoraphobia. If left to her own devices, Mrs. Undine would remain locked inside her air-conditioned house for the rest of her days, refusing to venture forth.

"Now, that's ridiculous," Mrs. Undine said when Dr. Bates tried to explain what was wrong with her. They were out back filling up the sinkhole next to the tulip tree with a shipment of sand. It had rained only a few hours ago and seemed to be threatening to pour again. Shoveling the wet sand, Dr. Bates heard Mrs. Undine worry aloud that he was going to ruin his school khakis. He should wait until his jeans were cleaned and dried. It would take only another minute or two. "They're about ready to go in the dryer, Martin. The washer's on spin."

"Look, do you want me to do this or not? Please move your foot," he added, tapping the spade next to the beige shoes she had ordered from a firm in Atlanta that specialized in narrow feet.

As she moved out of his way Mrs. Undine's worried gaze took in the gray sky and then a stack of paperbacks in the neighbors' carport. "Mrs. Keely is donating those books to the Lions, did I tell you? She said you should look through them in case there's anything you might like."

Dr. Bates ignored this and reviewed some of the highlights of her illness for her. He was often forced to repeat things to her because he could tell by the look in her eye that she was tuning him out.

"Well, if I'm so agoraphobic, Doctor, then why are you making such a fuss about my going out of the house and teaching? It seems to me you should be glad I'm trying to mix and mingle."

Her superficial logic gave him only momentary pause. "You want to mix and mingle, you go to the public school. What's wrong with the public school?"

"They don't need me, that's what's wrong. Robin Downs is very hard up. You realize I'm working for peanuts? They can't even afford to pay minimum wage." Her pale eyes came alive when she said this, not with anger but with pride. Mrs. Undine was never happier than when she was allied with some desperate cause, which was why he skirted the issue for now by saying, "But it's so obvious you *are* agoraphobic. Deep down, you really don't want to leave the house. That's why you go into a swivet about the gas, whether it's on or if the windows are open. Just yesterday, remember when you made me turn around when we were going out to the movies? You thought you had left the bathtub running."

"But I had, or rather, you had—the sink faucet. I don't know how many times I have to tell you, Martin: Be aware."

She picked up a branch while Dr. Bates chunked a few more spadefuls of dirty sand into the depression. He had tried to convince her that this whole project was a waste of time and money. In a month or two the sand that she had paid thirty-nine dollars for would have sunk into the pocket beneath the earth, and they would be back at square one with a mild, innocuous-looking crater about the size of her living-room rug. No one, except for Mrs. Keely, seemed to notice it. Mrs. Undine, though, was becoming less tractable these days, harder to manage. He supposed he never should have issued that ultimatum, either him or Robin Downs, for he really had nowhere to move. School was taking every last nickel, and he was in debt two thousand to VISA and three to Mastercard. Yet, knowing full well the state of his finances, Mrs. Undine had had the nerve to suggest the other day that he might like to begin thinking about paying something toward his room and board. Of course, as soon as he graduated and had a steady job, he planned to pay her a tidy sum. But this wasn't good enough for her anymore. She wanted him to ask his father for some money. If his father had enough money to gallivant around Alaska on a Royal Viking cruise, she had said, he could certainly cough up something for his son's upkeep. Dr. Bates had to explain to her yet again that the whole point was to be independent of his father. Sure, he could ask for money, and sure, his father would send it to him, gladly. But that would give his father a psychological hold on him, which Kay had warned him about. He simply had to make it on his own.

"I want it level," Mrs. Undine said when it became apparent that the depression was turning into a mound of sorts. There was too much sand. "The whole point is to make it level with the rest of the lawn."

Still holding the rusty spade, Dr. Bates collapsed into a nearby lawn chair and then, feeling moisture seep into his khakis, quickly rose. "So what do I do with the leftover sand?"

"Oh, dear, I don't want to call that sandman again." She unhitched the hem of her faded damask dress, which had somehow gotten caught on a stocking. "You know, when he delivered this, I'm just positive he was casing the house. He wanted to come inside for a glass of water."

"Heavens."

She directed an uncharacteristically sharp look at him.

"You may laugh, but just two blocks over Mrs. Walters was burgled. Her best silver tea service, the one that belonged to her grandmother."

"Not her grandmother's." He placed his hand over his heart.

"Martin, I don't know what's gotten into you lately. Sometimes you sound just like one of my students. They've always got a smart answer for everything. Here, give me. I'll smooth this over."

Without saying a word he handed her the spade and went back inside to his books. An hour or so ago she had barged into his room when he was trying to memorize a difficult list for his exam tomorrow in Conjoint Pain Control III. No simple word of thanks from her when he had agreed to come and help with the sand. And then when he had got out there, she had asked him to wait until his jeans dried. There was just no pleasing her these days. Of course, he realized that her irritability had little to do with him. The real trouble was that the life science course she was teaching was simply too much for her. Night after night she would sit up with a pot of tea trying to keep one jump ahead of her students. At breakfast, looking a wreck, she would try to pump him for information on such things as protozoans and cilia. But he was reluctant to help out, since it seemed to implicate him, however slightly, in creationism. To teach innocent minds, as Mrs. Undine was instructed to do, that mankind was somehow set apart, that it had nothing to do with the wonder of evolution, was to him on a moral par with murder. Mrs. Undine's so-called life science class had nothing to do with either life or science. It taught a contempt for both.

"Martin, please," she had commented after one of his 6:30 A.M. lectures when she was trying to consume a reheated Egg McMuffin. "And besides, you know very well that I'm a firm believer in evolution."

"That just makes it all the worse."

Mrs. Undine held vague, Unitarian-like beliefs about a Life Force and worshiped, undisturbed, at an Episcopal church that she could get to without having to make any left turns. She worried a lot about cutting across traffic.

"What do you want me to do, Martin? You know what will happen if I quit."

Yes, indeed he did, for he had been told often enough. Apparently Dr. Munrow was using Mrs. Undine as a stop-gap until the candidate he had in mind to replace the regular science teacher, who had decided to retire after her personal tragedy, was accepted by Robin Downs' Board of Regents. It seemed that Dr. Munrow was intent on hiring a black woman with a Ph.D., but the board was trying to push their candidate, a young white man who didn't even have a master's. Mrs. Undine had been told that if she quit now, the board was sure to have its way. Dr. Munrow must have time to persuade them that the school would not go into financial ruin because of one black teacher. Indeed, the school had no future at all, as far as he was concerned, if it continued with its de facto policy of segregation. Yes, of course, officially speaking, anyone was welcome as long as they could pay the tuition. But what black child could afford what Robin Downs was asking? Dr. Munrow was hoping, once his life science teacher was in place, to start a scholarship fund for minorities. As a result of all this Mrs. Undine was able to think of herself in the vanguard of Progress and Enlightenment, while her ex-son-in-law looked on in dismay from the sidelines.

"I don't mean to interrupt again," Mrs. Undine said only a few minutes after Dr. Bates had settled down to a review of anesthetics. It used to be that his room was sacrosanct. Never before would she have dared disturb him when he was working. "I wonder if you'd like me to put those khakis in the wash for you. I'm just about to put in another load."

He shook his head, keeping his eyes on the page before him.

"But, Martin, what will people think if you go to school with dirt on your pants? You forget, I'm afraid, that down here appearances count. Kay used to complain to me about the way you looked, and I would always take your side. I would say that people up North simply don't have the same standards, doesn't matter how much money they have. Last time I visited Kay in New York, she introduced me to a millionaire that I wouldn't have let in my back door."

The words swam out of focus, but he continued looking at the text.

"Now that you've been with us so long," she went on, "it's time you learned a few facts of life. Just because people can't *see* the holes in your socks doesn't mean they don't sense them. Do you realize that practically every pair you own has a hole? I couldn't believe my eyes. Yesterday I was going through your drawers and—"

"Fern," he said very gently, "how dare you go through my drawers?"

"I was putting away the clothes you asked me to launder, that's how dare I."

Even more gently—there was a slight quaver in his voice—he said, "From now on just leave them on the bed, please. There's no need to—"

"Good heavens," she said as the doorbell rang. "Now, who could that be? Excuse me a minute."

Dr. Bates sat in his room staring blankly at the word processor that had once accidentally erased half of Kay's dissertation. All it would take would be one simple phone call to New Jersey and he would be free of this woman. His father would wire him enough to allow him to move into one of those new spa apartments in Ozone, where he would be only a few minutes from school. But then, before he knew it, Cecil would be down to inspect the apartment, making sure that everything was all right with the toilet, the drains. First he would use a holiday as an excuse to visit. Then it would become a regular stopover on his way to see friends on the West Coast. Pretty soon they would be palling around like a couple of bachelor friends, his father staying weeks at a time. Then Cecil would start suggesting double dates again and would begin to grow jealous of Dr. Bates's friends. If Dr. Bates wanted to spend time alone, he would have to lie to his father. Cecil would suspect the lie, and the whole cycle of resentment and reconciliation would begin again until Dr. Bates met someone strong like Kay, who would make him realize how basically sick this relationship was. No, he simply couldn't go through another breakup with his father. It would be too much to cope with, what with finals coming up. Best to stay where he was. After all, Mrs. Undine did provide excellent natural protection. His father simply loathed her and had vowed never to set foot in her house.

". . . so I thought I'd see if maybe you'd like to put this up on your lawn," Dr. Bates heard after wandering into the bathroom. Curious, he zipped up his pants and then, in the hall, lingered close to the plaster arch that led to the living room.

"Well, I don't know," Mrs. Undine was saying. As a rule —Carol Deshotel being the one exception—Dr. Bates remained in his room whenever someone came over. This visitor, however, did not sound like any of the retired teachers who would occasionally drop over for a cup of coffee. And her voice seemed so familiar. Cautiously Dr. Bates peered around the corner for a glimpse, but all he could see was her hand. It was fiddling with the ivory elephant Mr. Undine had purchased on V-E Day in San Diego. Mrs. Undine worried a great deal about the elephant and was considering placing it in a safety deposit box.

"It's never too early to develop a recognition factor," the visitor said while Mrs. Undine cautioned her about the tusks, which sometimes came loose.

Of course, he thought, taking a step or two back over the floor heating grate. No wonder the voice was so familiar. It was Mrs. Mackie, the former patient who didn't have any space between her teeth. Never before had he seen such tight contact; it made working on her a nightmare. There was simply no room to maneuver. Just getting a dam on her, preparatory to drilling, was a major chore. He hoped to God there wasn't something the matter with her again. How many times during the last year had he thought he was through with her, only to have her show up yet again with a loose amalgam, a missing gold foil. As a matter of fact, he had almost failed his mock boards because of her. Luckily he was able to scrounge up a patient with a lot of space between his teeth for the real boards. Otherwise he wouldn't have stood a chance.

"What about the insurance?" Mrs. Undine was asking as Dr. Bates began to retreat to his room. But the word *insurance* caused him to pause. "You said a man from the insurance company is supposed to— No, on the end table there. Please set it down there."

"It will only take a few minutes. He's a nice man, really. I've already talked to him. And don't worry about lawyers. And oh, above all, don't mention this to you know who. At least not now."

"Oh, but I think . . ."

"No, Mrs. Undine, it would just complicate things."

Lawyers, insurance men? Dr. Bates had heard enough. After quietly bolting the door to his room he sank onto his bed. This was all he needed, a lawsuit. He tried hard not to imagine Dr. Schexsnyder's face when the school was served with papers, but the image soon seemed as real as a recent memory. Dr. Bates saw himself being summoned first to Dr. Schexsnyder's, then the dean's office. He would try to explain about her incredibly tight contact . . . But wait a minute. Didn't every patient sign a form stating that Gregg College of Dentistry could not be held legally responsible for any mistakes that were made in the course of treatment? If she had signed this, then he had nothing to worry about. Unless it simply meant that he himself would be legally responsible, not the school.

Worry soon induced a brief nap. Shortly after, he went into the kitchen—Mrs. Mackie had departed by then—and put on some water for one of those General Foods International Coffees that were helping him cut down on his coffee intake. This afternoon he thought he would try the Café Amaretto ("dipotassium phosphate, silicon dioxide . . ."). While he was standing there, staring bleakly at the saucepan of about-to-boil water, Mrs. Undine wandered in from the back yard with a handful of zinnias and asked him if it was mandatory for all atoms to have at least one electron.

"I don't know," he muttered.

She got down a vase. "I do hate to leave it bare like that. If there was only some sort of grass that enjoyed sand. Do you think Bermuda grass might?"

Anxious to ask her about Mrs. Mackie, he nonetheless couldn't resist this opportunity to chide her again about buying sand instead of dirt.

"Dirt is not cheap," she said, filling the vase with water. "And contrary to popular belief I am not made of money. By the way, I saw Mr. Keely out back, and he said he thought he could use our extra sand. He's taking it away now."

"Fern, what did that woman—"

"He just got back from a hunting trip, you know. Deer hunting. And you'll never guess what he found lying in the woods."

"The woman in the living room, what did she—"

"A dead deer, Martin. They figured it must have died of old age. You know, it's strange," she went on, clipping the stalks of the zinnias with a pair of kitchen scissors. "When you think about it, it's hard to imagine wild animals dying of old age. But I suppose they do. Do you think birds just fall out of trees when their time comes or—"

"Fern, what did that lady want?"

"Hm?" She plucked a few withered leaves from the stalks before replying. "Oh, Olive. She asked me to . . . Here, look." On the Formica counter, pocked by years of wear, was a printed sign. She held it up for his inspection. A few pieces of lath gave it support, while a sturdier piece was pointed to act as a stake. "TIME FOR A CHANGE. VOTE OLIVE MACKIE."

"Poor girl, she hasn't a chance, of course. Anyway, Martin, if you would stick it next to the persimmon out front, the ground is soft. Or do you think it looks too vulgar? Oh, dear." She contemplated the red, white, and blue a moment while patting her wilted permanent. "No, I don't think I *have* to do this to my yard. We'll just put it in the garage, and I'll tell Olive— Well, I'll think of something."

Trying to appear casual, he leaned against the Hotpoint refrigerator, sipping the coffee from a jelly glass. All the cups were in the dishwasher, which he had forgotten to run last night. "She want anything else?"

"Hm?"

Just last night he had asked her not to preface every single reply she gave with a "Hm?" Up North, he had explained, that was considered bad manners.

"Hm? What, Martin? Oh, well, as a matter of fact . . ." she said, walking out the kitchen door with the sign. He followed her down an oil-stained concrete step into the two-car garage. At present there were no cars in it since the electronic eye on the doors was malfunctioning and cost far too much to repair. She stood there a moment, surrounded by dimly discernible tools, a mower, extension cords, rags, scrap wood, cans of paint, varnish. "What am I doing here?" she finally asked.

"The sign."

"Oh." She stuck it behind some formidable-looking fishing tackle, one pole as thick as a man's arm. "All this space going to waste," she murmured. "I really should do something with it." She was talking to herself, of course, what she liked to term "thinking aloud." Lately, though, this thinking aloud seemed to be getting out of hand. Was it necessary, Dr. Bates wondered, for her to verbalize every stray thought that crossed her mind? "Maybe I'll get up now and get a paper towel," she would say in the middle of a television program they were watching. Or during supper: "I think I'm going to put some more salt on my peas."

"Is that all she wanted—Mrs. Mackie?" he asked, trailing her back into the kitchen.

"I'd rather not talk about it."

Of course. The one thing he needed to know about, and she was silent.

"I hope Mr. Keely doesn't strain his back," she said from the screen door which led to the back yard. Their neighbor, a hefty man with a kind, weathered face, was trying to back a wheelbarrow of sand through the azaleas that separated the two yards. Dr. Bates made another patient attempt at extracting some information from her while she winced in sympathy with Mr. Keely's exertions.

"I don't know why I should tell you everything when you snub my questions."

"What?"

"I asked you about atoms."

"Fern, I told you, I don't know."

The rusty screen she stood in front of filtered the orange and pinks of the sunset into a cross that hovered, garish and insubstantial, over Mr. Keely's bowed back. Dr. Bates shifted his eyes a fraction to the left, and the cross disappeared.

"Well, it's too much," Mrs. Undine said, breaking the stubborn silence between them. Dr. Bates shook his head. He had just had a curious, fleeting sensation of the earth, like a carnival ride, wheeling away from the sun. It left him slightly giddy and suspicious of his coffee intake. He simply must cut down.

"I don't want to talk to any insurance investigator," she went on, more to herself than in reply to him. "I'm just not the type to get mixed up with people like that—investigators and coroners."

"Coroners?"

She had gone to the counter, where she began putting away the peanut butter and jelly jars, first wiping them off carefully with a dishrag. "She says if I don't volunteer information now, I could be subpoenaed. Me, subpoenaed, like a common—"

"What are you talking about?"

"It's one of my exercise clients, Olive's uncle. His home attendant committed suicide, Mr. Versey—you know, Nesta's brother. The coroner looks like he might be changing his verdict, though. He's beginning to see some suspicious circumstances, and the insurance investigator has come here from Baton Rouge to find out why the verdict is being changed. I'm supposed to tell him whether or not I think it's possible Mr. Versey was despondent enough to do away with himself and I don't even know Mr. Versey. I only met him once or twice, and it's just not fair, dragging me in like this. I don't know what I'm going to do."

The more worked up she became, the more Dr. Bates rued opening up this can of worms. Relief that the worms had nothing to do with him made him initially good-humored. He listened politely, with half an ear. But then when she followed him into his bedroom, still going on about the deceased home attendant, Dr. Bates found it more difficult to sympathize.

"Look, Fern, you're making too much of this. So you spend five minutes tomorrow talking to the insurance guy, big deal."

She was sitting on the edge of the queen-size bed, where Kay and he used to sleep. "But what if I say something, accidentally, that makes everyone mad. Martin, I could get in trouble. Olive said I would be under oath." She twisted the edge of the bedspread. "There's only one thing to do. I better consult my lawyer. She'll tell me if I have to testify or not, what my rights are in this thing. What I'll do is maybe ask her over for dinner."

"What? Ask who?"

"Donna Lee, Mrs. Keely's daughter. She's the one who handled the sinkhole for me when I thought I was going to sue. I don't think she's a very good lawyer, really, but she'll do for this. I just want a little advice, and anyone else would cost an arm and a leg. We'll make it something of a social call, and I'll slip in the question offhand."

"You can't do that. If you want to see her, go to her office."

"Nonsense. That's what I did about the sinkhole, and she charged me fifty dollars. And I still don't know why there's a hole there. No, Martin, I'm afraid she owes me this."

Mrs. Undine went on to complain about the geologist whom Donna Lee had hired to come look at the hole, how incompetent he was, how he couldn't tell if an underground stream had caused it or what. Then she started asking Dr. Bates why he didn't use the word processor, why that expensive machine was just sitting there gathering dust. He sat silently through all of this, with what he imagined—secretly, barely acknowledging it to himself—was the patience of a saint. Saint or not, he did have to admit to himself that his self-control was quite remarkable. Kay had once said that she had never met a more even-tempered man in her life, and it was this, more than his looks, that had made her decide to marry him.

"Please have a fish stick, dear," Mrs. Undine urged at supper that evening. "We have plenty."

The lawyer had dropped by in the middle of the meal but did not commit herself by taking a seat. She had said she was in a hurry and really shouldn't have dropped by at all. But her mother had told her something urgent had come up. Although Dr. Bates thought she looked much prettier than what he remembered from a chance encounter in Mrs. Keely's drive a few days ago, he was still not pleased by the intrusion. Mrs. Undine knew full well he didn't like company at dinner. If she must have people over, she could at least wait until he was in his room.

"Please, just try one, dear," Mrs. Undine urged. "They're Mrs. Paul's, a new Crunchy Light Batter."

"No, thanks," the lawyer said a little brusquely while running her hands through her full blond hair, a gesture that for some reason aroused Dr. Bates. Usually he was not attracted to women taller than he was, which was one reason why his marriage had been a little confusing, since Kay was almost as tall as her mother—certainly as tall as this Donna Lee. But it seemed as if all the right-sized women were either married or engaged, at least the ones that crossed his path.

"I don't know where your mother got the idea it was so urgent I see you," Mrs. Undine said pleasantly. "I just told her it would be nice if you could drop over for a bite to eat. But you know your mother, how she tends to worry so. Please, dear, sit." The lawyer stayed where she was, leaning with folded arms against the counter.

"I was saying to your mother," Mrs. Undine went on, "how little I see of you these days. Do you know, Martin, it seems like just yesterday when I used to worry about backing over Donna Lee on her tricycle. She was always pedaling like fury up and down our drive. Never looked where she was going. By the way, Donna Lee, did you know that Martin was a dentist? He's over at the dental college in Ozone, and I tell you, dear, you could save yourself a bundle if you—"

"Fern," he said, looking down at his plate.

"Of course, he doesn't have his degree yet, but don't let

that bother you. He's thoroughly supervised by topnotch professionals. And they even let him be called doctor, although really—"

"I already have a dentist, Mrs. Undine." Her tone was civil.

"Yes, but Martin is so careful about hurting you, too, and—"

"Fern," he said softly, through clenched teeth. If it wouldn't have appeared too childish, he would have excused himself. But he was trapped. Donna Lee stood there, a stony look on her face, refusing to acknowledge the sheepish smile he telegraphed from his seat.

"Mrs. Undine, it's very nice to see you, but I've got a—"

"You know, Martin, Donna Lee used to be one of my better students. She was so conscientious, always followed instructions to a T. I'm sorry, did you say something?"

"I'm going to the symphony tonight, in Baton Rouge, and I'd like to change and . . ."

Demurely closing her eyes, Mrs. Undine swallowed, as discreetly as possible, a bite of Mrs. Paul's. "Oh, how lovely, the symphony. I don't suppose you have a little extra room in your car, do you? Martin really doesn't take up much space, and it would be so wonderful if he could get out of the house occasionally. You know, I sometimes worry about him, the way he never likes to leave the house—except for work, of course."

"Look, it isn't my car," Donna Lee said with a visible trace of panic. "I mean, it's my boyfriend, F.X.'s. He's taking me tonight."

"Dear, I was just joking," Mrs. Undine said gaily. Dr. Bates had stopped chewing. His face was grim, immobile. "You kids joke all the time, yet when one of us old folks . . . Well, never mind. Listen, dear, before you go, let me ask you a quick question. I do volunteer work for the Ladies' Aid Society, and one of my clients, a Mr. Loraine, his home attendant jumped out the window the other day and—"

"Right, I read about that." The lawyer hooked her thumbs in the belt loops of her jeans. They looked wrong on her, the jeans, Dr. Bates thought hazily through a fog of resentment.

She just didn't seem like the outdoors type, even though she wore a man's flannel shirt and some sort of work boots that women could have worn less self-consciously ten or fifteen years earlier, when protest was in.

"Anyway, an insurance investigator is coming in from Baton Rouge tomorrow, and they want me to talk to him. I just wanted to make sure that I won't get in any sort of trouble if I don't. You know I'm not the type for legal things, they make me too nervous. Just going through probate after Mr. Undine died, well, you remember me then, Donna Lee. I was a nervous wreck. Anyway, I'm afraid my nerves are going to start up again if I get involved with lawyers. I tried to tell Olive this. She's the one whose uncle—well actually, it's her great-uncle, he used to be married to Artis Young. Young was her maiden name. Miss Young used to teach my cousin, Lula Babco, grades one through eight all in one room, but then it got to be too much for her and she went up North somewhere and got a job in the lingerie department of some big department store and—Chicago, yes, that's it, and that's where she met her husband. They got married late in life and—"

"Mrs. Undine, really." The lawyer had opened the kitchen door. "I must—"

"Just a second, dear. Well anyway, Mr. Versey, he's the home attendant, and his sister is on the faculty at Robin Downs, or rather was. She quit when her brother died, and who can blame her. They lived together out near the doughnut place on the Old Jeff Davis Highway. Anyway, it seems she was the beneficiary of his life insurance policy, except that she can't collect one red cent on it if they stick to the results of the death certificate. The coroner had thought Mr. Versey took his own life, and of course, you can't get anything for doing that. Well, I do feel for Nesta, that's Mr. Versey's sister. I just don't know how she's going to get by on Social Security. Robin Downs really doesn't have a retirement policy worth a hill of beans. I tell you, if it wasn't for Mr. Undine's insurance—of course, it's almost all gone by now—I wouldn't have made it through those first years. Anyway, I don't want to say anything that might prejudice the insurance people against poor Nesta. But since I might be under oath, I can't tell a lie, either, can I? And besides, I really don't know Mr. Versey from Adam. It's so unfair to make me, of all people, go and . . . Donna Lee?"

"Why don't we discuss this at my office? Call Mr. Pickins and make an appointment, O.K.? I've got to run now. 'Bye."

"Of course, you realize, Martin," Mrs. Undine said after the lawyer had left, "that girl can be difficult. I can't begin to tell you the trouble she's caused her poor mother. That so-called boyfriend of hers—well, I don't think I'm speaking out of school when I say that he's an ex-con. That's right, straight from Angola, a drug dealer. Mrs. Keely is worried sick, just doesn't know what to do. She's afraid that if she protests too much, Donna Lee will marry him out of sheer perversity. I just don't understand what's gotten into young women these days. Take Kay, for instance, going off to New York City, of all places, as if she had an ice cube's chance in . . . in a hot place of finding anyone. Well, of course, not everyone up North is . . . I mean, it almost worked. But she could have saved herself and *you*, poor *you*—did Kay have any consideration for you? Dragging you out of your natural habitat like that. I just don't believe that people were meant to live all over the map. They were born in a certain place for good reason." She reached for the relish. "Well, Martin, you certainly make an enchanting dinner partner. I don't know when I've had so much fun. Honestly, would it kill you to be just a tiny bit sociable?"

"Pass the salt, please."

"Here you are, sir. Oh, I am glad that Mr. Keely took that sand away. Isn't that nice?"

"Wonderful."

Chapter Eight

For the first week or so Uncle L.D. was so furious he couldn't speak. Mistaking his complete and utter silence for a physical handicap, the staff of Azalea Manor was astonished when a clumsy nursing aide was cursed and reviled after spilling V8 juice on the old man. They tried everything they could think of to get him to talk again, including more V8 juice, but that was it—not another word. Olive, of course, knew full well that he was just being stubborn as a bulldozer. This was what she would tell him during visiting hours, when she would sit by his bed, listing on her fingers all the improvements that the move to the nursing home had brought to his life: A) He had three hot, well-balanced meals a day; B) there were nurses and doctors here to treat his bedsores; C) what about that beautiful view out his window of trees and things!; D) wasn't he always complaining that he had no friends? Well, here were three roommates just waiting to become his buddies. Uncle L.D. was never much improved by this recital, which on certain muggy, overcast days, might wind up with an E): "Don't forget, I could have left you in that dark old apartment with no one to look after you. But no, this is the thanks I get for running myself ragged, trying to find a nice home for you. You just don't realize how good you got it. There's a lot of rich people here, you know. Right down the hall from you, Uncle L.D., they got Mr. Dambar's mother. That's right, the man who owns that big house on Lewis Street with the heated pool—this is where his mother lives."

Uncle L.D., though, didn't care if Howard Hughes's mother was parked right outside his door; he wanted his own apartment back. Never would he get used to living with so much light. At seven every morning a bank of fluorescent tubes flickered on automatically, eliminating every shadow from the room. Squinting through his one good eye at a series of flat geometric shapes, he tried to determine, as in an abstract painting, whether this was a chair, that a desk, perhaps. The smells were also disorienting, mainly because, unlike in his own apartment, he noticed them and felt almost forced to label them. (Ammonia? But what about that sweet stench beneath it?) It was the same with the food. Vienna sausage and bananas he had learned to tolerate mainly because they had no taste to him. But everything they brought him now caused his taste buds to fire off queries to his brain. How mentally taxing it was to really taste, to be aware of something totally alien trying to force its way into his own system. The only relief he found during the day was when he dozed off, which he tried to do as often as possible. Then, even when he wasn't fully asleep, he would have a strong sense that he was back in the apartment over Sonny Boy. Often he would hear the girls talking downstairs and making change. But when he woke up, the dismay he felt upon realizing where he was almost made him sick. If Olive wanted to kill him, she couldn't have picked a surer way; a shotgun might have misfired, but Azalea Manor was foolproof.

On either side of him, so close that it seemed at times as if they were sharing the same bed, were two men who ground their teeth stereophonically all through the night. At the far end of the oblong room was a darkish-looking man who remained, because of the distance, something of a blur. Like Uncle L.D., he never joined in the mindless chatter of the other two. They at first tried to include him in their observations about the food here and the decline of the West. But after a while, when Uncle L.D. proved unresponsive, they talked right through him, as if he were already a ghost. The one on his left was a natty, fastidious type who had blue jays on his bathrobe, while the one on his right reminded Uncle L.D. of himself some fifteen years and thirty pounds ago. Indeed, there were times when Uncle L.D. watched himself get out of bed and wander out the door, which was very confusing, until he remembered who the departing gentleman was.

". . . little pinpricks in my legs like, I don't know," the nursing aide was saying as she led a man into the room. A hefty teenager, she pressed a finger into her dimpled knee, then added, "There he is." Picking up a towel from the floor, she walked out.

Having been enjoying the comparative luxury of a room to himself while the other men were out on the sun deck, Uncle L.D. was not pleased by the intrusion, at least initially. But then, noting the elegance of the visitor's three-piece suit, he felt a stir of interest. Pulling up one of the webbed lawn chairs, the young man settled into it as if it were the largest, most comfortable armchair in an exclusive men's club. Completely at ease, he gazed about the room with a proprietary air before addressing the old man.

"You remember me, Mr. Loraine. It's Dr. Munrow," he said, holding out a meaty hand. Uncle L.D. gripped it as hard as he could and held on, as if the feel of it would jog his memory. Although he knew this Munrow was someone important, someone who might be able to help him, the young man's smooth, broad face remained as puzzling as a *déjà vu*.

Suddenly aware of his own appearance, the old man attempted to apologize for the flimsy white robe he had on, more like paper than cloth. They had taken away his Hart Schaffner & Marx, he wanted to say, but all that came out was a slightly menacing growl. As if reading his mind, the visitor reached with his free hand for the turquoise pitcher on the nightstand and poured some water into a Dixie cup.

"By the way," Dr. Munrow said as the old man drank, "I thought you might like this." He pulled a thick yellow volume from his satchel and handed it to Uncle L.D., who regarded it a moment through spaghetti-stained pince-nez.

"It's got all the dates and facts—like here," the young man added, opening a page in the *Information Please*, "a list of all the prime ministers of England. And look, the distance to Arcturus."

"Very nice." A little miffed that the visitor thought he would ever need such a book, Uncle L.D. handed it back. "Now may I say—"

"It's yours. Keep it, sir," Dr. Munrow said, placing the book on the electric-orange bedspread.

"Now may I say what an honor it is to be called upon by a person of your intelligence?" Gently, with a foot that ached, he kicked the *Information Please* aside. "May I say that I think you're remarkable?"

"And may I say, sir, that I think *you're* remarkable?" The visitor leaned forward while Uncle L.D. searched his blue, childlike eyes for a trace of mockery; he found none. "I've heard from a number of sources what a remarkable memory you have, sir."

"Perhaps, in my own dull, retarded way, I've enlightened one or two people on that score." Although he was anxious to confide in someone, Uncle L.D. held back. Something about the visitor put him on guard. Perhaps it was the fact that his voice and bearing, both reminiscent of a man in his late fifties or so, did not jibe with his apparent youth. It reminded Uncle L.D. of college boys impersonating old men on stage with white shoe polish in their hair. "Does it perhaps strike you as a little odd," Uncle L.D. ventured, "that a man who could name you, right now, the dates of every important battle in the War of 1812 should be forcibly evicted from his domicile?"

"It does indeed. That's why I'm here, Mr. Loraine. I'm here to help you."

Uncle L.D.'s suspicion hardened. Those were the very words Olive had used just before carting him off.

"They told me you couldn't talk," the visitor went on, "and I thought to myself, *Yes, he's a clever man, a very clever man.* You're right not to talk. You must be so careful what you say—to them." He reached over and poured another cup of water, which he handed to the old man. "You know, it seems to me I'm just about the only person in town who believes in you. I don't care what they say: I know your memory is letter-perfect. They've been telling me you couldn't even remember your own mother's name, but I said—"

Uncle L.D. gagged on the water. "Who?" he demanded. "Who's been slandering me like this?"

Dr. Munrow's eyes went wide, like William Buckley, Jr.'s. "Your niece, for one. It seems there's been a slight discrepancy between something she told the sheriff and something you said to him, before you quit talking. You see, Mrs. Mackie claimed to have come and seen you on the day Mr. Versey passed away. And you had told the sheriff she hadn't. In fact, you were quite adamant about it. Afterwards, when the sheriff confronted her with this, Mrs. Mackie said, and I quote, 'The old bulldozer couldn't remember his own mother's name, much less how many times I've killed myself going up those stairs to visit him.' "

When Dr. Munrow said this about the sheriff, the ghostly outlines of the *déjà vu* were filled in by the memory of those endless questions about Olive and Mr. Versey. First it was the sheriff asking, then the coroner, and on one occasion Dr. Munrow himself, a schoolteacher, he remembered now, whom Mrs. Undine had brought over one day. Did Mr. Versey think this, did he think that, was he depressed, was he drinking? They all wanted to know every detail about Mr. Versey. Wasn't it enough that Mr. Versey had made his life miserable when he was alive? But now, even in death, he continued to have a hold on him, as if he were some sort of final exam. And look where all that talk about Mr. Versey had landed him, right in the middle of a nursing home. He knew it was better to keep his trap shut. If only he had been silent before, when they were questioning him earlier, he might not find himself in this wretched place now.

One hand stroking a palomino tie clasp, Dr. Munrow sat regarding the old man coolly until, unable to dam himself up any longer, Uncle L.D. exploded: "That girl doesn't know what she's talking about! She never came by that day. She's a dope!"

"You ask me, this town is chock full of dopes."

"Oh, Dr. Munrow," he said, reaching for the young man's hand and squeezing it. Those words were music to his ears. Perhaps, after all, he had found a soul mate.

"Only a dope could believe that a man like Mr. Versey would want to kill himself, right, Mr. Loraine? I mean, let's face it. It takes a certain amount of intelligence to want to do away with oneself."

"That man didn't have the brains to kill a flea. Why, I've seen him sit for hours staring at a crack in the wall and . . ."

"Yes, go on."

Realizing that he had perhaps said too much already, Uncle L.D. released his hand and lapsed into silence. Dr. Munrow did not seem the least bit concerned. Crossing his legs, he sat comfortably in front of the old man and watched him for a few moments, blankly, as if he were a tv.

"You told Dr. McFlug, the coroner," Dr. Munrow said finally, in almost a whisper, "that it was while you were napping. You had dozed off, correct? That was when Mr. Versey saw fit to throw himself out the window."

What business is it of yours what I said! Uncle L.D. wanted to shout, but he clenched his jaw, knowing that every time he opened his mouth, he seemed to get deeper in trouble. Yes, he had told the coroner about the nap. He did not want to complicate things by explaining what actually had happened. If he did, he would have to tell them how he had shaken Mr. Versey after prodding him with the umbrella. It was only after he had touched him that Mr. Versey had fallen out the window. But how could he explain this to the coroner when he couldn't even explain it to himself? What would they think if he told them that he had discovered Mr. Versey leaning out the window, so strangely silent? Perhaps he had been dead then. But if so, why? This was where Uncle L.D.'s memory failed him, or at least where it became murky. For Uncle L.D. did remember a struggle. He did remember striking the man with his umbrella . . . or was it only that he had wished to strike him? Had he actually struck him, perhaps hard enough to leave him unconscious there on the sill? But no—was it possible that he could knock someone out and then calmly wheel himself into a corner and fall asleep? The more he thought about it, the guiltier he felt. Somehow his sheets kept getting mixed up with the events—something Mr. Versey had done to his sheets.

"When I say this town is full of dopes, I'm including the sheriff and Dr. McFlug. Neither one of them said a thing about those bruises on your arm." The visitor had pulled his chair right up to the bed so that his face was only inches away. "In my heart of hearts," he whispered as Uncle L.D. turned his face away, "I think you, sir, have been sorely abused. I think Mr. Versey, if he were alive—God rest his soul—could be brought up on criminal charges of assault and battery." He leaned even closer, and even more softly than before, so that Uncle L.D. was not quite sure of the words, he said, "And I think, Mr. Loraine, that . . . particular day you had . . . limit. You . . . not take anymore . . ." Uncle L.D. had his eyes shut almost as tight as when Olive used to change his Pampers. He did not want to hear what he knew this man was going to say. And when he did say it, when he heard the still small voice (" . . . you hated . . . good cause . . . defense . . . wanted to kill . . ."), he thought, *This cannot be. I am not hearing this. I am only imagining I am hearing this.*

The relief, then, was tremendous when he opened his eyes and saw that there was no one there. The room was his, his alone. He had probably just dozed off and dreamed the visit. But this relief was short-lived, for his left foot, when it shifted under the bedspread, knocked against the *Information Please*, which tumbled to the floor with a dull thud.

Olive was in a stew. She had finally admitted to herself that, even though he was too small, too unmasculine, she was in love with Dr. Bates. But the question was, could she afford to have an affair with him now that her life was no longer her own? Soon she would be a public figure, one whose every move would be scrutinized by jealous rivals. Was it worth it to jeopardize the one chance she had of making something of her life? To say nothing of her family. What if Duane found out she was carrying on? Would she be able to explain to him that she still loved him dearly? That her passion for Dr. Bates was more like an illness, a fever, which would eventually pass, she was sure? Yet while it lasted she could not help thinking that there was something a little bland and unreal about Duane's own good health.

"I know it's yours, but still, Felix, it just isn't right," she was saying as she and her son entered the lobby of Azalea Manor. Felix had just informed her that his Harley-Davidson was on loan to a Mormon missionary, a friend of the bishop he boxed with. While pondering whose insurance would cover the motorcycle if it was wrecked by the missionary, her mind was also, on a slightly deeper, almost subconscious level, trying to gauge the effect an affair with Dr. Bates would have on her relationship with Felix. Was he mature enough to understand that such an affair would not be a betrayal of any of their family values? That it was something she had to experience in order to better understand herself and thus, ultimately, prove a better wife and mother? After all, she was probably the only one she knew who had never experienced an extramarital affair. Hadn't Carol told her that Desirée was carrying on with this ex-con who was supposed to be so good-looking, a guy she had picked up for shoplifting? And Carol herself had admitted to her that ten years ago she had fallen in love with someone from New Orleans. Even though they had never consummated the relationship, they had done a lot of heavy petting in his Porsche. He was a multi-millionaire, and Carol said that if she had wanted to, she could have been unbelievably rich today.

"Who's going to pay if . . ." She paused on the landing of a sweeping staircase that had once made Azalea Manor, before it was transformed into a nursing home, a highlight of many antebellum Home and Garden tours. Felix was dawdling below, next to a mural of giraffes in primary reds and yellows. "Are you coming?"

He tugged on his Everlast belt. "I'll wait here."

"Come on. It won't kill you." She moved to one side as an automatic chair lift ascended with its cargo, a steely-faced lady with a large bow in her hair. "Come on, you chicken."

"Uh-uh."

Olive made a clucking sound in the hopes that this might cheer him up. He had seemed depressed today when she had picked him up at the bishop's. She suspected that the Mormons might be making him feel guilty about his father's drinking. Perhaps it was getting a little out of hand these days, but that was nothing for Felix to concern himself with. As soon as Duane landed a decent job, things would settle down to normal. In the meantime the last thing she and Duane needed were those sunrise sermonettes on alcohol and the brain cells. Poor Duane had to let off steam somehow, and Felix just didn't realize what a huge capacity his father had.

She clucked again, louder this time, and then noticed that Mrs. Undine was at her elbow. "Oh," Olive murmured. It was as if the woman had materialized there in Star Trek fashion.

"Who is that down there?" Peering over her half glasses, Mrs. Undine said, "Is that Felix? I don't know if your uncle is really prepared to see anyone, Olive. He wouldn't say a word to me."

"Felix, come up here and say hello to Mrs. Undine. Felix!" He faded behind a cement pillar. "It's so sad Uncle L.D. can't talk anymore," she said with an ingratiating smile. "By the way," she added, placing a restraining hand upon the other woman's jersey sleeve, "how did things go with Mr. Ellen?"

"Mr. Ellen?"

"The insurance man."

Mrs. Undine said something vague, evasive. Apparently she hadn't spoken to him yet.

"You really must, you know," Olive said as Mrs. Undine took a step down. Ever since she had learned of Mr. Versey's demise Olive had been concerned that Mrs. Undine would worm her way out of the investigation. It had been Olive, of course, who had encouraged everyone to question Mrs. Undine by suggesting that the exercise instructor might be privy to some of the old man's secrets. At first Olive was only dimly aware of why she was doing this. But now, with Mrs. Undine no longer teaching Felix, she was desperate for some sort of natural link with Dr. Bates, some excuse to be around the house on Pine Street. And so, Olive did all in her power to embroil Mrs. Undine. This wasn't easy, since no one, including the insurance investigator, seemed particularly interested in talking to Mrs. Undine.

"To tell the truth, Olive, I'm on my way to my lawyer's now."

"Why? That's silly."

"I want to know if I must talk to that insurance man."

"But I told you, you don't have to worry about a thing."

Mrs. Undine pursed her lips. "I'm afraid I do. You see, the more I've thought about your uncle, the more concerned I've become. Do you realize how many times he's referred to guns in my presence? Now, what if someone asks me, under oath, if he ever talked violently, and I'll be forced to say—"

"Guns?"

"He was always saying to me, 'I could have taken out a gun and shot Mr. X; I could have taken out a gun and shot Miss Y.' "

"That's just an expression."

"Indeed—to you and me. But how is that going to sound to an investigator? I can't begin to tell you how nervous this makes me."

"Well, just leave that part out. Don't say anything about guns, hear." Then, as Mrs. Undine continued her careful descent, one hand gripping the dull, painted banister, Olive called out, "Come back and visit Uncle L.D. again soon. I know he appreciates it!"

"Isn't it nice that Mrs. Undine still comes and visits?" Olive was saying a few moments later in Room 2L6, where Uncle L.D. lay in stony silence between Mr. Higgins and Mr. Uwel. She liked Mr. Higgins the best, but she was careful to be equally nice to Mr. Uwel and the man at the other end of the room, an Arabic-looking man who, according to one of the nurses, had once made bricks. Trying to make conversation on a previous visit, she had asked him if it was true that they put straw in bricks. But like Uncle L.D., he wouldn't say anything back.

"Y'all want a Dynamint?" she asked. Uncle L.D. turned

his head away. Mr. Higgins, reeking of cologne, took one, and Mr. Uwel five.

"Did you talk to Mrs. P.?" Mr. Higgins inquired, his smooth, neat head to one side. Mr. Higgins was trying to help Olive with her campaign. On Olive's last visit he had suggested that she get in touch with his daughter-in-law, Mrs. P. Quaid, who had a hundred reams of Xerox paper just going to waste in her sewing room closet. As a matter of fact, Olive had given Mrs. P. a call, thinking that the paper might come in handy. But Mrs. P. had sounded decidedly hostile on the phone. For openers she didn't like being called Mrs. P. Furthermore, there were only three or four reams, which she used to print menus for the school cafeteria. She was the head dietician, someone Olive vaguely recalled from her own high school days. Olive had tried to end the conversation on a pleasant note by reminding Mrs. Quaid that they had met many times before "on opposite sides of the lunchroom counter." But Mrs. Quaid said she couldn't go voting for every Tom, Dick, and Harry she had served a hot lunch to.

"You tell her you're a good friend of mine," Mr. Higgins went on after Olive had made some sort of noncommittal reply. She didn't want to make him feel bad by telling him what really happened. "Tell Mrs. P. I said you could take as much as you want, understand?"

On the other side of Uncle L.D., Mr. Uwel cleared his throat. Apart from his bad teeth Mr. Uwel was a sturdy, handsome man who did not look as if he belonged here. This disturbed Olive and made her feel constrained when talking to him. "A schoolteacher," she replied when he asked who the lady was who was just here. "She used to give Uncle L.D. his workouts."

Both Mr. Higgins and Mr. Uwel said something at the same time. Catching neither comment, Olive patted Mr. Higgins's blue-jayed sleeve while Mr. Uwel repeated himself: "Do you know what Carlyle said about teachers? Well, goes double for me."

"Oh."

Again both Mr. Higgins and Mr. Uwel spoke at the same time, but this time they kept going, each trying to outshout the other.

"Boys!" Olive called out, holding up both hands. "Time!"

"It's my turn," Mr. Higgins declared.

"You hogged her last time. Why not give someone else a chance?" Mr. Uwel rubbed the thick stubble on his chin. "I got something important to ask."

"Now, look," Mr. Higgins said as he adjusted a knitted slipper-sock, "she hasn't got time for your Carlyle. We've got business to discuss—"

"Why don't you let her speak for herself—"

"Why don't you—"

Olive was about to squelch the bickering when, out of the corner of her eye, she thought she saw Dr. Bates walk past the door. It took considerable will power to stay seated, more, actually, than she possessed at the moment. She figured he must have come to pick up Mrs. Undine and had missed her downstairs. Well, she would just stick her head out and tell him that Mrs. Undine wasn't here.

"Hey, uh . . ." A vast disappointment gave her pause. It was only Felix. "Darling, over here. Here I am."

He turned around and strode over stiffly, in that exaggerated, macho way he had. "Don't call me that," he said, barely moving his lips as a juice tray clattered by.

"Come in and say hi." She gave him a nudge.

"Uh-uh."

"Come on."

"Uh-uh."

"Chicken."

"Fag."

"Chicken."

Back by Uncle L.D.'s beside, with Felix still lurking in the hall, she took a small Band-Aid and taped together as best she could the broken torso of Mr. Higgins's modernistic glass cat. "I was just lying here looking at it," he told her, "and the next thing I know, it falls right over and breaks in half."

"If I had some glue, it'd be better."

"Friend of my grandchild, she brought it to me. She comes

by, Mrs. P.'s child does, and never once brings me anything herself. I says to her, I says, 'Toinette, doesn't it shame you, girl, that your friend here always has something nice for me and you . . .''

"No, move your hand, Mr. Higgins. I can't see what I'm doing.''

Though it seemed sufficient, the overhead light in the room was not really adequate for any close work. Olive had to rest her eyes a moment before she finished mending the curio. While Mr. Higgins and Mr. Uwel started talking again her attention wandered, and she found herself in the midst of a daydream. There she was vacuuming, and in walks Duane with a strange look on his face. He tells her he knows all about her and Dr. Bates. She turns off the vacuum and faces him, unafraid. She is going to explain to him once and for all how Dr. Bates poses no threat to their marriage. He is enriching her life, bringing things to it that complement Duane's good qualities, a certain gentleness. A sweetness. But before she can get more than a few words out, Duane has smashed a pinkish elephant on the end table and is saying how he's going to kill Dr. Bates, tear him limb from limb. . . .

"Hide the cat.''

"Huh?'' Olive said, recoiling from a sharp poke on the arm.

Mr. Higgins squirmed in the bed. "Hide the damn cat.''

A chubby, tired-looking woman had wandered into the room, almost as if she were lost. When Mr. Higgins greeted her, Olive understood why he wanted the cat out of the way. It was most likely the girl who had given it to him, and he did not want her to see it was broken.

"I got to run, y'all,'' Olive said, happy for the interruption. It made her feel less guilty to leave if someone else was around to entertain them. As she got up it crossed her mind that in her daydream she had been vacuuming Mrs. Undine's living room. She had meant to be vacuuming her own, a chore she had been putting off for some time now.

"Miss Burma,'' Mr. Higgins said as Olive leaned over and pecked Uncle L.D. on the forehead, "this here is Miss Olive

Mackie. She's going to be our next Superintendent of Parks and things, and I want you to tell her right now she can count on your vote and the vote of all your girl friends."

Miss Burma loosened the belt of her green vinyl jacket, and Olive saw she had on a familiar uniform underneath. Forgetting her own personal problems, Olive smiled and held out her hand. "You work in Sonny Boy, don't you? I'm in there all the time. Just love that store."

Miss Burma's hand was a little sticky, clammy. Surreptitiously Olive wiped her own against her skirt after shaking Miss Burma's.

"Ask her if she'll distribute some fliers," Mr. Higgins urged Olive. "Miss Burma's good at volunteering. She mailed a lot of stuff for the Animal League last year."

Shifting her weight from one crepe sole to the other, Miss Burma smiled wearily through a blur of late-afternoon make-up. "I'd be glad to vote for you, but I'm afraid I'm sort of busy these days."

"Oh, don't mind Mr. Higgins," Olive said. "I got to run now. 'Bye, Mr. Uwel," she said, nodding in the direction of where he was sulking. She made a mental note to spend more time talking to him on the next visit. And then, patting Mr. Higgins on his rigidly parted hair, she whispered in his ear, "The cat's in the drawer there, hon."

Chapter Nine

"TERRIBLE."

"I know."

"The way things— Eighty-nine for legs . . ."

"Those are pretty."

"Huh?"

"The ones over there. Nice."

"Oh."

With a vague good-bye Olive rolled her cart away, leaving Mrs. Sanchez to contemplate the nice quartered fryers. Olive had run into her, had, in fact, been standing beside her a few moments, before she realized who she was. Then it had been too late to sneak away. For her part Mrs. Sanchez, who had not bothered to phone once since Olive had been fired, had seemed somewhat discombobulated when she noticed who was beside her. Both women immediately began to chatter away about how expensive everything was nowadays, and then, at the first opportunity, Olive made her escape. As she rounded the corner into canned soups she felt tight and hot in her chest, as if she had just finished twenty laps around the basketball court.

"Leo, where's your gun?" a voice said over the paging speaker. "I need your gun in produce."

The boy who had been shooting prices onto Campbell's wonton soup cursed as Olive swung by him. "Come get it yourself," he muttered.

Pausing farther down the aisle by the boxed soup, Olive

tried to decide what to do. She really would like to finish her shopping here at the Winn Dixie, yet she couldn't stand the thought of another encounter with that woman. What if they ended up together in the check-out line? After a moment's pause Olive abandoned her half-full cart. She would drive over to the A&P.

A gridlock on the corner of North Gladiola held her up for a minute or two, but before long she was pulling into the A&P parking lot on the other side of town. The violence of her aversion to the very sight of Mrs. Sanchez troubled Olive. After all, the woman hadn't done anything wrong herself. She was simply an innocent bystander. Nothing Mrs. Sanchez could have said to the mayor would have changed his mind. So what did it matter that she hadn't made any effort to keep Olive from being fired? Still, out of loyalty, couldn't Mrs. Sanchez have made some sort of token fuss? Why did she have to take everything lying down? Really, Olive brooded as she locked up the Cadillac, that woman was no better than the good Germans who just obeyed orders. Morally speaking, there was something even more reprehensible about this sort of behavior than out-and-out cruelty. If only she had had the courage to tell Mrs. Sanchez this while they were admiring the chickens.

". . . having a sale here, so I thought I'd . . ."

"A little cheaper here, I think."

"And I like the A&P coffee. Can't get that at . . ."

"Dark roast."

"Yes," Olive said as she wheeled her cart away from Mrs. Sanchez, whom she had just encountered, yet again. As she would later report to Carol, Olive liked to die when she rounded the corner in the A&P and saw Mrs. Sanchez examining a box of Shake 'n Bake.

"Did you tell her off?" Carol asked.

"I let her know what's what," Olive fudged and, by saying this, dimmed the memory of her own confusion and embarrassment. "I gave her the cold shoulder, let her stew in her own juice." She did not add that she had fled the A&P. Which was why, later that afternoon, she and Carol had gone to the Winn Dixie so that finally Olive could get her shopping done.

Carol paused in front of some baby carrots. "Maybe you should be nice to her."

"Why should I be nice to Nazis?"

"She might be able to help you out, O.K., election-wise, if you know what I mean."

Olive wanted to move on, but Carol, as usual, was setting the pace. At this rate, it would take them three hours to get done. "No, I don't."

"She must have friends, influence, that sort of thing. In any case, at this point in time you really can't afford to alienate anyone. Just think how bad you'd feel if you lost by one vote. You'd always be kicking yourself because of that one vote, Bunny."

Olive looked quizzically at her. Bunny used to be her nickname in high school. Carol hadn't called her that in years. "What'd you call me that for?"

"What?"

"Bunny."

"I did? I don't know—just slipped out, I guess."

They were regarding the no-cholesterol eggs in the frozen dairy products case when Carol, out of the blue, asked her about Dr. Bates. "Is he gay, you think?"

Flustered, Olive just shrugged. It was uncanny the way Carol could sometimes read her mind. Not that Olive had been wondering about Dr. Bates's sexual orientation, but he had been present in her thoughts just then. She had been imagining in detail the visit she was going to pay Mrs. Undine as soon as they were through shopping. "You know him?"

"I run into him every now and then."

Olive picked out some frozen pancake batter and put it into her cart. Casually she asked, "In Ozone?"

"Huh? No, here. He doesn't date, you know. At least not openly."

The chill of the interior of the case kept Olive's face from getting too red. It was almost as if she were already having an affair with Dr. Bates, the way her conscience was affecting her. She was reminded of her school days, when she used to confess to her mother that she had gone to a dirty Elizabeth Taylor movie before she had actually gone. With the spanking over with she could then enjoy the show with a clear conscience.

At the check-out line Olive began to brood about Felix. He was still bagging groceries here on weekends. Well equipped to deal with adolescent rebellion, Olive and Duane were prepared to listen to their son, to sit down and negotiate in a way their own parents never had. What they hadn't counted on, though, was this creeping orthodoxy. They could only hope it was just a phase he was going through. One vestige after another of good old red-blooded rebellion was being shed, starting with the Harley-Davidson, now in the hands of the Mormons. Cropping up in its place were such things as an electric shoeshiner and button-down shirts that Felix himself ironed with alarming dedication. Olive sometimes went through his drawers, hoping to find a stash of marijuana, perhaps some cigarettes, a *Hustler*, but came up with nothing but a few pamphlets about the end of the world. She wished vainly for another scene like the one that had taken place when she had discovered the snake on his arm. It was much more comfortable playing the role of the sinned-against parent. Lately all the scenes were askew, with Felix lecturing his father about his drinking and Olive for the shows she watched on tv. "They're rotting your mind," he would announce over the intercom as she tried to forget her troubles with a few moments of *Falcon Crest*. Of course, she didn't blame Robin Downs for this development. Almost all the boys who went there were quite normal, with nothing on their minds but football and girls. No, it was the darn boxing. She had to get him out of the clutches of that bishop.

"You haven't been listening to a thing I've said."

"I have," Olive said.

"One forty-nine," the computer said as the check-out girl swept a package of licorice over the scanner embedded in the counter. It was a woman's voice, somewhat disturbing to Olive, for it sounded a little like her mother's.

"The minute it isn't about you," Carol resumed as they wheeled the loaded carts into the parking lot, "you tune out. Everything's got to be about you."

The injustice of this remark made Olive accelerate her cart. How many hours had she sat and listened to Carol's problems about her hair, her Mercedes, her precious daughter's guitar teacher. And yet whenever Olive tried to suggest that she, too, might have problems, Carol's eyes would glaze over.

Olive was loading her groceries into the trunk of the Cadillac when Carol caught up. "I'm sorry," Carol said. "From now on I promise never to say anything critical. I keep on forgetting what a thin skin you got."

There was silence as Olive very carefully placed Carol's groceries in the trunk. Then, her jaw muscles flexing, Olive decided it would be a good idea to start over again. "You really think I ought to smooth things over with Mrs. Sanchez?"

"What? Hey, aren't we supposed to take the carts back?"

The Cadillac edged past the ungainly baskets, which Olive was too tired to wheel back. "You know, I've been meaning to ask you, Carol. You've got such a good feel for these things. There's this lady used to work in the lunchroom in high school, Mrs. Quaid, remember? I wonder if I should start to develop her, sort of as a touchstone for the working-class vote."

"I'd get the blacks behind me, O.K., if I were you."

"Oh, she's not black. But I'm covering that base, too. There's this black lady I know. I'm going to see her after I drop you off." Olive hesitated, wondering if it would allay or arouse suspicion if she mentioned that this black lady was Mrs. Undine's part-time maid. "What do you think about this: I'm considering letting my hair grow out. Don't you think voters will respond better to mid-length, something more conservative?"

"I'm trying out a new conditioner for my hair, you know, but so far I don't see any difference."

Olive counted to ten. "I can't make up my mind about this boat I'm forced to drive around in. At first I thought it had to go. A Cadillac might arouse too much resentment. But then I read something about projecting success—"

"Watch," Carol said as a car pulled out two blocks away.

"And with the working class it's not as simple as you'd think. They don't go for people who ride around in compacts. They like things to be obvious, sort of a wish fulfillment. Duane was saying to me the other day, he had his eye on this Nissan and . . . Hey, what's . . ."

A few tears were trickling down her friend's face. "Nothing, go on. . . ."

"Carol."

"It's nothing. I'm fine. Go on; I'm listening."

Olive was shaken. Carol had never cried in her presence before. Racking her brains, Olive tried to remember something she had said or done that could have given such offense. By the time they pulled in front of Carol's elegant house with its wrought-iron grillwork, Olive had apologized for several things that were not her fault. In the meantime Carol had shifted into her too-polite mode and made a big fuss over Olive when she brought her groceries in for her.

"That's all I need," Olive said aloud to herself when she returned to the Cadillac. During the past few days she had run herself ragged trying to get the campaign off the ground. When she wasn't at the printer's ordering flyers and posters, she was agonizing over speeches that she might be called upon to make. It was becoming clear that if she was ever going to get anywhere, she would need help. Carol being the obvious choice for campaign manager, she just couldn't afford for the girl to turn against her now. After all, Carol had plenty of time on her hands. Not only that, she knew tons of people and could afford to work for free. As Olive drove past a boiled-peanut vendor camped outside the new video store she went over everything she had said to Carol, trying to figure out where she had gone wrong. Had she perhaps been too pushy in the Winn Dixie, trying to get Carol to hurry up? Couldn't she have complimented Carol on the new ensemble she had on, or thanked her for the suggestion about Mrs. Sanchez? A compliment here, a compliment there could go a long way. Olive resolved that, from now on, she was going to try to be less abrupt with people. Although she hated small talk and liked to get right down to business, she was going to force herself to be nice and chatty.

As she pulled up in front of Mrs. Undine's Olive noticed Dr. Bates in the neighbor's drive, just standing there with a blank look on his face. For a moment she wondered if this could indeed be the man she was obsessed with. He looked so ordinary. But then, catching sight of her, he cocked his head in a way that brought him to life. Yes, this was him.

Getting out of the car, she was trying to think of a casual comment to make to him when Mrs. Undine, a sweater draped about her shoulder, called out from the front door. "Is that you? I just can't believe I was— Come in, Olive," she prompted as Olive paused to inspect the mud she had picked up from the drainage ditch bordering the lawn. Perhaps, she thought, it would be too pushy if she started the conversation. Men like to be the initiators. But Dr. Bates had turned away, and there was nothing to do but follow Mrs. Undine inside.

"When I saw your car drive up," Mrs. Undine said after shutting the fumed oak door behind Olive, "I said to myself, 'And they say there's no such thing as ESP.' "

With a polite smile Olive stepped into the living room, where a man on a stepladder was plastering the ceiling.

"I was sitting right here thinking I simply must talk to you, and the next thing I know, I see your car pull up." Mrs. Undine leaned forward in the chair she had settled into, a gleam of triumph in her eyes. In the wing chair Olive gazed across the room at the plasterer, an unsettling presence, for he looked somewhat like Felix's bishop. They both had the same build, stolid as a Russian peasant woman's.

"I wasn't sure how to get in touch with you," Mrs. Undine went on as Olive's eyes strayed to the newspaper on the chair arm. It was opened to the daily menu for the local hospital. "For some reason all I could remember was your maiden name. I just couldn't get Miss Barnell out of my head. Then the next thing I know, there you are, big as life." Noticing Olive's eyes on the plasterer's broad, speckled back, Mrs. Undine edged her Sheraton chair a little closer. "Don't worry about him," she said, almost in a whisper. "He's hard of hearing, doesn't hear anything but a shout. We can talk."

Somewhat puzzled by Mrs. Undine's eagerness, Olive forgot about the bishop's lookalike and leaned forward so she could hear better. "I what?" she asked after Mrs. Undine mumbled something.

"Have you heard?" Mrs. Undine enunciated.

"Heard what?"

A neat, tapered hand fluttered to Mrs. Undine's scalloped collar and picked at the grosgrain. Olive kept one eye out, waiting for the front door to open. "Of course, you must have," Mrs. Undine went on. "Well, you could have knocked me over with a feather when Mrs. Keely told me. Oh, Olive, it's so much worse than I ever thought. I never knew what I was dealing with, the type of person. It just goes to show, you never know."

Studying the teacher's face, Olive realized that she had been misreading her distress for eagerness. Glancing toward the front door, she asked Mrs. Undine to slow down, explain.

"Please promise me that this is the end, Olive. My nerves simply can't take any more. I'm in a state, I believe." And then, in a louder, strained voice, she called over to the plasterer, "Are you sure you have enough dropcloth? Mr. Ames!" He went on smoothing the ceiling, oblivious to the question. Satisfied, Mrs. Undine turned back to her guest. "You can't leave these people alone for one second," she confided. "Mrs. Walters had her best silver tea service stolen. She thinks it was the man who tried to sell her a subscription to *Esquire*."

Trying to clear a path through this canebrake of irrelevancies, Olive wielded a definite question over and over again: "What are you talking about, Mrs. Undine?" Finally it made an impression. "Why, Mr. Loraine, of course. Your uncle."

"What about Uncle L.D.?"

"You don't mean to say you haven't heard?"

"Heard what?"

"All this is strictly off the record, Olive. What I'm telling you now, you must pretend you never heard. And then that's it. I'm washing my hands of the whole affair. I've had enough."

The look in Olive's eye was by now somewhat baleful. "Mrs. Undine."

"Well, if you must know, I'm speaking of Mr. Versey's demise. It wasn't a suicide, like everyone thought at first. Nesta always insisted that her brother was happy and looking forward to retiring. He had a plot of land in Gulfport that he was going to build a fishing camp on." She leaned over and parted the curtains near her chair. In the late afternoon light, shaded by the persimmon, the green Cadillac appeared to be silvery, like Carol's Mercedes. The curtain fell back. "He confessed," Mrs. Undine said dully.

"Who? What?"

"Mr. Loraine. He admitted he murdered Mr. Versey. They had been arguing about his commode, and apparently Mr. Versey had manhandled him. You know what a temper your uncle has. Anyway, Mrs. Keely told me that Mr. Loraine had finally had enough bullying, and he . . ."

The front door opened, and Dr. Bates walked in.

"Did Mrs. Keely have it?" Mrs. Undine inquired brightly.

In reply he held up a formidable-looking waffle iron. "Hi," he said to Olive, who had slumped down in her chair, a dazed look on her face. Romance had been temporarily routed by a vision of herself as the niece of a murderer. She nodded perfunctorily in his direction as she tried to gauge the effect this would have on her campaign. Of course, he wasn't really a relative . . . only by marriage . . . But what did that matter? People still associated him with her.

"Well, it's too ridiculous," Olive was saying a little later as she got into her car. Mrs. Undine had come outside with her, leaving Dr. Bates to keep an eye on the plasterer. "He barely has the strength to raise his head."

"Still, when people are enraged." Mrs. Undine regarded a drooping banana plant across the street, somewhat the worse for wear after the previous evening's frost. "Mrs. Keely said—"

"I don't know what business it is of hers to begin with,"

Olive said, turning on the ignition. She didn't want to waste time speculating with Mrs. Undine about all the ifs and maybes. She was going to pay the old man a visit right this minute. The nerve of him, ruining her campaign before it even got off the ground. If there was one thing she was sure of, it was that she was going to nip this confession in the bud before it could do any more harm.

"Buckle up," Mrs. Undine said as Olive's tinted window purred shut. But then Mrs. Undine was rapping on the window.

"Yes?" The window slid down a crack.

"Olive, I never did find out. What was it that made you come over this afternoon? Did you want to—"

"ESP," she said, anxious to get rolling. Visiting hours at the nursing home would be over soon.

Although Mrs. Keely had invited him in, Dr. Bates preferred to wait outside for the waffle iron. Mrs. Undine's iron, which had been submerged in dishwater, was in a repair shop. In the meantime they were going to borrow Mrs. Keely's to make those banana waffles that Dr. Bates had taken a fancy to. Mrs. Undine had prepared them one Sunday evening after straightening her dresser drawers and coming across a recipe clipped from the pages of a ten-year-old *Louisiana Secondary Teacher*. Much to his satisfaction Dr. Bates had put on a good five pounds with the banana waffles and was eager for more.

He was standing in Mrs. Keely's drive, wondering if perhaps he should ask Mrs. Undine to substitute cranberries for the bananas this evening, when he saw the Cadillac pull up dangerously close to the rather steep drainage ditch that bordered the front lawn. Afraid that a small child might one day fall in, Mrs. Undine kept her chair next to the living-room window so that from time to time she might lift the curtain to peer out. Her concern had been absorbed, osmotically, by Dr. Bates, who turned for a moment to peer through a nearsighted haze at the woman edging past the ditch's slick, dull clay. It was only after he had gotten the iron from Mrs. Keely and returned to the house that he could see who the woman was—that former patient of his who had been dropping over lately on various obscure errands. He couldn't get over the feeling that this Mackie woman was up to something. Perhaps one day, during an unguarded moment, he might be slapped with a subpoena. But was it his fault that she had such tight contact? Any dentist would find it hard to work with teeth set that close together.

Over cranberry waffles that evening Dr. Bates inquired how the plastering was going. Mrs. Undine explained that the man had crawled into the attic and discovered a leak in a pipe that was causing the cracks and bubbles in the living-room ceiling. "The pipe has twelve separate joints, though, and has to be fit together exactly right, simultaneously. So he's coming back tomorrow with an assistant." She closed her eyes and swallowed. "And then he discovered there's some sort of infestation in the roof."

"Termites?"

"No, some sort of beetle. I forget what he called it."

They were eating on tv trays in front of a fire which Dr. Bates had discovered could be built in the supposedly non-working fireplace. Mrs. Undine was quite amazed that for all these years she had assumed she shouldn't be using the hearth. "I guess I was just afraid that Mr. Undine would be careless," she had explained on the day Dr. Bates had surprised her with a neat fire made with a chemical log from the A&P. Ever since, on the cooler evenings, they had made it a habit to dine in the living room before the sparkling blue and lime-green flames. One day, when Dr. Bates had more time, he was going to buy some pine logs, which would emit less disturbing colors.

"Beetles?"

"Mm," she said, looking preoccupied.

After removing the cozy, Dr. Bates poured himself another cup of tea from the flowered pot. The tea was helping him cut down on coffee. "I suppose when you look closely at anything," he began, meaning to end with "you'll find it's falling apart." But he did not complete the sentence for fear she might think he was making a personal allusion. They had been getting along quite well in the past few weeks. All the turmoil about life science and a possible parting of the ways had, in a curious way, cemented their relationship. Before, what with so much smooth sailing, there had been something unreal about the emotional landscape, too flat. But now, after the eruption, there were definite ups and downs, peaks and valleys adding another dimension. She herself had become more substantial to him, a woman with a mind of her own who was quite willing to live without him. This was what he found most attractive, that she really preferred to live alone. And since, for now at least, this was also his wish—to live alone—he felt they made a matched set.

"By the way, Fern, what was Mrs. Mackie doing here?"

"Hm? Oh, Dr. Bates, I wish I had never heard of her." Mrs. Undine put down her fork. She had barely touched her food this evening. "You know, it's strange, but the minute I joined the Ladies' Aid, I had a feeling that I shouldn't. It was Mrs. Keely who talked me into it, you know. She's the one who said they needed someone to teach exercise. She gave me a big song and dance about the article in *Reader's Digest* she had read, how exercise helps old people's memories. I was doing it for their mental health, you understand—to help them cope. But as far as I can tell, no one's improving. And besides, I'm so worried they might strain themselves, and I might be held responsible. Sued."

"What?"

"Sued. How would that look when I took the stand? No, Your Honor, I haven't a medical degree, but Mrs. Keely said it would be all right. She said it wouldn't matter. Why, Dr. Bates, I sometimes wonder if I'm not half-cracked, letting myself be talked into such a thing."

With a sympathetic nod Dr. Bates acknowledged her plight. He appreciated her not calling him Martin anymore. It gave their relationship a certain formality that made it easier for him to be kind to her. "Well, I often did wonder how you could . . . I mean, it just seemed you weren't exactly the type. Are you sure that plasterer knows what he's talking about?"

"Hm? No, I am not." She lifted the dun curtain by her

chair and took a peek out the window. "But what can you do?"

"Mrs. Keely said her daughter knows something about plaster," he said innocently. "She just had her apartment walls redone, Donna did."

No fool, Mrs. Undine caught his drift immediately. In a neutral voice she said, "You know, I've been meaning to ask her over for a real dinner someday. It wasn't right to try to pawn off fish sticks on her. Perhaps she will know something about these beetles. Her name, by the way, is Donna Lee."

"Oh?"

"When do you think would be a suitable evening? Sometime soon, I would think."

While Dr. Bates contemplated being "forced" to dine with the lawyer, Mrs. Undine went to the worktable set up next to the somewhat overbearing Victorian breakfront and resumed work on a diorama of the aftermath of Noah's flood. Quite pleased that he had eluded the personal rejection that might have come had he asked Donna Lee to dinner himself, Dr. Bates bolted down a fourth waffle.

"I'm sorry," he was saying into the phone a few minutes later. He was in the kitchen washing up the dishes. "I can't hear very well. Can you speak up?"

"It's me, Carol," came an unhealthy-sounding whisper on the other end of the line. "I can't talk too loud. My husband's trying to get me to cut down . . . much phone and . . ."

"What?"

"I'm so tired of life, Marty. All I do is shop and be the perfect little housewife. I hate everybody . . . myself . . . meaning and I think sometimes there's got to be more than . . . useless . . ."

Stretching the cord as he walked into the doorway, Dr. Bates held up his index finger. Mrs. Undine, who was shaping a piece of violet construction paper, put down her pinking sheers and called out, "Dr. Bates, please hurry."

He held out the receiver in her direction and motioned impatiently. With a certain flatness she obliged: "Hurry, you'll be late."

"Oh, that's Fern," he said in a complaining tone of voice. "I got to go now."

"Well, can't you tell her—"

"No, she's in a terrible rush. She's not feeling well."

"So why doesn't she lie down?"

"I've really got to go, Carol."

After he finished tidying the kitchen, he passed through the living room on his way to the bedroom. "Dr. Bates, this is the last time," Mrs. Undine said, peering critically at a small drowned dinosaur. "From now on you just tell your friends you're busy."

He paused, noticing that Kay's pastel was a little crooked. "Hm?"

"It's the second time you've said I was ill," she went on while he straightened the portrait over the mantel. "I don't like it. I have never intentionally deceived anyone in my life. Really, I don't know how I let you talk me into this."

"Never intentionally deceived, huh? And what is that you're doing now, Fern?"

Mrs. Undine hunched her narrow shoulders defensively. She had a bad conscience about evolution, which he felt it was his duty to prick from time to time. Satisfied, he continued into his own room.

Chapter Ten

AS SHE CLIMBED THE STAIRS to his apartment Olive wondered if the reason she was unable to feel as bad as she thought she should was because she wasn't absolutely one-hundred per cent certain that Uncle L.D. was dead. Yet even if she were sure, it might be just as difficult to work up a proper amount of grief. After all, these last few years had not been easy for the old man, what with his being bedridden and his mind all but shot. Was it possible that, toward the end, as more and more of his memory went down the drain, Uncle L.D. had forgotten who he was? This was the only explanation Olive could come up with for Mr. Versey's so-called murder: The old man had simply thought he himself was someone else, someone capable of murder. And if he had thought he was someone else, if he had no memory of the man who never cursed, who, despite all his other faults, was honest as the day was long, then in a way the person who had passed away was not really Uncle L.D. Perhaps this was why it was hard for Olive to mourn. The real Uncle L.D. had long ago been forgotten—not by her, but by himself.

In spite of this reasoning she had nevertheless suffered considerable alarm earlier that day when the receptionist at the nursing home had informed her that Uncle L.D.'s bed was occupied by a Mr. Norwood. As for the whereabouts of Uncle L.D. the lady had nothing on her computer other than PC. When pressed about the meaning of PC, she had to admit that these initials didn't mean a thing to her. A timid, motherly woman with a premature Christmas tree brooch pinned to her collar, the receptionist explained that she was just a temp. Olive demanded to see the director, but it turned out she was away at a conference on gerontological sex at the Marriott in Salt Lake City. Mr. Higgins, who might have been some help, had been transferred to the hospital for some tests, while Mr. Uwel had been granted a two-day pass to visit his sister-in-law. When she checked back at the desk a few hours later, Olive was told by the teary-eyed lady, who seemed to have a good heart, that she had figured out what PC meant. Passed Away. The C, it turned out, was really an A when you looked real close on the computer screen. She told Olive that as soon as possible she would round up all the papers for her concerning cause of death and disposition of the remains. "You see," she patiently explained, "the man in Billing and Records who has all this information, hon, he's taken a half day off to price mirror wall tiles for his living room."

Olive kept a set of keys to the apartment on Flat Avenue just in case she and Dr. Bates might need a quiet place to go and talk in the afternoons. (Of course, she planned to give it a good cleaning before she brought Dr. Bates there.) Having nothing better to do while she waited for the papers, she thought she would drop by the apartment to check the closets and see what, if any, funeral insurance Uncle L.D. might have stashed away. He was never one to tolerate any discussion of the future, and so Olive hadn't the vaguest idea if he carried insurance or had left a will. Not that he had anything to will anyone, except perhaps for the furniture, which was too dark and heavy for Olive's taste, anyway.

She was musing on the legality of scattering ashes, a somewhat romantic gesture that she thought the old man might appreciate, when she finally managed to turn the rusty lock.

"Mrs. Mackie," came a voice from the far end of the room. Olive's mouth tightened. Ensconced in the four-poster amid a generous array of bananas and Vienna sausage, Uncle L.D.

looked almost dapper in a brand-new three-piece suit. "In the future you might have the courtesy to knock."

Her nose started running, as if with choked-back tears. Fumbling in her bag for a tissue, she felt strangely capable of mourning now but put on a brave face. "Well, I thought I'd find you here."

"The keys, Mrs. Mackie." He held out his hand.

"What?"

"My keys."

Something was missing from his voice, that playful edge of irony; the dull, flat insistence made her wary. "Sure, have the keys," she said, approaching the bed. "But how do you expect me to look after you if I can't get in?"

"Your services are no longer required."

The disdain in his voice made her bridle. Who did he think he was, talking to her like that? Flinging the keys onto the bedspread, she let him know just what an ingrate he was. And what did he mean by checking himself out of the nursing home? How in the world had he gotten himself back over here without anyone knowing? And just who did he think was going to feed and bathe him now that he had finally gotten his own selfish way again?

Uncle L.D. remained calm as a Buddha throughout this tirade. When she finally got around to mentioning the murder, he even had the gall to smile. Just what the hell had gotten into him? she wanted to know. Was he trying to ruin her? "Is that it? You can't stand to see me succeed, huh? You're going to make sure I lose this election. Sure, who's going to vote for the niece of a darn murderer? I'd like to know.

"And if you think that after all this I'm going to come traipsing up and down these stairs for you," she added, picking up a banana peel, "you got another thing coming. And furthermore . . ." She went on at some length in this vein, which she capsulized, not long afterwards, while it was still fresh in her mind, for Mrs. Sanchez. She had run into her former colleague in Housewares on the way down from Uncle L.D.'s. Remembering Carol's advice, Olive had asked

Mrs. Sanchez to join her for a cup of coffee at a nearby café. After offering two or three reasons why she couldn't Mrs. Sanchez had finally capitulated when Olive told her that she would not take no for an answer.

"Don't ask me how he did it," Olive said after a young woman in a folk-style long skirt had brought their cappuccinos. Although it was near City Hall, Olive had rarely eaten at Isola Bella, mainly because it was so pricey and the portions so small. The owner, she had heard, was from Dayton, Ohio. "He's come up with someone to look after him. And remember how I told you what a bitch it was, trying to get Four Sisters to replace Mr. Versey?"

"They finally found someone?" Mrs. Sanchez asked in a low voice. The café was empty at this hour, which made both of them somewhat self-conscious. Outside on the sidewalk a middle-aged couple were peering through the plate glass with cupped hands.

"No, see, there was this girl who used to visit Uncle L.D.'s roommate at the nursing home, and it turned out she wasn't happy with her job. She used to work at Sonny Boy, in notions, I believe. Anyway, she's the one who's looking after him now. Miss Burma, he calls her."

Mrs. Sanchez just sat there, her pretty face as blank and plump as a doll's. Patiently Olive took up the slack: "She came in after I'd been talking to Uncle L.D. awhile. She was nice enough, sort of down at the mouth, if you know the type." Olive grudgingly recalled that the apartment had smelled nice and clean, thanks to Miss Burma, who had gone out with the laundry. "I tried my best to be pleasant, even though I was pretty steamed. Anyway, she told me it was this friend of hers who got her the job, a lawyer. She's the one made all the arrangements and got Uncle L.D. checked out of the nursing home. I have her name written down here." Olive poked around in her handbag but couldn't find the coupon she had written it on. Meanwhile Mrs. Sanchez said nothing. She just sat there looking strained and uncomfortable without volunteering even a cluck or two of sympathy. "Anyway, it's pretty shocking, don't you think, the way lawyers victimize people. This dame must have been pretty hard up for business if she had to scare up clients at a nursing home. I told Uncle L.D., fine, you want yourself a lawyer? You got one. But don't expect me to pay one red cent when she comes around to collect. In fact, to tell you the truth, Mary, I'm afraid to even get on the phone with this woman. I mean, I'd like to give her a piece of my mind for butting in like this—but I just know what will happen. She'll start thinking I'm the responsible party, and all the bills will come zeroing in on me like homing pigeons."

Mrs. Sanchez glanced at her jeweled watch.

"Should we get some gelato, Mary?"

"I really should be going."

Olive would have liked to be able to say, "Good, go; it's been so charming." But if she did that, she might as well say good-bye to the mayor, who hadn't returned any of her phone calls so far. The time had come to stop pussyfooting around. She would confront the issue of Mrs. Sanchez's disloyalty head-on—though, of course, in a calm, rational manner that would leave plenty of room for Mrs. Sanchez to repent. "Look, Mary, let's face it. When I saw you at the Winn Dixie, I really didn't want to talk to you. I guess I was ashamed for you. I just couldn't understand how, after fifteen years, you could betray me so easily, not make the slightest effort on my behalf."

Mrs. Sanchez had cried when Olive had told her about an old mutt of Felix's who had been put to sleep because of liver problems. She had sniffled when Olive and she had discussed Ali MacGraw in *Love Story*. But now her face was a mask of rigid indifference. "It's not as if I didn't try to warn you."

"Oh, come on."

With a creamy, dimpled hand Mrs. Sanchez straightened the hemp placemat beneath the earthenware mug. "Olive, if it hadn't been for me, you would have been fired fourteen years ago. I never wanted to say this, but I guess, since you brought it up . . ."

The waitress appeared beside them with two cinnamon sticks. Taking one, Mrs. Sanchez stirred her cappuccino while commenting on how terrible it was, that earthquake yesterday that had killed hundreds of people in Chile. Olive, appalled by what she had just heard, was not going to let her weasel out of it so easily. "What do you mean, fourteen years ago?"

"Well, it's true," Mrs. Sanchez replied in a small voice, glancing meekly over at the waitress, who was polishing a pewter sconce with Noxon. "I've been pleading your case ever since I can remember, and quite frankly, I'm somewhat hurt. You've never been grateful. You've always looked down your nose at me."

Olive's voice was remote. "I don't know what you're talking about."

"Twice I threatened to quit if they fired you. Right after Felix was born, when you were so tired out with the baby, I told them it wouldn't be fair. And then that time you and Duane almost got a divorce, remember? About five years ago."

Not five, but seven. That was when Duane had lost interest in her sexually. Olive had overreacted at first, threatening him with divorce. But then after consulting Carol, Olive had taken a more mature view of the matter. Carol had told her it was not at all uncommon for husbands and wives to live chastely together after a certain number of years. So Olive stopped demanding attention. Oddly enough, this made Duane a little more affectionate. Not long afterwards she discovered that when she pushed him away, he became positively amorous. Duane, it seemed, was turned on by women who were turned off. That was his secret. Once she had learned this, she had no more trouble with him in that department. In any case, she began to realize that she had gotten a little bored with Duane's lovemaking. Perhaps this explained why more recently, after Duane had lost his job selling real estate and had again stopped sleeping with her on a regular basis, Olive could shrug it off. Working in a cheese shop probably didn't make Duane feel very sexy.

"Mary, if you don't mind, I don't see what good it'll do for you to dredge up the past like this. Let's let bygones be bygones." She smiled brightly to cover her consternation. (To think that they had wanted to fire her that many years ago!) "Now, here's what I'd like you to do, hon. First, I'd appreciate it if you'd set up an appointment with His Honor for me, tell him I'll take him to lunch. You know he hasn't returned any of my calls, so I guess we'll have to go *mano a mano*. I've got to find out just how he plans to support my campaign."

"What campaign?"

Olive studied her face a moment to see if she was serious. How could the mayor not have told her? "I'm running against Vondra this spring."

"You're joking."

Ignoring this last remark, Olive skimmed along: "Now, this is where you could be a big help. I need you to get me those computer printouts of the voter lists. I'm helpless without them. See, I want to mail out personalized appeals and—"

"But I can't just—"

"And I want to find out which voters need to be picked up on election day. I'm going to get Felix and some of his friends to drive around in vans, getting out the vote, as they say. And, of course, I'm counting on using you, too. It'll be a lot of fun."

"Well, I . . . Is Felix old enough to drive?"

"He'll have a learner's permit by then."

"Olive, really, about those printouts. You know I can't just—"

"It's no big deal. I used to mail them to a friend of Vondra's who was thinking of opening up a mini-mall or something. Just get an authorization code from the registrar, say it's for the mayor."

When Mrs. Sanchez began to insist that she really had to get back to the office, Olive told her to hurry along; she would take care of the check. It was sinful how much they charged for a cup of coffee, Olive thought as she dug out a VISA card from her Organizer, which included a calculator, printed shopping lists, a date book, threader, checkbook, emery board, mirror, horoscope, change purse, and a can of Mace disguised as deodorant. Felix had given it to her for her birthday.

Waiting for the girl to return with her card, Olive examined the framed Merit Award of Suitableness that the city had given the renovated café for not making itself look too modern. Olive had forged Vondra's signature on all these certificates one busy morning when Vondra claimed she had no time.

"I'm sorry," the girl said, handing back Olive's card. "You're over your limit."

"Oh, for cryin' out loud. Here." She pulled out her Organizer. "I'll write a check." For some reason she didn't have any cash on her. Duane must have gone through her purse again that morning.

"I'm sorry. We don't accept personal checks." The girl flicked a strand of long brown hair off her peasant blouse.

"Well, what am I supposed to do?"

After some discussion Olive agreed to leave her driver's license behind while she went back to Uncle L.D.'s to borrow a few bucks. Five or ten years ago she never would have submitted to such an indignity. The tradespeople would have taken her word without a second thought. But there were so many new people in town these days that no one trusted anyone anymore. A somber couple from Ecuador had opened a video store, and someone from Delaware had gotten run over on Myrtle Street last Thursday.

"Look, I know you're in there," Olive was saying a few minutes later as she pounded on Uncle L.D.'s door. It was really stupid of her to have given him those keys back. How was he supposed to get out of bed and unlock the door if Miss Burma wasn't there? "It's me, Olive. Let me in."

After giving the door a good kick she retreated down the stale-smelling stairway and, composing herself with a smile, entered Sonny Boy. As Carol had stressed, it was important that Olive look pleasant whenever she went out. After all, everyone she saw was a potential vote.

"A quarter pound of those Turtles," she said at the candy counter, where a sullen redhead was thumbing through a worn hairstyles magazine. "And a quarter pound of cashews," Olive added. Her blood-sugar level was low; she needed a lift.

"How much?" Olive asked after the girl handed over two white bags. With a jerk of her head the clerk indicated the amount showing on the cash register. But Olive had asked a civil question and expected a civil reply. "How much?"

"Can't you read?"

Olive did not think of herself as being either old or reactionary, but sometimes, when faced with this new breed of clerk, she heard herself sounding like Mrs. Undine. It would be one thing if the incivility were coupled with a little competence. What was intolerable was the combination of rudeness and total ineptitude. A good three minutes Olive had spent trying to get the clerk's attention when she wanted to order, and then she had spooned out only broken bits and pieces. Not one whole Turtle in the bag.

"Yes, ma'am, I can read," Olive said, squinting at the clerk's plastic name tag. "And I want to tell you something, Toinette. Long as you don't feel like telling me how much, I might not feel like paying."

"Code three," the clerk said into a microphone to the right of the computerized register. "Code three," she repeated in a lazy, weary voice that nevertheless resounded mightily against the store's cinderblock walls.

"What's up?"

Feeling a hand on her elbow, Olive looked around and saw a security guard at her side, a diminutive black man with piercing blue eyes.

"She won't pay," the redhead said, looking up from the magazine she had started to read again.

Olive was indignant. "I never said . . . I just wanted her to . . ." A few shoppers drifted nearer. "She wouldn't . . . Oh, never mind," she said, pulling out her Organizer. The last thing she needed now was some sort of scene. She would pay and get out—except that she just remembered she didn't have any cash on her. "Here, I don't want them," she said, plopping the two bags down on the glass counter, or at least meaning to. Instead, one of the Organizer's secret compartments came open, and trying to prevent a newspaper photo of Dr. Bates from fluttering out, she accidentally let the white bags drop to the floor.

"What's this?" the security guard asked, picking up the clipping. " 'New Jersey Not All Cracked Up To Be, Says Aspiring Dentist.' You from New—"

"If you don't mind," Olive said, snatching it from him.

By the time she got out of Sonny Boy, she was so rattled that she didn't remember where she had parked the car. Summoned by the code three, the assistant manager had turned out to be extremely shy and easily cowed. Olive had let him know that she wasn't about to pay for candy and nuts that had been on the floor. Then, while the security guard was giving his version of what had happened, she had managed to slip away.

Peering about her, Olive trudged down the street, knowing the Cadillac couldn't be far. The main thing now was to get some distance between herself and that darn store.

"Now, where were we?" Uncle L.D. inquired once the banging on the door had ceased.

"I was fixing to trim your hair," the girl said from the sink, where she was finishing up the dishes. Although she fussed about far too much for Uncle L.D.'s taste, this new attendant was an infinite improvement over the one he had murdered. Already he had cured her of saying *hopefully*. On top of that she seemed genuinely impressed that the Battle of New Orleans had taken place after the Peace of Ghent. Yes, Uncle L.D. knew a good thing when he saw it, and he was going to do everything he could to make sure she was happy here.

Of course, he was still a little concerned about his new status as a hero. Dr. Munrow had assured him that there would not be any undue publicity, that he would be left in peace, but surely Tula Springs was being far too discreet. Not one reporter had called upon him. And the phone might as well have been off the hook for all the congratulations he was getting from ordinary citizens. Was it not something for a man like him, not exactly in his prime, to have stood up to a despicable blackguard like Mr. Versey? Who knew—he might very well have gone on to torture and abuse other senior citizens. Yes, Dr. Munrow was right. It had been a courageous act, the act of a man of conviction, a warrior in the fight against the barbarism that was eroding Western civilization. The only trouble was, Uncle L.D. was still a little fuzzy about the exact nature of his courageous act. Had he indeed defended himself with an umbrella and then, as a last resort, pushed an enraged and murderous Mr. Versey out the window? Well, whatever he had done, it had been effective—and necessary.

One side effect of those long talks he had had with Dr. Munrow—who had persuaded him to admit what he had done by convincing him that there was nothing to be ashamed of, that his repressed rage was truly a righteous anger—was that Artis had ceased to haunt him. Uncle L.D. had married her because she had thought she was pregnant, when actually she had only missed a period. But by then it was too late. Ironically enough, Artis and he were unable to have a child. This had always been a thorn in his side, a grudge that he thought he would carry to the grave. But when he was finally able to admit that yes, it was he who had shoved Mr. Versey out that window, something inside him was freed. He could finally forgive her, and with this forgiveness came a flood of energy, bringing with it new memories of the genuinely good times he and Artis had shared. It was a whole new vista, one that had been closed off to him for years: There in the distance were Artis and he, crouching in the shrubs of a Lake Michigan mansion as they eavesdropped on a live chamber music concert. A little closer, in the mid-ground, he could see Artis in pink mittens trying to learn golf on an icy course, her mouth crammed with saltwater taffy. Off to the right, blurring into the horizon in a blue haze, they stood beneath the Lincoln Memorial, where Artis was telling him that she had once confounded Carl Van Vechten with a difficult question at a free lecture.

All this was restored to him. He hadn't felt better in years. And yet, wouldn't you know, Olive was doing everything she could to spoil things. Instead of congratulating him, or at least sympathizing with him, she had tried to stir up his fears: What about jail? Do you want to spend the rest of your days in jail? Fortunately Dr. Munrow had prepared him for just such an onslaught. He had told him not to say a word to his enemies, to keep perfectly quiet. Because anything he said in his own defense would be used against him, twisted to suit *their* meaning. All he had to do was trust in Dr. Munrow, and he would make sure that no harm came to him. Uncle L.D. did not find this a difficult task. Hadn't Dr. Munrow already saved him from a fate worse than death? Everytime Uncle L.D. woke from a nap and saw where he was, back in his own apartment, his heart nearly burst with joy and gratitude. There just wasn't enough he could do in one lifetime for that fine young man.

"You got cute ears, you know," the girl said as she trimmed the down on his lobes.

"And in my own dull, retarded way may I say that your ears also, Miss Burma, are most becoming."

She slapped his head lightly. "I told you, I don't want to hear no more of that. You aren't dull or retarded. You're just about the smartest thing I've ever seen. Oh, Lord." She paused as a metallic-sounding "Code three" came up from the grate near the sink. "Shoplifter." She nipped at the Band-Aid on her ring finger, trying to make it stick better. "I tell you, Mr. Loraine, I am so glad to be out of that place. Hold still." She straightened his head and resumed clipping. "I would have gone to work for the sewer company—anything to get out of that place. My boss was so mean, and anyways—"

"Anyway."

"Huh?"

"You got a beau, Miss Burma?"

"I go out. No one serious, though. Not too long ago I almost got married, but then I decided not to. He played the clarinet."

"Every girl should be married. You stick with me, and I'll show you how it's done. Now, I bet you don't realize what the one thing is a man looks for in a girl, the major feature that hooks him. Take a guess."

"Well . . ."

"Go on."

"I don't know—legs?"

"No, Miss Burma. It's systematization. A systematized woman always gets her man. I've never seen it fail. You can take all your looks and charm and brains, and if you don't have systematization, then you might as well give up."

The girl snipped a hair off her arm while she considered this. Then, hearing a key rattle in the lock, she reached out for the pocket watch dangling from the bedpost. "She's late."

It was the lawyer Dr. Munrow had hired to look after Uncle L.D.'s legal interests, a bright, attractive young lady who seemed to have stepped right out of one of Uncle L.D.'s YWCA classes. As she approached the bed Uncle L.D. felt his heart swell painfully. He could not take his eyes off her when she was in the apartment.

"May I say that I think you're remarkable?"

The lawyer took his hand and squeezed it. "No, you may not. How are you, dear?"

He waved away Miss Burma's scissors. "That's enough."

"But I'm not through."

"Enough."

"Donna Lee, make him sit still."

Uncle L.D. had asked the girl to address the lawyer properly, as Miss Keely, but the lawyer herself had forbidden this. Apparently, despite the difference between them on the social scale, Miss Keely and Miss Burma were friends of sorts, having met through a previous legal case. It was perhaps the one thing about the lawyer that Uncle L.D. disapproved of, her spurious belief in a classless society.

"All right, you two." The lawyer took the scissors from Miss Burma and told her she could finish later. Yanking the towel from around his neck, Uncle L.D. asked the girl to get Miss Keely a cup of tea, but the lawyer said she didn't have time. "I got to get back to the office. Now, listen." She perched on the edge of his bed and once again took his hand. "The coroner's going to come by tomorrow morning to interview you," she said, patting his hand. "I don't want you to say a word until I'm here, understand? He'll probably have the sheriff with him, but don't you worry. They can't do a thing to you. The important thing is to keep quiet till I'm here."

"You don't have to worry none," the girl commented from the rocker, where she was touching up her nails with an emery board. "That lady was here, Miss Mackie, and he kept those lips of his zipped up good and tight. I swear, Donna Lee, she was doing everything she could to make him talk, trying to scare him with all this nonsense about jail and all."

The lawyer's clear, oval face was solemn, her blue eyes dark with thought. Uncle L.D. was so absorbed in contemplating the way her blond hair framed her remarkable face that she had to repeat herself: "Just who is this woman again? I know you told me once before."

"Mrs. Mackie is my late wife's niece, grandniece," he said as she plucked a long hair from beneath his eye. "She's been poking her nose where it doesn't belong ever since I can remember."

"I seen her at the beauty college," the girl offered. "My mamma does her hair."

"L.D., you just let me take care of her, understand? She looks like she could be trouble." She went on to tell him what time Dr. McFlug, the coroner, was supposed to arrive, but he was too intoxicated by the smell of her—how utterly fresh and delicate!—to attend to any details.

"Oh, listen, Burma," Miss Keely said from the door just before she was about to leave. "F.X. and Carl and I are going to Baton Rouge to see *A Passage to India*. It's something you really should see. Why don't you come along?"

"I don't know. I don't like India that much. Well, O.K., I guess."

"We'll come by about seven. Just dress casual."

When the lawyer had gone, Uncle L.D. sat there wondering what this world was coming to. Imagine, taking a maid out to the movies. Next thing you knew, people would be inviting their garbagemen over for tea.

"All right, Miss Burma. Let's see if you can remember. What's the secret of a successful lady, the lady that always gets her man?"

"Oh, hush up," she said, prying herself from the rocker with a moan. Giving the air a practice snip with the scissors, she added in a weary voice, "I'm not through with you yet. We got to make you look nice and neat for the coroner."

Chapter Eleven

"WELL, OF COURSE, Mary will be glad to get you those printouts," the mayor said as he rose from the chesterfield in his office. He was known to conduct all his business from this hundred-year-old divan; rarely, if ever, did he make use of his desk. Olive had decided not to wait for Mrs. Sanchez to schedule an appointment for her. She had looked in, on impulse, while she was at City Hall on other, unrelated business.

"I really would appreciate it," Olive said as she felt herself, psychologically at least, crowded toward the door. "Those voter lists would be a big help. Mary seemed a little reluctant, you know, when I asked her."

The mayor frowned. He was handsome in the bland, neutered style of a soap-opera patriarch and sweated profusely, as if he were under a klieg light. Mrs. Sanchez kept laundered shirts in her drawer for him to change into after lunch. "Don't you worry, Olive. I'll make sure she gets them to you right away."

"Oh, and by the way," she added, pulling the unrelated business out of her handbag. "Do you think Mary could take care of these for me?"

He examined the pink slips she handed him, a ticket for running a red light and a summons for driving without a license. "You got it," he said, tossing them onto the chesterfield, which was piled high with memoranda and letters.

"Oh, and this," she said, fishing out the complaint that

had been filed by Isola Bella with the Citizens Patrol. Olive had been so upset after her run-in with the Sonny Boy security guard that she had forgotten to return to the café to pay her bill and pick up her license.

Telling her not to worry, the mayor ushered her out of the office with a hearty handshake and a few questions about young Felix's health and happiness.

For a moment or two she looked around halfheartedly for Mrs. Sanchez, who had not been at her desk when Olive had popped in on the mayor, unannounced. But it was too painful to remain in these old haunts for any length of time. A few familiar faces smiled at her, and a couple of times, when it couldn't be helped, she stopped and chatted with a former colleague about how wonderful it was to be free.

Once outside, though, she felt a rush of energy. Finally some definite progress had been made on her campaign. Binwanger had reassured her of his support—though it had to be covert for now—and he had promised her those printouts. Yes, she had had a setback this week, when Carol had refused to be her campaign manager. But as they say, there was more than one fish in the sea.

After fortifying herself with chicken nuggets from the BurgerMat Olive drove out to the old section of town where Judge Henley lived. Pulling up in the front yard next to the yellow school bus the judge's wife drove, Olive glanced warily about to make sure none of his hounds was loose. As the judge never tired of telling visitors, he and his grandfather had built the cypress house themselves in the midst of the Depression without using a single power tool. Judge Henley had been the last person to see Olive's father alive. They had been out hunting alligators one night when Olive's father had suffered a fatal heart attack. It had been a terrible shock to Olive, this sudden bereavement six years earlier. Unable to face anyone for a while, she had declined the two or three lukewarm invitations for dinner that had come from the judge shortly after the tragedy. As for Olive's mother, she had always resented the judge for taking up so much of her husband's time. In a fit of grief she had called the judge, to his face, an irresponsible nincompoop and then moved out to her sister's in Twentynine Palms, California. Judge Henley had taken umbrage, for he was known to be a stern man of honor. If she had been a gentleman, no doubt he would have challenged Olive's mother to a duel. In any case, it was yet another reason why Olive had been disinclined to pay the Henleys a visit. But now, having heard from the mayor that Judge Henley pulled a lot of weight with the D.A., Olive felt that a little social call might be in order. The D.A., it appeared, would decide whether Uncle L.D. was going to go before a grand jury. Dreading the publicity such an appearance would generate, she thought she might help the D.A. make up his mind.

"Yes, and he's joined this choir that goes around singing all over the parish," Olive was saying to the judge in his austere living room. Mrs. Henley, who was in the kitchen putting up preserves, had seated her on a shiny black bench. When he had clomped in a few moments later, the judge had sat himself down on a hard, high-backed chair, emblazoned with an angry-looking eagle. Olive found it easier to look a little to the side of the judge, at a stack of *National Reviews*, while she talked. "Of course, I'm a little bothered that it's Mormon."

"What's Mormon?"

"The choir. But there's some nice young people in it. I'm just glad he's out socializing. For a while he was spending too much time on individualistic things, like his target practice and boxing."

"Indeed." The judge had a twin who for the past thirty years had sold tickets at the Leon Cinema. Both men had a tendency to glare at people and make them feel guilty. Even today at the Leon, Olive would always stand behind Duane when he bought their tickets.

"So I guess you take the good with the bad." Olive sighed and smoothed her skirt. "He's really a good boy."

"Now, who's this we're talking about?"

"Judge dear," Mrs. Henley called out from the kitchen, "that's Olive Mackie, your late friend Norvil's daughter, and she's talking about her little boy, Felix."

"Yes, I know, I know," he said, squirming irritably in his chair. "Be quiet, please, Mrs. Henley."

"She works for Mayor Binwanger down at City Hall," came the imperturbable voice from the kitchen.

"Yes, I know. Silence, please."

"Well, actually . . ." Olive began to explain. "I don't . . ."

"A dreadful man," the judge said, plucking a brown leaf from the muddy Army boots he had been gardening in. The judge was well-known for growing practically everything he ate; what he didn't grow he shot. "Of course, you realize what's keeping that scum in office. Toxic waste. Bumwanger gets a nice healthy kickback from the Baton Rouge companies that can't find any other town dumb enough to bury their poison. Trouble is, no one's been able to pin anything on him yet. He's a sly one. But believe me, his day is going to come."

Olive made a token gesture of surprise, raised eyebrows, even though she found the judge's strait-laced probity somewhat tiresome and prejudiced. After all, how was the poor mayor supposed to make a decent living on the salary the city gave him? So he made a few bucks that were laundered through the Citizens Patrol, the guys who guarded the dump. Big deal. If it was a crime, it was certainly a victimless crime. He wasn't taking the money out of anyone's pockets, no one's but the chemical companies'. And as Olive viewed it, they deserved to pay through the nose for leaving such a mess behind.

"Judge Henley, I'm all for ecology, but I guess it's better than just pouring all that stuff into the rivers, killing the fish."

"Don't hand me any of that crybaby ecology blather." He drew a cigarette from the pocket of his plaid lumberjack shirt. "I'm talking . . ." He lit the cigarette and puffed. "I'm talking plain and simple corruption."

"Judge dear," the pleasant voice came from the kitchen, "I'm sure Olive didn't drop by to discuss business. Let's be nice."

Poor Mrs. Henley, Olive thought. The judge was so narrow

about his honesty that he wouldn't let her join the country club or any other social group where people might try to influence her. He wouldn't even allow a tv in the house, much less show a little good will by helping the Lions at Christmas with their tree sale. No, the only people he ever associated with were folks like Olive's father who could care less about politics. It was a wonder he stayed in office. Every election the mayor would put up someone to drive him out, but somehow the judge always squeaked by. He had a following among ignorant farmers and that sort of people.

"You remember my uncle, don't you?" Olive said after he returned from the bathroom. "L.D. Loraine."

"Loraine, Loraine—sounds familiar."

"Years ago he used to go deer hunting with you and my father. He's ninety-one now, can you believe it? Poor man, he's been bedridden for years, broke his hip and something happened to his joints. I feel so sorry for him. He's a widow, you know—widower."

Picking up the trowel he had set down on a lovely, antique side table, the judge tapped his head. "Someone just brought him up the other day—wish I could remember. Strange, these coincidences. Did you ever read Mark Twain on coincidences? Of course, he didn't believe they were co-incidences. He believed in mental telepathy. That's why so many letters cross over, people answering questions before they're asked. Have you ever found that to be the case, Olive?"

"Having a question answered before I asked it?"

"Yes."

"No. In fact, just the opposite," she added, not quite sure what she meant.

He looked sternly at her, as if he were about to reproach her, when there was a clatter in the next room.

"Oh, for corn's sake," came the sweet voice. "I dropped my ladle. I'm such a clumsy."

"You ever read Twain on the 1897 Vienna Parliament?" the judge demanded.

"1897? No, not that one."

"Loraine, Loraine," the voice said. "Judge dear, isn't that

the man Dr. McFlug is so worked up over? The one whose maid jumped out the window?"

"Yes, that's my uncle," Olive said, tears coming to her eyes. They were real tears, for she did feel just awful about this whole mess. "It's so unfair, the poor man." She pulled out a tissue and blew her nose. "And, Judge, I know, being a close personal friend of my daddy's, you'll do everything you can to stop the D.A. from putting my poor uncle on trial. If you could just see how weak and helpless he is. And everyone knows the D.A. adores you—he'll do anything you say. If you just asked him to . . . Judge, are you all right?" His face was so red that Olive was afraid he was having an attack of some sort. "Judge?"

The next thing she knew, he had picked up his trowel and bolted from the house. With a long sigh Olive got up and went into the kitchen for some girl talk with Mrs. Henley, who really was a dear. Then, after giving the judge some time to cool off, she wandered out back into the garden, where he was yanking up turnips like there was no tomorrow.

"You could do me a big favor," Donna Lee said as she took the waffle iron from Dr. Bates and set it on top of her mother's refrigerator. When Mrs. Undine's iron had come back from the repair shop, Dr. Bates had walked next door to return Mrs. Keely's. To his surprise, since he hadn't noticed her bicycle in the drive, Donna Lee had answered the door. She told him that she had just dropped by to pick up a hacksaw that she needed for her apartment.

"You were saying something about a favor?" Dr. Bates said as they walked out into the living room. Donna Lee had lost the thread of conversation when the waffle iron knocked a can of Raid behind the refrigerator. They had fished for the Raid with a broom and a clothes hanger but couldn't get it out. Dr. Bates had even tilted the refrigerator toward him, but that hadn't done much good, either.

"Oh, right."

Mrs. Keely's living room was larger than Mrs. Undine's and, even though there was nothing fancy about it, somewhat more gracious. Indeed, the furniture in Mrs. Undine's was probably more expensive, but there was something self-conscious about its arrangement. Every piece there seemed to betray much thought and second thought, whereas at Mrs. Keely's the rather beat-up but comfortable-looking arm-chairs and sofas all seemed to belong exactly where they were.

"If you could somehow hint to your mother-in-law—"

"She's not really my mother-in-law anymore."

"Well, whatever. I hate to be making up excuses all the time, but it just doesn't seem fair for her to be asking me to dinner in order to get free legal advice." She had perched on the worn arm of an overstuffed chair so that she was no longer looking down at him. "You don't know what I went through with that hole in her back yard. I must have given her about five hundred dollars worth of my time, and then my mother gets mad at me when I bill Mrs. Undine for fifty."

"I suppose there must be a fine line between being polite and being taken advantage of."

She frowned, as if he had said something critical of her.

"You see, I meant . . . Well, anyway, I think she was planning to ask you about this plasterer your mother found for her. He discovered some beetles in her attic."

"See? I was right. I *told* Mother Mrs. Undine was after something, and Mother gave me this big lecture about how unsociable I am." Donna Lee gnawed on a hangnail with masculine determination. "What the hell do I know about beetles, anyway? Lord."

Dr. Bates shrugged and, with a bemused smile, commented, "Well, you know Mrs. Undine." Through an oval window he could see an old black Lincoln weaving from side to side of the road as the driver tossed out the Tula Springs *Herald*.

"Did you know Kay?" he asked with a slight adolescent squeak. He cleared his throat. "Her daughter?"

She shook her head. "Not really. She was a little older. Why?"

He shrugged. "Just wondering. I was married to her, you know."

"Yes."

Feeling foolish, he was about to make his exit when she said, "I remember her riding in the back of a Cadillac convertible for one of those homecoming parades. She was the Queen, and I used to boast to all my girl friends: 'She lives next door to me. I live next door to the Queen.' "

"Well, I guess the Queen has flown the coop."

Silence again. He gave a discreet cough, wondering if his last remark had sounded sexist.

"Are you really a dentist?"

Her dark blue eyes, which had been averted, now searched his face, as if she were expecting to find some explanation there. "It's so hard to imagine you like that. I mean, you don't seem the type at all."

"The type?"

"You know."

Resentful—and yet secretly pleased that he didn't seem the "type"—he wondered if she realized how terribly racist she sounded. "I'm Jewish, you know."

"What? Oh, Lord, I didn't mean *that*. Did you think . . . Come on, there's not one dentist I know who's Jewish, not one."

Having gained the upper hand, he was reluctant to let her off the hook too easily. Let her squirm a bit. "Mm."

Idly she ran her hand over the brittle, micalike petals of a dried hydrangea in a nearby vase. "Besides, I happen to admire Jewish people tremendously. I've always thought that if I ever got married, it would have to be to a Jew or something like that."

"Something like that?"

"I mean, I can't stand all these good ole boys." Then, somewhat belligerently, she asked him if he'd like a cup of tea.

"No, thanks," he said while his heart begged him to please stay. But he knew there would be another invitation if he just held out for now. "I'm sorry. I've got a lot of studying."

"Oh. Well."

Humming to himself, he crossed the lawns back to the

Queen's house. Some part of him that had lain dormant was, unseasonably, coming to life. He had always thought there was something vulgar about spring. How much less beastly, in a literal sense, did it seem for a young man's fancy to turn to whatever at the onset of winter. Of course, he wasn't that young any longer. But still . . .

When he got back, Mrs. Undine, who was in bed with a cold, asked him if he would mind going out and buying a drain guard for the bathroom sink. She just couldn't sleep knowing that minute by minute the pipe must be clogging up. Someone in town *must* have the right size drain guard. "Ask," she said. "Don't be afraid to ask the sales personnel for help."

"O.K. By the way, don't ask Donna Lee for dinner."

"What?"

"It's not right. I'll find out about the beetles myself."

"The Beatles?"

"You were going to ask her about the beetles."

She picked up the *Ladies' Home Journal* on the counterpane. "I was? Oh, that can't be right. Me? Why would I . . . Go on now. Hurry up before the stores close."

Her loss of memory he charitably ascribed to the cold medicine she was taking. Still, it was annoying. It reminded him of Kay, who would forget things she herself had told him and then try to make him think that he had imagined them. What made it all the worse, he thought as he pulled out of the driveway directly into the path of an oncoming moped, was that Kay considered herself to be scientific and precise. So naturally she couldn't be wrong. The moped swerved, honked, and then continued on its way.

"This is the pool."

"Oh." Dr. Bates looked obligingly at the murky water in the kidney-shaped pool, where several lean frogs, some dying, some dead, were congregated.

"I don't know where they come from," Olive commented. "Would you like a gin and tonic?"

He looked puzzled. "No, thanks."

"I've got some good English gin."

"No, really. I better be going."

She realized that it was now or never. A step had to be taken, either forwards or backwards. She simply couldn't go on being in love with this man from afar, like some silly adolescent. Having made good progress today at City Hall as far as her professional life went, she felt she owed it to herself to resolve this personal dilemma. The house was empty. Duane was at a job interview in Baton Rouge and wouldn't be home till late this evening. Felix was singing in Thibodaux. So. She took a step toward him, her heart beating violently.

"How are your teeth, Mrs. Mackie?"

She could not reply.

"Do you mind if I take a look?" he asked.

She closed her eyes and lifted up her face. So this was what love felt like, the grand passion she had always wanted to experience. Apparently guilt was the secret ingredient of those passions. This was what had been missing from her love life: the tremendous guilt that she never felt with her husband.

"Mm." His fingers stretched apart her lips. "They look pretty good, Mrs. Mackie. The number five is holding up well, but you might want me to check that molar in six months or so. Well, so long. I got to run."

"Did you get it?"

"Get what?"

Mrs. Undine put down her *Ladies' Home Journal.* "Dr. Bates."

She had anointed the area between her nose and lips with Vicks VapoRub, and the effect was most unbecoming.

"Oh, the drain thing," he said from the hall. "They didn't have the right size." He drifted off to his room, ignoring the remarks from the sick room.

Seated at his desk, he switched on the word processor and searched for a letter he had started to a friend from Wesleyan. But after a moment or two he was staring blankly at the screen, trying to make sense of his visit to Mrs. Mackie's pool. Offhand, it seemed to be nothing but a singularity, an event without a cause. Although this was common enough in quantum physics, one encountered it less often in the everyday world. One minute he was standing in a hardware store, the next he was looking into a former patient's mouth by her pool. The question was, what was the connection between these two events? Surely he had sensed something phony the minute she had come up to him in the hardware store. There was something too studied about her "surprise" at seeing him there and all the excuses she had for being there herself. The fact was, he had been followed. Why, then, hadn't he simply made up some excuse why he couldn't drive her home from the store? That baloney she had given him about her car being stalled —the obvious answer to that was to have taken her to a garage.

Yet he had driven her home. And not only that, when she had asked him if he would like to look at her pool, he had said, without thinking, yes. Now, why in heaven's name should he have been interested in seeing her pool?

"Please, it's important," he was saying on the kitchen extension a moment later. "I *have* to talk to you."

"But, hon, I'm in the middle of an audit," Kay said from her office in New Orleans. "The IRS is coming next week and—"

"Please, it won't take long. Now, look, I had this dream last night. I was standing by the pool of a former patient of mine." He had decided to turn this experience into a dream for Kay. If she knew it had actually happened, she wouldn't be interested in exploring the deeper meanings. Instead, she would try to find out who the woman was, what she looked like, how old . . . "There were these frogs in the pool, and I saw some vines floating around"—he added this touch on the spur of the moment to make the whole thing sound more like a dream—"and the next thing I know, I was pulling back her lips and staring at her teeth. I had this funny feeling inside me, it's hard to describe. And she was so weird, sort of standing there limp, like a dummy—you know, a ventriloquist's dummy."

"Well, Martin, those vines intrigue me. Why vines?"

"No, that's not really important."

"Why not? You know it's the things that you don't think are important, the little incidentals, they sometimes carry the weight of the dream."

"I know. But anyway, I was wondering what made me want to look at her teeth. It's such an unnatural thing to do in that context. And they're so close together. She has trouble flossing."

"It's so interesting how you deny those vines. Why don't you want to talk about the vines?"

"That's not really the point. The question is, why would I suddenly part her lips and—"

"Something disturbs you about those vines. You said they were floating. What does floating mean? Floats? You float on your back—there's floats in a parade—waves . . . And the vines. What comes from vines? Grapes, right? You're really talking about wine. Something Bacchic is going on here. But listen, Martin, I love you very much and all, but I absolutely must go. You have no idea what I'm going through. Brett is in a snit and not giving me any help. Anyway, how about tomorrow night? Let's talk tomorrow. I'll call you, hon. Bye-bye."

"Who was that?"

He started, not expecting to find Mrs. Undine up and about. Her quilted bathrobe was tied at the throat with a yellow bow.

"No one," he muttered, peering into the refrigerator.

"That was Kay, wasn't it?"

"What's for supper?"

"I wish you hadn't hung up. I wanted to ask her something."

"I didn't know you were there."

"I wanted to ask her about those books of hers. I'm tired of having all my closet space taken up with her books. I need the room. There's just not enough room in this house for everyone to use it as a warehouse." She retied the yellow bow. "I don't like having a lot of dead space. There's some things I'd like to take out of the living room and store in the closets, but I can't."

"Mm." Kraft Miracle Whip, ReaLemon, an open box of baking soda—he gazed absently at the shelves.

"And that picture. I'd like to know what she wants done with that picture."

"What picture?"

"Shut the door please. That picture of her over the mantel."

He closed the refrigerator. "Fern."

"It's silly, really. I never did like it."

"But she's your daughter."

"Yes, and I'd rather not have her hanging around like a dead ancestor. That was her father's foolishness. He had to have a portrait. Didn't you ever notice how one eye is bigger than the other? If Kay doesn't want it, I'm going to give it to Mrs. Keely. She's in charge of the rummage sale at her church, I believe."

"Well, I don't know," Dr. Bates demurred.

"Well, I do. Now, why don't you put on some hot water. I think I'll have a cup of tea."

Chapter Twelve

On a gray, bleary afternoon Olive had driven over to Carol's to work on personal letters for the most active voters on the printout from City Hall. If the voter was a senior citizen, Olive would promise that she, as Superintendent, would make the parks safe for sitting. ("Sitting?" Carol had asked. "Like on benches? That makes them sound like idiots." And she would cross that part out.) If the voter was a fireman, Olive was able to say that their chief was endorsing her. (He had laid the tiles for her patio and had apparently felt an obscure loyalty.) To a member of the Preservation League: "As far as I'm concerned, history has always overridden all priorities. I will do everything in my power to restore Tula Springs to its original historical charm and beauty." Nineteen members of the National Rifle Association were told of her plans for a shooting range in Ferguson Park. ("Over my dead body," Carol had said, and Olive had reassured her that there was no chance of this getting through a council meeting.) It was exhausting work.

"You're crazy not to use a word processor," Carol said after switching off the two typewriters.

"Hey, people are on to those phony personal letters. There's something about the typeface. You can tell."

They adjourned to the kitchen to refresh themselves with Sara Lee brownies and coffee. "How much is all this going to cost you?" Carol asked.

"I'm keeping it to a minimum," Olive said, thinking sadly

of the C.D. she had cashed in, with a penalty charge. "But I expect to get a lot of help. You don't realize how many people here can't stand Vondra. You know Mr. Dambar, the guy who owns the creosote factory? I once heard him tell Vondra to go to hell. They were arguing about zoning or something. Anyway, I'm seeing him tomorrow. And yesterday I got a contribution from Judge Henley." Actually it had been Mrs. Henley who had slipped her a twenty-dollar bill on the sly. Judge Henley was still being difficult and obnoxious.

Carol sipped from the Lenox cup. She sighed. "I don't know."

"Well, I do. Deep down, I know I'm going to win. That's how I can risk my savings, everything. I believe in myself. I believe I have something really valuable to offer. And I know people are beginning to recognize it. It's like a new me."

"Your eye looks better."

"Really?"

"Uh-huh."

The other night Duane had struck Olive in the eye with his elbow. He was drunk and hadn't meant to do it, yet this spastic, unpremeditated blow had served a purpose. It had made her feel much less guilty about her disturbingly chaste relationship with Dr. Bates. Apparently Duane had been upset that she was using her savings on the campaign. What about Felix's education? he wanted to know. Well, Felix wouldn't be eating, much less going to school, if she didn't haul ass and win this election. Anyone could see that. Because they certainly weren't going to make it with Duane working at a cheese shop. If he was really that worried about Felix's education, Duane would get out and start looking for a serious job and stop complaining about how tired he was all the time.

"You know, Carol, I really appreciate all this work you've been doing for me," Olive said as they walked along the miniature box hedge to the Cadillac. "I don't know why you won't just let me call you my campaign manager. You're doing practically all the work."

"No, really, I don't want to get that involved. I mean,

something might come up. I've had time lately, but I can't promise anything for the future."

"Well." Unlike many women, Olive and Carol never exchanged a hug or kiss when saying good-bye. Olive had felt many times like taking the initiative and breaking this silly barrier, but something about Carol warned her away. "I'll call you. Really, thanks so much."

Four houses away the Cadillac pulled into the drive. Olive had originally planned to go on from Carol's to Uncle L.D.'s, but she was weary and needed a rest. All this self-motivation, making her own schedule, scaring up things to do, was such an effort. There were days when, after making Duane and Felix breakfast, she would plop down on the méridienne in the living room and for an hour or so just lie there in a stupor. Despite what she had told Carol, she could not still the voice inside her that told her she was a failure, she didn't have a chance. *Give up. Go out and get yourself a real job. You'll never be anything but a secretary, admit it.*

Kicking off her shoes, she picked up the phone and punched out a number. When Mrs. Undine answered, Olive hung up without saying anything. A few minutes later, after staring blankly out the window, probing her tender eye, she tried the number again. Again Mrs. Undine. Olive hung up.

For the next two days, sick to death of the campaign, Olive moped about the house, daydreaming about Dr. Bates. At times she tried to imagine what it would be like to live in New Jersey, the wife of a prosperous dentist. In an *Information Please* that Uncle L.D. had thrown at her, back when he used to be in the nursing home (and by God, she had kept the book, brought it home for Felix, who had sense enough to know that books are meant to be read, not aimed at people) she found out that New Jersey was called the Garden State. The state colors were buff and blue. The state animal was the horse, the state insect the honeybee, and there was no state song.

"Sure, come on in," Olive said, answering the door. It was her third day of moping, which had not been entirely unproductive. In the perverse way some marriages have, Olive's busy campaigning had seemed to discourage her partner, but now, seeing her laid low for days on end, Duane had experienced a sudden burst of energy and purpose. He was in the bedroom dressing for an interview with a real estate firm in Baton Rouge.

The woman who came into the living room was young, slender, and, in jeans and a parka, somewhat casually dressed for an attorney. Although she was pretty in a fresh, interesting way, she had a dour look, as if she were consciously trying to cancel out her attractiveness. "I suppose you know I represent your uncle," she said, taking a seat.

Olive had guessed as much when the woman had introduced herself at the door. She was glad she had the opportunity now to let this girl know, once and for all, that she was washing her hands of Uncle L.D. The less she had to do with him, the better. To put it bluntly, he was a campaign liability. The sooner he was written off, the better. Furthermore, she was going to make it perfectly clear that she was not going to pick up one red cent of his legal expenses. "Ms. Keely, could I—"

"Excuse me, Ms. Mackie, I realize you must be very busy, so if you don't mind, I'd like to get right down to business."

"But—"

Ms. Keely slipped off the parka hood. "I'm sorry, I don't drink coffee or tea, so if we could just . . ." She pulled out a yellow note pad from her attaché case. "Now, number one, I wonder if you're aware that Mr. Versey was a member of the Ku Klux Klan from 1963 to 1965. Oh, by the way, I hope you don't mind if I record you?"

"What?"

Ms. Keely pulled out a slim metal box from her attaché case and set it on the blond Danish-modern coffee table. "Just talk in a normal voice."

"I'd rather you didn't use that thing."

"What? Now, Ms. Mackie, moving right along. I want you to have a look at this." She thrust a blurred Xerox of some official-looking document into Olive's hand. "What do we see here? It's Mr. Versey again. Confinement for nine months at the Pine Hills Forensic Institute, 1957. Charges? Theft."

"Good, I'm glad." Olive held her hand over the recorder, which didn't seem to have any buttons. Somewhat more softly she added, "See, I don't care if Mr. Versey gunned down the Archduke Ferdinand. It has nothing to do with me, understand? I've given all the testimony I can, and that's that. If the old man wants to end his days in jail, that's just fine with me."

Before Olive could finish speaking, the lawyer was already going on to her next point. "Now, here, Ms. Mackie"—she was consulting her notes—"I see here that as a result of a violent altercation with his supervisor Mr. Versey left his job at the Mildred Post Office, threatening his supervisor with these words, and I quote: 'You're short, Mr. Samuels, real short for a man, but I promise to make you a good two feet shorter before I leave.'"

"Good, I'm glad." Surreptitiously Olive pocketed a roach clip she noticed on the coffee table. To help him cut down on drinking, Olive was encouraging Duane to take an occasional joint whenever Felix was out of the house. "And by the way, I believe the reason Mr. Versey left was because of the jiffy bags."

"Yes, that's what *he* says." She looked up from her notes. "You know, it's curious, Ms. Mackie. It's curious how eager you are to take this man's side, a man with a record, a man who burned crosses and terrorized the black population. It's even more curious that you hired such a man to look after your uncle. I've grown to have the utmost respect for Mr. Loraine, you know. I don't think I've ever met a man with more guts and integrity."

"Does a man of such integrity throw his housekeeper out the window?"

"Yes, sometimes he does. When his back's against the wall, when there's no other alternative to being brutalized."

Olive wiggled her bare toes. "Really, how you can believe such nonsense . . . A ninety-one-year-old invalid tossing a man half his age out the window."

"Your uncle was fighting for his life." Ms. Keely unzipped her bulky Army surplus parka a bit more but still kept it on. "I suppose you've heard of judo. An opponent's own weight and strength, you understand, can be used against him. A child could toss a full-grown man employing these principles."

"Since when did Uncle L.D. get his black belt? And by the way, he's not really my uncle, you know. He's a great-uncle by marriage."

"You needn't take everything so literally. I'm aware of your relation to my client, and I also realize he knows nothing of judo. The point remains that it *is* possible. Especially since he says so himself. I refuse to believe that your uncle could lie about anything, much less something so important to him. And furthermore, if you want to talk about nonsense, let's talk about suicide. Do you actually think for one minute that Mr. Versey, if he were serious about killing himself, would toss himself out a second-story window?"

"He wasn't in his right mind. Anyone who spent over eight hours a day with Uncle L.D. wouldn't be in his right mind. Come here, babe," she added as Duane emerged from the bedroom. He looked handsome in his gray European-cut suit, but his tie needed fixing. Standing on the sofa, she redid the knot for him.

"I have here an affidavit from Nesta Versey, his sister. In it she makes it quite plain that he was a happy man, that he had no reason to do away with himself."

"Are these cuff links too much?" Duane whispered while the lawyer read an excerpt from the affidavit. "Should I wear the jade ones instead?"

"No, these are fine. Good luck, hon." She gave him a pat on the behind. "Break a leg."

" . . . get up and fix me a glass of fresh-squeezed orange juice." The lawyer paused until Duane had made his exit and Olive had turned her attention back to the matter at hand. " . . . fresh-squeezed orange juice."

"Right, I heard." Looking out the window behind the sofa, Olive saw Duane start toward his Nissan. But then he remembered and walked over to the Cadillac. Olive had told him that the Cadillac would make a better impression.

"By the way," Olive said, interrupting the lawyer, who had gone on to read more of the affidavit, "do you mind if I ask who it was that got you hooked up with Uncle L.D.? I assume he didn't just look you up in the Yellow Pages. Oh," she felt compelled to add since Duane had been too preoccupied to introduce himself, "that was my husband—I mean, is, is my husband."

"Fine. Ms. Mackie, do you have any idea what the psychological effect of a nursing home is on someone? It's really about the worst place in the world for an older person. I personally find it hard to comprehend how anyone with an ounce of compassion could—"

"Who told you about him?"

The lawyer kept her eyes on the yellow note pad. "I am acting on behalf of a friend of Mr. Loraine's whose confidentiality I'm bound to respect."

"Very modest, this friend."

"As a matter of fact, this friend has no bearing on the case whatsoever. The friend happened to show a little compassion and paid me a nominal sum to help get Mr. Loraine out of the nursing home. I'm on my own as far as this case goes. I hope to make that quite clear."

"Of course. You just tell Mrs. Undine she doesn't have a thing to worry about. I won't tell a soul."

"Mrs. Undine?" The lawyer gave a good imitation of looking confused, which made Olive smile. "What makes you think . . ."

"Please, Ms. Keely, I wasn't born yesterday. She's the only other person who visits him. Who else could it be? So, good, she's done her quota of meddling this month and gotten him out of the nursing home. But I want to make something clear myself: You tell her I'm not setting foot in that apartment of his anymore. And if she thinks I'm going to take any responsibility for your fees—you can both forget it, right now." She leaned over toward the recorder on the coffee table: "Hear? I'm not responsible for any legal fees incurred by Mr. L.D. Loraine. This is Mrs. Duane Mackie speaking."

"It's not on."

"What?"

"I thought you told me you didn't want to be recorded. I turned it off. In any case, you have nothing to worry about as far as that goes. However"—she reached for another sheaf of papers in the attaché case—"there is something you might want to start thinking about. I have here statements from four separate sources saying that you were not in the apartment on Flat Avenue on the day you claimed to be, in your own statement to the coroner, the day Mr. Versey died. As a matter of fact, when I reviewed your statement to the coroner, it simply didn't make much sense. First you told him that Mr. Versey was sick and wasn't even at the apartment that day when you went there. But obviously he had to be if he was found dead on the sidewalk. Then you said Mr. Versey might have gone to the floor above to throw himself out—an apartment, I might point out, that is currently occupied by a dog-grooming academy. Now, his sister, Miss Nesta Versey, stated here that Mr. Versey has never owned or been interested in owning a dog. She also claimed, by the way, that he had gone to work that day even though he was, and I quote, under the weather with a cold. Furthermore, in your same statement to the coroner—and by the way, the coroner really shouldn't be taking these statements, legally speaking. He should stick to the medical facts and stop acting like a sheriff. Anyway, be that as it may, in the very same statement you made to him, page three, paragraph two, line six, you contradict everything you said before by saying that Mr. Versey had probably been depressed after spending *eight hours* in Mr. Loraine's apartment."

"I—"

"Please, let me finish. So you yourself admit that it was improbable that he threw himself from the window of a dog grooming academy. Furthermore, besides Miss Versey's statement, I have a statement from Mr. Loraine that Mr. Versey was in the apartment that day. And, to remove any doubt from your mind, just in case you're having trouble remembering, I have signed statements from Mrs. Vondra Hewes, Mrs. Louise Waling, and Dr. Martin Bates that you were being treated with expired composite at the Gregg College of Dentistry in Ozone from two-thirty-five P.M. until three-fifty-five P.M. Which meant that you had to leave Tula Springs at approximately one-fifty P.M. to get to Ozone and that you returned to Tula Springs at approximately four-fifty-five in time to hurry with your husband, Duane Edward, to a dinner party at 82 Ile de France Place given by Dr. and Mrs. Emile Deshotel (I have here a signed statement from Mrs. Deshotel), which you did not leave until eleven-forty-three P.M. Oh, and I forgot . . . Here, look." She held up a paper that had been lying in her lap. "Mrs. Undine has given me a signed statement that that morning you were in attendance at her class in domestic science at Robin Downs. So, Ms. Mackie, just when did you find time to squeeze in a visit to your uncle? Every minute of your day is accounted for here." She gently shook the sheaf of signed statements.

Olive was appalled. It was bad enough that this girl had been able to ferret out statements from Vondra and that awful receptionist. But to have gone to her dear friends . . . One of her recurring dreams was that for some reason she had decided to go to a country-club dance in her undies and was, of course, mortified when she got there. This was how she felt now.

The lawyer had taken out a red bandanna and sneezed into it. Sniffling, she tucked it away in the parka. "To be quite frank, this is the one piece of the puzzle I can't put together. Everything else fits in quite nicely, but your perjury just doesn't make sense."

"Hey, now, hold on a second. Don't you go throwing around words like that."

"Well, call it what you like." Her face had softened somewhat, so that it was more of a match for her disconcertingly sweet, breathy voice. "I must admit I'm curious, Ms. Mackie, why you seem to insist you were at the scene of the crime. Most people would bend over backwards to claim just the opposite. Here you have the perfect alibi and—"

"Alibi?"

"I don't mean alibi."

"But you said alibi."

She glanced at her watch. "I've got an appointment downtown. Perhaps someday you'll have time to drop by my office. I'd like to continue this discussion, if possible."

Olive followed her to the door. Confused, vaguely guilty, she nonetheless felt her fighting spirit roused. She wasn't going to take this lying down. "Ms. Keely, if I were you, before I barged into too many more houses and made too many more veiled threats, I think I would stop and consider who I'm dealing with. It might be worth your while to know that I just happen to be a close personal friend of Judge Henley. He's known me ever since I was in diapers."

"Indeed?" The lawyer zipped up her parka and pulled up the hood. It was chilly out, but not *that* cold.

"Yes. As a matter of fact, I just saw him the other day at his house, and he assured me . . ."

Ms. Keely smiled encouragingly. "Yes? Go on."

Olive had the feeling she had gone far enough.

"Ms. Mackie, I resent the term 'veiled threats.' I'm simply letting you know what the facts are concerning certain matters. And as for Judge Henley, I appreciate the information. Thank you very much."

The lawyer's bicycle was chained to the gas lamp at the end of the drive. Seeing that she was having some trouble unlocking the chain, Olive started out across the lawn in bare feet. She was having second thoughts. Maybe it would be best if she smiled and were a little more polite. After all, there was an election coming up. But before she could offer any help, Ms. Keely had removed the chain and mounted the bike.

Olive hurried back into the house. No, she thought, revising these second thoughts. She was not going to kowtow to anyone. She had her pride.

"Believe me, she and Henley are in cahoots," Donna Lee insisted, but Dr. Bates still looked sceptical. Earlier that afternoon Donna Lee had dropped by Mrs. Undine's to see if Mrs. Undine would mind spending a couple hours with Mr.

Loraine. Burma had gotten something in her eye and was at the doctor's. When Mrs. Undine bowed out, explaining how busy she was, Dr. Bates had volunteered to take her place. "Good. You can bring your books and study," Donna Lee had said. Dr. Bates hadn't been able to read more than a paragraph or two, though. The old man was a tireless talker, and by the time Donna Lee arrived, Dr. Bates felt as if he had spent an entire week with him.

"Can't we go somewhere else?" he asked under his breath. From the four-poster on the other side of the room Mr. Loraine was keeping a sharp eye on them. Donna Lee had asked the old man to please bear with her and let her talk to Dr. Bates a few moments.

"Burma ought to be back any minute," she said. "Now, listen, Judge Henley has always had this holier-than-thou reputation, like some sort of goddam preacher. I've known all along, though."

"What?"

"That he's crooked as a two-dollar bill. And now I have proof. He's been discussing the case with Mackie, can you believe it? She told me so herself."

"So?"

"So! Don't you realize that when this goes to trial, he'll be presiding? And there she is cozying up to him. I'm telling you, this man is a menace. Something should be done about him. You can't believe how right wing he is. Every time I've argued a case in front of him, he's tried to make me look foolish. He doesn't believe women should be lawyers, period. We're talking Stone Age, Martin."

"Finished?" the old man called out.

"Just a minute, sweetie." Donna Lee waved childishly to him. "Now, listen, Martin, this is important. If you see her again—"

"Who?"

"Mackie. Draw her out as much as you can on all this. Dig into just what went on between her and Henley. And then try to find out the angle on her perjury, why she said she was here on that day."

The rocker squeaked as Dr. Bates stood up to give his

bottom a rest from the tv tray. "I'm not sure it's such a good idea for me to see this woman. To tell you the truth, I think she has a thing for me."

"She's married, right?"

He nodded.

"Well then, it's wrong for her to have a thing for you. She's only getting what she deserves."

Although he was pleased by the friendship that seemed to be developing between himself and Donna Lee, he was hoping for much more. Perhaps this was why he objected to being used as bait for her fishing expeditions; he would have liked to see some sign of jealousy, but there was none. "Don't you think it's slightly callous to use someone like that? Lead her on?"

Donna Lee smiled sweetly. "My dear boy, Mackie's been up to her ears in City Hall for ages. She's thick with all the good ole boys. I hardly think we can teach her anything about using people. What do you want to do? Sit back and see this poor man end up in jail?"

"Well, hold on now—" Feeling a sneeze coming on, Dr. Bates tensed; but the feeling went away. "Isn't Mrs. Mackie the one who said he *didn't* do anything?"

"A cover-up for something, and I mean to get to the bottom of it. She's just worried about the effect all this will have on her campaign. You know she's running for office, don't you?" She directed a sharp look at the open window. The neon *N* had just given a particularly loud and alarming pop. "Which reminds me, Martin, just in case your conscience is still bothering you. Did I tell you what Dr. Munrow said about her? He told me that Mackie paid him a visit not long ago and tried to bribe him. She told him that if he supported her campaign, she would give the school free landscaping and garbage service. I got that from the horse's mouth."

"Yeah, but what about him? I mean, there he is, the head of a racist school."

"Which he's trying to integrate, singlehandedly."

His eyes drifted to her blond hair, a disturbing sight. "O.K., but still, they teach creationism."

"Look, Martin, down here you can't have everything. Besides, he's not one of those fake Christians. He actually believes what he preaches. I was really touched by his concern for Mr. Loraine. Look what Mackie had done, just dumped him in that horrible nursing home. Have you any idea what life at Azalea Manor must be like? How you can feel concerned at all about that woman is beyond me."

"Well, I know those places—"

"In my own dull, retarded way may I suggest that you two have had plenty of time. It's my turn now. Come on over here, Miss Keely. I want you to tell me the exact date the *Titanic* sunk. Remote ice . . ."

"Wanders thoroughly," she said, completing his mnemonic formula.

"Excellent! Oh, Dr. Bates, what a mind that girl has! She's going places, let me tell you."

"You'll never believe what happened to me today. This horrible woman came barging into my house, and the next thing I know, she was practically threatening me at gunpoint. I've never seen such a pushy woman in all my life. It makes me want to hand in my card to Women's Lib."

Olive and Dr. Bates were walking in the narrow strip of woods bordering Mrs. Undine's yard. Although it had been chilly in the afternoon, it had warmed up enough by early evening for Olive to feel uncomfortable in her cashmere sweater. She had driven over to Pine Street to give Mrs. Undine what-for concerning Uncle L.D. When no one had answered the door, she had gone around back and found Dr. Bates spreading a layer of dirt over some sand. Mrs. Undine, it seemed, was out Christmas shopping at the mall in Mississippi.

"Well, you know, it really wasn't Fern who got Donna Lee involved in this thing," Dr. Bates said as he plucked a burr from his sleeve. Not far ahead was the Tula Springs water tower, its struts graffitied with adolescent hieroglyphs. Olive was silent until they were almost upon it. She was trying to concentrate upon the romantic aspect of this unforeseen opportunity to be alone with Dr. Bates. But Mrs. Undine kept nagging at her.

"Why must you always stand up for her?" Olive demanded.

"What? It's true. She could care less about the old guy."

A Cyclone fence ringed the asphalt at the base of the tower. Listlessly they strolled past the Keep Out sign. "You know, when I was in high school, this guy I couldn't stand, he climbed up to the top of this thing and painted his name next to mine. I nearly died. I really felt like killing myself."

She noticed an auburn tinge in Dr. Bates's fine dark-brown hair and wondered if it had always been there. Or maybe it was just something caused by the light, with the sun so low. "Then about a week later I found out he hadn't done it. It was Kay Undine. She had got her boyfriend to climb up and do it. You can still see parts of it now. Look, see that *v* there?"

He muttered something about being sorry.

"I thought I'd never forgive her. But now it just sort of makes me smile. You know, the guy up there, the guy she knew I hated, it turns out he's a deputy. He questioned me about Mr. Versey and all. It was weird. He's got three kids and he's a poet."

"Mm."

"I'm sort of ashamed of myself now. I shouldn't have been so mean to him just because he didn't go out for sports. People are very cruel in high school, don't you think? It's like people used to be in the Middle Ages, torturing each other, ostracizing anyone who's different."

"And now here we are in the humane twentieth century."

She looked quizzically at him. It was always difficult to decide if he was being serious or not. That apparent niceness about him, that also she was unsure of. The more she was with him, the more she could sense something hard, almost cruel, about him, a certain steely core of resolve. Unfortunately this only made him seem more desirable to her. It would have been easier to forget a marshmallow. "Dr. Bates, will you answer one question?"

"Hm?"

"Will you tell me why, the other day, when we were

standing by the pool, why did you put your fingers in my mouth?"

"What? I was examining your teeth."

"They were trembling."

"Well, you'll have to get them screwed in tighter then, those teeth." He smiled feebly. "Oh, by the way, I meant to ask you how things went with that judge. I really hope he can help you out."

"Be serious," she said as he was talking. "I want you to tell me why you opened my mouth and looked at my teeth. I— Judge? How did you know I talked to Judge Henley?"

"What?"

"What do you mean, what? I asked you how you knew I—"

"Oh, Fern. I believe it was Fern. She must have said something or other . . ."

"Goddammit. That woman can't leave well enough alone, can she? You know, I just don't get it. She didn't seem that interested in Uncle L.D. before all this business. I got the feeling she didn't really care for him. And now . . ."

Dr. Bates stopped to pluck a piece of tissue off a bush. "I can't stand litterbugs, the way they . . ." It turned out to be a late blossom, somewhat limp and faded, but a flower nonetheless. "Uh, yes, he's quite a character, that uncle of yours."

"You've met him?"

"Yeah, he . . . I mean, not really. Fern . . ."

"She took you over there, didn't she? Look me in the eye, Dr. Bates. You've been over there, haven't you?"

"Not really. She just talks about him a lot."

He changed the subject, chattering mindlessly about the trouble he was having with his left contact lens, but Olive was not listening. Gnawing the inside of her cheek, she wondered what in the world Mrs. Undine was up to. The only conclusion she could reach was that she was out to ruin her. For some reason Mrs. Undine wanted to make sure Olive didn't win that election. She was going to make sure Olive's name was mud by dragging her uncle before the public as a murderer. "Why does she hate me?"

". . . like today I didn't even put them in. I get so tired of all those lens solutions, and then I'm afraid I might get some infection on my eyeball or something."

"Why does Mrs. Undine hate me? What have I ever done to her?"

"I don't think she hates you."

"She wouldn't even put up a sign for me in her yard. And she gave Felix a C in Life Science, and science is Felix's strongest subject. I helped him— Dr. Bates, is that smoke?"

They had been strolling aimlessly around the perimeter of the water tower when her eye happened to alight on a bluish haze atop a clump of honeysuckle. "You think it's a fire?" she asked as they hurried toward the dense undergrowth.

"Hey, Mamma, get your hoof out of here," a boy's voice croaked as Olive prodded with her foot to get a better view.

"Y'all shouldn't smoke," Olive called into the brittle, yellowish leaves. Beneath, a vague cluster of heads, like the purplish corolla of a huge, meaty tropical plant, was just visible. "Who are y'all? I bet I know y'all's mothers."

"Come on," Dr. Bates muttered, pulling her away.

As they headed back for Mrs. Undine's, Olive told him he should have said something. They might burn down the woods. He said they might be hoods or something; it wasn't a good idea to get mixed up with them. When she pretended she was going to go back to them anyway, he restrained her, physically. She struggled against him, and they sort of wrestled a little. Then after that they went into Mrs. Undine's living room and made love on the couch.

PART THREE

Chapter Thirteen

"SIT DOWN."

Dr. Bates sat down.

"Cigar?"

"No, thanks."

Taking a platinum clipper that was chained to his vest pocket, Dr. Schexsnyder snipped the end off his Corona Royale. Without the slightest regard for Dr. Bates's own pressing schedule Dr. Schexsnyder had summoned him to his office just as Dr. Bates was about to undam Carol Deshotel's mouth. Deep down, Dr. Bates knew this was it. He was going to be told that he wouldn't be able to graduate this spring. He had been expecting this interview for some time, and he had promised himself that when it came, he was not just going to sit there, meekly accepting his fate. No, he would deliver a tirade against Dr. Schexsnyder's money-grubbing mind-set that would make Donna Lee proud.

"It's been a tough year for you, hasn't it, son?"

Dr. Bates shrugged.

"Everything all right at home? Getting enough shut-eye?" The sapphire on the instructor's little finger gleamed dully as he turned the pages of Dr. Bates's file. "I don't understand these grades, C here, D in Temporomandibular Joint Dysfunction, Incomplete here." He picked at some dirt under his nail. "What's this you're up to with Mrs. Deshotel?"

"I'm trying to repair a porcelain-jacket crown."

"Why is it taking so long?"

Dr. Bates rubbed his palms against his white coat. "She talks a lot. And that D I got, it really wasn't fair, you know. Dr. Renshaw got confused about the exam last semester and gave it a week early. Half the class failed and—"

"Martin, my boy," Dr. Schexsnyder said, slapping the file onto his desk, "I'm going to give it to you straight. No beating around the bush."

Dr. Bates's courage deserted him. He felt far too old to start searching for a new career. If only he could be given another chance. He would work hard; he would concentrate. . . . "Dr. Schexsnyder, I—"

"Hear me out, son. You'll be finishing up in May, right? Well, I want you to do me a big favor. Take June off, the whole darn month. Go down to the Caribbean, Florida, get yourself some sun. Relax. You've been looking pale as a ghost, boy. Then come July, I want you to find yourself an apartment in New Orleans. I got a friend can help you find a one-bedroom that's pretty reasonable. What's that frown supposed to mean?"

"I don't understand."

"You're coming to work for me, boy." He gave Dr. Bates's limp, sweaty hand an extremely painful squeeze. "We need someone like you to help take up the slack. I think you'll fill the bill."

Dr. Bates tried to damp the sweet pleasure that welled up in him. Could he have heard right? Did Dr. Schexsnyder mean that he wanted him to join his group in New Orleans?

"You're a smart boy, that's why I don't understand these grades. But I'm betting on you. I think with time you'll straighten out the kinks."

"But what about Frank Estee? He told me last semester you had already chosen him."

The instructor tapped a neat ash into a Sugar Bowl ashtray. "Yeah, I had my eye on him for a while. But the boy's offsides. He's a little too pushy, if you know what I mean. I'd be the last to deny he's got a good pair of hands—but see, the very fact that he told you something like that. It's not quite the tone I'm looking for in my practice. I need class, ole boy. I think you understand what I'm getting at." He stretched luxuriously in the cramped office. "Yeah, I like the way you work with your patients. You've got a nice personal touch, gives them a sense of loyalty."

The receptionist stuck her head in the door. "I'm going to leave Jones tied up here," she said, indicating her three-year-old, who was leashed to her desk. "Keep an eye on him while I go get you your Tab."

Dr. Schexsnyder grunted, and Louise was off. "I don't have time now to go into details. We'll talk later. O.K., son, let's get out there and play ball." He gave Dr. Bates a slap on the fanny. With a garbled thank you Dr. Bates returned to his patient.

"What's got into you, Marty?" Carol asked after he had finished with her and was escorting her to the door. "You haven't listened to a thing I've said."

"I'm sorry. I've . . . Now, remember, try not to eat anything for three hours. And nothing hot to drink for one hour."

"Yes, Doctor."

With a vague smile he wandered off to the reference library, where he sat for a while pretending to read. Was Dr. Schexsnyder really such a dreadful person? he asked himself. In all honesty, had he taken a dim view of Dr. Schexsnyder simply because he had thought Frank Estee was his favorite? And as far as the poor and disadvantaged went, wouldn't Dr. Bates be in a better position to contribute to their welfare if he had plenty of money? Wouldn't he be able to do far more good by influencing the opinions of the movers and shakers of society than by fixing a few teeth in a free health clinic? Surely this latter road was only a superficial, cosmetic way of dealing with a pernicious problem that had to be attacked at the root. And as someone with influence, a person of substance, wouldn't he be better equipped to make some real changes in the structure of society?

The answer to all these questions was no—at least as far as Donna Lee was concerned. They were dining together that evening at Isola Bella, something he had been looking forward to all week. But she seemed rather distracted, anxious to get back to her office to finish up some work. "Don't you think you're being a little simplistic?" he asked.

"No."

Progress had been slow on this front, his relationship with Donna Lee. She was still spending most of her free time with the steady boyfriend her mother disapproved of. On the other hand, Donna Lee had never said anything to discourage Dr. Bates. They both held each other in the highest esteem, though he was beginning to wonder if there wasn't something a little chilling about esteem. With Victorian restraint they would clasp hands before saying good night and perhaps exchange a comradely kiss on both cheeks, in the European manner. A few times, in order to spark jealousy, he had come close to telling her that he had slept with Mrs. Mackie, but he always pulled himself up short. Instead of jealousy, he was afraid her reaction might be amazement or even outright scorn. How would he ever be able to explain to her the strange chemistry between himself and Mrs. Mackie when he couldn't even explain it to himself?

After their initial encounter in Mrs. Undine's living room Mrs. Mackie, guilt ridden and bewildered, had avoided him for a while. Regarding the whole thing as an aberration, he had made no effort to get in touch with her himself. But then, not long after the Christmas holidays, circumstances had thrown them together again. Before he knew it, he was making love to her in her living room on an awkward piece of furniture known as a méridienne. Quite frankly the sex was as stiff and uncomfortable as the furniture in the respective living rooms. And afterward Mrs. Mackie felt so guilty she could hardly bear to look at him. For his part Dr. Bates was always glad to make his escape. Deep down—or perhaps, not so very deep down—he knew he did not respect her as he should. She was far too shallow and opportunistic, and she wasn't even very good-looking, not by his standards, at least. All this made it hard for him to comprehend the lust she aroused in him, a kind of primitive eroticism that was cued not so much by sight or touch as by smell. Her unique scent was like the furniture polish he used to sniff at home in New Jersey as he trailed the Finnish maid from chair to chair. He was only five then and was excited by the idea of being alone with Hulga while his mother was out at Elizabeth Arden having her legs waxed.

"Look at you," he said after Nancy, the owner and cook, had set down a plate of linguini. "You're hardly working for Legal Aid. You're in the fanciest law firm in town. I don't see how you have much room to talk."

"Martin, do you realize how many hours I've spent, days, weeks, working for nothing? Do you have any idea how much time I've put into this Loraine case alone? My boss is furious. I'm falling behind on the real work I'm supposed to be doing. And I just hate the stupid contracts I'm supposed to be working on." Deftly she wound her pasta. "If you want to help people, then help people. If you want to make money, then make money. But for God's sakes, don't try to help people by making money. You'll end up like me, doing neither."

"Yes, but . . ."

"I can't begin to tell you all the grief I've been through trying to help that old man. It's been a nightmare, and it hasn't earned me a cent. The coroner's intent on getting the body disinterred—"

"He died?"

"Mr. Versey's. The coroner said the Xerox place lost two pages of his evidence, and they claim he never brought those pages in. It's stupid things like that, me having to threaten a copy shop as a favor to Dr. McFlug." Holding the fork in front of her mouth, Donna Lee stared out into space, as if she were dining alone.

"Is this linguini going to be enough for you?"

"What?"

"Should we order something else?"

"Oh, and the D.A., he's been sitting on this for months now. I suspect Judge Henley's got to him. No grand jury, nothing. Someone's got to light a fire under him. The old man can't sit in limbo for the rest of his life. He's got to get his name cleared."

Dr. Bates gazed sullenly at the neighboring table, where

three well-dressed women were carrying on an animated conversation. "It's an odd way of clearing someone's name, getting him accused of murder."

"Justifiable homicide."

He shrugged.

She put down her fork and looked him in the eye. "Do you realize how much you shrug? It's the one thing about you I don't like."

"I don't shrug."

"You shrug all the time, my dear."

After dinner Dr. Bates walked Donna Lee the few blocks to the Bessie Building, and then, because the stairway wasn't lit, he felt he should accompany her up to her office. A single pole lamp was on in the reception area of Herbert, Herbert, and Associates, leaving most of the room in the dark. Following Donna Lee down the hall, he strained his ears for any noise coming from the somewhat eerie, darkened offices. Hers turned out to be almost bare, impersonal, as if she were either just moving in or moving out. Not a single photo or diploma decorated the wood veneer walls. Besides a desk, a chair, and a few perfunctory bookshelves, there was only a wooden pew, which made the room seem vaguely conventual.

"Thank you, Martin. Now that you see I haven't been robbed or raped, you can say good night." She held out her hand and gave him a brisk, mother-superior smile.

"Doesn't it bother you, being all alone in this building?"

"Hm?" She sat down and reloaded her staple gun. He hadn't grasped her hand. "Oh, before you go, take a look at . . . I know it's here somewhere." She riffled through some papers in a metal box marked IN and pulled out a sheet. "I thought you'd get a kick out of this."

"Dear Ms. Keely," the letter read. "As a long-time member of the Sierra Club I want you to know how much I applaud their efforts towards conserving Louisiana's irreplaceable waterways and wildlife. I have always been behind any and every effort to preserve the ecological balance, our most precious heritage. And I want you to know that if I am elected Superintendent of Streets, Parks, and Garbage, I will do everything in my power to make the Sierra Club proud of Tula Springs' contribution to a clean and ecologically sound Louisiana. May I count on your support? Sincerely, Olive Mackie." At the bottom of the letter was a form: "I would like to pledge [   ]$10 [   ]$25 [   ]$100 [   ]Other for a clean Louisiana."

"Can you believe?"

Dr. Bates handed the letter back with no comment.

"That woman is just too much." She flicked a strand of blond hair from her eye. "Anyway, Martin, I had fun tonight. Thanks a lot. Now, smile and say good night."

Wishing she were back home curled up in bed with a Louis L'Amour, Olive shook hands with almost every parent in the Blue Room. Although the school was in a state of virtual civil war, Robin Downs had gone ahead with its annual fund raiser, a fifty-dollar-a-plate dinner at the country club followed by an auction. The pro-Munrow faction was clustered about the melting ice swan near the punch bowl, while the much larger group of anti-Munrovites was scattered among the elegant candle-lit tables where the five-course dinner had been served. Seeing how outnumbered the principal was, Olive was glad now that Dr. Munrow hadn't endorsed her campaign. She could joke with a clear conscience among the anti-Munrovites, yet at the same time, because she was entirely in sympathy with the idea of a black science teacher, she could drop a sincere word or two of encouragement in the enemy camp.

"Yes, Duane is working in Baton Rouge now. It's a terrific job," she was saying to Mrs. Jenks, one of the principal's few supporters on the Board of Regents. Mrs. Jenks was leaning upon a docile great-grandson, who was munching ice from a coffee cup. When she wanted to move on, she would call out, "All right, Walter!" and the pale boy would shuffle along by her side.

Noticing that her purse had popped open, Mrs. Jenks tried to close it while saying, "Isn't that quite a piece to drive every day?"

"Well," Olive replied, giving her a hand with the beaded

evening bag, "he's got a little apartment and stays there a few days a week, so it isn't so bad."

It was such a relief to have money again. Duane had finally landed a job at a real-estate firm in Baton Rouge through a friend he used to play football with. Of course, Olive was anxious about Duane's having his own apartment there. But she simply couldn't uproot herself now, in the middle of a campaign, and move to Baton Rouge. Secretly, although she complained to him, she was glad for the four days alone each week. They gave her some time to sort out her feelings about Dr. Bates. Yes, she supposed she did still love him even though he wasn't really the world's greatest lover. At the same time some deep feminine instinct told her that she could not count on him. He was not in love with her, that much she was sure of. And he lacked the solidity of character that Duane had. In fact, she was forced to admit that, despite her having once thought he possessed a steely, willful core, Dr. Bates was perhaps a rather frivolous and shallow man. She found it hard to imagine that he had any deep feelings about anything but himself. Yet knowing all this, realizing what a conceited snob he was, did not make her any the less attracted to him. She had also discovered that she had more religion in her than she had counted on. The guilt she experienced after lovemaking was so debilitating that she could barely live with herself. Perhaps this was why the campaign had acquired such tremendous importance for her lately. It was almost as if every vote was a way of reassuring her that she was not so bad after all. And soon, with the primaries, she would know for certain what the judgment was, guilty or not guilty.

"Look at Dr. Munrow over there." Mrs. Jenks jabbed a crooked finger into the dense smoky air, clogged by quips, rumors, half-smothered laughter, and much politeness. "Trying to butter up the Sandersons. Now, you know the Sandersons are going to pull their child out the minute Dr. Munrow installs that colored girl."

"You think he'll win out?" Olive was surprised to hear the black teacher spoken of as a *fait accompli.*

"Doesn't matter if he gets the votes or not. He's going to do what's best for the school whether they like it or not."

"But Mrs. Jenks, do you think that's right? Shouldn't he listen to what they—"

"All right, Walter!" she commanded, and the boy and she were off.

Worried that she had spent too much time by the swan, Olive made a strategic move in the direction of the tables. She was anxious to talk to Mr. Dambar, the wealthy man who seemed to dislike Vondra. Olive had been meaning to pay a visit to the creosote plant he owned and have a chat with him, yet what with one thing and another she had never gotten around to it. The opportunity was perfect now because he was standing beside a friend of Olive's who could introduce her. Betty Ogleby, the friend, was a flying instructor who worked free-lance for a greeting-card company. She had already contributed fifty dollars to Olive's campaign, in return for which Olive had promised to take at least one flying lesson.

Oh, Martin, Martin, a small voice called out as she waved to Betty.

"Yoo-hoo, excuse me, please," a pretty older woman said, intercepting Olive before she could get to Betty. The woman had been sitting at a table with Mrs. Undine, whom Olive had been carefully avoiding all evening, along with Dr. Munrow. A couple months earlier, shortly after New Year's Day, Mrs. Undine and she had had words over Uncle L.D. It had been an unpleasant scene. Mrs. Undine insisted she had had nothing to do with the old man's release from the nursing home when it was patently obvious she was behind it. Wasn't it true, after all, that her next-door neighbor was Uncle L.D.'s lawyer? Olive had warned her that if she tried to interfere anymore, Mrs. Undine would live to regret it. Of course, Olive had no idea what she had meant by "live to regret it," which was why she was avoiding Mrs. Undine. Besides, she was a little nervous that Mrs. Undine might start prying into Dr. Bates's private life.

"Are you Mrs. Mackie, Mrs. Duane Mackie?"

The woman's smile was so frank and engaging that Olive couldn't help smiling back. "Yes, that's me, I'm afraid."

"Do you remember me, dear? I'm Mrs. Woody."

There was something vaguely familiar about the name and the face, which was pretty in a blatant, fifties sort of way.

"I'm Sarah Woody's mother. You remember Sarah."

Olive smiled, even though she was still puzzled.

"Oh, my, Sarah used to think the world of you. She used to go to all the away games to see you play ball. Even made Mr. Woody put up a net at the end of our driveway."

Suddenly it came to her: Why, of course, Sarah was the dumpy eighth-grader who had had a crush on Olive when she was a senior and captain of the basketball team. Olive had always been embarrassed by this girl, especially when she began copying the clothes she wore.

"Well, Mrs. Woody." Olive took the lady's hand and gave it a squeeze. "How is Sarah?" Time had made her feel more magnanimous toward this old admirer.

Mrs. Woody's false eyelashes fluttered demurely; strangely enough, they looked fine on her. "Me and Mr. Woody are so proud of our Sarah. She just had a baby boy, twenty-three and a half inches long, if you please."

"How nice!" Glancing anxiously over at Betty to make sure Mr. Dambar was still by her side, Olive added, "By the way, I'm running for Superintendent of Streets, Parks, and Garbage, and I would—"

"Oh, Olive, you don't have to tell *me* that, dear. I know all about you, and I'm sure you're going to eat them up alive. Why, anyone as pretty and smart as you—and just look at those shoes, how sweet they are."

Coming from anyone else, all this extravagant praise would have sounded phony, but Mrs. Woody carried it off with aplomb. For a moment or two Olive and she beamed at each other, a mutual admiration society.

"By the way." Olive caught a strong whiff of sweetish perfume as Mrs. Woody leaned over and whispered, "Sarah asked me to give you this." Confidentially she tucked a white envelope under the flap of Olive's Diane von Fursten-berg evening bag.

Olive flushed with pleasure. Undoubtedly a discreet contribution. With a murmured thanks she pecked Mrs. Woody on her powdered cheek.

It's people like her who make the world go round, Olive thought as Mrs. Woody returned to her table.

Although Betty did introduce her to Mr. Dambar, a handsome man with the nicest manners, Olive wasn't able to get very far with him. Every time she tried to steer the conversation around to the upcoming election, he would slide off into an unrelated subject. And then Dr. Munrow had taken it upon himself to mosey on over. With a nod and smile to the principal, who was in one of his down-home moods, Olive gave up on Mr. Dambar for the time being and drifted off.

When she got back to Cherylview that evening, Olive put away the cretonne drapes she had bought at the auction and went into the bathroom to see if there was any Preparation H. Betty had told her that everyone in Hollywood was using Preparation H to shrink the bags under their eyes. In a way Olive was relieved when she didn't find any.

"Where were you?"

"Oh, hi, Felix." Her son was standing in the door to the bathroom. He looked tense and disapproving, a fresh pimple marring his chin. "I was at the auction."

"You put on all that make-up for an auction?"

For years it had been her mother complaining about her make-up; now it was her son. Olive sighed as she applied Noxema to her face. "Honey, why don't you go read Leviticus or something. I'm tired."

After changing into a terrycloth robe Olive brought the phone to bed with her and called her mother in Twentynine Palms, California. She told her about the drapes she had bought at the auction and the new dress she was thinking of buying for herself. Her mother asked her please not to say drapes—"A lady never says drapes"—and wanted to know where she planned to hang them. "I'm going to turn them into slipcovers," Olive explained. "And another thing," her mother said, "I hope you don't talk out of windows anymore. A lady never talks out of windows." "What makes you think I talk out of windows, Mother?" "You've been doing it all your life."

Duane had a Baggie full of grass stashed away somewhere in his desk. After hanging up, Olive pawed through the drawers, anxious to find something to calm her nerves: Talking with her mother always upset her, especially when there was an echo in the connection, as there had been tonight. She sometimes wished she didn't love her mother so much. It would make life much easier. "Don't talk out of windows," Olive muttered and then suddenly leaned over and sniffed. Her nose almost touching the bills, old Christmas cards, insurance forms, she caught the elusive scent again. It was familiar, yet, wracking her brain, she still drew a blank. Finally, after uncovering a stack of misprinted checks ("Mr. or Mrs. Duane Macke"), she came across the source:

> Woolite
> croutons
> insoles
> Fantastik
> coasters
> Secret
> nail remover
> dill
> stamps

She was staring at this list—it was unmistakably Carol's handwriting and her perfume, Joy—when Felix walked into the room. "What?" she murmured, her hand reflexively covering the pink list.

"What are you doing?"

"What does it look like I'm doing?" she shot back with adolescent pique.

"If you have to smoke grass, Olive, I'd rather you did it in front of me."

"I'm not smoking anything." She tried to lighten the mood. "I'm sneaking a cup of coffee." Felix's Mormons forbade coffee and tea.

The levity went unappreciated. Felix stood there, pantless, in his gartered black socks and stiff white shirt, with the sad, lost look of a character in an old-time stag film. "You realize you're going to hell, don't you?" he said solemnly.

She squeezed back the tears in her eyes. It was just beginning to dawn on her, what that shopping list must mean. She tried hard not to believe what she knew she must believe while at the same time searching for some way to get rid of Felix without causing a scene. "Baby, listen, Mommie's tired. She go night-night."

"I found it in the middle drawer there, so don't try to pretend. I guess you don't realize what you're doing every time you take a puff. Every puff means you're saying yes to the drug pushers who sell this stuff to children. Every puff means you're casting your vote for child pornography, gun-running, heroin addiction, armed robbery, murder, wife-beating, child abuse." He was perfectly calm while reciting his list. "Enjoy."

"Oh, Felix, don't," she pleaded as he walked off. "Don't be mean to me now. Not now."

Strangely enough, as she lay on the bed smoking a joint—Felix was right; the grass was in the middle drawer—it was not Duane's deceit that hurt so much. Somehow she could cope with this. It was almost as if she had been preparing herself for it, in a half-conscious way, for years. What really hurt, almost more than she could believe, was Carol's betrayal. If it had been anyone but Carol . . .

Rolling herself another joint, she consoled herself with the thought that maybe she was just imagining things. After all, what did a shopping list prove? Why was she so quick to jump to conclusions? Unfortunately she was able to come up with too many answers. Hadn't Duane gone steady with Carol all through high school? Was it so easy for a man to forget his first love like that? And why had Duane been so eager to buy this house only four doors down from the Deshotels?

Still, it was just a shopping list.

But why was it kept, so neatly folded, hidden away in his drawer like that? Why, unless he attached some personal value to it?

Two joints later Olive discovered within herself, beneath

the tears and jealousy and vexation, a strange calm. It was almost as if somehow she had finally gotten what she wanted. But this calm did not last long. With an electronic beep her waterproof watch sounded an alarm—for what? why had she set it?—and she felt herself rising, too fast, toward the choppy surface. She was headed for a case of the bends.

Driving back from Donna Lee's office, Dr. Bates soon found himself adrift in the winding, looping drives of Cherylview Estates. Twice he thought he was on a Place where Olive lived, but it turned out to be a Way—Burgundy Way. And when he thought he had crossed back to a Place, he found he had somehow circled onto Burgundy Way again. When he finally did manage to find Ile de France Place, he pulled up in front of the Tudor house and got out. Strange, he thought, how all the trees in Cherylview were mere saplings; not one full-grown oak or pine. He was halfway across the lawn before he noticed the woman peering out at him from a lighted window, a grim, wrinkled face that gave him a start. Not Olive—could it be? No, her mother maybe. But then he realized this must be the wrong Tudor.

A few minutes later, as he was driving slowly past the right Tudor, the Volks almost, but not quite, came to a stop. Through gauzelike curtains in the living-room window he could see the wavy silhouette of a man bobbing and weaving about, in and out of focus. "Damn," he muttered. Wasn't her husband supposed to be in Baton Rouge tonight? Oh, right, that must be her boy.

In the rearview mirror, as he rounded a curve, he caught a glimpse of turquoise, probably the pool.

Chapter Fourteen

As OLIVE WAS GOING OUT THE DOOR to pick up another batch of campaign posters from the printer, she remembered the envelope Mrs. Woody had put in her purse the night before. Perhaps it would be enough, this contribution, to cover the cost of the posters. That would be nice.

The contribution, however, turned out to be a summons. Olive read it through twice as she stood by the Cadillac, the key in the door. Mrs. Woody had served her with a summons to appear before a grand jury the following week at three-thirty on Wednesday afternoon in Room 312 in the Parish Courthouse in Ozone.

"So he says to me, 'Look, Dr. Bates, I've always admired your work a great deal and the way you get along with your patients. There's not many people who have your finesse' and so on and so forth. And I'm sitting there thinking, well, maybe I could do more good for people, I mean the people who are down and out, if I have the right connections, if I'm someone who, you know . . .'"

"Yes, fine, take the job," Olive said impatiently. "So anyway, like I was saying, I open up my purse and see the envelope, and it turns out to be a *summons*. My heart just— I can't imagine why, what this is all about. I mean, it doesn't seem possible that . . . So I hopped in the car and sped over to Judge Henley's, and he wasn't there, but Mrs. Henley told me she was sure this didn't have anything to do with Uncle L.D. because she would have known."

"Mm. Well, I wouldn't get all worked up about it. What do you think about New Orleans? If I work for Dr. Schexsnyder, I'd have to find a place there. He's not too far from Audubon Park. I could run there, I bet. Anyway, he said . . ."

After dropping by the judge's, Olive had hurried over to Mrs. Undine's. Dr. Bates, though, was turning out to be no help whatsoever. She had wanted a shoulder to cry upon, but he was obviously preoccupied by his own worries. They were sitting in the living room, whose ceiling had just been repainted, rather unsuccessfully, for there was a large grayish patch that looked sort of like South America. Yet this wasn't what disturbed her about the room. Somehow it seemed bare, even though when she looked about, she didn't notice any furniture missing. It was only toward the end of Dr. Bates's rehash of his interview with Dr. Schexsnyder that she noticed what was missing. Pink. Yes, the orangish pink of Kay's dress in the portrait. The pastel above the mantel was gone.

"What? Oh, that," Dr. Bates said when she interrupted him. "Yes, Fern gave it away."

"Why?"

"I don't know—something about Kay not being dead. Anyway, you know how Schexsnyder—"

"Please, Martin, if you'll just give me two seconds, that's all I'm asking for. I need to talk to you. I've just had a terrible shock."

Dr. Bates shifted on the sofa, recrossing his legs. "Yes, well, I really can't tell you anything about that summons."

"That's not it. It's something more important." She reached for the ivory elephant on the coffee table.

"Careful, those tusks come off."

Offended, Olive put the elephant down. "You sound just like Mrs. Undine."

"Well, it *is* valuable," he muttered, his face red.

Allowing a moment for the mutual hostility to settle down, Olive resumed her bid for sympathy. "Look, it's bad enough that I don't have anyone to talk to, that I have to come here when I know it's wrong. And by the way," she added, not looking at him, "I'm not here for anything but . . . I mean, don't get any ideas. I've got too much on my mind for that. So look, to make a long story short, I guess I wouldn't be here if I still had a best friend. But I don't anymore."

Dr. Bates looked at her with the exaggerated interest one applies to the wallet baby pictures of casual acquaintances. "What happened?"

"I found out about Carol and . . . and . . ." The room blurred, and in a childish way her nose began to dribble. She groped for a tissue in her purse but couldn't find one. "She, all this time . . ." The taste of salt, the blur, her constricted throat—she felt as if she were going under.

His face looked stricken. "Oh, no . . . You found out." He closed his eyes and swallowed, like Mrs. Undine at the table. "It was nothing, Olive. You've got to believe me. I swear, I've forgotten all about it."

"You've? What do you mean? Uh, do you have a handkerchief?"

"No." He got up and went to the window and, parting the curtain, peered out. "She was upset about some personal things, and then she starts coming to me for checkups, and it turned out she needed a crown, and all right, so I drove her home once or twice, and we stopped off and big deal— back seat of the car. It was stupid, nothing. And besides, why should you get so upset? We're not exactly, I mean, we're just, you and me . . ."

"Are you telling me that *you* and Carol . . ."

"Well, isn't that what you were . . . Oh." He winced. "Damn."

Still numbed by the shock of the first betrayal, Olive found it difficult to properly respond to a second. Sitting there in the wing chair, she felt like a patient recovering from surgery. The pain lay dimly below the surface, waiting for the anesthesia to wear off.

"You should be grateful to her," Dr. Bates said, pacing in front of the window. "She made a big sacrifice for you.

Duane wanted to run off and marry . . . Well, anyway, it was Carol who called off the whole thing."

"Which whole thing, Martin? Your whole thing or the other whole thing?" All hope was lost now; she had not been mistaken about the shopping list.

"There was never anything between me and her."

She said dully, "All this time you've known about her and my husband and you never said a word to me. I don't understand. I thought we were . . ."

"It was all over by the time I knew Carol. She and Duane were past history. What good would there have been in telling you something that wasn't true anymore? Besides, when I first heard, I didn't even realize he was your husband. It was just a name, didn't mean a thing. And she kept on changing the name, too. She was trying to call him someone else. I didn't know. Didn't care. And anyway—"

The front door opened. Olive gripped the worn padded arms of her chair.

"Oh," Mrs. Undine said, glancing in Olive's direction. "I didn't expect to find you home, Dr. Bates," she added in an attempt to cover her quite evident consternation.

"I told you I didn't have to go to school today."

"Oh, yes, of course. Could you give me a hand, please?" Laden with groceries, a handbag, and the rubber floor mat from her car, she advanced a step or two into the living room. "I simply must clean this," she said, nodding at the floor mat, and as she did so a jar of spaghetti sauce slid out of the A&P bag. All three of them stared at it a moment as it rolled over the shiny woodlike floor. Finally, just as Mrs. Undine was beginning to stoop, Dr. Bates walked over and picked the jar up for her.

"That reminds me," Mrs. Undine said as she handed him the groceries, which he took into the kitchen. "I just saw young Felix, Olive. He was bagging me and said something about the petition—you know, the thing the students are circulating for Dr. Munrow. It's to show their support and— Dr. Bates," she called out in a tremulous voice, "please don't put the groceries away. He's always putting everything where it doesn't belong," she added confidentially to Olive, "and I'm forced to do it over again."

Olive had risen from the wing chair. She wished now that she had made her exit before Mrs. Undine had appeared. The woman's presence was no help to Olive's current mental condition. She felt a total wreck. "Mrs. Undine, I don't want Felix getting mixed up in school politics."

"You don't think it's a good idea to get a colored woman there?"

"Of course, I want one," she said wearily. "But that's beside the point. Felix is having enough problems now. And . . ."

"Fern!" Dr. Bates called out from the other room.

"Now what?" Mrs. Undine said, going into the kitchen. Olive trailed behind.

"What is it, Dr. Bates?"

He was looking terribly stern and attractive, Olive thought. "Look, just look." He pointed to a knob on the stove.

"Well?" Neither Mrs. Undine nor Olive saw anything unusual.

He turned the knob so that there was a gentle hiss. "It was on full blast, Fern. You left the gas on all afternoon without a flame."

"Oh, no, I couldn't have. Dr. Bates, it must have been you."

"Me? I was here."

"Yes, of course, dear."

Gassed to death in Mrs. Undine's living room, Olive mused. That's all she needed. While the two of them tried to pin the blame on each other she mumbled a good-bye. The anesthesia was wearing off; the pain loomed closer.

"Are you leaving, Olive?" Mrs. Undine asked. "Maybe you can give me a lift. I don't want to drive without my floor mat."

"Well, I . . ."

"Oh, never mind, dear. I'll get Dr. Bates to drive me. I'm already late for my appointment and . . . No, you won't, Dr.

Bates? Well, then, it looks as if I'll just have to drive without a floor mat."

"Now, let's see. Mr. Loraine, I think it would be better if we moved you away from the window. This is in color, you see, and you'll look a little too green."

Mrs. Undine obliged the coroner, who was aiming his Betamax at Uncle L.D., and moved the old man's wheelchair a few feet from the unshaded window. Dressed in a three-piece suit, Uncle L.D. had been in the midst of an exercise session when Dr. McFlug had arrived with his video camera. Although Mrs. Undine had seemed a little flustered at first, she agreed to stay until Miss Burma returned from the laundry on South Wesley. Of course, the old man knew he should not say a word to the coroner without Miss Keely being present, but the idea of being on tv was too tempting to pass up. The only other time he had been on tv was when Earl Long had walked past him with a paper bag over his head. Uncle L.D. had been out looking for a sparkplug and had ended up in the background on the six o'clock news.

"This is for court?" Mrs. Undine inquired after she was safely positioned behind the camera.

"No, ma'am. This is just something to prod the D.A. to get a move on. I thought a little audio-visual aid might help him and his staff make up their minds. They've been sitting on this thing for months now, even though I've reversed my suicide verdict. Still no formal charges against Mr. Loraine, can you believe? I won't rest until I have this whole affair properly settled. It's a blot on my good name. Forty-seven years I've held this office without anyone questioning my judgment. I don't like it one bit."

Upright and spindly as a Shaker antique, the old doctor moved stiffly from one side of the room to the other, checking angles through the lens. Uncle L.D. was not sure, but he thought this was probably the same doctor who had pronounced Artis dead. Back then, though, the doctor's hair had been gray. Now it was quite brown, alarmingly brown.

"Mrs. Undine, is my cravat—"

"It's fine, Mr. Loraine. No, don't muss your hair. Doctor, please, before you start, let me fix his hair."

While she combed the old man's fine reddish hair she once again made sure that there would be absolutely no mention of her on this tape. "You promise?"

"Indeed," the coroner said. "Now, first I'm going to take a shot of this window so that . . ." As he advanced on the window with the camera Mrs. Undine, spotting a banana skin in his path, deftly yanked it away.

"Oh, do be careful, Doctor," she advised while he aimed the camera straight down on the sidewalk. "Don't lean out too far."

She then looked around for a garbage pail.

"Please, Mrs. Undine, we must keep still," the coroner said as the foot pedal on the lidded pail creaked.

"You mean this is sound?"

"Indeed."

"Oh, Doctor, you'll have to erase this part. I'm not here, remember?"

"Right. Now, Mr. Loraine, I think I'm ready for you. When I say action, why don't you identify yourself and then give the address and date and time." The camera was raised to the bony shoulder, where it swayed uncertainly for a moment before being steadied. "All right, action!"

Uncle L.D.'s heart pumped violently, his eyes watered. He was going through the same terrible stage fright he used to get before a YWCA speech. They were always such an agony to begin, even with only ten or fifteen girls in the audience. "Good evening, ladies, it's a pleasure to be here tonight, and I'd like to thank each and every one of you for coming. I'm reminded of the time the rooster came into a bar and ordered a—"

"Mr. Loraine, please!" the coroner croaked. Then in a more professional tone he added, "If you don't mind, I'll ask the questions. Just answer as plainly and factually as you can, understand?" Up went the camera again. "This is Dr. Gabriel McFlug, coroner for St. Jude Parish, and I'm in the apartment of Mr. L.D. Loraine, who sits before me. The apartment is located at— Where? Where are we?"

"Six oh two North Tenth Street," Uncle L.D. said.

"Oh, no, no," Mrs. Undine put in. "This is Flat Avenue, isn't it?"

Uncle L.D.'s lips turned grim and bloodless. "I thought you meant where I was born. I was born at six oh two North Tenth Street in the city of—"

"Never mind," the coroner said. "We'll get to that later, sir."

Mrs. Undine waved at Uncle L.D. "Don't touch your hair," she mouthed silently.

"Would you mind telling us exactly what happened on the afternoon of uh . . . the day Mr. Versey passed away?"

"What?"

"The day that your housekeeper, Mr. Ernest Versey was—"

"Are we on?" Uncle L.D. inquired.

"Yes. I'm asking you, sir."

The old man cleared his throat, then spat on the floor. "I recall vividly every detail of that day. You ask me, how is this possible that you, a man nearly three score and ten, can remember every detail like that? I'll be happy to oblige you." He pointed a thick index finger at the ceiling. "The answer is mnemonics. The science of mnemonics."

"Wait a minute, hold on." The camera stopped humming. "I thought you were ninety-one."

"Oh, that's a good one." Uncle L.D. couldn't help chuckling silently to himself. This poor old bird who called himself a doctor could use a memory lesson or two himself. Imagine, thinking he was ninety-one years old! Why, he hoped to be six feet under long before he became that old and decrepit. Ninety-one!

"Now, if I may continue," Uncle L.D. said, looking hard at the camera. "So I say, folks, if it's possible for me—and I don't count myself to be in the least bit above average in talent, though perhaps in looks . . ." He smiled wryly. "If it's possible for someone like me . . . All it takes is five minutes a day, five minutes that I positively and absolutely guarantee will change your entire life. Tell me, ma'am, you over there, what is your current salary?"

Mrs. Undine pretended not to see the finger pointed at her while Dr. McFlug put the camera down on the dresser. "Water, please," he said, mopping his brow with a pressed handkerchief.

"What?"

"A glass of water, please, ma'am."

With a distracted look she went to the sink. When she returned with a glass, she asked him how dangerous a houseful of gas was.

"Pardon me?" he said after gulping the water.

"I'm having trouble with a boarder. He's always forgetting to turn things off, and this afternoon he left the gas on and . . . Yes, dear?"

Uncle L.D. had wheeled himself over. "What's the matter? Why aren't you filming me?"

"Mr. Loraine," she said patiently, "you must remember, this is for a judge."

Dr. McFlug looked dubiously at his Betamax. "I don't believe Judge Henley's going to see this, Mrs. Undine. He's under investigation, you know. It's part of what's holding up this whole case."

"Oh, my."

"The assistant D.A., a gal called Markett, I believe—Sarah Markett. She's got everyone in a swivet. Went right to the attorney general, she did, and now he's going to bring a case before the grand jury to look into Judge Henley's ethics. The lady lawyers around here don't take too kindly to Henley, it seems. Even Miss Keely, she's in on this, too."

Mrs. Undine's hand went to her throat. "Really, I can't approve of this."

"Obstructionist if I ever saw one. No wonder we can't get anywhere on this Versey business. Miss Markett and Miss Keely are after the judge for ethical misconduct or something, making a big stink. The mayor smelled blood, and now it looks like he's in on the kill with them. Of course, he never did like Henley, always had it in for him." He flicked the camera with his thumb, then shook it. "That's why it's important to get this confession on tape as soon as possible. Make it neat and clean, no mess."

"What confession?" Uncle L.D. asked, wheeling an inch closer.

"Why, sir." The coroner turned and regarded him curiously. "What you've been saying all along, the fact that you killed Mr. Versey."

"I never . . . What in blazes! *Me* kill someone? Why, I happen to be one of the most highly respected citizens . . ." Suddenly the blood drained from his choked red face. "Oh, yes, that's right. I did."

The coroner and Mrs. Undine regarded each other a moment. "He does this from time to time," Dr. McFlug commented. "Forgets. Then it all comes back to him. I must say, it is unnerving. That's why it's of such prime importance, ma'am, for us to get this down on tape today before he forgets everything for good."

"I've never forgotten a thing in my life." With a jerk the old man wheeled himself backwards. "I can tell you exactly what I had for breakfast on the day of my majority. And you, sir, can you tell me what you had for breakfast TODAY?" His hand came down with a whack on the arm of the wheelchair.

"I had an Egg McMuffin," Mrs. Undine said.

"I'm not asking *you.*"

"Oh."

"All right, Mr. Loraine," the coroner said, taking aim once again, "let's take it from the top."

When Mrs. Undine returned from her appointment, she found Dr. Bates stretched out on the living-room couch, a chintz cushion covering his face. Having devoted a good half hour to feeling guilty about Carol, he was now mulling over the gas incident. Was it possible that Mrs. Undine harbored a violent antipathy toward him—subconsciously? Was she a latent anti-Semite? What other explanation could there be? She was such a careful woman, always turning things off. Her true self must have spoken through the "mistake" of leaving the gas on. Despite a thin veneer of so-called tolerance, she was, after all, the product of generation after generation of racism and repression.

"I was thinking we might have veal marengo tonight," she said as he strolled idly out to the back yard, where she was picking up sodden pine cones. Quite warm for February, the late afternoon had an unsettling, summerish feel that was aided and abetted by the boisterous chirruping of vigorous insects.

"Why veal marengo?"

"I don't know. Does there have to be a reason? Dr. Bates, when you mow, I hope you check the ground first. These pine cones can be terrifically dangerous. They might lodge in your eye."

He went back inside and read a few pages from *Middlemarch* on the toilet. He was determined to get through the book before he started working for Dr. Schexsnyder in the summer. After flushing he decided he had better take out the extended wear contact lenses he had worn for eight days straight. Cleaning them was a depressing, complicated chore that he would put off for as long as possible. When the delicate lenses were safely in the solution, he went back outside. Mrs. Undine was over by the azaleas talking with Mrs. Keely.

"I was just asking her about that poor judge," Mrs. Undine said after Mrs. Keely, with a little wave for him, returned to her house. "It looks like Donna Lee is mad at him."

"What judge?"

"I forget his name. He's mixed up with Mr. Loraine somehow. Oh, Dr. Bates, you'll never imagine what I went through this afternoon. The coroner was over at the apartment trying to film Mr. Loraine's confession, and I'm not sure, but I think my voice got on the tape. I asked the doctor to erase it, but I can't trust him. Oh, my back. Help me up."

She had been leaning over to pick up a strip of rubber that looked like a dead snake. Dr. Bates gave her a hand, and she straightened up.

"You know, I think this *is* a snake," he said, squatting down to examine the dubious black strip from a respectful distance.

"Snake? Dear, it's just some old hose the children next door . . . They're always trailing things into my yard."

"No, look here, Fern, doesn't that look like . . ."

Mrs. Undine lifted the half glasses that were hanging by a silver chain from her neck and peered. "I'm sorry, Dr. Bates. That is a piece of hose that I haven't time to discuss. I've got to make supper."

Later that evening, while he was eating a Pizza-burger, he asked her what had happened to the veal marengo. She told him she couldn't find the recipe in her card file. Someone must have taken it.

"Why do you ask that woman over?" she asked after the generator from the Keely's central air-conditioning unit whirred on. It made Dr. Bates feel as if something large were about to take off.

"I've never asked her. She just comes."

"You know it doesn't look good, her popping over here all the time. People are beginning to talk."

Dr. Bates turned red. He thought he had been so discreet.

"Mrs. Keely said she saw you two walking round out back in the woods the other day."

"What? I never . . . Oh, you mean Olive and me."

"Why, of course. Just whom did you think I meant, Dr. Bates?" She raised the half glasses and peered curiously at him, as if he were a strip of rubber. "Are you feeling all right, dear? You've been behaving so peculiarly these past few weeks."

"I'm under a lot of strain, Fern. School is really killing me. I've got so much to memorize, and Dr. Schexsnyder is watching me like a hawk."

"I see. And is that why you've taken to scribbling on your hands?" She regarded the blurred crib on his palms.

He removed his free hand from the table. "O.K., so I'm human. And besides, I *tried* to wash it off."

"Well, I'm relieved to hear there's *some* explanation." She closed her eyes and swallowed. "I wasn't going to bring it up, but I must admit you were beginning to worry me. Especially after you left that gas on. Quite frankly, I was tempted to consult Dr. McFlug this afternoon. I thought you might be having a nervous breakdown, what with writing all over yourself and seeing snakes and all."

The Pizza-burger caught in his throat. After a brief coughing spell and a swig of water he said, "Fern, I didn't have my contacts in. And furthermore, it wasn't me who left the gas on. As a matter of fact, I'm glad you brought it up. I've been doing some thinking lately. I don't think you're agoraphobic after all."

"Indeed?"

"I think that deep down, you want to—" He broke off abruptly. It had occurred to him that if he said what he really thought about her latent homicidal tendencies, it would only confirm her own opinion about his precarious mental state.

"I want to what?"

"Nothing."

"Dr. Bates, please don't leave me hanging. I want to know what's wrong with me."

"Let's drop it, O.K.?"

"Well, if you insist."

At eleven o'clock that evening Mrs. Undine rapped lightly at his door and brought in a tray of cookies and warm milk. They talked for a few moments about Mrs. Keely. "I do think she likes you," Mrs. Undine said. Unbidden, she perched on the edge of his bed, where he was memorizing various antiemetics for a pharmacology exam. "She says you're about the most handsome man she's ever met."

Dr. Bates made a wry face to cover his pleasure.

"Please, though, do be more careful about appearances. I know you're not doing anything wrong, Dr. Bates, but people down here are very conscious of what is and is not done. You mustn't give Mrs. Keely any food for thought."

"Look, I'm not interested in *Mrs.* Keely."

"That's where you're wrong, Doctor. The way to a girl's heart is through her mother—and don't you forget it. Good night, Dr. Bates. Sleep tight."

But it was a restless sleep he endured that night. There was something unsettling about an ex-mother-in-law playing matchmaker. Shouldn't she at least make some effort, however vain, to get him back together with her daughter? Somehow she wasn't playing her part right.

Twice during the night he got up and went into the kitchen to make sure the stove was off.

Chapter Fifteen

SINCE THERE WAS NO MIDAS MUFFLER in Tula Springs, Olive figured the sensible thing to do was drive to Ozone. She had had so much trouble with the service at the Cadillac dealer, first with a knocking under the hood, then with a clicking noise in the dashboard, that she had little faith in their ability to properly install a muffler. While she was waiting for the Midas men to finish the job she peered up at the windows of the dental college across the street and found the dimity curtains. But because of the daylight reflection it was impossible to see inside. Her feelings for Dr. Bates were still in turmoil, but overall, she would have had to say that she probably hated him. What she had loved in him, she realized now, had not been his good looks or personality. Rather, it had been his goodness, the wonderful caring quality that was so rare in most men. But finding out that he was as callous and disloyal as all the others, she couldn't help thinking of him as being lower than a worm. Had he no idea what she had given up for him when she had permitted him to make love to her? She was a virgin as far as adultery was concerned. It had been a very tender, precious event in her life, one that he had permanently soiled by going off with Carol.

"Is that you?"

Looking over her shoulder, Olive saw Mrs. Henley coming out of the Dunkin' Donuts next door to the muffler shop.

"Oh, I'm so sorry—it's not," Mrs. Henley said, squinting at the dark glasses Olive was wearing.

"Mrs. Henley, it's me, Olive Mackie."

"Well, I thought you were Regina Lawson. I was wondering what in heaven's name you were doing in Ozone. She lives in Jackson, Mississippi, you know, a marvelous girl. Her aunt and I used to be the greatest friends, and then she had some complications from a nose operation, and the next thing you know, she was dead." She shifted the pink-striped bag of crullers from one arm to the other. With her close-set, slightly protruding eyes and her head cocked to one side Mrs. Henley called to mind a charming lemur peering from behind the bars of a depressing cage. Overcome by a rush of pity and affection, Olive took the woman's gentle hand and said, "I'm so sorry for everything, Mrs. Henley."

"Tut, Olive, Wilma passed away ten years ago."

"No, I mean about the judge. I wish there was something I could do."

"Oh, honey, he's going to be fine. As a matter of fact, I'm just on my way over to the courthouse to cheer him up." She smiled at the bag. "You know, the NRA offered to pay all his legal expenses, but the judge wouldn't hear of it. I sometimes wish he wasn't so stubborn, but I guess boys will be boys."

"You wouldn't believe what I went through on Wednesday," Olive confided, referring to her recent appearance before the grand jury that was investigating Judge Henley's ethics. "Somehow they had found out I had been to your house that day—remember when I stopped over to say hello? And they tried to get me to say that I had bribed the judge so he'd go to the D.A. and get him to forget about my uncle. It was a nightmare, just awful." Worst of all had been the cruel question posed by her old admirer, the once fat, ungainly Sarah Woody Markett. Transformed into an assistant district attorney, she was tan and fit, with no memory, it seemed, of having once treated Olive like a goddess. Not that Olive had any chance to remind the girl. Sarah was coldly professional and didn't leave any opportunity for Olive to talk to her either before or after being sworn in.

"You should have heard me, Mrs. Henley. I said to them, 'Yeah, sure I bribed him. I told the judge if he fixed things, I'd give him the five bucks I have in my checking account, and for good measure I'd throw in the lawnmower that's on the fritz.' The nerve of those idiots. I was so mad I could barely breathe. By the way, how do things look for Uncle L.D.?"

Mrs. Henley peered over her shoulder before replying. "To tell you the truth, dear, he's not been thinking about your uncle much, what with all this ethical business. The mayor and his friend the D.A. are out to get him this time."

"The D.A.? I thought he was a good friend of the judge's?"

"Lord, child, whatever gave you that idea?"

"The mayor, that's what," Olive said grimly, filing this bit of information away. His Honor would pay for this double-dealing someday.

"Well, in any case," Mrs. Henley went on, "the D.A.'s not really pressing this murder business very hard. Seems that it's the coroner who's stirring up all the trouble." She patted her tightly permed gray hair. "Anyway, the judge has never had a case where someone *wanted* to be a murderer, especially such a nice old man. Even if it is justifiable homicide, it's going to be a mare's-nest if there ever is a trial. People are going to be so upset if they see a poor old man on trial like that. Yet neither the D.A. nor the judge can really believe in the suicide theory, either. The coroner's pretty well convinced the D.A. that it couldn't be suicide. And what with the old man himself confessing . . . I heard just the other day from Bill—he works for the D.A. He told me they got a videotape of the old man's confession."

"Lord."

"Yes, the coroner taped it himself. They're pretty sure it's not admissible, but still . . ."

Olive and Mrs. Henley had been walking arm in arm toward the Dunkin' Donut corner. When they got to the stop sign, they turned and started back the other way. "I can't understand why that darn coroner can't just leave him alone," Olive commented.

"It's not just him. It's your uncle's lawyer as well. She's a friend of Mrs. Markett's, and they're spurring each other on."

"You'd think a lawyer wouldn't try so hard to get her client accused of murder. Oh, excuse me." Mrs. Henley and Olive were having trouble walking in rhythm; Olive had just accidentally pulled on Mrs. Henley's frail arm.

"That's another thing that worries the judge. He thinks something crooked is going on with this Miss Keely. She's a radical, you know. When she was in college, the judge found out, she used to picket all the time. She was given a summons at a sit-down, and now she goes to all the Sierra Club meetings. And, of course, I don't have to tell you about the Sierra Club."

Actually Olive thought it was quite foolish of the judge to let himself be sidetracked by the Sierra Club, a perfectly respectable organization. But she let Mrs. Henley have her say. It just wouldn't be worth it to try to explain about Mrs. Undine. She, of course, was the one spurring everyone on because she didn't want Olive to win the election.

"You know the Sierra Club is trying to make things difficult for the poor Army Corps of Engineers in the Atchafalaya basin," Mrs. Henley said. "They're squawking about the birds and the fish and aren't giving the least little thought to human beings. I simply can't fathom such selfishness. Can you, Olive?"

"Miz Mackie! Yo!"

One of the muffler specialists had emerged from the shed and was motioning to her. Giving Mrs. Henley a squeeze on the arm, Olive told her she had better go now and see what they wanted. "You know, you really do look like Regina. I can't get over it," Mrs. Henley said as she headed off for the courthouse.

"Yeah, right, so here's . . ." The man, a boy really, pointed with a grimy finger at something on his clipboard.

"What?"

Wiry, with a pock-marked face, he looked everywhere but at her. "Exhaust needs . . . I'd really see, like I said before, huh?"

"Well, I don't think there's anything wrong with the exhaust. It's the muffler that's making the noise."

"Naw, it's like there's this—can't, you got a, see . . ."

If there was anything Olive hated to talk about, it was her car. And yet so many hours of her life seemed to be spent discussing the inner workings of the Cadillac. And the emotion that was involved: She was often reduced to tears of fury and despair, knowing she was being had but unable to get her point across to the obtuse, patronizing mechanics. Invariably the discussions would spiral upwards, becoming more technical and abstract the more she protested, until they all seemed to wind up in a realm of vehicular metaphysics, where she was defeated. This afternoon was no exception. Soon she found herself trying to defend cause and effect against the boy's Alice in Wonderland logic. An uncanny feeling crept over her, as if she were in a bad dream. As a matter of fact, there was a good reason for this feeling. Only a few days ago she had dreamed about arguing through a dimity curtain with the legendary king, who was trying to sell her a gold-inlay shock absorber. This Midas certainly didn't look like a king. He was scrawny and pimply and, Olive would remember later that afternoon, when she was in the middle of a speech to the Tula Springs Garden Club, quite dirty.

". . . then my mother, whom most of you remember, she became something of a specialist on the question of interference. Now, for instance, the topmost leaves of a ficus grow straight out, parallel to the earth. They would completely overshadow the ones below, as far as getting light is concerned, but those little leaves at the bottom have a trick. They bend down, more like vertical, and that's how they get their share of the light." Here she paused, and in an instant the dream of the muffler shop was recalled. When she started to speak again, she realized that she had forgotten what she was talking about. Something to do with ficus. . . . "So anyway, that's the way that goes. Now, are there any questions?"

"I heard that if you're elected, you're going to open a firing range in Ferguson Park. Is that true?" a somewhat stern, middle-aged woman in red asked. She was seated next to Nesta Versey, Mr. Versey's sister, and they seemed to be on good terms.

"I don't think it would be possible to open a firing range there," Olive replied. Usually the garden club met at one of the member's homes. This month, however, because of a special exhibition of shrubs that required more space than a living room, they were meeting in the VFW Hall. Some of the VFW men, leftovers from a previous meeting, were moping about in the back of the room. Aware of their presence, Olive tiptoed around the subject of firearms.

Nesta Versey held up her hand. Wondering if Nesta realized who she was, Olive attempted a pleasant smile. It had been a little disconcerting to see this bland oval face peering at her during the speech with myopic intensity.

"Yes?"

"Would you recommend planting ficus next to kumquats?" Nesta asked. Neither fat nor thin, short nor tall, attractive nor unattractive, Nesta was one of the extras who floated about in the background, giving a semblance of life to supermarket scenes, taking up a place in a post office line, buying a trinket at a distant counter. For someone like this to make one's heart pound was perhaps a little ludicrous, but Olive couldn't help it.

"Sure, why not? I think that would be a very nice idea. Just make sure that the kumquat doesn't overshadow the ficus."

After a few other questions Olive received a polite hand and was invited to pour. A photographer from the *Herald* took Olive's picture as she tilted a silver coffeepot into a cup held by a guest of one of the members, Mrs. Louis Coco. After exchanging a cordial word or two with Mrs. Coco, Olive was escorted around the hall by the president of the garden club, Mrs. Hal Bingham. Mrs. Bingham had been a friend of Olive's great-aunt Artis and was also Olive's mother's godmother. "I hear that a certain Mr. Dambar has made a generous contribution to someone's campaign," the old lady said softly, in between introductions to various members.

"He has," Olive said, recalling the thrill she had gotten the week before when she had opened the mail and found a five-hundred-dollar check. She had not given up on Mr. Dambar after the Robin Downs auction but had finally managed to track him down at the Steamboat Lounge of the Ramada Inn in Ozone. There, over a couple drinks, she had learned that he was indeed angry at Vondra. It wasn't about any zoning law, though. Rather, their quarrel was over the new organ at the Baptist church. Vondra was trying to cut corners with an $85,000 organ from a second-rate manufacturer, while Mr. Dambar was insisting on the best, a $110,000 organ from Germany. Two people had already resigned from the congregation over this issue and become Methodists.

"I would be very careful if I were you," Mrs. Bingham said. Though in her late eighties, she still gardened and drove and looked none the worse for wear than a sixty-five-year-old. "Vondra is steamed. She's out to get you, Olive. I heard that she said some very disparaging things about you to the Knights of Columbus."

"So she's already started her mudslinging. Well, that's too bad. I plan to run a clean, issue-oriented campaign myself. Hello, Mrs. Rawlins."

Carol's mother had emerged from behind a huge potted rhododendron with a cup of coffee in each hand. "What happened to Mabel? She asks me to bring her some coffee, and then she disappears. Olive, dear, that was a very nice speech. We're all so proud of you."

A tense "Thank you" was the best Olive could manage. She knew that Mrs. Rawlins, a hearty, florid, athletic woman, was not responsible for her daughter's conduct, but even so, there was only so much Olive could be expected to endure. When Olive had confronted Carol herself with her treachery and disloyalty, Carol had gone into hysterics, denying everything. The next day, though, Carol had been in a cold fury. She couldn't believe how ungrateful Olive was after all that she had done for her, sacrificing her last chance of happiness on earth by giving up Duane for good. Didn't Olive realize that Duane had been ready to leave her and go off with Carol? If it hadn't been for her, Olive would have found herself alone in the world, without a cent to her name. But no, this was the thanks she got.

"And as if that's not enough," Carol had gone on, following Olive around her kitchen, which she was trying to mop, "not only do you have to ruin things between me and Duane, but then, O.K., you have the gall to come between me and Marty. I know about you two. Don't try to deny it. Marty told me everything."

Stunned though she was by Dr. Bates's betrayal of their secret, Olive managed to take the offensive. "Listen, girl, I was in love with him first. Besides, he could care less about you. He told me so himself."

"Is that right? Well, you ought to hear what he says about *you*."

Olive braced herself, tightening her grip on the self-squeeze mop.

"Marty told me he thinks you might be a dyke."

"You're lying."

"I am not. He thinks you're a latent dyke."

"You two fags should know," Olive had said—or something equally inane. For days afterwards she had chided herself for not coming up with a more devastating reply. But she was so wounded by what Dr. Bates had said—or at least by what Carol had said he had said—that she could barely get up off her méridienne. It had taken a supreme effort of the will to rally her forces and get her muffler fixed, much less appear at the garden club. She did this by forgetting with all her might everything Carol had said. If she brooded upon it or, worse, tried to discuss it with Dr. Bates, she knew she would make herself unfit for any sort of campaign work.

Mrs. Bingham patted Olive's hand. "Doesn't she look nice?"

"She always looks nice," Mrs. Rawlins said. "Oh, there's Mabel. And now the coffee's cold."

"What?" Olive said, feeling Mrs. Bingham tug on her arm.

"I want you to meet Dewey Fitt. See him over there? He's a Republican. I was thinking, if you lose the primaries next month, you might want to run as a Republican. Come along."

"But I'm a registered Democrat," she protested as the old woman piloted her around a clump of forsythia to a wiry gentleman in a VFW uniform. He was talking in clipped, abrupt tones, using plenty of hand gestures, to the woman in red who had asked Olive about the firing range.

"Now, when I first moved here," Mr. Fitt said after being introduced to Olive, "people would laugh if you said you were a Republican. There weren't one in a hundred in all Louisiana."

"My uncle's always been a Republican," Olive put in, wishing instantly that she hadn't.

Up close the red dress the woman was wearing looked much more expensive and cranberry than it had at a distance. Olive was trying to figure out what the material could be when Nesta Versey appeared at the woman's side.

"You've met Nesta Versey, haven't you, Velmarae?" the woman in red said to Mrs. Bingham. "And this is Dewey Flitt, Nesta."

"Fitt."

"And I believe you know the guest of honor."

Olive nodded. "Oh, sure, me and Miss Versey go way back. She used to teach me chemistry at Tula Springs High. It was one of my favorite courses." She was hoping that this slender association might dim their more glaring relationship.

"When was that?" Nesta asked.

Olive could read nothing into her voice or look; she was as neutral as a valence chart. "Let's see, I graduated in the late sixties. My name was Barnell, Olive Barnell."

"Barnell . . . I don't seem to recall any Barnells. There was a Barnes, though, a very bright young thing. She became a doctor. Myra," she said, looking at the woman in red, "I've got to get home."

"Well, run along then. I think I'll stay a bit. Now, remember, Nesta, we're going to the mall tomorrow."

Feeling a little piqued that she had made no impression as a student, Olive nonetheless breathed easier as the teacher made her way to the door. Myra—or Mrs. Wedge, as Mrs. Bingham had introduced her earlier—hardly waited for Nesta to get out of earshot before she began talking about her. "I'm so worried about her," she confided to Mrs. Bingham while Mr. Fitt, with a stiff nod, broke away from the group. "Nesta's yard is a mess. I tried to prune for her and do a little weeding in her begonias, but then she just let it all go." Olive recognized the Brooklyn-like tones of a New Orleans accent. Mrs. Wedge must be a native New Orleanian. "She just hasn't been the same since Ernest was moidered. Poor Nesta spends all her time in her room watching those tv preachers. You don't know what I had to go through to get her out today. She's really afraid not to have a preacher around."

Mrs. Wedge was very purposefully not looking at Olive, making her feel a little like a criminal herself. Wanting to flee, yet somehow paralyzed by this irrational guilt, Olive was finally rescued by Mrs. Bingham. "Why is it mine always fog up?" Mrs. Bingham exclaimed, plucking off her extra-large Dior glasses. "No matter where I am, these things always fog up. Olive, dear, you better run along, hadn't you? I imagine Felix is beginning to wonder about his supper."

"Oh, right, I better go," Olive said meekly as she turned and drifted toward the Exit sign Nesta had passed under only a few moments before.

The fullness was too much. Perhaps if he were able to see more clearly, it would not be so overwhelming. But in the impressionistic haze afforded by his one good eye, the waves of green broke atop one another not just to the horizon but somehow beyond any imaginable curve of the earth. Pale clusters of jessamine and wisteria drifted by on contrary currents and faded with the dizzy hum that follows an ear-splitting blast. Almost as if he expected an explosion, the old man gripped the sides of the chaise longue, his pulse skimming lightly over the regular beat. Yet he did not complain, fearful that they might take him back to the apartment and leave him alone.

"You sure you wouldn't like some iced tea?" Mrs. Undine asked, waving a yellow jacket away from his lap.

Trying to sound as normal as possible, he said, "How about a smidgin of port?" The two young people, purplish shadows in the distance, would have disapproved, but he thought he might be able to wheedle some out of Mrs. Undine while they were taking their walk.

A few moments later she returned from the kitchen and, with a guilty look, handed him a jelly glass. "Here. It's a little cream sherry. I don't have any port, Mr. Loraine."

He was about to refuse it when he noticed the ice cube floating in the sherry. "This will do. I thank you, young lady."

If only he could think of a way to get them all inside Mrs. Undine's house. There, in her drawing room, he would be able to collect his thoughts and entertain them with feats of memory. But sitting in the back yard like this, he felt blurred around the edges. He was not himself.

"I said, are you having a nice time, Mr. Loraine?"

"What? Yes, yes, fine, very nice."

The purple shadows had risen into the trees. No, that couldn't have been them, the two young people. He would like to meet the young woman who had come to chat with Dr. Bates. From a distance she had seemed fresh and attractive. His eyes teared as he squinted at the yard, trying to see where they had gone. But they were camouflaged by the swaying seaweed green of shadow and leaf. Yes, he was always open to meeting a new face. That was the secret of staying young.

"See over there, Mr. Loraine, by that tulip tree? There's a hole there, a sinkhole that worries me to death. And no one's able to tell me a thing about it. I've had all sorts of experts poking around, lawyers, geologists, field service agents—and what have I learned? Nothing. All my money is going into that hole, thirty-nine dollars a load for sand, fifty for the lawyer, twenty-seven for the geologist. I might as well just take every penny I got and dump it into that hole."

Again the old man gripped the edge of the cushioned

chaise longue. He did not like the idea that he was not on solid ground.

" . . . feel as if I'm going in all sorts of directions at once —pulled this way and that," Mrs. Undine went on, oblivious to his distress. He needed to regain his balance, and this took concentration. But how could he concentrate with her nattering away like this? On and on she went about her crabgrass, Dr. Bates's appetite, her unruly fifth-period class while beneath her the flimsy deck of earth seemed to shudder.

He gulped what was left of the sherry and, as was his custom, ate the ice.

A sudden click, a loud whir caused Olive to pause. Dr. Bates looked over at the offending central air-conditioning unit in the neighbor's yard. "Fern claims she doesn't hear it," he said, glancing in Mrs. Undine's direction. She was sitting across the lawn next to the old man, whom they were baby-sitting for Donna Lee. Miss Burma, his home attendant, had taken the day off to drive to the zoo in Baton Rouge with Donna Lee's receptionist, Mr. Pickens. Not able to stand the idea of being cooped up in the old man's apartment on such a nice day, Dr. Bates had transported him to Mrs. Undine's back yard. Donna Lee had promised to fetch him when she was through defending a woman in Ozone for assault and battery against a sexist bartender.

"Can't we go somewhere?" Olive said urgently. "I've got to talk to you."

"Listen, I told you, I'm supposed to watch him."

"Let her."

"She's going somewhere soon. I promised Donna Lee."

Olive's jaw muscle bulged. "What are you promising *her* things for? Now, look, Martin, I can't talk in front of Mrs. Undine, much less my uncle. Come on, let's get out of here."

"You shouldn't have come over, you know."

Mrs. Undine had stood up and was waving at them.

"I better see what she wants," he said, heading toward her. Olive followed at a distance.

"Why don't you young people come sit with us," Mrs.

Undine said when they approached. "We're beginning to feel left out. Olive, you look dressed to the nines."

"I was the guest speaker at the garden club." Shading her eyes, she added, "Hello, Uncle L.D."

"What? Oh, it's you." He turned his head away.

"I used to belong to the garden club," Mrs. Undine said. "But then I found out I just didn't have the time. One can't do everything." She moved the biology text in her lap so that it would be in the shade of the lawn umbrella.

Olive turned to Dr. Bates and whispered in his ear, "If you don't come with me right this minute, I'll scream."

Seeing the look in her eyes, he started toward the house.

"Where are you going?" Mrs. Undine asked. "You know I have to leave in a few minutes."

"I'll be right back, Fern."

They did not get farther than the kitchen before they were in the midst of a bitter argument. Dr. Bates told Olive she was insane to come marching over to his house like this. He wasn't thinking of himself, but of her. What chance would she have in the election if people began to think things about her? And people were beginning to talk; he knew. While he was trying to get this over she was inserting bitter remarks about Carol, a subject he had hoped was dead and buried. "I don't know where you get off telling her I'm abnormal." "What did you have to go and talk about me for, anyway? What happened between us was something sacred. Then you got to drag it through the mud by talking to Carol." "You think if I were a pervert, I'd risk everything I value in life to be with you? Are you nuts or something?"

Progressing to the living room, they found their anger dampened by misery. From misery to pity was not such a big step, and it was only a short hop from there to sex.

"Why are we doing this?" Olive asked as she unfastened his belt. "Let's not, please. What if Mrs. Undine . . . Oh, Martin."

The complications of the false buttons on her dress made the matter seem more urgent to him. "Darling, don't . . ."

"Huh?"

"Don't talk, please."
"But I think we should discuss this."
"Oh, darling."
"Martin."
"You smell so nice."
"Oh."
"Oh."
"I think I love you."
"Oh."

PART FOUR

Chapter Sixteen

OLIVE STILL COULDN'T HELP THINKING of it as Vondra's office, at least for the first week or two. There was something unreal, almost spooky, about its being hers now. Her friends told her not to worry. Before long the oak desk, the swivel chair, the dictaphone would be second nature to her. Yet for a good while the new responsibilities seemed so great, she felt so unworthy, that she almost wished she hadn't won the election. Of course, part of this feeling was perfectly understandable, seeing as how Vondra had trounced Olive in the primaries. Were it not for certain irregularities that Olive had discovered in Vondra's filing for candidacy, Olive would not have found herself on the Democratic ticket in the May election. Yes, Mayor Binwanger might have scoffed at Olive's report on these irregularities, claiming they were just nit-picking. (Vondra, according to Olive, had filed eleven days late. There was no signature on page iiiA. She misrepresented her income by $1537—an adding mistake, Vondra claimed. Mrs. DeLisle signed and stamped page 3 for her boss, the election commissioner. Vondra misrepresented her birthday—1931 not 1936. Campaign contributions from Stukkie's Ambulance Service and Ulmer Foods were not acknowledged.) But after Olive had taken the mayor aside and expressed her deep personal concern about the environment and toxic wastes, it became clear to him that, legally speaking, Vondra was not a valid candidate. And so, in a close race against the Republicans, Olive shaved past with a two-per-cent margin and was duly installed as Superintendent of Streets, Parks, and Garbage.

Her first week was spent interviewing secretaries. She was looking for someone bright and competent, but not too bright, too competent. Finding someone in between was extraordinarily difficult. Toward the end of the week she detected a slight edge on the voice of the normally obsequious man at the employment agency. If only Mrs. Sanchez were available—that was what she needed, a Mrs. Sanchez. Finally, in her second week of interviewing, she found just what she was looking for, a bland, conscientious, middle-aged man who had been a receptionist-typist at the law firm of Herbert and Herbert for the past fourteen months. He told Olive that he had become disillusioned with his job there.

"Why?" she inquired.

Somewhat overweight, but not unpleasant-looking, the man seemed reluctant to talk at first. After some prodding and many assurances of complete confidentiality he relented. "It's Miss Keely, my boss. She's beginning to get on my nerves. Always, like, 'Why didn't you do this?' 'Why didn't you do that?' You know. And I try to explain, Mr. Herbert is giving me things to do, too. He's really her boss, not mine, except that half the time I have to answer the phone and take messages for him. Then Miss Keely tells me not to, that I'm supposed to do her work first before I do anyone else's. I just can't take it any longer."

"Will she be surprised if you leave, Mr. Pickens? I mean, have you told her you were unhappy?"

"Not really. She says all the time she can't do without me. There'd be a big to-do if I left. We're in the middle of all this work now, and she's given me about a million pages to type."

Olive did not need to hear any more. She hired him on the spot with a promise of a raise in six months.

Although hiring Mr. Pickens away from Ms. Keely gave her some satisfaction, it was not enough to offset Olive's general displeasure with this woman. When Ms. Keely and her cronies had failed to oust Judge Henley from office, Olive's delight had been short-lived. For not long afterwards

Olive had come upon Ms. Keely and Dr. Bates eating at Isola Bella, and twice she had seen them driving together in Ms. Keely's Volvo on the Old Jeff Davis Highway. When she had asked Dr. Bates what all this was supposed to mean, he was evasive and muttered something about Donna Lee already having a boyfriend. If she did, then why couldn't she leave Dr. Bates alone? The only answer Olive could come up with was that Ms. Keely was out to hurt her, Olive, any way she could. She was probably jealous of Olive's winning the election. When Dr. Bates pointed out that Donna Lee didn't even know there was anything between Olive and him, Olive shrugged it off. Somehow the woman must know.

"As a matter of fact," Dr. Bates had said during this same discussion, "just what *is* there between us? I don't understand how you can keep on being jealous of me when we don't see each other anymore."

Dr. Bates was, in general, speaking the truth. They had both decided it would not be such a great idea to start having a real honest-to-goodness affair. Yet they had experienced one or two aberrations similar to the one earlier that spring, when Mrs. Undine, coming inside for a glass of Kool-Aid, had nearly caught Dr. Bates with his pants down on the couch. Olive was making a sincere effort to patch things up with Duane. This was hampered, though, by her being unable to let him know how furious she was about Carol. If Olive ever did give Duane the good blasting he deserved, Carol, fearing that he would then of necessity learn about herself and Dr. Bates, threatened to tell Duane all she knew about Dr. Bates and Olive. Of course, Duane would murder Olive if he found out about this. Despite his video games, his home computer, Duane was basically antediluvian and still subscribed to both the *Reader's Digest* and the double standard.

Speaking of murder, Olive was still wondering what was going to become of Uncle L.D. When Nesta Versey had heard of the move afoot to have her brother's body disinterred, she had threatened the coroner with a lawsuit if he touched a single flower on his grave. Her religious scruples forbade tampering with the dead. The D.A. would have let the case rest at that point had not Nesta, at the same time, insisted in a vehement letter to the *Baton Rouge Advocate* that justice be carried out. Her brother's soul would not rest until his murder was avenged.

"If you ask me, somehow it just doesn't sound like her, those words she used," Olive commented to Mrs. Sanchez in Dead Records. They were in the middle of a coffee break, a practice Olive insisted on continuing, not just to show Mrs. Sanchez that she wasn't a snob but also for very practical reasons. Mrs. Sanchez knew what was what at City Hall, from the mayor's office on down, and Olive had come to find her advice indispensable. Besides, in a way Olive owed her job to Mrs. Sanchez. How else would she have found out about the mayor's cozy arrangement with the Citizens Patrol were it not for an indiscreet word or two from Mrs. Sanchez last summer? It was this which had put Olive on the trail.

Mrs. Sanchez took a delicate bite from a Danish butter cookie. "You mean in the *Advocate*? That letter she wrote?"

"Yes. I saw her just before the election at a garden club meeting, and she seemed nice enough. I mean, she had her chance then to let me have it right between the eyes, but she wasn't mean at all. Then in that letter she was out for blood, couldn't wait to see the whole lot of us hang. She thinks there's a conspiracy or something because the D.A. still hasn't done anything."

Mrs. Sanchez washed down a Nite Diet pill with a sip of coffee. She had lost sixteen pounds in the last month by taking these pills both day and night. "You know, Olive, if you don't mind my saying so, you were maybe a little hard on Emery this morning in the council meeting."

Olive still wanted to talk about Nesta Versey, but Mrs. Sanchez's attention span was limited when it came to anything not directly related to City Hall. "I won't have public property going to a private school, Mary, and that's that."

Emery Joyner, the head of the Zoning Board, had suggested that the yews that were left over from the cemetery road might be donated to Robin Downs. "Over my dead body," Olive had said with surprising vigor. Mrs. Sanchez now wondered aloud if Olive might learn to get her points across less strenuously. "You're only going to wind up alienating everyone that way."

"I don't care. It's something I feel very strongly about. I will not have my department compromised."

A loud beep made Mrs. Sanchez start. It wasn't her pager, though; it was Olive's. She had asked Mr. Pickens to beep her when Felix called.

"I've got to go pick Felix up," Olive said as she screwed the lid back on the Cremora. "Would you do me a favor, Mary, and check on Mr. Pickens in about half an hour? Make sure he's got those bids out for the wading pool, O.K.? I'll be back at the office around four-fifteen, I imagine."

Felix was standing in the psychologist's front yard when Olive pulled up in the Cadillac. Dr. Lahey was a pleasant young woman whose husband, a retired, forty-one-year-old stockbroker, had added a second story to their wood-frame house. They lived in Judge Henley's neighborhood, an older section of town where many of the houses were falling into disrepair. The yards there tended to be overwhelmed by magnificent live oaks that vaulted in a gloomy, year-round shade. The psychologist's yard, though, was somewhat cheerier. Many limbs, probably old and rotten, had been cut down.

"How did it go?" Olive asked when Felix had roused himself from the huge stump he was sprawled upon and gotten into the car.

He grunted.

Three weeks ago, not long after Olive was installed in office, Felix had been engaged in an exhibition boxing match with the bishop in an attempt to raise money for the chorus's trip to Meridian, Mississippi. Reluctantly Olive had attended, even though this was really Felix's father's duty. But Duane was tied up with a closing in Baton Rouge. During the first round the bishop appeared to be giggling, and the sparring seemed rather childish and awkward, even to Olive's untrained eye. The second and third rounds were even sillier; Olive wished the bishop would stop smirking. In the fourth round Felix, who had been somber and listless, smiled, and the next thing Olive knew, he was beating the bishop to a pulp. Along with Olive, a few fathers had jumped into the homemade ring to pull Felix off the bishop. It took twenty-two stitches to sew the gash over his eyebrow. The bishop's estranged wife had called Olive and told her that she was going to have Felix arrested for assault and battery. The bishop himself, however, seemed reluctant to press charges, and a compromise was worked out: Felix was to be expelled from the chorus, grounded at home for the entire summer, and required to undergo therapy for at least a year.

"It's thirty-five bucks a shot, Felix. Don't you think that entitles me to know something about what's going on?" Olive stopped the car in the middle of the oak-shaded street to let an old, grossly overweight dog, its head bent blindly toward the asphalt, jaywalk across.

"Just a lot of bullshit," Felix said, heaving his sneakers onto the dashboard. Olive dared not tell him to put his feet down; she was still afraid he might become religious again. Although she had been horrified by the beating, she couldn't help feeling secretly glad to witness the gradual return of the old Felix, the boy who had gotten a tattoo and stolen hubcaps.

"What do you mean?"

"Like all this crap about, you know, did your mother make you wear wet diapers, did she paddle you?"

"What in God's name is she talking about *me* for? Doesn't she talk about that bishop?"

"We haven't gotten to him yet. Let's stop at BurgerMat. I want a crab-burger."

"Felix, did that bishop ever say or do anything funny around you? You know you should never be ashamed to talk to me about anything at all. I understand a lot more than you may think. Now, as for *my* mother, you couldn't tell her—"

"Ol, stop! You're going right by!" He kicked his white high-tops against the Cadillac's windshield as the drive-in's neon sign drifted past.

"Enough!" She slapped out at his shoes, which had cost an exorbitant sixty-three dollars and eighty-eight cents. But this was what they were wearing at Robin Downs this year

—untied, of course. Only a nerd would lace and tie his shoes, Felix had informed her after he had tripped and nearly cracked his head wide open on the patio yesterday. "You're going to have a decent home-cooked meal tonight."

"Give me a break."

"You and Duane are always going out to eat junk, and everyone knows junk makes you crazy. When Duane gets back on Tuesday, I'm going to lay down the law."

"He's not coming back from Baton Rouge till Friday."

"Well, whatever, I'm putting you both on notice. We're all going to start eating healthy. I realize I've been spending too much time at the office to cook properly, but from now on . . ."

When they got home, she told him he could swim for half an hour, then he must go read *The Mill on the Floss* until it was time for supper. Dr. Bates had given Olive a summer reading list for Felix and had advised her to severely limit his tv intake. According to Dr. Bates he would rather feed his child—if he had one—a pint of whiskey every day than let him be exposed to tv's mind-rotting idiocy. Olive had taken the tv out of Felix's bedroom and put a special lock on the cable box in her own bedroom.

"I really am beginning to wonder about that shrink of his," Olive was saying a few minutes later, after returning to the office. "All this prying into childhood. I don't think that has anything to do with it. It's that bishop. I think there's something weird about him."

Poised for dictation, Mr. Pickens relaxed and balanced the steno pad on his knee. His round face, which had seemed rather heavy and dull at first, was beginning to grow on his boss. She suspected that it masked a great deal of kindness, and from time to time a sly, furtive intelligence peeked out. "Of course, they say that the first four or five years of a child's life, that's when you're made, so to speak."

Olive nibbled at her pen. "But we're not trying to remake Felix. We're just trying to figure out why he lost it at the boxing deal. It's a very specific problem, very localized. If someone has a broken arm, you don't do a major overhaul, trying to get him to lower his cholesterol."

"Yeah, I can see what you're saying." He loosened the large knot in his chocolate-brown tie. An ink stain marred the pocket of his beige shirt. "But still, what the shrink is probably aiming at . . . When we do anything, it all comes from what we remember. I mean, we're always remembering, like when I look at you now, I don't see just you but I see like this female authority figure, and you're young and sort of remind me of my other boss, Donna Lee, and maybe about half of me is still reacting to Donna Lee instead of you. And then when I was with Donna Lee, I was remembering someone else and—"

"Right," she said, glancing down at the figures on her desk. L&M Mixers, the concrete company owned by Mr. Dambar, had delivered the lowest bid for the road repairs in the Sixth Ward, and she was anxious to get a letter out to them today. Mr. Pickens's theories would have to wait.

"By the way," she said after he read back the letter she had dictated, "remember that dentist I was telling you about, that short guy from up North? Did you ever see him drop by Donna Lee's office?"

He adjusted a strand of fine, lusterless hair on his balding pate. "Oh, him, that sort of cute guy. Yeah, he'd drop by every now and then."

"You think there's anything going on between those two?"

"Lord knows, Miss Mackie." Glancing at his watch, he yawned and shifted in the Morris chair that she had borrowed from Dead Records. "I wouldn't begin to try and figure out what's going on in that woman's head. She's got every kind of weirdo going in and out of her office all day long. There's this lady who works for a chiropractor. I saw her trying to snap Donna Lee's spine one day—she just *works* for a chiropractor, does his bills and stuff. Then there's this preacher who comes and preaches at me while he's waiting on her. He used to go on about how he climbed up in this tree one day when he was at divinity school in Nevada, and he told God that he was sick of Him. He wanted to be free to be himself, so for three years, he said, God gave him permission to lie and cheat and steal and sleep around, and that got it all out of his system. Now he says he can't be tempted by anything."

Olive had been only half listening as she filed some letters in the oak cabinet behind her desk. "This preacher," she said, "he wasn't sort of young-looking, was he?"

"Yeah, sort of."

"By any chance, was he also a school principal?"

"Huh?"

Perspiration beaded Mr. Pickens's nose. She asked him to wipe it off. "Does he teach or anything?" she asked after he had passed a finger over his nose, resentfully.

"How should I know?"

"Do you remember his name?"

"Good Lord, you're beginning to sound just like her. She was always giving me the third degree."

"I'm sorry, Carl. I don't mean to . . . Was his name Munrow, Dr. Munrow?"

"It was Dr. something, could've been that. Now can I go type this up?"

Secretaries were a diffident lot. Olive realized she had pumped him for all he was worth today, and let him go type. But tomorrow she would see if there was anything else she could get out of him concerning that man. After all, it seemed so peculiar that Dr. Munrow would be visiting Ms. Keely. What business could he have with her? Perhaps, Olive thought, she would buy Mr. Pickens a po-boy tomorrow, and they could eat lunch together in Dead Records.

"Night, buttercup," Olive heard Mrs. Sanchez say as she walked past the outer office, her keys jangling pleasantly like cowbells at the end of the day. Olive was about to call out "Night" when she realized it hadn't been meant for her.

" 'Bye, Mary," Mr. Pickens said in a low voice. "She's got me here doing . . ." He glanced over his shoulder at the half-open door to Olive's office. Somewhat shamefully his boss looked away and pretended to be absorbed in her work.

Yes, he knew who that man was, but for the life of him Uncle L.D. could not put a face to the name. Mr. Versey, Mr.

Versey, Dr. Munrow kept repeating that afternoon as he sat beside the old man's bed, quizzing him in preparation for this final test. Uncle L.D. was anxious to cooperate, but it felt so odd not being able to remember the home attendant's face. Why was it that when he closed his eyes and tried hard to remember, he saw the pretty, heart-shaped face of the girl who used to work across the aisle from Artis at Marshall Field's? Or sometimes it was the colored girl, Jimmy, who used to iron for Artis three days a week.

"You understand, Mr. Loraine? Try to be as clear and precise as you can. Say everything exactly like you just told me, and if you forget something, don't make something up to take its place. Do you want to run over it once again? No? All right then, let's see." Dr. Munrow leaned over and straightened the old man's cravat. The judge was due at the apartment any minute. He was going to decide once and for all whether there was any reason for the D.A. to pursue this case any further. From the grim look on Dr. Munrow's sallow face Uncle L.D. could tell there was no margin for error. If he failed to convince Judge Henley, he would no longer enjoy the protection of Dr. Munrow. Olive would have him back at that wretched nursing home in no time whatsoever.

"May I say, sir, that it's a privilege and honor to know you?" he said as Dr. Munrow, in his wilted seersucker suit, cast an appraising eye on him.

Shaking his head, the young man said, as if to himself, "No, this won't do."

Although Uncle L.D. had become fond of Dr. Munrow, he still was a little afraid of him. There was so much about the young man that reminded him of his own youth, the intelligence and drive, the immense self-discipline. At the same time, though, there was a hint of ruthlessness that was alien to him. It was the one ingredient, the old man often thought, that had been left out of his own make-up, the one thing that had kept him from getting to the top. Yes, as far as Uncle L.D. could see, this Dr. Munrow was going places. He was going to count for something in this world. If only the young man would let him, he could show him how to avoid the pitfalls and get to the top that much quicker.

"Did I ever tell you about the day I met Dr. Engel, a scholar of the first order?" he asked as Dr. Munrow rolled the wheelchair across the room toward the bed. "He was the one who put me on to the Peace of Ghent. I met him at a truck stop just outside of Kankakee in— Say, what are you doing?"

"I'm sorry, Mr. Loraine, but you got to get up. Let's get in that chair."

"But, my dear sir, didn't I tell you that this is impossible? I can't be moved." Bright as he was, Dr. Munrow still seemed unable to grasp the simple fact that he must remain where he was. Any attempt to get out of bed had become unspeakably painful. Even Miss Burma's gentle touch, when she rolled him over to change the sheets, was like being burned with a lit cigarette.

"I'd like you in that chair," Dr. Munrow said as he checked his own tie in the mirror above the bed.

"But why?"

"How do you expect Judge Henley to believe a word you say when you can't even get out of bed?" Mopping his boyish face with a handkerchief, he added, "Do me this favor."

"As you know, sir, I've always been interested in improving myself, and I was wondering if you might take a minute or two of your time now to sit down and think of two or three ways that I might substantially improve myself in any— Oh, no, stop." The old man stiffened as Dr. Munrow began canting his legs, gently, toward the edge of the bed. Like distant thunder, the pain was delayed a second or two after the initial shock of being touched.

"There, thata boy."

"Oh, oh, not my arms, don't touch my arms."

But Dr. Munrow already had a firm grip there and was levering him upright. This pain was worse than anything the old man could remember. Crying out, he tried to squirm away.

"What are you doing?" Dr. Munrow demanded. "Stop that."

"Help! Help!" A nightmarish sense of knowing what was going to happen next added mental anguish to the old man's physical torture. He had been through all this before, he felt. It was almost as if he were living a memory. "I don't have to go!"

"What? Now, come on, stop your babbling." He tugged the frail arm. "I'm not hurting you."

"I already went! Look in the potty there. Please."

The wheelchair squeaked as Dr. Munrow jerked it closer to the bed. "All right, here we go."

Knowing he was too small now for the potty, knowing he would be sucked in, the old man let out a piercing shriek.

"Stop that!" Dr. Munrow shook him. "Stop that this minute, you old—"

"Dr. Munrow."

Looking over his shoulder, Dr. Munrow saw Mrs. Undine at the door. In the struggle to get the old man into the chair, he had apparently not heard her enter. She was standing on the other side of the room, clutching her purse to her chest. "What's going on?" she asked in a high, unnatural voice. "What do you mean by . . . "

"Ah, if it isn't my favorite science teacher." Letting the old man slump back onto the bed, Dr. Munrow straightened up and smiled warmly at her. "I suppose you're here to—"

"Yes," she said, her voice quavering, "it's my day to give him his exercise."

"Well, we won't have to worry about exercise today. He's having one of his spells. You know how ornery he can get when he's having one of his spells." Dr. Munrow beamed aggressively at her. She took a tentative step into the room.

"Where is Miss Burma?"

"She has the day off."

"Out," the old man groaned feebly from the bed. "Get out."

Dr. Munrow had advanced a step or two toward Mrs. Undine as she looked anxiously toward the bed. "Hello, Mr.

Loraine. It's I, Mrs. Undine. Are you all right, dear? Is everything O.K.?"

"For God's sake, shut the window. Shut the goddam son-of-a-bitch window!"

"Now, what sort of language is that to use in front of a lady?" Dr. Munrow said in a rich, deliberate voice, as if he were addressing a roomful of people. "You must forgive him, Mrs. Undine. He doesn't realize what he's saying when he's like this."

"That's all right." Somewhat hesitantly she approached the bed. "What are you doing here?"

"Me? I came to visit my friend. I found myself with a few spare moments, and I said to myself, 'Dr. Munrow, why don't we go visit Mr. Loraine. It's been a while since we've seen him.' And so here we are. And," he added, laying a hand on her arm, "I don't think you'll be needed today. Good-bye, Mrs. Undine."

She tried, delicately, to free her arm but found this was impossible. "But I can stay."

"No, no, you run along, dear. I'm sure you have a lot to do."

"But, Dr. Munrow"—she was being edged toward the door—"you must not be so rough with him. He's an old man."

"Yes, of course, Mrs. Undine."

The door was already closing on her as she said, "I simply must say that I don't approve of such behavior, Dr. Munrow."

"Yes, of course. Good day."

"Oh, Mother, really," Kay said when Mrs. Undine returned from the kitchen. Seated on the living-room couch, Kay and her ex-husband had exchanged a look when they saw Mrs. Undine check the knobs on the stove. In a few moments Kay would have to return to New Orleans, where she and Dr. Bates had spent the weekend looking for an apartment for him. On a whim Kay had driven Dr. Bates back to Tula Springs for a quick visit with her mother—and to pick up the word processor, which she had decided she might need after all. Dr. Bates appreciated the ride since something was wrong with the brakes on his Volks. He would have had to take the bus back.

On the drive from New Orleans, Dr. Bates had told his ex-wife how her mother had left the gas on one day, and Kay had agreed that it was an unconscious manifestation of hostility. It was probably a good thing that he was leaving and taking that job in New Orleans with Dr. Schexsnyder. The conversation had been a little strained in Kay's BMW, mainly because they had both had too much to drink on Saturday night and had ended up in bed together. Dr. Bates wanted to tell her all about his obsession with Donna Lee. He wanted Kay's opinion about whether he was falling in love with the lawyer in a healthy way or whether he was neurotically attracted to her simply because she wouldn't go to bed with him. But because of his aberration with Kay he didn't bring up the lawyer at all.

"I just went to get some more ice," Mrs. Undine defended herself.

"We saw you check the stove," Kay said, picking up her white wine spritzer. Like her mother, Kay was tall and, aside from her shapely legs, not particularly well built. But because she knew how to carry herself and what to wear, the two of them seemed like night and day. Women would stare at Kay when they passed her on a sidewalk. Everything she wore was terribly expensive and understated, and with her cold, icy stare she always gave the impression that she was someone who might be famous. Dr. Bates had never realized what clothes meant to women until he had started going out with Kay. It was a revelation how much thought went into her "look," which was somewhat reminiscent of the Alain Resnais antiheroines.

Mrs. Undine resumed her seat by the window and took a sip of sherry. "Anyway, as I was saying, I stood outside the door a few minutes, wondering if maybe I should go back in. I—"

"Mother," Kay said, winding a strand of black hair around her index finger, a nervous habit that became more pronounced in her mother's presence, "since when do you put ice in your sherry?"

Mrs. Undine looked at her glass and seemed surprised to see the ice cube. "Oh. Well. Please, Kay, let me finish. I was thinking maybe I should go back in, but then he wasn't making any noise anymore, the old man wasn't. And I knew you would be coming back and wanting supper, so I just had to hurry back."

"He was hitting the old guy?" Dr. Bates asked.

"Not really, no. But he was so rough. Something in his voice . . . I once heard him talking like that to a woman on the Board of Regents. I was in the outer office and heard him saying to her—well, calling her a bigot, a racist, that sort of thing. My ears were burning. I felt so ashamed. There's simply no call, ever, to use language like that."

Kay removed a gold earring and rubbed her lobe. "This is great. Here I come all this way to visit, and no one asks me anything. You sit there gabbing about people I never heard of. Let's talk about something we can all . . ."

Mrs. Undine leaned over and scratched a mosquito bite on her ankle while Dr. Bates apologized. Soon they were involved in a discussion of the secretary Kay had just fired, a young Tulane graduate who was overqualified for the job. Then they talked about whether Kay shouldn't stay and have a bite to eat before going back to New Orleans. "I don't think it's a good policy to drive on an empty stomach," her mother advised.

"I really got to get back." She set her glass down and seemed about to stand up but hesitated as she looked at the blank space over the mantel. "What happened to my portrait?"

"I gave it to Mrs. Keely. She's donating it to the Baptist church."

"Mother, I don't want my picture hanging in the Baptist church."

"It's not going to hang there. They're going to auction it off for underprivileged youths."

Kay nibbled the rough skin around her nails. "God."

"Well, you always said you hated it, dear."

"I thought you were just going to put it in the garage or something."

"I'm not running a warehouse anymore." She parted the curtains and glanced out at the ditch. "There's not enough room in this house for my things, let alone yours and everyone else who happens to . . . I feel so cramped. There's no room in the closets; my dresses are squashed. And there's too much furniture here, in this room. I've been wanting for years now to sell off some of this. That cabinet over there, those end tables, the chair in the corner—it's all clutter. I've always liked the idea of a few good pieces of furniture with a lot of space in between. But your father, he was always bringing home one thing after another. I never did have anything the way I wanted it."

"You've had all these years to fix things up, Mother."

"Look at Mrs. Keely's—all that space she has. You never see Mr. Keely buying furniture, I guarantee. And let me tell you something, Kay." Mrs. Undine leaned forward in her chair, peering at her daughter over her half glasses. "I never did like wicker."

Looking around the room, Dr. Bates noticed for the first time how much wicker there was—the seats of three, no, four chairs, the tops of three end tables, a lowboy with wicker shelves, a wicker frame to the picture of Mr. Undine with the fish. While Kay and her mother went on discussing the furniture and what could be done about it Dr. Bates experienced a brief eerie sensation. It was as if the room were one of the displays in the Museum of Natural History, totally authentic in every detail (yes, this was what those people sat on, this was how they lived), and yet somehow unreal, disconnected. He was on the other side of the glass, peering in. Soon he would move on to the next display.

I got to get laid, he thought desperately. *I got to.* And he began trying to think of a way to get Kay into the bedroom.

"Well, I kept it this way for your sake, Kay. I thought it might upset you if I changed it all around."

"That's ridiculous. I don't care what you do to this room."

"You were always defending your father, you know, always taking his side."

"Oh, Mother, really. That's ancient history."

"Kay," Dr. Bates said, "why don't you come look at the word processor before you go? It's in my room."

"Yes," Mrs. Undine prompted, "go on, dear. I really do wish you'd take that thing back with you. It's just cluttering up the room."

Chapter Seventeen

"O.K., MEN, JUST ANOTHER MINUTE," Olive said as she looked into the living room on the way to the kitchen. Felix and Duane were sitting on the couch, each with a joy stick on his lap. They were playing a video game with fighter planes and an animated color landscape.

"Would you like another 7-Up, honey?"

Duane shook his head. Since getting the job in Baton Rouge he had gone on the wagon and lost fifteen pounds. She was proud of his appearance, and proud that he was making the effort to sleep at home four or five nights a week. Felix's therapist had recommended that Duane spend more time around his son, even if this meant getting in from Baton Rouge at nine-thirty or ten in the evening. As for Felix, he was earning good money this summer mowing lawns in Cherylview, and although he had never finished *The Mill on the Floss,* he had become interested in scuba diving. Olive worried a great deal when she watched her boy submerge in the pool out back. She could not breathe easy until he surfaced. It was very trying, this new hobby, but she kept her mouth shut.

In the kitchen Olive checked on the chicken Florentine in the oven and then spread garlic butter on the French bread. She was enjoying a sense of accomplishment, a feeling that was new to her and one that she figured she had earned. To begin with she was making good money in a highly respected job that was making her new friends every day. But what was even more important was that she had managed to salvage her foundering marriage. How many other women would have been able to forgive what she had forced herself to forgive? And then there was her infatuation with Dr. Bates. There again her whole life could have gone on the rocks. If she had really let herself go, she imagined she could have ruined things forever with Duane. But something inside her had always made her hold back from Dr. Bates, and the love she felt, which still pained her, had been kept under control. Yes, she could congratulate herself for not actually having had an affair with him. There was simply some experimentation in that direction. When she thought hard about it, she realized that it must have been her deep and unswerving love for Felix that had tamed her feelings for Dr. Bates. She had managed to save Felix from those dreadful Mormons in the nick of time. And now she and Duane were going to devote their lives to the boy's welfare. They had both discussed it and decided that there was nothing more important to either of them.

There was one other reason for her to feel a sense of real accomplishment. She had finally cleared the way for the old man to be readmitted to Azalea Manor, where he could be properly taken care of with round-the-clock nursing. And if anyone thought that had been easy, they had another thing coming.

"I want you two to go out and visit Uncle L.D. next week," Olive said a few minutes later, when they were seated in the alcove just off the kitchen. Behind Felix the off-white wall shimmered with the reflected light from the pool, suggesting the uncertain depth of a photographer's backdrop.

"Honey," Duane said, "he's not my uncle."

"Listen, after what he's been through, he deserves all the visitors he can get. You remember how I told you about what Dr. Munrow was doing to him, how that man was—"

"Pass the salt."

Her jaw muscles tensing, Olive pushed the shaker over to Duane. She was aching to tell the story again, how she had rescued Uncle L.D. from those dreadful charges hanging over his head. The first time she had told it, she was sure Duane and Felix weren't really listening closely enough. They had missed all the finer points. And she had left out a few important facts. For instance, it was Mrs. Undine who had put her on the trail. She was the one who had really got Olive thinking when she had come up to her in the hardware store with a drain guard in her hand.

"Listen, Olive, I know you don't want to talk to me, but—"

Olive had turned and walked away. But Mrs. Undine persisted. Catching up with her, she began to tell her about seeing Dr. Munrow at the old man's apartment. "It's been worrying me so, I can't get it off my mind. The way he was manhandling your poor uncle—it just wasn't right."

Olive had relented. There was something different about Mrs. Undine. The undertow of complaint was absent from her voice. In its stead was simple, direct concern. Olive listened. And as Mrs. Undine spoke, Olive remembered her talk with Dr. Munrow outside the gym. Even then, months ago, she had felt there was something funny about the man. He gave her the willies.

"Duane, I was wondering if maybe you shouldn't go talk to that bishop."

"Huh?"

"Hey, Ol," Felix said, his mouth full, "lay off."

"I think he got off too easy."

Duane put down his fork and stared at her a moment. "What did *he* do? He didn't do a thing."

"Is that right, Felix?" Olive looked steadily at her son. "Did the bishop never do anything to deserve what you did to him? I just can't believe that a son of mine would, for no reason at all . . ."

"Now, honey, you know what Dr. Lahey says. We're not to cross-examine anyone. Felix is in a confidential relationship with his therapist, and we've got to respect that."

"Yes, that's just great. A confidential relationship with a perfect stranger, and his own mother . . . Want more bread?"

Olive got up and went into the kitchen to heat up the other loaf. She had already told Gail, her friend at the bank, how her suspicions had been aroused by Mr. Pickens when he informed her that Dr. Munrow used to visit Donna Lee. Of course, she had to leave out a lot in this account. She certainly couldn't mention her rivalry with the lawyer. And Gail really didn't get the full import of all that was going on at Robin Downs. She should have filled in a little background for Gail, things that Mrs. Undine had told her.

"I guess Dr. Munrow can't help being a little worked up these days," Mrs. Undine had said in the hardware store. "It looks like the Board of Regents might fire him."

"Because he wants to hire a black science teacher?"

"Oh, dear me, no. It's just the way he's going about it, Olive. Lots of folks wouldn't mind a black teacher at all. But he's gotten pretty highhanded, stepped on a few toes. He sees everything in black and white. Either you're for him or you're for Satan. There's no two ways about it."

Gail, of course, didn't have any children. So this wouldn't have meant much to her anyway.

Coming back with the garlic bread, Olive remembered that Mrs. Sanchez had met Mrs. Bingham once or twice through a mutual friend. It was Mrs. Sanchez who should have heard about the Mrs. Bingham part of the story—not Harry Leroy. To Harry Leroy, Bingham was just a name. It meant nothing.

"Yes, this is the best part," she had told him on the phone that afternoon. "I went over to Mrs. Bingham's pretending it was just a social visit. Then in a real natural way I eased into a topic I thought she might be able to say a few interesting things about. See, she's friends with this lady who knows Nesta Versey. Myra Wedge is in the garden club, and so Mrs. Bingham has known her for years. Mrs. Bingham told me that Mrs. Wedge had some sort of breakdown after her husband died. That's how her and Nesta became good friends. Mrs. Wedge is interested in bereaved people and joined the group at the Optimist club that visits widows and all. Anyway, just sitting there over tea with Mrs. Bingham, I found out all I had to know: It's amazing how everything is right in front of us, staring us in the face."

"Oh, yeah, that's it—couldn't agree with you more," Harry Leroy had said. "Listen, Olive, got to run. I—"

"But aren't you going to ask what it was? How I knew? It was when Mrs. Bingham told me that Nesta was having a hard time making ends meet. She had been cheated out of an insurance policy on her brother's life. That was all I needed to hear—insurance policy."

"Hey, terrific. Now, like, there's this client here I got to—"

"Wait, please. You got to hear this. So when Mrs. Bingham mentioned the insurance policy, it suddenly struck me what Myra Wedge had said about Nesta. She said that Nesta spent a lot of time watching tv preachers. Somehow I knew I was on to something."

"Tv preachers. That's it, great. Just got to run, kid. I'll give you a buzz."

Duane and Felix were talking about NFL statistics. Olive waited patiently a moment, then felt she just had to interrupt: "It was the part about the tv preachers, that was really the best, don't you think? I mean the way I put it together with the insurance."

Duane and Felix looked glumly at her. Then, after breaking off a hunk of bread, Felix began quoting a few more statistics to his father.

"Did I tell you boys that that lady, Myra Wedge, she's Mr. Pickens's next-door neighbor? I drove him home from work one day and saw her out in her front yard. So I decided it might be a good opportunity to—"

"Olive," Duane broke in. "Felix and I were talking."

"I know, but I thought you might find this interesting."

"We did, the first twenty times."

Olive had not told them twenty times. She had not told them once the way she wanted to tell them. When she thought about it, her best audience had been Mrs. Sanchez. It was a shame, though, that the recital had had to be squeezed into coffee breaks. Sometimes Mrs. Sanchez would ask a really good question in Dead Records, but Olive wouldn't be able to answer it because she or Mrs. Sanchez would get paged.

"So you see, Mary," she had informed Mrs. Sanchez after

her visit to Mrs. Wedge's front yard. The lady had been more than happy to tell all she knew about her friend, Nesta. "Mr. Versey had been paying on a term life insurance policy since he was in his twenties. When he died, his sister was supposed to get a nice round sum of two hundred and fifty grand."

Mrs. Sanchez's plump hand went to her heart. "My."

"The only trouble was, when the coroner gave his initial verdict of suicide, she couldn't collect a cent."

"But how could anyone change a coroner's verdict? Wasn't it plain what happened?"

"No, not really. To begin with, the coroner is a bumbling idiot, as you well know. He didn't order an autopsy, nothing. He simply looked at the bump on Mr. Versey's head and concluded that he had been killed by the fall from the window. Actually what else could he conclude at the time? It was the only logical thing to believe."

Mrs. Sanchez sipped thoughtfully from her cup. "Well, either that he had accidentally fallen out the window . . ."

"Yes, if he were an infant."

"Or that he had been pushed."

"By a ninety-one-year-old, right?"

"I see. So it had to be suicide."

"Exactly. Until Dr. Munrow came along. See, Nesta Versey was teaching at Robin Downs then. That's how he knew about it. Apparently after the suicide—or whatever—she had told him she couldn't go on teaching. The shock had been too great—and she was getting on in years anyway. She was worried about finances then, too. Since she wasn't collecting any insurance, she would have to get by on Social Security and what little retirement benefits she had from when she was teaching years ago at the public school. You see, Robin Downs was strapped and had nothing to give her, no decent retirement benefits at all. Anyway, as they talked—" Here there was a beep for Olive, and she was not able to continue till two days later.

"Like I was saying," she had resumed after some initial chitchat with Mrs. Sanchez about the mayor's mood that day, "when Dr. Munrow talked with Nesta, he found out how unlikely it was that her brother would have killed himself. They had lived happily together. Neither one had ever married, and they looked to each other for mutual support, in a nice sort of way. That was why the shock was so terrible. She had always been religious in a conventional way, but after her brother died so suddenly, so comparatively young, she became much more susceptible to that sort of influence."

"So that's why she was watching tv preachers all the time."

"That's right, and why she was hooked by Dr. Munrow. He's ordained, you know. He's very good at making a person feel sinful and unworthy. In any case, he was able to work out a deal with her. He told Nesta that he would see what he could do to get the money out of the insurance company. All she had to do was let him invest it for her. He would provide her with a monthly income that she could live on comfortably. Well, Nesta apparently wasn't that interested in getting rich. She figured that if Dr. Munrow could help her, it was better than nothing—which was what she had at the moment. And furthermore, her money would be invested with God. That was a big thing, to see her money going for God's work."

"You don't mean . . ."

"Exactly. Dr. Munrow had every reason to squeeze that money out of the insurance company. It was all going for Robin Downs' building fund. Don't you see? If he could bring in half a million in one lump to build some decent classrooms, the Board of Regents couldn't very well get rid of him. And they would be blackmailed, in a way. They would have to say yes to his science teacher and begin integrating the school. As long as he had that financial power, he held the reins."

"Wait a minute, I thought you said it was a quarter million."

"Double indemnity, Mary. If Dr. Munrow could prove that Mr. Versey had been murdered, the insurance company would have to double the amount."

Mrs. Sanchez's finely plucked eyebrows went up. "So that's when he began talking to the old man."

"Yes—and was able to confuse, frighten, and bribe him into making a confession. After all, Uncle L.D. did hate Mr. Versey. Anybody could see that. So all Dr. Munrow had to do was offer the old man a free ride out of that nursing home, let him have his own way, and the rest was easy. Don't forget, the idea of suicide was easy for Dr. Munrow to ridicule. Who would believe that even if Mr. Versey had wanted to kill himself, he would have done it from a second-story window? So when Dr. Munrow started a campaign to bring this to light, Dr. McFlug got worried about his reputation. He realized how silly it was, a suicide verdict. Then Dr. Munrow spurred things along by helping Nesta write letters to the papers. That was when the D.A. got worried about his reputation as well. Everyone was in a stew. No one knew what to think, except Dr. Munrow. He had a definite goal in mind."

"Isn't it scary how clever Dr. Munrow was?" Olive couldn't help saying as she helped herself to more chicken.

"Who?" Duane mumbled.

"Your son's principal. Now, why do I say he was clever, boys? I want you to tell me why he was clever."

"Oh, come on. Let's not have any more of this Mrs. Undine business. Felix and I have heard enough."

"If you've heard enough, then you can tell me. And I didn't explain the part about seeing Mrs. Undine in the hardware store. That's when I really got suspicious of—"

"Felix, didn't I ask you not to leave those scuba tanks out like that?"

"I'm going in after supper."

"Well, you should put them away, you know."

Olive picked at her food. Thinking back, she realized that Mrs. Sanchez was just being polite when she listened. There was no sense of involvement with her. Her questions were merely dutiful. To her dismay Olive finally understood who the perfect audience was for her story. Deep in her heart she had to admit that there was only one person with whom she could share it fully.

"So you see," she would have told him, "the smartest

thing he did was to bring Ms. Keely into the act. Dr. Munrow got her to feel sorry for Uncle L.D., making him out to be the victim of physical abuse. Then Dr. Munrow faded into the background and let that dumb blonde do all his work for him. She was determined to make Uncle L.D. seem like a hero for defending himself, the Rambo of the old-age set. It never crossed her mind that there was something fishy about Uncle L.D.'s confession."

He would take her hand and mutter some apology about the dumb blonde, how he never really cared for her. It was just that she had pursued him and he hadn't wanted to hurt her feelings. "But anyway, that's all over now. Back to your uncle, Olive. I just can't see him lying. He never seemed the type to lie."

"No, he isn't. He just wasn't remembering right."

"But how did anyone find that out?"

"Simple, Martin. You know Judge Henley is a good friend of mine. If it weren't for me, there's no telling what might have happened to my uncle. I talked to the judge a few times, and then I found out from his wife that the D.A.'s office had questioned Nesta and learned that her brother had suffered chest pains for the past few years. Mr. Versey hated doctors, though. He had some sort of conspiracy theory about them. They were all supposed to be tied in with the insurance racket and were out to cheat folks out of every cent they were entitled to. He was afraid, if he reported these chest pains, they'd raise the premium or might even cancel his policy. Anyway, when the judge heard about this, he decided it was high time the D.A. got the facts and laid the case to rest. But, of course, Judge Henley couldn't trust the D.A.'s staff to do anything right. Don't forget, Sarah Markett, the assistant D.A., had just caused him a hell of a lot of trouble. So the judge took the bull by the horns and went over to Uncle L.D.'s apartment himself. Mrs. Henley said he was fed up and decided to get the story straight from the old man's mouth—everything the old man could remember that had happened that day. It turns out that what he really remembered— Oh, right, the judge had to throw Dr. Munrow out of the apartment first. Dr. Munrow was messing up the old man's memory, it was pretty obvious. Anyway, what Uncle L.D. could remember was one simple fact: Mr. Versey lying across the sill. The window was open. Then, when he shook Mr. Versey, that's when he apparently began to fall out. But it was obvious to the judge that Mr. Versey was already dead or unconscious *before* he fell out the window."

"But that would mean the old man had hit him or something. That can't be right."

"No, Martin. Of course Uncle L.D. wasn't strong enough to do any real damage, even if he had wanted to. That's why Uncle L.D. felt so guilty. He wanted to hurt Mr. Versey, and Dr. Munrow had convinced him that he actually had. But it was me. I was the one who gave the answer to Judge Henley."

"You?"

"He was puzzling over what could have happened to Mr. Versey, and I remember having told Mrs. Henley once about how hard it was to open that big window in Uncle L.D.'s apartment. I remember saying to her that every time I tried to get it open, it almost gave me a heart attack. And she told me she repeated this one evening to her husband, in passing. She really wasn't making any connection herself. Anyway, that's what did the trick."

"So Mr. Versey died opening the window. Fell across the sill—and that's how your uncle found him. Poor man. It must have been hard on him."

"You can see why he was so confused and guilty."

"Sure. But one thing I don't understand. Is a judge supposed to act like a detective? I never heard of anything like that."

"That's part of why Judge Henley is always getting into hot water. You know those lady lawyers tried to get him indicted with a grand jury not long ago. He's always bending the rules a little. Anyway, when I told Mrs. Henley about the insurance deal Dr. Munrow had cooked up with Nesta, the so-called endowment she was going to make to Robin

Downs, the judge hit the roof. He laid down the law to Dr. Munrow and told him he better not see him meddling in Nesta's affairs anymore."

"But if it was an accident, she'll get some money then."

"Not a half million, but maybe the original amount, minus the lawyer's fees. She's going to have to sue the insurance company since they'll want to stand by the coroner's original verdict. It'll be a hassle, I'm sure. But anyway . . ." Sadly Olive realized whom it was she was speaking to—or rather, not speaking to. She had thought it was Martin. But it wasn't. It was Dr. Bates, the kind and considerate student dentist, who would blush when you stared at him too long or accidentally touched his hand.

"Felix, have you heard anything about who's going to be teaching y'all science in the fall?" Olive asked, anxious to start up a proper dinner-table conversation. Duane and Felix had stopped discussing statistics and had just been sitting there eating while she was daydreaming.

"Far as I know, Mrs. Undine will be back again."

"But I thought she was just a substitute."

"She is. But Dr. Munrow never did get the O.K. from the board for that other teacher."

"You mean the black lady?"

"Yeah. Roger's ma knows her. He told me she's not sure she'd want to teach there anyway." Roger was Felix's black friend. Dr. Lahey had encouraged Olive and Duane to let him visit as often as he liked, and so Felix had been seeing quite a lot of him recently. Olive always went out of her way to be polite to Roger and to make him feel at home.

"I think it's pretty silly. A woman who doesn't know the first thing about science . . ." Olive said.

Duane flashed her a warning look. "Just because she's black, honey."

"I'm talking about Mrs. Undine. She has no business teaching science. She was a civics teacher, Duane. Now, boys, I want you to promise me you'll go see Uncle L.D. next week. I went to a lot of trouble to get him back at Azalea Manor. If it weren't for me, he'd be all alone in that apartment, no one to feed him, nothing. Now that Dr. Munrow can't get anything out of him, he doesn't care a fig. And that Ms. Keely, boy, she sure dropped out of the picture quick enough. I tell you, it's really awful the way some people *use* people. The minute you're not serving any purpose, they drop you like a hot potato. Sure, when he was the symbol of all the beaten and abused senior citizens of the world, then Ms. Keely found him interesting enough. But now that he's back to being just a plain old man, she suddenly realizes she hasn't the time to look after him anymore. And these were the people who claimed *I* was the one without a heart, huh. I like that."

"Must you go into this again, hon?"

"All right, I won't say another word about it. But I just hope everyone understands how much I've done for him. I hope they realize how much better off he's going to be with someone to look after him twenty-four hours a day and feed him three square meals."

"And now he can look at trees and grass," Felix mimicked. "Yeah, Ol, great. You're terrific. Kind to dogs and all. Now, what's for dessert?"

After dinner Olive suggested that they drive to the mall in Mississippi to see a movie. Felix, though, had already seen all four movies at the Quad with Roger, and so, excusing himself, he slid out the glass doors to the pool.

"Has he talked to you about his therapy?" Olive asked her husband as they stood side by side at the sink, doing the dishes. "He won't talk to me. I don't have a clue about what went on with that bishop."

"You know we're not supposed to pry."

"O.K., fine. But, Duane, if you could have seen how horrible it was, to be sitting there and suddenly all that blood and violence, the way Felix was hitting him. I don't think I'll ever forget that for as long as I live. I was so mortified. I thought I'd never be able to show my face again in this town."

"Honey, that's not really dry," he said, tapping the platter with the stylized pink fish on it that she was putting away. "Can't you dry it a little better?"

She passed the towel over it a few more times. Of course

she loved Duane. If necessary she would throw herself in front of a speeding train for him. But there was no doubt that it was a little difficult being alone with him for any length of time. She had asked Gail to dinner that evening, but Gail had a date. Harry and Desirée Leroy were visiting Desirée's stepmother in Opelousas. The new neighbors next door were coming over on Saturday. Across the street Georgette McClusky was going out to her three-year-old's dance recital. She had thought about asking Mrs. Sanchez over, but Mrs. Sanchez was sure to make a big production out of it and insist on repaying the invitation. Anyway, it was probably better not to get too involved socially with Mrs. Sanchez, Olive's instincts told her. Normally she could have counted on Carol to take up the slack. But there was no way she could even begin to imagine forgiving that girl, not after all she had said and done.

"What's the matter with you?" Duane reached into the cupboard and took out a glass she had just put away. "Look at this." Taking the towel from her, he wiped off the drops inside.

"Honey, it evaporates. Really, it makes more sense to let it evaporate naturally than to run a towel over it."

"Who told you that? Germs thrive in water. You've got to leave everything really dry."

"Listen, we learnèd in home ec that it was better—"

"Cut it out. Just cut it out. No one ever went to school to learn how to dry dishes."

"I beg your pardon, but I just happen to have taken four years of home ec in high school."

"Whoever taught you must have been a nut, then. You don't put dishes away wet."

Quivering with suppressed rage, Olive was afraid to look at him. He had become so critical ever since giving up drinking. Nothing she did was ever right. At dinner this evening every time she poured herself a glass of wine, he would glare at her. Need he be reminded that she wasn't the one with the problem?

"You mean to tell me, Olive, that Mrs. Undine taught you

to put dishes away wet?" His voice sounded tight, constricted.

Olive took a deep breath, hoping to sound more normal. "Mrs. Undine taught civics. We did not study dishes in civics."

"Good, there she is again, Mrs. Undine." He manhandled a saucepan, banging it against the porcelain sink. "That's all I've heard from you tonight—Mrs. Undine this, Mrs. Undine that."

"What are you talking about? I never—"

"Oh, now you deny that you brought up her name even. That's great, Olive."

So maybe she had brought up her name a couple times, Olive thought. Couldn't he see that she was talking about Uncle L.D., not about that woman? "Duane, why are you acting so strange? Are you allergic to her name or something? Why does she make you so hot under the collar?"

He was scouring the Teflon coating with a steel-wool pad, but Olive kept her mouth shut.

"Me? Don't make me laugh. Just what is it between you and that dame? I can't figure it out. For the last year there hasn't been a day when you haven't brought up Mrs. Undine. First, she's bothering the old man, then she's out to ruin your campaign, then you say she's the one behind all that murder business—and now, tonight, suddenly Mrs. Undine is Miss Innocent. You want to know something, babe? I think you got some sort of complex, some sort of fixation. And you want to know something else? I don't think it's Felix who should be seeing a shrink. It's no riddle to me why he went nuts."

She turned away so he wouldn't see the tears that had welled up in her eyes. For a moment she thought about letting him have it. How dare he suggest she was the cause of Felix's problems when he had been carrying on with Carol like that! The gall of him. Had he no conscience, no morals at all? And what was so unfair was that she would never be able to confront him. He would never understand that she had never had a real affair with Dr. Bates, that it wasn't anything like his sordid lust for Carol. All her denial and restraint, all she had suffered—and yet in the end, in his eyes, she would come out looking just as unfaithful as he.

"I've got to go to the office tonight," she said, hanging up the striped towel. She was afraid of what might happen if they talked about Mrs. Undine anymore. She had to get out of the house, away from him.

He was silent, still scrubbing at the same saucepan.

It would have been gratifying to storm out of the kitchen. But she must remember Felix. Duane and she couldn't afford to indulge their own grievances. "I'm so backed up at work," she said wearily as she plucked her keys from the cup hook in the cabinet. "Mr. Pickens and I are swamped this week. I can't get out from under . . . There's a council meeting Thursday and . . . Anyway, will you keep an eye on Felix, hon? Those tanks make me so nervous. I hope he knows what he's doing."

In her office that evening Olive was able to drown her anger and frustration in a steady inundation of mindless paperwork. After her initial sense of not belonging she had found herself becoming more and more attached to this windowless rectangle, twelve feet by nineteen. Before, when reports or statements were incorrect or overdue, she not only felt it didn't concern her, but she had to admit that it actually gave her a perverse pleasure. Ultimately everything could be blamed on Vondra, her boss. But now she experienced genuine pangs whenever something went wrong in her department. Her work had begun to have real meaning for her, and this somehow made it easier to put up with Duane. Indeed, without her work, with her identity totally dependent on her husband, she knew she would have failed Felix and given up on Duane for good. Every time she felt she had reached the boiling point, all she had to do was go to the office and her equanimity was restored.

"Hello? Hello, who's there?" Mrs. Undine's voice came over the wire. "Yes, hello?"

Olive gently put down the receiver. She had felt an overwhelming urge to talk to Dr. Bates, to tell him all she had gone through tonight. And she wanted so much to talk to him about Uncle L.D. He would tell her that she was doing right; she knew he would. But it was just her luck to always get Mrs. Undine whenever she phoned the house. Why was it that it was always *her* voice on the other end of the line?

Chapter Eighteen

HE KEPT ALL THE LIGHTS ON AT NIGHT NOW for fear they might come for him when he was asleep. And so, forcing himself to stay awake, he felt for the first time in years what a blessing sleep was, and yearned for it. But no, they would not catch him unawares. He planned to put up a fight this time. They were not going to take his room away from him.

"Mr. Loraine?"

Startled, he opened his eyes and held up his arms, as if to ward off a blow. "No, no, I won't."

"I'm so sorry, dear. Did I wake you? It's just me." Mrs. Undine was holding a Corning Ware dish covered with aluminum foil. "Dr. Bates is moving out this evening, and I discovered all this food in the freezer that I won't be able to deal with by myself. I thought you might enjoy something a little different. It's a Chinese casserole."

"So you're the one they sent. Well, that's fine with me. I think I can take you on, woman."

"I have lots of other things I'd like to give you," she said, setting the dish down on the coffee table. "There's plenty of nice shirts and trousers you might enjoy, something to vary your wardrobe. Oh, my." His fist had struck out and grazed her arm. "Did you mean to do that, Mr. Loraine? I must say, it's not very nice."

His legs tangled in the yellowed sheets, he vainly tried to kick free while waving his arms about. "Come on, I'll take you, you scrawny old bat. I'll teach you to fool around with L.D. Loraine. You think you can get me out of this bed, you got another thing coming."

"For heaven's sake," she said, gazing down at the shirt that was buttoned up wrong, the suit coat that was only half on, "I'm not planning to get you out of bed. I have nothing to do with all that, sir. You're not going to be moved to Azalea Manor until the day after tomorrow, you know. The idea, trying to strike me like that."

The old man's body slowly wilted as he closed his eyes, trying to catch his breath.

Mrs. Undine spread some tissue on the cover of the potty and sat down. "Now, Mr. Loraine, don't you think we should be mature about this? Surely you can't blame Miss Burma for finding herself a much better job." Gently she reached out with another tissue and dabbed at his glistening forehead. "You'll be happy there. There will be lots of nice people for you to meet."

"No, here. Let me be, please. I don't want to move."

"In my own dull, retarded way may I suggest, Mr. Loraine, that you might . . ." He opened his eyes, and they regarded each other for a moment. "You really can't leave, can you?" she whispered, as if to herself.

His gray, drawn face seemed to almost visibly suffuse with hope. "You'll help me, won't you, Mrs. Undine? You'll tell him I did it, won't you? Make him believe I killed Mr. Versey, please. It's true, I'm not lying. I did it."

"Please don't talk such nonsense. Why, never for one second did I believe you could ever hurt a fly." Stretching a long thin arm over his head, she switched out the harsh light above the bed. "You won't ever again have to worry about Dr. Munrow, hear? He's not going to bother you anymore, I guarantee. He's leaving Tula Springs. He got appointed dean of a Bible college out in California, so he'll be miles away. When I think of the way he was using you, it makes me see red."

"No, I did it," he feebly protested. But he was not a very convincing liar. When Dr. Munrow had been so rough with him on the day of the judge's visit, Uncle L.D. had vividly recalled his own helplessness and known for certain that he had done nothing to Mr. Versey. Yet to be relieved of this guilt was like suddenly becoming weightless, with no center of gravity. When he was guilty, didn't he have friends then, a wonderful new housekeeper, his own lovely lawyer, a school principal, all these highly educated people visiting him almost every day? But now that he was innocent, where was everyone? He felt almost as if he had become invisible, disembodied, a vague, confused memory in everyone's mind, including his own. Oh, so what if that young, scheming whippersnapper thought he was using him? So what if everyone thought Dr. Munrow was bad— evil incarnate? Uncle L.D. didn't care if he was Satan himself: He would have welcomed Dr. Munrow back with open arms and a cry of joy!

Mrs. Undine had gotten up and switched off the naked light bulb in the ceiling fixture. An unearthly green bathed the room as she returned to the old man's bedside. "Tell me about the Peace of Ghent, will you?" she said, leaning close. "I've been thinking about it lately, Mr. Loraine."

"If he just let me, I could explain." His voice, dry and cracked, sounded curiously adolescent. And his body, lying there on the worn mattress, seemed boyish, a teenager's at the awkward age when hands and feet and sometimes even the head seem disproportionate.

"The Peace of Ghent, what happened?" Mrs. Undine prompted. Her voice was a soft, bedtime-story whisper.

"Ghent?"

"Yes, didn't it . . . You were telling me once about the Battle of New Orleans."

"Oh, of course, the British, they had concluded a . . . In Belgium there was . . ." *The news of peace, how slowly it travels —and yet,* the old man thought, *I can feel it. When you're weightless like this, you can feel the earth rushing through space with the news, and the sun itself hurrying towards Hercules.* Dizzy, he groped for her hand on the bed. "Twelve miles a second," he said. Where was it? Where was her hand? He needed something to hang on to at this speed.

"That's right," she said as his eyes closed. "Sleep, Mr. Loraine. You look so tired."

Mrs. Undine sat silently by the bed for some time as his breathing became regular. She had taken his hand and held on to it firmly, almost as if she, too, needed steadying.

He was loading a cardboard box into the trunk of the Volkswagen when she pulled up in the Cadillac. Finally a few precious moments had been granted to her. There was so much she wanted to tell him before he left, and yet it seemed that Mrs. Undine was always around. But tonight, leaving the office late, she had stopped by Uncle L.D.'s meaning to cheer him up and make him feel better about the move. The door had been ajar, though, and looking in, Olive had seen Mrs. Undine by the bed. Her heart thumping wildly, she had crept silently down the stairs and raced to the Cadillac.

"Hi."

"Oh, hi," he said, looking startled.

"I was just on my way home, and I thought I'd . . . I saw you out here and . . ." *Oh, Martin,* she thought, *please, darling, take me in your arms one last time.* "You're getting ready to leave?"

His head was in the front of the car, rearranging boxes and suitcases. "Mm. Driving out tonight. Thought there'd be less traffic."

Oh, my darling, if you only knew what I've been through. Did you hear about how I saved Uncle L.D.? And Duane, he's being so mean to me. I have no one to talk to, Martin. I think I might die without you.

"Boy, you got a lot stuffed in there," she said, peering into the trunk with feigned interest.

He had walked away from the car and was headed for the front door. She followed, resolving not to let him touch her once they were inside. All she wanted to do was talk. That was it. Because she couldn't live with herself otherwise. She couldn't look Felix in the face again.

Lingering a moment on the stoop, she let her gaze wander

to the bluish streetlamp atop a telephone pole. Like a cloud of electrons, hundreds of moths and June bugs danced madly in the light, urged on by the cries from Mrs. Undine's persimmon, the tree frogs'. Her stomach knotted as a soft breeze wafted over the pungent smell of freshly cut grass. Never before had a summer evening seemed so real and wonderful—and yet he was leaving. She would probably never see him again.

Oh, Martin, my darling, my love.

"Hi."

"Hi," Olive said automatically as she stepped into the living room.

"This is Kay," Dr. Bates said, nodding towards his ex-wife. Barefoot and in jeans, Kay was struggling to shut a bulging suitcase. Caught off guard like this, Olive felt panicky, defensive. Why hadn't he warned her? She never would have come inside if she had known.

"Hi," Kay said again. Then, "Oh, *hi.* I didn't recognize you at first. You've changed, Olive. It is Olive, isn't it? Olive Barnell?"

"Kay! You look great!" Olive exclaimed with excessive enthusiasm.

"Yeah," she said, glancing down at her jeans.

"No, I mean it. How've you been, girl? It's been so long."

"I know. Ages. God, almost twenty years."

"No, it can't be. You look great."

"You look great, too." Kay gave up on the suitcase and stood up. "You've met Martin?" she asked, looking over at Dr. Bates. He was sealing a cardboard box with electric tape. "I drove over from New Orleans today to help him take his stuff there. He's got so much junk. Martin, doesn't Mother have any packing tape? It would work much better. Well, girl, what are you doing here? It's so good to see you."

"Oh, I just dropped by to see your mother."

"Mother?"

"Well, you see, my son goes to Robin Downs, and she teaches there and all. You got any children, Kay?"

Kay's mouth tightened just like her mother's would. "Oh, I've been too busy. I was in New York and got my doctorate, and now I have this job that's just killing me. I have to supervise fifteen therapists plus do my own therapy, thirty patients, if you can believe. Of course, some of them are group."

"I know just what you mean, Kay. Lord, I've got a hundred people in my department alone. I've got to supervise all of them, plus I'm responsible for overseeing a lot of these peripheral jobs that don't fit in any one department."

Kay was winding and unwinding a strand of black hair on her index finger. "I thought Mother told me you were a meter maid or something."

Olive had been a meter maid the summer she had graduated from high school. "I was just elected to the City Council. I'm a superintendent."

"Oh. You know, Olive, you really have changed. You look really good, so much more . . . You must have lost weight."

"No, not really." Although she was still wary, Olive felt a warm glow. Seeing Kay here, she had felt foolish, stiff, and awkward and had simply said the first things that had popped into her head. After the meter maid crack Olive had almost lost her cool. But then she realized that that was probably the last Kay had heard of her. Kay was not being snotty, not really. And with the compliment about how she had changed, Kay was not saying that she had looked so terrible in high school. No, she was simply saying that Olive had grown better-looking, right? Politics had taught Olive to give people the benefit of the doubt.

Twisting the silver bracelet on her wrist, Olive realized that this would be a good time to make her exit. After all, Mrs. Undine would be returning any minute, and she would have to pretend that she had something to say to her. "I actually have put on a pound or two."

"Huh?" Kay started looking through A&P bags filled with what looked like old letters and bills. "Do we bring all this, Martin?" she asked as he wandered into the kitchen. "You're divorced, right?"

"Oh, no. Still happily married."

"That's funny. Someone told me that you and what's-his-name were divorced."

Leave while you're ahead, Olive told herself. "Oh, no. Duane and I, we live over in Cherylview."

"Duane? Not Duane Mackie? That gorgeous hunk?"

"Yes," Olive said, her face flushed with pleasure. It was a dream come true to be suddenly transformed like this in front of Kay, who had always looked down her nose at her. Like Cinderella, Olive felt she had finally come into her true estate. From an unpopular meter maid she had blossomed into a svelte, chic (oh, she was so glad she had dressed carefully before going to the office today) career woman with a son (yes, Kay had winced when she heard Olive had a son) and a gorgeous husband.

"You mean Carol's boyfriend?"

The blood drained from Olive's face. Did Kay know? Or maybe she was simply referring to the fact that Carol and Duane had gone steady in high school. "Uh, well."

"The Duane Carol used to date all the time?"

"Yes," Olive said, breathing easier. *Now leave,* she told herself sternly. *Say good-bye before the clock strikes twelve.* "They broke up senior year, you know."

"But didn't they get back together that summer?"

"Sort of. But you know . . ."

"Is that when you started going out with him? When you were a meter maid?"

"I met Duane in college. He was the beau of my sorority and . . ."

Dr. Bates stood by the screen door in the kitchen, wishing Olive would go away. The tension in the living room between the two women was too much for him. He had never told Kay anything about him and Olive—not directly, in any case—but even so, Kay by instinct was behaving like a catty rival. And what was so absurd was that neither Kay nor Olive was his girl friend. They were both just friends. Oh, he was so tired of friends. As soon as he got installed in New Orleans, he was going to break that pattern once and for all. He would find a woman to be his *lover.* They would be passionately and romantically involved, with sex at the very center of their relationship—not as an aberration.

Of course, if he had had any sense, he would have said a pleasant good-bye to Olive in the driveway. He didn't have to walk away so abruptly. He had been afraid, though, that she was going to start gushing tears, and everything would get messy again. It was strange what a tug she was still able to give his heart, altering his self-contained little orbit around Mrs. Undine's.

"Do you have any eggs?"

Dr. Bates switched on the light outside the screen door. The stars were immediately canceled out, and there stood Donna Lee. Apparently she had crossed over from her mother's house by way of the back yard.

"Eggs?"

"Mother has to bake some brownies for church, but she doesn't have enough eggs."

"I'll look."

Going to the refrigerator, he found six brown and a white in the plastic niches in the door.

"Three is all I need," she said, holding out her hands. She took two in one, one in the other, and then said, "Listen, Martin, this is silly. When you said good-bye the other day, you seemed mad or something. Resentful. It bothers me a lot. I don't want you leaving like that. I like you a lot, Martin. I want you to be my friend."

He slammed the refrigerator shut. On the other side of the sink a roach hesitated in front of one of Mrs. Undine's Roach Motels, then turned abruptly and disappeared behind the counter.

"I'm sorry I made you feel bad about taking that job with Schexsnyder. It isn't the end of the world, Martin. I know you'll make the best of it. You'll do a lot of good for people."

He shrugged. When he had said good-bye to her on Wednesday, he had made a move on the steps of her apartment to embrace her, and she had jerked away, as if he were some sort of crazed rapist. So much for Donna Lee: not even a single kiss, much less an aberration.

"Is it the old man? Is that why you're mad at me, Martin? Listen, I swear to you, I didn't know a thing about that insurance money. I just thought Dr. Munrow was trying to help the guy, like a good Samaritan. I never had a clue about what was really going on. Mr. Loraine had confessed so many times that he had done it. What was I supposed to think?"

"Mm. So you just stood by while they sent him back to a nursing home. That's just great," Dr. Bates said warmly. Seeing that this was a sore spot for her, he was determined to use it for all it was worth. In truth, though, he hadn't thought of the old guy in weeks, not since the last time Donna Lee had brought him by to get some sun in the back yard.

"What did you want me to do?" She was aroused, her dark-blue eyes suddenly focused and alert. "I did everything humanly possible. I called every single home-care agency in the parish, and no one had anyone available. So am I supposed to let him lie there in that apartment all by himself? Even if I dropped by every day to see how he was, that wouldn't be enough. I've got a job to do, and sometimes I don't get home till nine or ten. You want to know whose fault it is, huh? It's that dear friend of yours."

In her prim gray skirt, plain blouse, and jogging shoes Donna Lee leaned forward slightly with the eggs in her hands, as if she were about to start a ladies' obstacle course at an Episcopal church social.

"What friend?"

"Your dear Mrs. Mackie. She's the one who stole my secretary away. If I had Mr. Pickens, I wouldn't have had to ask Burma to come help me out."

"There's plenty of other people you could have asked besides Burma. She was perfectly happy looking after the old man."

"For your information, wiping up an old man's crap was not Burma's idea of being perfectly happy. *You,* you spend five minutes in his apartment and you can't wait to get out of there. But Burma, she's perfectly happy being there eight hours a day, six days a week, right?" The disgust on her face made him wonder if she knew what he was really angry about. Was she, too, talking in code? "Burma happened to be doing it out of the goodness of her heart. She was going nuts there, you know, and besides, she was barely getting minimum wage. So was it so evil of me to give her the chance to make almost twice as much working in a clean, air-conditioned office? And even if I hadn't given her this out, she would have quit anyway. She couldn't have lasted another day with him."

"Well, you did happen to need someone pretty desperately."

"Thanks to Mrs. Mackie. Besides, do you know what those people at the home-care agency told me? Did you know that before Mr. Versey the old man had gone through five women and two men, and none of them had lasted for more than a week? They refused to try anyone else at that job, Martin. They told me it was a waste of time. The old man was too difficult. And Mr. Versey was the only one who could put up with him. He was the only one who could take it. So really, Martin, I think it's grossly unfair for you to lay this one on me. I've already killed myself trying to help him out. Do you realize how much free legal advice I've given him?" Tears filled her eyes. "Oh, you're impossible," she said, trying to run out. But he was blocking the way to the screen door, and somewhat confusedly she headed the other way.

Remorse gnawing on him, he followed her into the living room.

"Hi."

"Oh, hi."

"Hi, Martin."

"Hi."

Donna Lee was standing somewhat awkwardly between Kay and Olive, who had still not left. At the door stood Carol Deshotel in a simple white frock that showed off a ravishing tan. "Hi," Carol said again, giving him a childish wave of the hand. "My mother wanted me to tell Mrs. Undine that she couldn't make it to canasta this week," Carol said to the room in general. "I was coming out this way anyway, so she asked me to 'cause there's something wrong with her phone, and then I saw Kay's car out there, and I thought I just had to stop and see Kay. It's been ages, and Kay you look so good. I'm so jealous I could die."

This was all Dr. Bates needed. Hadn't he already given Carol an official good-bye on Tuesday evening while her husband was at the Kiwanis meeting? What could she mean by dropping over like this? They had had their last aberration; he had been quite clear about that.

"Martin," Kay said, "do you know Carol Rawlins?"

"Deshotel," he said.

"What?"

"Nothing."

"Uh, Carol," Kay went on, "this is my husband, Martin Bates."

Leave, Olive kept telling herself. And she would have if she hadn't heard voices coming from the other room. Who was he talking to in that kitchen? Why didn't he come out and pack? Then she thought she recognized the voice. It was Ms. Keely. The nerve of her to just pop over like that. And she was sounding so emotional. Olive walked a few steps into the living room, trying to position herself nearer the kitchen so she could hear what they were saying.

The next thing she knew, Carol had walked in the front door with hardly a knock. The gall of that woman to wear such a sexy dress. And she could smell her Joy clear across the room.

"Hi," Carol was saying to Kay and then to Olive, as if nothing untoward had ever occurred between them. Olive was too choked up to say anything back. All she wanted to do was flee. If she didn't, she was afraid she wouldn't be responsible for what happened. Oh, Carol looked so gorgeous. How in the world did she do it?

But just as she was about to deliver an appropriate exit line, Ms. Keely had burst into the living room, tears streaming down her cheeks. And three eggs in her hands. Well, of all the excuses. Eggs.

"Martin," Kay said, "do you know Carol Rawlins?"

"Deshotel," he said, his face red as a beet.

Why, look at him, he can barely take his eyes off that hussy in her white dress, Olive thought.

"What?"

"Nothing."

"Uh, Carol," Kay went on, "this is my husband, Martin Bates."

"Oh."

Oh, she says. Olive gave her a long hard look, and Carol smiled back shamelessly at her.

"Husband?" Carol murmured.

"What?" Kay asked sharply.

"Nothing. Olive, you look so sweet," Carol added. "This is like a class reunion, isn't it? Everyone all getting together, except for her."

Her meant Donna Lee, who was trying to wipe the tears from her eyes with the backs of her egg-laden hands.

"Oh, Donna Lee went to TSH, too," Kay said helpfully. "She was a few classes behind us."

"Really." Carol beamed at her. "And now you've caught up with us, I see."

For a few moments there was a terrific silence. Everyone was obviously just dying to leave, but for some reason no one could make a move. The living room, crammed with suitcases, books, overstuffed A&P bags, deep-sea fishing tackle, a leather jacket, ivory elephant, Mr. Undine holding a bass, wilted chrysanthemums, hair mousse, coffee, Hermès cologne, a corkscrew, a waffle iron, lens solution, a drain guard—this living room would not let them go.

"Do you remember the Silver Tea we had here?" Kay said finally.

"Oh, God, the FHA," Carol said.

"What's the FHA?" Dr. Bates asked.

"Future Homemakers of America," Carol said. "I wore this ridiculous pillbox hat that I had to beg my mother to let me buy. Can you believe we all wore hats? *Hats.*"

"And gloves. White gloves," Kay said.

Feeling that they were ignoring her, Olive cut in on them. "And Mrs. Undine, remember, she—"

They went on talking as if Olive hadn't said anything. A

vague panic seized her. She found it hard to breathe, as if there were a weight on her chest.

"I got mine at the Vogue. Mother wanted me to go to Penney's, but I told her I'd rather die than wear something from Penney's. Everyone would know it was from Penney's."

"Mine was from Penney's," Kay said.

"Yeah, but you could wear anything, girl. You—"

Floundering, Olive said, in a loud, forceful voice, "Yeah, and Mrs. Undine, that was the time she slipped up and said— You remember, she was trying to say, 'I don't want you girls to muck up my living room' and she said by mistake 'fuck up.' 'I don't want you girls to fuck up my living room,' and we all nearly died, and your mother had to run out of the room. She was in tears, and God that was funny."

Carol and Kay exchanged a look.

"What are you talking about?" Carol said. "She never . . ."

"Oh, yes, surely y'all remember. It was the funniest thing I ever heard in my life."

"Oh, come on, Olive, you're making that up."

"No, I'm not. I swear. Kay, you remember . . ."

Kay looked doubtfully at her. "Well . . ."

"Don't humor me. Just say if you remember."

"Personally I don't, but, Olive, there's a lot I forget. I mean, that was an awful long time ago."

"But you couldn't have forgotten. Carol, Kay, please." Olive turned to Dr. Bates, to Ms. Keely, as if she were on trial. "Really, I swear, you would have died laughing. No one could forget. Mrs. Undine, you know how she is—and then to come out and say . . ." Suddenly she lashed out at a wicker end table with her foot. A glass toppled to the floor and shattered; in a puddle was a single ice cube. "She did say it! She said fuck!"

Everyone, including Olive, looked somewhere else, desperately: at the window, the mantel, the couch, anywhere but at another pair of eyes.

And then the door opened. "Oh, my," Mrs. Undine said. "What have we here? Oh, what a mess this place is. Kay, darling, I was hoping it would be all cleaned up by the time

I got back. Oh, why, hello, Carol. And Olive. What a surprise. Oh, my, and you, too, Donna Lee?"

Mrs. Undine didn't seem to take in anything but a general picture of the room. But then, when she had had a chance to look a little more closely, she saw how stiff and unnatural their smiles were.

"Why, girls," she said, her weary face suddenly illuminated with genuine concern, "whatever is the matter with you? You all look like you've just seen a ghost." And with that, Mrs. Undine, who seemed a little unsteady on her feet, walked somewhat stiffly into the kitchen. She said she would make some refreshments. It was quite warm this evening, wasn't it?

But everyone politely declined. They didn't have time for a drink. They all had to leave.

"Mother needs these eggs," Donna Lee said.

"My husband is waiting," Carol said.

"Felix," Olive said, going out the door.

$\mathcal{V}$OICES OF THE $\mathcal{S}$OUTH

Hamilton Basso
  The View from Pompey's Head
Richard Bausch
  Real Presence
  Take Me Back
Robert Bausch
  On the Way Home
Doris Betts
  The Astronomer and Other Stories
  The Gentle Insurrection and Other Stories
Sheila Bosworth
  Almost Innocent
  Slow Poison
David Bottoms
  Easter Weekend
Erskine Caldwell
  Poor Fool
Fred Chappell
  The Gaudy Place
  The Inkling
  It Is Time, Lord
Kelly Cherry
  Augusta Played
Vicki Covington
  Bird of Paradise
R. H. W. Dillard
  The Book of Changes
Ellen Douglas
  A Family's Affairs
  A Lifetime Burning
  The Rock Cried Out
  Where the Dreams Cross
Percival Everett
  Cutting Lisa
  Suder
Peter Feibleman
  The Daughters of Necessity
  A Place Without Twilight
George Garrett
  An Evening Performance
  Do, Lord, Remember Me
  The Finished Man
Marianne Gingher
  Bobby Rex's Greatest Hit
Shirley Ann Grau
  The Hard Blue Sky
  The House on Coliseum Street
  The Keepers of the House
Barry Hannah
  The Tennis Handsome

Donald Hays
  The Dixie Association
William Humphrey
  Home from the Hill
  The Ordways
Mac Hyman
  No Time For Sergeants
Madison Jones
  A Cry of Absence
Nancy Lemann
  Lives of the Saints
  Sportsman's Paradise
Beverly Lowry
  Come Back, Lolly Ray
Willie Morris
  The Last of the Southern Girls
Louis D. Rubin, Jr.
  The Golden Weather
Evelyn Scott
  The Wave
Lee Smith
  The Last Day the Dogbushes Bloomed
Elizabeth Spencer
  The Salt Line
  This Crooked Way
  The Voice at the Back Door
Max Steele
  Debby
Walter Sullivan
  The Long, Long Love
Allen Tate
  The Fathers
Peter Taylor
  The Widows of Thornton
Robert Penn Warren
  Band of Angels
  Brother to Dragons
  World Enough and Time
Walter White
  Flight
James Wilcox
  Miss Undine's Living Room
  North Gladiola
Joan Williams
  The Morning and the Evening
  The Wintering
Christine Wiltz
  Glass House
Thomas Wolfe
  The Hills Beyond
  The Web and the Rock